TETHERED IN BLOOD

H. L. Rillon

For more information, or to book an event, contact:

H.L.RillonBooks@gmail.com

Cover design by H. L. Rillon

Map design by Saumya's Vision

Paperback ISBN-13: 979-8-218-62767-6

eBook ISBN-13: 979-8-218-62768-3

Library of Congress Control Number: 2025906446

Content & Trigger Warning

Dear readers,
Tethered In Blood is a tension and action-riddled, (very) slow-burn gothic romantic fantasy that ends on an intense cliffhanger (don't worry, they get their happy ending!) As much as I hope you laugh through this book, please note that it *does* contain horror, graphic, and dark themes. Each of the main characters has a painful backstory. The FMC has CPTSD, and her flashbacks are depicted throughout the story. If any of this may upset you, this book might not be the right fit.

This book contains violence and sexual content. It is not intended for anyone under the legal age of adulthood. All characters depicted are over eighteen years of age.

Trigger warnings include but may not be limited to: violence, murder, torture (severed fingers, gauged eyes, slit throats), restraint, rape mentioned and hinted in flashbacks, child abuse/neglect mentioned, vivid descriptions of decayed corpses and smells, poisoning, drowning, whips, weapons (arrows, swords, knives, and daggers), and obnoxious amounts of flirting from the best friend *(I'm looking at you, Garrick)*.

Please note: *Chapters 5 and 25 may be especially triggering.*
Your mental health matters!

Playlist

The full *Tethered In Blood* playlist can be found on Spotify.

To my friends and family, who helped make this a reality,

&

To those who learned to care for others in a world that never cared for them,

May you find the peace that you've given so freely.

EXCERPT FROM THE SCROLL OF BINDING
(VERSE I: THE BURIED ROOT)

SHE WILL WEAR THE NAME OF ANOTHER.

BORN OF ROOT AND RUIN,
POISON-FED AND HOLLOW-NAMED.

RAISED BY HANDS THAT MARKED HER FATE.

THEY WILL MISTAKE HER FOR SOFT,
FOR SAINT, FOR STRAY.

HER HANDS WILL HEAL.
THE DEAD WILL RISE.

THE LAND WILL WITHER WHERE SHE TREADS.
THE TREES WILL BEND WHEN SHE BREAKS.

FOR HER BLOOD IS THE LOCK.
HER BODY, THE THRESHOLD.

WHEN THE STORM FINDS HER, THE VEIL WILL STIR.

AND FROM HER BLOOD, THE GODS WILL WAKE.

LET IT BE KNOWN: THE HERBALIST MUST BLEED;

THE GODS ARE WAITING.

Aurelith

Wickloe

Ashthorne Docks

Veilwoods

Ruvenmere

Capital

Vaelwick

Emberhollow

Bandit Camp

Hollowbrooke

Silverfel

Black Lake

The Fae Border

Blacksmiths Guild

VALEITDWYN

WELCOME TO THE KINGDOM OF AURELITH,

DILTHEN ARAS.

Let's go dig up some nightmares.

1

EDEN

THE WORLD HAD never been kind to me, but I never needed kindness to survive. I learned early that survival was an act of will, a lesson instilled by my parents. While most children lay in warm beds, I spent my nights in Veilwood. My hands trembled as I foraged for something useful: roots to numb the pain, berries to stave off hunger, and bark to brew into a sense of warmth.

My father referred to it as building resilience. My mother said it was necessary. But I considered it abandonment.

Wickloe, like every village in Aurelith, had its superstitions. Some whispered of the Veilwood's ancient hunger, warning that those who wandered too deep never returned the same. Others swore the river carried the spirits of the forgotten, pulling them under when the moon hung low.

My mother used those stories as cautionary tales, but I learned the truth early: real monsters didn't lurk in the shadows of the trees. They sat at dinner tables where they bargain with their blood.

The hood of my cloak slipped from my head as I kneeled by the river's edge, plunging my fingers into the icy water. The crisp, clean flavors of stone and soil offered a momentary relief from the exhaustion weighing on my limbs.

The Veilwoods were nearly behind me. The twisted trees had thinned, their gnarled roots no longer reaching out to trip me with each step. Although the air felt lighter, alive with the hum of insects and free of the mossy decay, my chest felt no less heavy. I should have felt relieved. I should have felt something other than this endless, gnawing fatigue. But the capital was a day away, and I couldn't afford to think beyond the next step.

Crunching over frosty leaves, I moved away from the water to find dry ground beneath an oak. The rough bark scraped my spine as I sank to the ground, trying to focus on my surroundings and stay present.

My limbs felt heavy, and my breath misted in the frosty night air. The wind stirred the trees above, rustling brittle leaves that never fell. An owl hooted in the distance, its call low and haunting, while something small scurried through the undergrowth, unseen yet near. Veilflies glimmered in the air with tiny blue pulses of light against the darkness. A fox padded along the riverbank, its ears flicking toward me before it vanished into the underbrush, leaving only the whisper of rustling ferns behind.

My eyelids closed for a moment, yet the darkness behind them pulled at me. Echoes of nightmares lingered at the fringes of my mind.

Not yet. I couldn't sleep yet.

My grip strengthened on my cloak. Clutching onto something could secure me here, in this instant, and not where my mind attempted to take me. The muscle ache told me I needed rest, but sleep was dangerous. Sleep meant lowering my guard. It meant slipping into dreams where hands reached for me from the dark, the smells of iron and fire coated my throat, and I woke gasping with a heart that sputtered and a pulse deafening in my ears. The faint sound of a snapping branch made me stiffen, though it was too light to be anything other than a deer moving through the trees.

Still, my pulse stayed tight in my throat.

The river's rhythmic murmur wove through the rustling branches. When exhaustion sank deep into my bones, my body slumped more heavily against the tree. I intended to rest for only a moment, long enough to gather my strength. But the river's insistent lullaby beckoned to me, and the darkness enveloped me.

The damp soil pressed against my knees as I plucked feverfew from the tangled roots of an oak, my fingers brushing against the delicate white petals. A fragrance of pine and loamy soil filled the air. Distant insect calls blended with the hush of the wind as it swept through the trees.

It should have been peaceful.

But something felt wrong.

My skin prickled at the nape of my neck, an instinct older than reason. My pulse slowed, then pounded.

I turned.

Marcus stood just beyond the tree line. His leather shoes were too pristine for the forest trail, and his tailored jacket was immaculate, as if he had stepped from a ballroom, not from my nightmares. He was as calculated as ever. Entitlement clung to him like a second skin.

"Hello, Darling." His silky, almost pleasant voice sent ice threading through my veins. He rolled the leaf between his fingertips, then let it fall, before wiping his hand against a crisp white handkerchief. "I thought I might find you here. You always did love your little..." He paused. "Plants."

My stomach tightened, but I kept my voice even.

"I'm busy, Marcus."

"Busy avoiding me, you mean? You've been doing that an awful lot lately." He took a slow step closer, and his head tilted as though he were considering a misbehaved pet. "Haven't you?"

My eyes remained locked on him. "I don't know what you mean. I've been working."

"That's cute," he laughed.

I narrowed my gaze. "What?"

"The way you play healer." His lips curled as his mask slipped enough to show the underlying disdain. "We all know what you're really doing here, Eden." My name dripped from his tongue with venom, stealing my breath. I had to get past him, and my best option was to move before his patience snapped.

"I don't have time for this," I clipped, pushing past him.

"I think you do." His hand closed around my arm, his fingers dug deep, and I lost my balance. I stumbled, but he didn't let go. The amusement in his voice vanished, replaced by indifference. "You have to stop running away from us like this. The dramatics have lost their flavor."

"There is no us, Marcus," I gritted through clenched teeth. "Now let me—"

"Oh, but there is. There has always been, Darling." His smile twisted into a predatory hunger. "You and I are soon to be married. I'm sure you already know."

His words struck hard, and a sick weight settled in my stomach. "Let. Me. Go." He shoved me back. The breath rushed from my lungs when my boots slid over damp leaves, and I landed hard on the forest floor.

Marcus didn't move to help me. He only watched, wiping his hands as though touching me had dirtied him. His silken and cruel voice carried through the frosty air. "Go ahead. Play your little games while you can. But don't think for a second that you're free of me." He turned and walked back down the path with confidence. "You'll come back," he called over his shoulder. "You always do."

I woke with a gasp, my heart slamming against my chest and my breath shallow. The river still murmured beside me, and the wind whispered through the branches above.

The freezing air bit at me as I sat still beneath the tree. I pushed a hand against the rough bark at my back to secure myself in the present. The Veilwoods stretched behind me, filled with the sounds of the river's steady murmur, crickets, and the occasional rustle of unseen creatures moving through the underbrush. The sky above had deepened into the darkest shade of blue, with stars peeking through the canopy in pinpricks of light.

I wasn't in the past.

I was here. Alone.

Forcing my stiff limbs to move, I reached for my satchel. My fingers grazed over the worn leather before slipping inside, grasping the small paper tucked between vials and dried herbs. The edges crinkled beneath my touch as I unfolded it.

Court Herbalist Needed.

The handling blurred the ink in places, but the words remained legible.

A strange, heavy sensation curled in my chest. It had only been a day since I had taken it, but it felt as though the slip of paper had been waiting for me much longer. I traced my thumb across the parchment and reread the words, even though I knew them by heart.

This was my way out. My chance to put distance between myself and the past that still haunted me—to be more than a ghost gliding through forests and back alleys. I wanted to step into a world where Marcus's reach couldn't find me.

I took a deep breath and folded the flier, slipping it back into my satchel. Its weight suggested a quiet promise. There was no time for ghosts.

The river ran shallow where I crossed, the icy water swirling around rocks as I crept over the bridge. With each step, the past tugged at me, urging me to linger and hesitate.

When I reached the other side, the land expanded. The trees receded, and the Veilwoods, once dense and endless behind me, loosened their grip, yielding to open space. However, with that openness came an unease coiling low in my spine.

Pulling my hood to hide my face, I crossed the old dirt path toward the bridge. Thick, swirling fog clung to the wooden planks and crept along the edges like ghostly fingers. The air smelled of damp soil and something faintly metallic, sending a chill down my spine.

A crow cawed from the railing, its dark eyes gleaming in the soft light. Another responded from the trees beyond, the sound piercing the muffled silence of the mist.

My fingers burrowed into my cloak. I was still shaking off the nightmare when the past came clawing at me again.

The wood beneath my feet gleamed with rain, and the air was heavy with wet pine and dampened lantern oil.

I was running.

My ragged breaths constricted my chest. My boots struck the wooden planks in rapid succession. Each step echoed with the pounding of a drum. The fog swallowed everything beyond the bridge and left shadows in its wake.

Marcus's men weren't far behind when I looked back. Their torches flickered in the mist, and their cruel and amused voices echoed. "She won't get far."

"She never does."

The words scraped against my mind.

The village lights of Wickloe ahead glimmered in false salvation once I crossed the bridge. My lungs burned. My legs ached. But I kept moving. I had to—

A hand caught my wrist.

No.

The world spun, and the bridge beneath me tilted. My hip hit the railing, and pain lanced through my bones. Their fingers tightened with a bruising force as a voice murmured in my ear.

"Going somewhere, Darling?"

The memory snapped, leaving me cold and unsteady. The bridge lay behind me, the crows still watched from their perch, and the river whispered without care.

I wasn't there.

I wasn't running.

Willing my breath to steady, I unclenched my fingers from the hem of my cloak. My pulse hammered at my temples, but I continued forward, one step at a time.

The past held no sway over me here. Yet, as I walked into the mist, I could still feel Marcus's fingers ghosting over my wrist and hear his voice curling in the depths of my mind. The farther I walked, the thinner the trees grew, their skeletal branches bending under the weight of the morning frost. Soon, the road widened, bordered by brittle fields and the first hints of distant hills. By midday, the silence pressed in, leaving too much space for thoughts to creep in, unwelcome and sharp-edged.

What if they don't accept me?

Doubt constricted in my chest, colder than the wind that bit at my face. I knew the experience. My journal hadn't been filled with observations and theories; I had earned every remedy, every antidote, and every detailed note of pain.

Burning fevers. Stomach cramps. Weakness in the limbs. Blurred vision. Hallucinations.

I learned the signs of poison not from books, but from my body. I learned the cures because I needed them to live. *But would that be enough?*

The capital was filled with people who had studied in halls of marble and gold. These men and women learned from scholars, not through suffering. Their hands had never trembled from fever as they scrawled notes by candlelight, desperate to comprehend what threatened their lives before time ran out. I didn't look the same as them, or like I belonged in a palace. That thought sent a familiar ache crawling through me, sinking deep into my ribs. My steps faltered, and the world grew hazy.

The fire was dying in the hearth, casting shadows that crawled across the wooden walls of our home. The scent of dried herbs and candle wax hung in the air, yet it did nothing to soften the sharp bite of my mother's voice.

"You have charcoal on your hands again."

I rubbed my fingers against my skirts, but the smudges wouldn't come off. "I was writing."

Her gaze flicked to my open journal, to the pages spread wide with careful notes, pressed flowers, and sketched diagrams. Her expression twisted in neither anger nor approval.

My father set down his pipe, watching me from across the room. "You've been spending too much time with that book."

"It's important," I said. "I'm learning."

My mother's sigh was sharp and final. "You can't change what you are with books and pressed flowers, Eden."

She didn't have to say it outright. I didn't learn from books or study in a grand hall beneath candlelit chandeliers. My knowledge came from bitter-tasting drafts given to me with lies and calculated intent.

"Drink this. It will help with the fever."

"This will warm you."

My mother's hand smoothed my hair as the poison took hold, my vision blurred, and my heartbeat stuttered. My father watched as I writhed on the floor, fighting to purge whatever mixture they had given me this time. They never explained why or provided a reason.

But I learned. I wrote everything down and tracked the symptoms, their duration, and the lingering effects. When I had recovered enough to move, I searched the area for herbs that might counteract the effects of what had been done to me. I tested doses on myself and observed whether or not the antidotes worked. I discovered what kept my pulse steady, what cleared my mind, and what stitched me back together after they tried to break me.

Marcus's poisons were more cruel. His touch was excruciating. His voice coiled deep within me.

"You always had such a talent for healing, Darling. I wonder how much you'll have to break before accepting that you belong to me."

The icy air stung my lungs. The empty road stretched endlessly ahead, and the sky was a pale shade of blue above it. I set my jaw and compelled my feet to move.

"This isn't real." Another breath. "I'm on the road to the capital." Another. "The sky is clear. The wind is cold. The air smells of frost and dirt."

My voice was a faint murmur, but it was enough. Enough to ground me, to break the memory's grip, and to remind myself that I wasn't there. I wasn't a child waiting for an answer that would never come. I wasn't his.

The charcoal on my hands was nothing to be ashamed of. It proved my hard work. I had my journal, knowledge, and skills. That had to be enough.

If it weren't, I would make it.

2

EDEN

THE SUN HUNG low in the sky, casting long shadows across the land. Its dying light washed the castle in amber, violet, and crimson hues. The white stone gleamed beneath it, creating a stark contrast against the darkening sky. Its towers pierced the evening haze like silent sentinels. The pristine walls stretched high. It was a fortress built for protection and power—a symbol of the monarchy that ruled within.

The road to the gate was quiet, save for the distant murmur of the city behind me. A scent of damp stone and fresh-cut hay lingered in the air, mingling with the faint traces of burning oil from the torches lining the outer walls. Beneath it all was the aroma of steel, blood, and the weight of expectation.

Two knights stood at the entrance, clad in polished armor that captured the last glimmers of sunlight. The metal was delicate, not gaudy, just intricate enough to remind one that even the lowest castle guards stood well above those outside these walls. They held practiced, unmoving postures, their stillness born from familiarity. This was their usual post, and the boredom of routine had settled into them.

A strange sensation coiled in my stomach when I paused before them. I had come this far, but as I stood before the castle and gazed at the imposing gate, the unknown bore down on me.

I didn't belong here. The courts of Aurelith were for the refined, well-bred, and well-groomed—not for a girl with scars concealed beneath layers of frayed and muddy cloth. Nor for someone who had learned to heal out of necessity, not luxury.

An impatient grunt jolted me from my thoughts.

One knight shifted. The other turned his head. The metal of his helmet glinted in the dim light as he regarded me.

I schooled my expression into a harmless smile that masked sharp edges. "Must be boring, standing there all day like that," I greeted, tilting my head. "Do they at least let you blink?"

A long sigh echoed from the knight on the left, his vexation palpable even through the metal. He didn't move, didn't react beyond that drawn-out breath. But the knight on the right's gaze flickered. Through the slit of his visor, emerald-green eyes narrowed on me. "State your business, commoner."

Commoner. As if I needed the reminder.

My fingers tightened against my cloak. The fabric restrained me while I swallowed the sharp retort that threatened to emerge. The weight of my satchel dug into my shoulder and reminded me why I was here, the proof that I had something to offer beyond my bloodline.

I lifted my chin and met the knight's gaze with defiance. "I am here about the herbalist position."

The knight to the left let out a long, weary sigh, as if he had decided that this was a waste of his time. "Another one."

The knight before me shifted his weight, and his eyes, sharp despite the barrier of his helm, once again locked onto mine. "Do you have proof?" His voice held a slight edge, not quite impatience, but close. "Too many have been seeking the position in the past few days."

A gentle breeze stirred the air, carrying the aroma of frosty stone and the lingering smoke from the torches above. The last rays of sunlight reflected off the knight's polished pauldrons and gilded the metal in a fading golden glow before the shadows crept in.

"Our people have work to do," he continued. "Don't waste their time."

I held his gaze, refusing to waver. "Of course." From my satchel, I retrieved the folded parchment—the Court Herbalist Needed notice—along with my journal. This was my proof: not just charcoal on parchment, but experience.

I straightened and extended my hands, keeping them steady. Let them think what they wanted of me. The words on those pages held more importance than any assumptions they had about who I was.

His helmet darkened in the fading light as the sun dipped below the horizon. I couldn't determine the point of his stare, yet I felt his eyes on me as the heavy silence settled between us. After a few slow breaths, he reached out. His gauntleted hand closed over the journal and lifted it from my grasp with a gentle, almost weightless touch. The parchment whispered as he skimmed the notes, the pressed herbs, and the sketches.

He lifted his head. "These are yours?"

"Yes."

His fingers lingered on the edge of a page. The leather of his glove brushed against an old ink stain I had tried and failed to scrub clean. He snapped the journal shut with a decisive movement and handed it back. The other knight, who had shown no interest until now, turned his gaze to watch him. Perhaps curious about what had made him pause.

I took the journal from his outstretched hand and slipped the flier inside, folding my hands over it and pressing them against my waist. The cool leather felt soothing and prevented my mind from wandering further into doubt.

"You are to go straight to the infirmary," he said. His tone was as firm as before, though it was now less detached and more deliberate.

He rattled off directions, a series of turns and hallways I was expected to follow. The words blurred. My focus shifted between the overwhelming weight of the moment and the looming gates that separated me from whatever awaited inside. When he stopped, I nodded.

Glancing at the other knight, he turned and raised a hand in silent command. The heavy gates groaned as the guards pulled them open, the iron hinges echoing in the evening air. Beyond, the castle loomed taller, its archways swallowing the last sliver of light.

The gates groaned shut behind me, sealing me within the castle's hold. The path stretched ahead, winding toward the grand archway, its stones darkened by shadow. The remaining traces of snow, thin but stubborn, crunched softly under my boots, the sound swallowed by the vast silence pressing in from all sides.

Thick clouds concealed the moon, offering only fleeting glimpses of silver light breaking through the shifting veils of darkness. It cast pale, fractured beams across the yard that caught in the delicate frost clinging to the iron railings and the sculpted stone of the castle walls. The crisp, cold air nipped at my exposed skin, curling in soft, ghostly wisps with each breath I took.

The castle walls loomed high. Its white stone glistened under the feeble light in a stark contrast against the night sky. The architecture featured intricate turrets that towered over arched windows, flickering with the faint glow of torchlight. A grand crest adorned the façade above the main entrance, a symbol of power carved into the bones of the structure.

Lanterns lined the pathway. Their golden light flickered against the snowfall drifting by. Banners hung from the stone, their edges stiff with frost, and the sigils embroidered upon them dimmed in the soft glow. With each step, I ventured deeper into something vast and unshakable. The prestige of the castle and the history embedded in its walls swayed me.

My attention shifted to a faint trickle of water flowing over smooth rocks in the first corridor. Floral and rich scents, inappropriate for castle halls that should smell only of cold stone and burning torches, filled the air. Their insistence curled around me, guiding my steps.

The corridor led to a series of archways, their stone filigreed with ivy. The tendrils stretched along the columns as if reaching for the sky. A garden bathed in moonlight rested beyond them. The night's silver glow poured in from above and illuminated the space in a way that made it seem untouched by time. It should have been barren, stripped of life by the frost.

Frostflies drifted lazily through the air, their wings pulsing in shifting shades of blue, gold, and violet- embers stolen from a dying star. They fluttered between blooms of flowers I had never encountered before. The petals curled in strange, intricate formations, their colors both unnatural and mesmerizing. Roses, dark as wine and tipped with silver frost, climbed the walls and wrapped around the pillars, their thorns gleaming in the faint light.

In the heart of the garden stood a willow tree that whispered in the breeze, its branches draping low. Beneath it, nestled in a bed of moss and pale winter blossoms, sat a birdbath of polished stone. Its basin rippled with liquid moonlight. I stepped forward, drawn by the unspoken secrets.

Aurelith's courts may have condemned magic, but within these walls, it breathed.

My fingers grazed the cool stone of the archway while I basked in the sight before me. Every instinct I had—to look, touch, learn—pulled me forward, deeper into the garden's embrace. But reason whispered its warnings: I wasn't yet official here, not yet safe. In a place where magic endured despite its ban, touching the wrong object could lead to unforeseen consequences I couldn't manage.

Still, the ache to understand burned in me.

Glancing around, I scanned the shadowy corridors and searched for any sign of movement. The castle had been quiet thus far, but that didn't mean unseen eyes weren't watching. Confident in my solitude, I shut my eyes and inhaled deeply.

Layered and intricate scents filled the air. Damp soil, dewy petals, and the crisp bite of frost nipped at the edges. The rich, dark rose perfume mingled with the peculiar, sweet scent of flowers I couldn't name. The water in the birdbath held a faint mineral tang, and its rippling surface sang softly in the wind. And magic dwelled there, humming beneath it all, not in the manner of spells or raw power but in a more profound way, woven into the roots of the place. I dissected each aroma and sound, cataloging them.

One could forget the outside world here.

With reluctance, I opened my eyes and compelled myself to return to the present.

My time to comprehend this garden would come, but not tonight.

"Dilthen Doe."

The deep, commanding voice echoed through the corridors. Each syllable bled into my skin, felt rather than heard. My breath caught when the figure emerged from the shadows. The torchlight flickered against black armor gilded with intricate etchings. The dim glow of gold veins ran through the obsidian plates, signifying more than just armor. It stood as a statement, a warning, a legacy carved in steel.

His helmet bore horns that weren't ornamental nor for spectacle. Purposeful and thoughtful carvings framed him, a creature forged in battle, not merely a soldier in its service.

I had met powerful men who sought to own, control, and break others. But he was different. There was no pretense of civility and no need for manipulation.

This man didn't go to war; he *was* the war. He didn't need to seize power; it yielded to him.

His intense gaze fixed on me, and my grip tightened around my journal at my front. He carried an air about him, like the moment before a storm, when the air pulsated with unseen energy, poised to break.

I had been cautious. I had touched nothing. I had broken no rules. Yet, the air grew charged with inescapable tension.

One thing was sure: I wasn't supposed to be here.

"I presume the guards allowed you entry," he said, smoother now but no less fierce. "State your purpose."

I swallowed and turned to face him fully. "I am seeking the herbalist position," I said, lifting my chin to feign confidence. "I was instructed to visit the infirmary."

A sharp huff echoed from behind his dark helmet, little more than a breath but loaded with meaning—judgment, displeasure, or perhaps simple impatience. For a moment, he said nothing, remaining unreadable until he spun around with the effortless authority he possessed in his solitary presence. "Follow me."

I blinked.

His strides were steady yet swift. His armor produced no extraneous noise, only the subtle sound of metal shifting as he moved.

"Oh." The word slipped out while I adjusted my grip on my satchel before rushing to keep up. He turned a corner, never looking back to see if I was following, as if he knew I would. I hurried to catch up to him. The stone walls closed in around us, and the scents of the strange moonlit garden faded as I was drawn deeper into the castle's embrace.

3

OBERON

AURELITH'S HALLS WERE never truly silent—not in a place founded on politics, war, and ambition. At this hour, the sounds that remained were distant: the whisper of wind slipping through stone crevices, the occasional murmur of shifting guards, and the rhythmic echo of my footsteps. Beyond the narrow windows, the sky stretched in shades of black and silver. The clouds parted, allowing the moon to spill through in scattered beams of light. Those fleeting slivers of light cut across the stone floor, illuminating the polished marble for moments before darkness consumed them again.

Tonight, it was my turn to make the rounds. It was a tedious, mind-numbing task that tested my patience. I was ill-suited for such duties. My purpose wasn't to patrol the hallways and ensure that the castle remained undisturbed, but Alric required it.

A knight. That was what I had to be. Not an assassin, nor the blade that severed threats before they took root. A knight. A soldier of the crown. To wear that title, I had to play the part. Part of that meant enduring the dull routine of men who had never tasted war outside of an open battlefield.

I exhaled sharply, my breath swirling in the frigid air as my mind recalled the command I had received before nightfall.

"We caught wind of a rebellion leader," Alric said while he slid a map across his desk. The parchment was old, edges softened from wear, but its contents were fresh. Marked routes and crude circles converged on a forest outpost. "His name is Rhys Carrow." A familiar name, spoken in hushed warnings and in reports that have surfaced often. A man operating in the shadows, coordinating attacks from the forests beyond the capital's reach.

I studied the map, noting the terrain, weak points, routes of entry, escape paths, and the distance between the outpost and the nearest village or safe house. "The orders?" I asked, though I knew the answer.

Alric's expression hardened, accentuating the traces of an individual who hadn't yet learned to wield the ruthlessness his father once had. His hesitation was brief.

"Bring him back alive. I need answers, not a corpse. Enter through the eastern gates and take him to the cells. Get as much as you can out of him. If he resists..." There was a flicker of hesitation before his expression smoothed into cold calculation. "Do what you must."

I nodded, memorizing the map, tucking away every detail of the mission ahead.

Now, I walked the corridors, my mind already planning and hunting beyond these walls. The halls stretched on, lined with flickering torchlight, and the faint scent of melting wax wafted through the cold air.

A figure at the archway of the inner garden caught my attention. It seemed to be just another shape in the periphery, another servant, or a lost court member wandering the halls where they didn't belong. But something about her drew me in. It was a novel sensation, an invisible string pulled taut and anchored to the unseen, to the inevitable.

She stood shrouded in the glow of the fading moonlight from the garden beyond. Silver light caught the edges of her figure, outlining her too delicately for this place. Her simple clothes, made from worn and well-used fabrics, showed signs of mud and frayed seams. She didn't belong among the silks and perfumes of the court. No noble would dare wear clothing like hers.

She wore a well-maintained cloak, too well-maintained and too large. It was made for a man, not for someone of her stature. The contrast struck me.

From whom had she taken it?

Her hair was untamed, a wild halo framing her face, a testament to hours spent in the wind and under the sun. A few loose strands caught the silver light and shimmered softly. Nestled behind her ear was a sprig of lavender—an intentional touch.

But neither the lavender nor the unruly waves of her hair captured my attention. It was her posture. She clutched a tattered leather journal to her chest, her fingers gripping it until her knuckles turned pale. She hesitated, caught between stepping forward and bolting back. She gazed at the garden as if it were the most beautiful thing she had ever seen. Or perhaps it was the magic that, though forbidden outside these walls, thrived here.

The hypocrisy of it all didn't escape me.

Her skirt brushed against the stone floor, and the softest scent of wildflowers reached me. It wasn't perfume, nothing crafted or intentional. It was simply her.

She was trying too hard. Her shoulders were too relaxed, and her posture appeared too deliberately casual. A radiance that felt feigned rather than genuine. A mask she had worn for so long that I wondered if she even knew how to let it fall.

I wanted to walk away. I tried to ignore whatever pull I felt. But I couldn't stop staring.

So, I ordered her attention.

"Dilthen Doe."

She turned at my voice. Her gaze searched my armor as I exited the shadowy corridor, eyes flashing with an emotion that carried too much depth and weight. In that quiet moment, a soft blush crept across her cheeks. Her lips parted, and my heart skipped a beat. It was an intense and unwelcome experience. One that I detested.

"I assume the guards allowed you entry," I said, maintaining distance in my voice. "State your purpose."

She swallowed before turning to face me fully. "I'm seeking the herbalist position," she explained. Her voice was soft and decadent. It clung to the recesses of my mind and refused to let go. "I was instructed to visit the infirmary."

Yet she stood in the inner garden. Far from the infirmary, far from where she was supposed to be.

The garden's soft glow framed her, making her seem out of place. She didn't belong here any more than I did. I continued to stare, searching for a clue in how she carried herself and spoke to determine whether she was another fool, unaware of the position she sought or just another waste of time. But I found nothing. Tension seized my jaw, and I pivoted abruptly, indifferent to whether she followed or remained at the garden's threshold.

"Follow me."

As we stepped into the next corridor, the air grew colder, the warmth of the day long since swallowed by the castle's stone walls. The chill was deep, damp, and creeping beneath my armor, sinking into my skin with an unwelcome touch. She followed behind me, her presence impossible to ignore, like a too-bright candle in a dim room.

It had been silent, except for the measured echo of our footsteps. I focused on my immediate objective—getting her to the infirmary, passing her off to Calder, and being done with it. Done with her and whatever unsettling feelings she had stirred within me.

When that wasn't enough, I let my mind drift back to something more significant: Rhys Carrow, the rebellion, the mission ahead. *His outpost was exposed in three places. To the east, through the tree line, if I went in alone. North was a more direct route, but riskier. To the west, where his men—*

"Do you always patrol the castle at night?" Her voice interrupted my thoughts, rich like honey dissolving in hot tea. I didn't respond, assuming she would pick up on it. "It must get lonely, all this quiet," she pressed. "Or is that something you prefer?"

I kept walking with my gaze fixed ahead. My patience wore thinner by the second. She would stop eventually; she had to.

"I imagine this gives you plenty of time to think," she continued. Her voice became lighter, amused by my silence. "That could be pleasant... Or maddening."

Like you?

My jaw tightened, and my eye twitched as I fought the urge to snap. *She was deliberate in this, wasn't she?* A woman like her—a traveler, a commoner, someone who didn't belong within these walls—had no right to sound so damned confident. She shouldn't have sounded so at ease with the silence I wielded as a weapon.

When she continued her rambling, I exhaled in pure exasperation. "Do you ever stop talking?"

To my further annoyance, she laughed, seemingly unbothered. "Only when someone answers," she mused. "It's more fun that way."

"Fun," I muttered. "That's what this is."

"See? I knew you could make a joke."

The adaneth was insufferable.

I halted and spun to face her. As expected, she walked straight into me. The impact was a faint thud against my chest. Her body was too small, too light to do more than falter. She stumbled back. Her hand flew to her nose, and she righted herself, rubbing the spot where she had collided with my armor.

I hoped that hurt as much as she had been irksome.

She blinked up at me. Her lips parted to speak, but she didn't say a word. I savored the moment until that damned smile returned. She was too sure. Too bold. "Let me guess," she said. Her tone was far too casual for someone who had just walked straight into me. "You're about to tell me I talk too much?"

"No," I insisted, leaving no room for jest as I leaned in, letting my words settle. "I'm about to tell you that I see right through you."

Her smile deepened. "Well, aren't you perceptive? I hope you like what you see."

The audacity of her.

My muscles locked with the irritation curled low in my gut. She played a game that held no appeal to me. But the way she stood, the way she looked at me, made it impossible to ignore.

The moonlight filtered through the arched window behind me. Its fractured glow broke through the clouds, softening the hard edges of her face. The silver sheen made the planes of her cheeks and jawline otherworldly, which didn't belong in these halls of detached stone and sharper intentions.

Yet it was her eyes that held me captive.

Amber. Rich. Firelight shone over polished gold. Warm but deceptive—capable of being soft or passionate depending on the light. They locked onto mine through the narrow slit of my helmet, wide and searching. She tried to read something in me I wasn't willing to share.

My breath hitched. It was a faint lapse in control that infuriated me the moment it happened. My eyes narrowed, and my heart kicked against my ribs.

She had been too close. The scent of wildflowers and elduvaris clung to her, carrying the night's lingering chill. Now that she was within arm's reach, the imperfections that distance had dulled became painfully clear. The faint dusting of freckles across her nose and cheeks reflected time spent in the sun, the wind, and the world outside these walls. She stood, wearing defiance as effortlessly as she did that oversized cloak. Her skin flushed a delicate pink that crept up her throat, spread over her cheeks, and bloomed beneath the pale light.

Was it the proximity? Embarrassment? Something else?

The thought had been irrational in its persistence, like a burr caught in fabric—slight but impossible to shake. My chest constricted, and my breathing threatened to slip from its steady rhythm. I took a slow, deep breath, as if that would prevent whatever this feeling was from taking root.

Her mouth parted as if she intended to speak, but no words came. The stillness between us stretched taut. Heat raced up my spine and twisted at the base of my skull, making the limits of my self-control fray at the seams. My leather gloves creaked from the force of my fists clenching at my sides.

No.

I gritted my teeth and buried the feeling deep inside. *It meant nothing. She was insignificant.*

Yet I stood, trapped in a moment that shouldn't have existed. The blush on her cheeks deepened as her gaze dropped to the ground. I huffed. The pressure in my chest eased just enough for me to regain control and push away the unsteady tug she had wedged beneath my skin. She was another distraction in a night I wanted to forget. Nothing more.

Her forced cheerfulness grated on me in a way I couldn't identify or dismiss. It made me want to tear down whatever walls she had built and discover what lay beyond them.

I pivoted and stalked toward the infirmary doors. "Stay here," I snapped over my shoulder before pushing the door open. It creaked under my touch, and the aroma of dried herbs and burning oil wafted into the chilled corridor. "Calder!" My voice pierced the silence.

Even with my back to her, she remained bright as ever. *Damn her.*

Footsteps shuffled inside, followed by the slow scrape of a chair against the stone. A tired voice drifted out before its owner appeared. "I'm coming, I'm coming," Calder's tone conveyed the weariness of someone who hadn't slept in days. "If it's another one of those so-called 'herbalists,' you can spare me the trouble and send them right back out the—"

The faint glow from within the infirmary backlit her figure, highlighting the distinct features of her face. Calder was tall and built from efficiency and endurance. She had pulled her chestnut-brown hair into a tight, practical bun, but stray wisps escaped, curling around her temples and defying her usual precision. A streak of dark herbs, ink, or dried blood smeared her cheek, a testament to the long hours she spent tending to the sick and preparing remedies.

Her sharp hazel eyes flicked toward me, ready to argue and protest, before settling on the young woman behind me. She stilled. There was a brief pause—a flicker of calculation. I didn't understand what Calder saw in her, but something changed, and I didn't like what that meant. Stepping aside, I crossed my arms while Calder studied her.

The corners of my mouth pulled into a faint scowl behind my helmet. "She claims she's here for the position."

Calder offered a dry, humorless laugh and shook her head. "They've been emerging from the woodwork—desperate, clueless, and barely skilled enough to bandage a finger. I—"She paused, her gaze sharpening as she reassessed the woman.

The woman shifted on her feet, her earlier ease faltering under Calder's scrutiny. Her smile held a newfound tension. Her fingers tightened around that damned journal of hers, and she dipped her head, avoiding Calder's gaze. Whether it was a sign of submission or strategy, I couldn't tell. I should have been pleased, but that moment of uncertainty—the brief fissure in her carefully crafted mask—unsettled me.

"I must take my leave," I announced with a stiff bow. "The castle doesn't inspect itself."

Calder scoffed.

I straightened, flicking a final side glance at the woman. "Good luck."

4

EDEN

THE INFIRMARY WAS inviting, quite unlike the cold, harsh stone corridors I had traversed to reach it. The room was warm and soothing, filled with the calming scents of lavender and chamomile. Their soft floral aromas blended with the faint tang of medicinal herbs. A golden glow spilled from a modest chandelier. Its flickering light danced across the pale plastered walls and exposed wooden beams, casting a gentle haze of comfort over the space. I hadn't expected the sense of safety it presented.

The front room appeared quaint yet organized. It served as a place where order met care, where everything had a purpose beyond mere functionality. A large wooden desk stood at its center, worn smooth by time yet polished to a warm sheen. Neat stacks of parchment, ink bottles, and quills covered its surface. Their careful arrangement suggested routine—someone who knew where everything belonged. A vase of dried flowers rested to one side, with their muted hues adding a personal, homely touch, a softness that felt out of place within the castle walls.

Beside the desk, a chair upholstered in faded fabric sat waiting, inviting despite its age, as if it had witnessed countless hours of quiet contemplation, with careful hands tending to more than just wounds. My gaze drifted toward a corner shelf filled with jars and vials. Their contents comprised a collection of dried leaves, ground powders, and tinctures suspended in glass. Each jar was labeled in careful, slanted handwriting, though the ink had faded with time.

I stepped closer. My fingers itched to reach out, trace the delicate loops of the script, open a jar, and breathe in the knowledge contained within it. Whoever worked here took pride in this place. Every carefully arranged item and every softened edge made the room resemble a sanctuary more than an infirmary. Even the stone beneath my feet had been softened by a rug with a faded floral pattern, warming the space in a way I hadn't thought possible. This served as a restorative space, not just for bodies.

As I peered around the desk, I was left speechless. The second room opened into a larger, more enchanting space, which was an unexpected contrast to the quaint front room. Shelves stretched from floor to ceiling, crammed with books, journals, and scrolls—a scholar's trove and a healer's sanctuary. The faint scent of aged parchment and dried ink mingled with the ever-present fragrance of herbs, filling me with a sense of dedication and wonder. My fingers brushed the cracked spine of a worn leather-bound tome as I approached.

At the room's core stood a long wooden table cluttered with the unmistakable tools of the trade—mortar and pestles, small cauldrons, and cutting boards darkened from use. Tiny glass bottles filled with amber liquid and powdered mixtures lined the surface. Above, bundles of drying herbs hung from the ceiling beams, their green, and brown stems swaying in the still air, filling the space with a rich, forest aroma.

A window at the far end allowed a sliver of moonlight to filter through. Silver streaks spilled across the wooden floor, catching on the edges of scattered parchment and polished glass vials. The way the light danced in the room made the space pulse with far more than just knowledge.

I could spend long nights hunched over this table, my hands dusty with crushed petals and ground roots, ink, and charcoal staining the creases of my fingers as I scribbled notes into my journal. I would wake to the smell of steeped tonics, the soft flicker of candlelight illuminating unread books waiting to be devoured. I had spent years learning in darkness, in silence, and in secrecy. I would have a space to work, study, and heal—something I had never experienced before. A home, of sorts. The thought took my breath away.

No.

It wasn't home. It wasn't mine to claim. I forced a breath and steadied myself, tracing the rim of an empty glass bottle with the tip of my finger. It could be... if they let me stay.

Calder's voice brought me back to the moment.

"Your name?"

I hesitated, not having given it much thought. I hadn't needed to until now. Eden Therrin was a name too heavy with old wounds, one I wanted to leave behind me. If I spoke it here, in this place, it would tether me to everything that had been. I wanted a fresh start. An alternative name.

One of my own.

"Quinn Larkspur," I said, the name unfamiliar yet fitting.

Calder arched a brow. If she suspected the lie, she didn't press. Instead, she held out her hand. I offered her my journal, placing it into her palm. She took it with care, as though its weight might betray its secrets, and flipped it open, scanning the pages with an intensity that tightened my chest.

The silence stretched before she spoke again. "The beginning," she murmured, tilting the journal toward the light. "It's all herbs and flowers—basic uses, trial and error notes." She paused. A faint crease formed between her brows as her fingers traced the edge of a page. "Topical ointments, salves... nothing too intricate, but detailed. Painstakingly so."

I resisted the sting of her words. It had taken years to compile those notes, test every mixture on myself, and record the effects. The writing and diagrams on those pages exceeded mere study—they were survival.

Calder continued. Her fingers flipped through more pages. The candlelight caught in her expression—a mix of curiosity and skepticism wrapped in exhaustion. "Later," she muttered, "it changes. General remedies, tinctures, poultices..."

She stopped, tapping her finger against a section where I had scrawled names and ailments in uneven handwriting.

"Other people's needs. Their pains and illnesses. You started keeping track of them."

I nodded. "I did."

Calder lifted her gaze from the pages, fixing me with a stare that saw far too much. "Why?"

The single word reverberated in my mind. *Why?* Because nobody had ever kept track of mine.

I hesitated, unable to speak. Her gaze was too steady and perceptive, squeezing the truth out of me regardless of whether I wanted to give it.

"It started as a matter of survival," I admitted, my voice just above a whisper. "I needed to learn to keep myself alive. But... it became more. I saw how much I could help others. Their needs became just as important as mine." It was the most straightforward answer I could give—the truth, but not all of it.

Calder's assessing eyes raked over me, peeling back layers I had kept hidden my entire life. Her gaze lingered in places that left me exposed and raw.

"You've spent much time under the sun," she murmured, her tone soft, as she read the unspoken story etched into my skin. Her words became a blade pressed to a nerve. "Freckles, tinted skin... even the way you stand. You braced against the elements. It's all written on you."

A piece of me wanted to recoil from her words, deny them, and correct her. But she was right, and that unsettled me the most. She had unraveled me piece by piece, with observations that felt too personal and precise.

I nodded, unsure how to respond. My hands clasped the hem of my cloak, my fingers gripping the fabric to anchor myself. I had spent so long hiding behind masks, careful smiles, and chosen words. Yet she tugged at the fringes of everything I had been reluctant to let show.

Calder straightened. The fleeting softness in her tone vanished as quickly as it had come. The moment of quiet assessment had ended. She snapped my journal shut and set it on top of the desk with a decisive *thud*. Her lips curved into a faint, testing smile.

"Create three things from your journal—ointments, tinctures, or anything else." Her eyes turned to me. "But you won't be using your notes. If they are truly yours, you won't need them."

My hand lingered on the journal for a moment, fingers twitching over the worn leather cover, before I resolved to let it go. Its weight had always been a comfort. It proved my knowledge and everything I had survived. Now, it amounted to an untouchable test.

My fingers quivered as I withdrew my hand. "What would you like me to make?"

"That's for you to decide," she said, turning toward the opposite end of the room and glancing over her shoulder. "Follow."

Although smaller, the next room had shelves covering the walls, filled with jars, vials, and bundles of dried herbs. The aroma overwhelmed me—elduven, sharp, medicinal. Layers of dried roots, preserved flowers, and infused oils created a dense fragrance that lingered on my skin.

Calder gestured around us. "Everything you need is here," she announced, eliminating any space for doubt. "You have until sunrise."

The flickering light of the sconces cast long, shifting shadows across the stone floor. *Breathe. Stop shaking.* I had to prove myself. I memorized my notes, each formula, and each ratio etched into my memory, scarred.

Her gaze made the room suffocating. Every move I made gave the impression of being watched, weighed, and dissected. My fingers clung to the worktable. "Well," I said, forcing a smile that felt like wearing an ill-fitting mask. "Let's see if I can impress you." The words came laced with the same constructed ease I had mastered over the years.

Calder only clasped her hands and watched. Scanning the shelves, my mind sorted through the possibilities before settling on the first remedy—a simple burn salve I had made countless times. My fingers skimmed the jars and bundles, selecting comfrey root, calendula petals, and beeswax. Each ingredient had become an old friend—familiar and reliable.

I arranged them with precision, hoping Calder would notice. With a quick strike of flint and steel, I ignited a small flame beneath a brass cauldron, the metal catching the warm glow of the firelight. The wax melted, and the scent of honey infused the air as I mixed in the herbs. The once-separate elements blended into a smooth, golden balm that was thick and glistening when I lifted the spoon.

Calder's silence hung heavy, but I fixed my smile and glanced at her with a practiced air of ease. "First one's done,"

I chirped, sliding the jar toward her. She didn't respond or acknowledge the effort, but her eyes tracked my every move.

Next—a joint pain liniment. I reached for dried arnica flowers and cayenne pepper, a potent combination. The pestle was heavy in my hand as I ground them into a fine powder. My movements remained calm and measured, but inside, my nerves buzzed like a hive of bees. The powder combined with oil and alcohol, and I shook the jar until the scent of spice and medicine permeated the air, stimulating my senses.

"Be careful with that one," I joked, even though my stomach knotted. "It'll wake you up if you're not prepared for it."

Calder's brow twitched. *Amusement? Annoyance?* I couldn't tell.

The final remedy was more personal, more daring. I hesitated before reaching for what I needed to create a frost salve I had crafted during one of the darkest winters of my life. The nights had been long with biting frost, and I needed something to keep my fingers from stiffening beyond use. I gathered pine resin, chamomile, violet petals, and a pinch of myrrh, their scents wrapping around me with a memory. My hands trembled while I measured and ground, but I disguised it with a cheerful hum, keeping my movements fluid. I couldn't falter. Not where she could see.

When the resin melted, I stirred in the herbs. The mixture thickened as it became fragrant, elduven, and familiar. A warmth spread through my chest from the comfort of doing something I understood.

Calder stepped closer and studied my work. "What is that?"

"A frost salve," I replied, ensuring my voice remained bright and steady. "For frostbite and cracked skin. The violet petals help circulation, and the resin forms a barrier against the cold."

She cocked her head and inspected the jar as I poured the finished salve inside, the smooth liquid settling into the glass. "Where did you learn that?"

"I made it up," I admitted. "My cracked, bleeding hands left me with nothing else. It took weeks of trial and error, but I got it right."

Calder's eyes flicked to mine, searched and peeled me open without touching me. "And it worked?"

I nodded. My heart beat against my ribs, but I kept my mask in place. "It did. For me and others in the village. I've used it ever since."

She picked up the jar, turned it in her hands, and watched the salve shift against the glass. The flickering light softened her features, blurring the sharp edges of her face. "Interesting." She set the jar on the table and looked at me again. "Resourceful. Precise. Perhaps you'll prove useful after all."

"I'll take that as a compliment," I said lightly.

Calder gave me one last careful look before disappearing into another room, leaving me with a lingering sense of uncertainty and a growing unease. The fire's heat licked at my skin, but a chill ran through me. *Useful.* Not skilled or talented. The word lingered in my mind, a reminder of the thin line between acceptance and exploitation. I shrugged my shoulders, trying to shake off the feeling. It wasn't acceptance, but it was a start.

Calder reappeared from the back room, a measuring tape coiled in her hand, her brow furrowed in concentration. She strode toward me with the quiet authority of someone who didn't need to announce their importance, and I couldn't help but tense, my instinct to step back and brace contained beneath my controlled expression.

"What is that for?"

"For your uniform," she said, unraveling the tape with a snap of her wrist. "Stand straight."

"Uniform?" The word felt foreign to my tongue, a weight I was unsure I could carry.

"Yes. You won't work in the infirmary in patchwork gowns and scavenged boots." Her eyes perused me, lingering on the frayed edges of my sleeves, the scuffs on my shoes, the signs of life outside the castle walls. "This is a place of healing, not charity," she added. "Appearances matter here."

I stifled the irritation bubbling in my throat and pressed against the instinctive bitterness that twisted in my chest. "I assumed my skills might speak louder than my hemline."

Calder's eyes narrowed. I thought she might scold me, but the most minor twitch pulled at the corner of her mouth—a near imperceptible smirk. "Skills are a good start," she admitted, voice still brisk. "But they're not what the castle remembers. Stand still now."

Her hands were efficient and no-nonsense, and the measuring tape brushed against my shoulders, waist, and arms with quick precision. The sensation was foreign and impersonal, yet unsettling. When was the last time someone had taken my measure? Since no one had bothered?

"What colors do you favor?"

Colors? As if my opinion even mattered. I hesitated because I didn't know, but the first answer that came to mind blurted out before I could overthink it. "Green, I suppose. Or red."

Calder hummed. "Dark colors, then. Something useful."

"Like me."

She stepped back, scrawling notes on a scrap of parchment that she withdrew from her apron pocket. "You'll have your garments in a few days. Until then," her gaze flickered toward my sleeves again, "try not to ruin what little you've got."

I let out a slow breath as the weight of expectation settled deeper into my core. I had wanted this. Had fought for it.

Now, there was no turning back.

5

OBERON

'*DO WHAT YOU must.*' My jaw clenched as Alric's words echoed and curled around my thoughts. It was my duty, the sole purpose carved into my bones since I took my first life.

'*It will be done.*'

The thick forest canopy above filtered the moonlight into scattered, fractured beams. Gnarled trees surrounded me with skeletal branches that reached toward the sky like bony fingers clawing for salvation. The air hung damp and heavy, thick with the decay of leaves and the musk of wet soil. My boots pressed into the ground silently.

A flicker of movement caught my eye. Moths danced around the distant firelight, their fragile wings casting fleeting shadows against the trees. Near my boot, a beetle skittered across a twisted root, its carapace glinting wet obsidian. In the underbrush, nightchimes droned, a restless, ceaseless hum. Their translucent bodies pulsed with a faint bioluminescent glow, and their wings shimmered as they rubbed against each other, releasing a sound of distant thunder in a whispering chorus that breathed with the night itself.

The forest was alive, breathing, and writhing, claiming me as one of its own.

Beyond the tangled branches, the firelight wavered, a dull ember against the darkness. I crouched low as the shadows wrapped around me. The camp sprawled ahead, basic but practical. Mismatched tents leaned against one another, their fabric stained from weather and battle. A thin coil of smoke curled toward the sky, carrying the acrid scent of charred wood and the pungent aroma of roasted meat. The embers crackled and spat sparks that died before they touched the damp ground.

Stolen provisions lay scattered—barrels pried open, grain sacks spilled across the dirt. Crude but effective weapons glinted in the firelight. A rusted sword rested against a tree, its edge nicked from overuse. At the heart of the camp, a larger tent stood, its canvas patched and fraying at the seams.

Rhys Carrow.

Their vigilance was laughable. Two sentries paced the perimeter with the awareness of men who had never faced death in the dark. Their movements were slow and predictable. One scuffed his boot absently against the dirt, the other rubbed the nape of his neck as if the weight of his helmet was too much effort to bear. Near the fire, another rebel sat slouched, his laughter too loud and careless, his guard forgotten in the warmth of drink and cheap entertainment.

The narrow paths between the tents were worn by use, slick with mud, and strewn with debris. A broken cart was propped against a tree with its remaining wheel half-sunken into the dirt. Moths flitted in languid spirals above the fire. Their wings caught the light before they vanished into darkness. A spider spun its web between two crates, its delicate strands glistening with trapped dew.

Even the insects thrived on the negligence of these men.

The details settled into my mind—every weakness, blind spot, and gap in their defenses. My fingers brushed the handle of my dagger. No alarms. No mistakes.

I became a specter, a shadow between flickering firelight and shifting darkness. My breath was steady, and my pulse was a measured drumbeat in the silence. The night welcomed me and wrapped me in its icy embrace. It rendered me a mere whisper of movement against the endless drone of insects.

The first watchman lingered nearby, his boots still scuffing against the dry dirt in a sluggish, thoughtless rhythm. He was a man accustomed to the illusion of safety. His weight shifted from one foot to the other, his spine slouched with boredom, and his hands rested on his belt. He was oblivious to the death poised mere inches from his elbow, to the way the shadows had deepened around him, swallowing the moment whole.

Fool.

My blade extended my will. It whispered through the air, a fleeting caress of steel against flesh. His skin parted like silk, the muscle split, and his windpipe's wet, fragile cartilage collapsed beneath the edge.

His breath hitched in a soft, strangled choke before his mouth gaped open in wordless shock. His blood welled against his lips, bubbling. The light in his eyes flickered. Recognition. Realization. Fear. Then nothing.

I caught him before his body could betray him with a thud, lowering his weight into the undergrowth. The ground welcomed him greedily, drinking deep as his life drained into its hungry maw. His limbs jerked once, twice—as he held onto the last wisps of existence before they eluded his grasp.

The fire crackled, and laughter murmured from the camp. Unconcerned. Unaware.

I exhaled through my lips to steady the rush of iron and instinct that curled through my veins. I had no time for satisfaction. No time for hesitation.

The second watchman was sharper. His head twitched, and his shoulders stiffened with a hound's nervous awareness, sensing the subtle change. He sniffed and turned, fingers brushing his sword's pommel.

Too slow.

In a seamless glide of motion, I surged forward. My dagger's hilt met his skull with a brutal crack and an impact that reverberated through my arm. Bone crunched, his breath hitched, and his mouth opened into a half-formed sound that never reached his throat.

His eyes were glazed, pupils wide with unfocused shock. He swayed as his body betrayed him, and consciousness slipped before he had the chance to fight for it. He crumpled in a lifeless husk of meat and bone, hitting the dirt with a *thud*.

The firelight flickered, painting the world in amber and blood. The smell of smoke, roasting meat, and fresh death curled around me.

Two dead.

Each step held a calculated breath as I moved deeper into the camp. The laughter by the fire swelled, raucous and careless, their voices thick with ale and the fleeting illusion of safety. They remained oblivious. One of them gestured wildly with a half-eaten hunk of bread clutched in his greasy fingers. Crumbs tumbled to the dirt as he bellowed something crude, and his companions doubled over in drunken amusement.

Disgust roiled in my stomach. *These were the men who sought to overthrow the kingdom? These undisciplined fools, these slovenly brutes who couldn't even hold their posts with vigilance?* They had no honor. No caution or understanding of what a veritable war required. They were children playing at rebellion, unaware of the blood that would drown them before they ever reached their throne of fantasies.

The air shifted when I neared the main tent. The fabric danced with false movement, but beyond the illusion, Carrow, and another man's voices whispered plans over stolen maps. I stilled, waiting. *The other man should leave soon.* His tone became weary, and his words faded into dismissal. A moment later, footsteps scuffed the dirt, growing more distant.

Carrow was alone.

The tent flap remained silent as I slipped inside, my movements honed to instinct. The interior featured sparse yet practical furnishings. A heavy wooden table dominated the space, its surface cluttered with maps, ink-stained parchments, and the remnants of a half-melted candle. A battered chest sagged in the corner, partially hidden beneath a moth-eaten blanket.

Rhys Carrow stood hunched over the table, his fingers tracing a path along the map. He looked younger than I expected, just a few years past boyhood. He wore his dark hair in a loose knot, allowing stray strands to fall around his face. His clothes were a mix of leather and rough-spun cloth—practical and worn—not the silks and embellishments of a noble-born rebel. He was a warrior, not a schemer.

He didn't hear me until the callous press of my blade kissed the bare skin of his throat. "Don't move." My voice was a low growl edged with finality.

He stiffened. His fingers hovered above the map, and his breath hitched before he concealed it. His pulse quickened beneath the steel, like a rabbit caught in a snare, weighing whether to fight or surrender. His lips curled into a sneer. "So, the prince sent his lapdog." His words dripped with derision, resentment lay beneath—not just for me, but for the reality of his weakness.

The blade pressed harder against the strain in his throat. One slice, and he would drown in his own blood. "Your life is forfeit unless you comply." My hand was steady, but my patience was thin. "Your choice."

He huffed, his jaw muscles tightening. "You'll get nothing from me." The venom in his tone resembled a dying man's last defense—full of bravado but devoid of leverage.

I moved closer, near enough for him to sense the pressure of my presence behind him, close enough that the icy bite of steel against his skin turned into a tangible threat. "Then you will regret surviving tonight."

The camp stirred. Laughter had dulled into hushed murmurs. The sharp clatter of weapons broke through the night. Someone had noticed the missing guards. "Your men are smarter than you," I muttered as I cinched the rope tight around Carrow's wrists, feeling the muscle tense in my grip.

His smirk wavered. He heard it, too. Shouts rose, and torches flickered to life. Their glow stretched between the trees' hungry fingers. "You won't survive this," he taunted, but the bravado couldn't mask the flicker of uncertainty in his eyes. He knew the tide had shifted, and control had slipped from his grasp.

I hauled him forward, sticking to the narrow paths that the firelight couldn't reach. The rebels scrambled, their movements frantic, disjointed, disorganized, and afraid. They had never expected that the shadows would fight back.

A cluster of them blocked the path ahead, weapons drawn, but hesitation thick in their stances. Their grip on their blades was too tight, their breath too fast. Inexperienced. Predictable. They weren't ready for death.

Shoving Carrow behind me, I seized the handle of my blade. "Stay down." My blade passed through the air in a whisper of finality. Its silver edge gleamed before it struck flesh. The steel parted a man's throat, severing his jugular in one clean, merciless stroke.

Blood gushed, hot and viscous, against the cool air. He staggered backward, hands scrabbling at his throat, his eyes wide with the stark, horrifying realization that he was dead. His knees buckled, and his body twitched in its final, futile rebellion against the inevitable. Then he crumpled with his essence pooling beneath him in dark rivulets.

A second man faltered, and his blade shook. My dagger plunged into his chest with a wet, sickening crunch. His ribs caved in around the intrusion. Bone and muscle scraped against steel as the blade found his heart.

His mouth opened in a soundless scream, breath stolen by the impact of the strike. His body spasmed, and his fingers twitched as he grasped for redemption in an irrevocable act of defiance. His legs gave out, and he slumped against a tree. He slid in a slow, agonizing descent, leaving a thick smear of crimson in his wake.

Another man hesitated, his sword half-raised, eyes flicking between me and his fallen comrades.

Too late.

My dagger found its mark before he could retreat. The blade punched through the soft flesh just below his jaw. He gurgled and choked on his blood, clawing at my wrist in a wasted effort. I twisted the blade, severing what brief life remained in him. His form slumped against my shoulder before I shoved him off of me.

The camp had awakened. There were more torches, more shouting, and the odor of blood thickened the air, mixing with smoke. Carrow stared at the bodies and swallowed hard, his throat bobbing. I wiped my blades clean against a fallen rebel's tunic, flicked the excess blood to the ground, and met Carrow's gaze. "Still think I won't survive?"

The last man stood frozen, caught in the liminal space between fight and flight. His eyes darted between the bodies at his feet and the predator that stood before him. His skin had gone pallid, a sickly shade of green, and his mouth fell open in shallow, panicked gasps. *He was breaking.*

Terror locked his limbs, and his sword trembled in his grasp. There was a moment when his mind flailed for a decision, a flicker of desperate thought that might have led him to run, call for help, or take another action. But I didn't allow him the opportunity.

Steel flashed in the dim moonlight. A clean stroke. His throat parted with ease, and the air left him in a wet, ragged exhale. The sword slipped from his fingers before his body followed, crumpling to the ground in a heap of dead weight.

With the path open, I wrenched Carrow forward and hauled him into the dense forest. His steps faltered, his balance unsteady, as I dragged him through the underbrush. His earlier taunts had quieted, and his voice dwindled to bitter murmurs. The weight of reality had settled over him. His people were dying, his rebellion was crumbling, and he was at the mercy of the one thing he had no defense against:

The prince's lapdog.

The shadows swallowed us once more. The chaos of the camp dimmed behind us, replaced by the whisper of wind through the branches and the distant chorus of nocturnal creatures. The terrain beneath my feet became uneven, slick with moss and damp soil, each step measured to keep us silent. Hot pain flared along my shoulder, a reminder of a blade that had grazed me in the skirmish. A shallow cut, but enough to burn as sweat seeped into the wound. I had endured worse.

Carrow stumbled, wrenching us both off balance. I held tighter on his bindings and jerked him upright. The deeper we went, the more the sounds of pursuit faded. They hadn't found us in time. They couldn't halt the events underway. Carrow had only begun to grasp the full extent of his failure.

And I would ensure he felt every second of it.

❧

I THREW CARROW against the bitter, unforgiving stone of the cell. He landed hard. His breath knocked from his chest in a ragged gasp.

The damp air reeked of mildew, iron, and the lingering smell of old suffering. Shadows clung to the corners of the walls that had absorbed the agony of those who had come before him.

His defiance had worn away on the journey back, eroded by exhaustion and the knowledge that there was no escape. But he hadn't broken. Not yet. His silence now wasn't submission—it was resignation. A man staring at the inevitable, teeth clenched around whatever scraps of dignity he thought he had left.

"You should have cooperated, Rhys," I stated, my voice devoid of emotion, flat and absolute. "Now you will have to tell me everything I want to know. One way or another."

I dragged him by his bound wrists until his back met the damp stone wall. He gritted his teeth as I unfastened the ropes, replacing them with iron shackles. His ankles followed, the metal clinking as the locks snapped shut. He winced as the steel bit into his raw flesh but refused to yield.

Shame.

The blade of my dagger slid free from its sheath in a whisper of steel. The metal drank in the faint light, its honed edge reflecting the raw, flickering terror in Carrow's eyes. I inched close enough to let him feel the weight of what was coming, close enough that he could smell the blood dried into the leather of my gloves.

The first cut was shallow. Only a whisper of pressure against his forehead. A scratch. A single bead of blood welled up, trembling before it carved a slow path down his face, a crimson tear against the pallor of his skin.

My dagger traced a deliberate path, slicing through flesh with precise, practiced strokes. The blade marked his skin, parting it in thin, glistening lines. Each fresh wound brought a new shudder through his body, a tremor in his breath, a tightening in his muscles.

He held out longer than most. The first scream came when the cuts deepened. The dagger bit into the sinew beneath his skin. A raw, strangled sound burst from his throat that echoed off the stone walls and filled the chamber with a haunting symphony of pain.

Sweat beaded on his brow, mingling with the blood as it dripped from his chin. His breathing turned ragged, shallow, and quick between shuddering gasps. But I wasn't done. The blade worked with precision, carving slow, intricate paths across his chest, arms, and ribs. Several cuts were shallow, others deep enough to expose the pale, glistening fat. The smell of iron thickened in the air.

His body drooped against the shackles. His muscles twitched with every fresh wound, every new flare of agony. His screams faded, swallowed by silence, his mind reeling, struggling to withstand what his body couldn't. Still, he refused to speak.

I inclined my head, examining the ruin of him. The once-bright defiance in his eyes had dulled, reduced to a glazed, unfocused stare. His lips trembled.

"You will talk," I murmured. An involuntary shudder rolled through him, his body betraying what his mind refused to yield. My dagger hovered over his chest, the tip poised against sweat-slicked skin, catching the dim light.

I leaned in, my voice emotionless and steady. "I will ask again, Rhys Carrow, before I make this worse for you. Who are your allies? What are their plans?"

He shook his head in a slow, weak movement. Not defiance anymore—just the hollow remnants of a man trying to hold onto something that had slipped away from him.

"Wrong answer."

The dagger arced downward in a single, precise motion. The blade met flesh, then bone, and in a swift, clean separation, his pinky severed. The digit hit the stone floor with a wet thud. Carrow's cry ripped through the cell, his body jerking against the restraints. His breath hitched, shuddering, his eyes wide—panic and pain warring in their depths.

I let the pause expand between us while he gasped, writhing against the chains and curling his fingers inward to reclaim his lost possession.

Then I did it again.

The ring finger next. Another clean cut. Another ragged, keening cry reverberated against the stone walls. His body convulsed, muscles spasmed, and his breaths came in ragged, wet gasps. His head lolled forward, blood dripping from his ruined hand onto his lap.

Then the middle.

His shriek shattered through the cell, but it didn't last. His body betrayed him. His eyes rolled back as his mind fought to escape the torment.

My fingers curled into his matted hair, yanking his head with a sharp jerk. "No," I hissed. "You don't get to leave yet." His lashes flickered, and his pupils dilated, his breath shallow and wheezing. He swayed in the shackles, teetering on the edge of unconsciousness.

I pressed the blade to his chest, letting the slick metal graze his skin. A reminder that there was still more to come. His body shuddered beneath it, his mind clawing back from the abyss. His breath came in sharp, uneven bursts. He hung onto life by a thread.

Leaning in, I whispered again, my tone softer this time. "Let's try again. Who are your allies? What are their plans?"

His lips moved, but the sound was a rasp, a breath of surrender lost in the still air between us. Watching the dull glaze settle over his eyes, I cocked my head and leaned closer, my ear inches from his mouth. A smirk ghosted across my features as I murmured, "Don't make me work for it, Rhys. You only have so many fingers left."

He drew a ragged breath, his entire body trembling with the effort. The fight was gone.

Carrow's breath rattled as he whispered, "The... the Blacksmith's Guild..." His words trembled, slipping past bloodied lips. "They're planning... a ritual... a sacrifice." His head lolled, his body sagging further against the restraints. "In five full moons... the bleeding must be done."

I stilled. The words were a slow-drawn blade against my spine. "Sacrifice?"

Carrow gave a weak, shuddering nod, his eyes glassy and unfocused. "The Guild... they need blood... something old, strong..." He swallowed hard, his head rolling against the stone. "The uprising depends on it."

I processed the words, turning them over, searching for meaning. It was vague: a ritual, a sacrifice, blood, five full moons. It was superstition, another misguided effort to harness old magic for their cause. It didn't matter. What mattered was that they planned something, and I had the means to end it. A whisper of satisfaction nestled in my chest.

My gaze didn't leave his face as I lifted my dagger and plunged it into his eye with a *pop*. Steel met little resistance before the familiar wet squelch of muscle gave way, and I twisted the hilt. His body jerked once, twice, then stilled.

A final, rattled breath escaped him before his life faded into the hollow silence. His blood dripped slowly and thickly as I pulled the dagger free. The smell of iron, sweat, and urine clung to the air.

The following silence was deafening. Only the soft, wet patter of blood broke the stillness. I stepped back, my chest heaving with exertion, my breath slow as I studied my handiwork. His body sagged in the iron shackles, limp and lifeless. His fingers—what remained of them—hung in grotesque angles, and his ruined eye socket was a gaping hole. A crimson trail streaked his cheek, soaking into the drenched fabric of his tunic.

The slow, gnawing burn in my shoulder became impossible to ignore. The dull ache from earlier had sharpened into something more sinister. It burrowed beneath my skin, radiating outward, setting my veins alight with fire and ice. My pulse pounded in my skull, and my breath came in shorter, shallower gasps.

The wound wasn't deep. It was a grazing cut, at best. But it was wrong.

Cold sweat broke across my brow. My fingers twitched at my side, a tremor I hadn't willed. I spun around, striding toward the stairs, but the world around me shifted with each step. The stone beneath my boots felt unsteady, the air thick and stifling.

Shadows stretched along the walls, twisting in the flickering torchlight. I blinked hard, but my vision swam. The flames formed shifting halos of gold that danced at my periphery.

Poison. Someone had coated their blade. I swallowed back the nausea that churned in my stomach and pushed forward. I had endured worse. My body had weathered wounds far beyond this—deep, gaping slashes, broken ribs, even the bite of steel through my abdomen.

When I approached the infirmary, my chest heaved. Each breath was labored and jagged. My limbs grew heavy, and my steps faltered. The world tilted beneath me.

I compelled my body to comply and staggered the last few paces until the infirmary door stood before me. My hand pressed against the wood, and my body's weight sent it swinging open. I collapsed against the frame, weak fingers curling at my side as I struggled to keep myself upright. The room spun and blurred into indistinct shapes.

The figure at the infirmary desk jumped to their feet. I pushed forward, reaching them before my legs wavered. My body felt detached, and the ringing in my skull drowned out everything else. The figure was there before I could fall. Their hands pressed against my side, steadying me.

Warm.

Firm.

"Poison," I rasped. The relentless, pulsing roar in my head didn't allow me to hear a response, if there was one. Dark ink bled into the boundaries of my vision. My knees buckled, and the ground beneath me tilted.

The world fell away, enveloped by the unforgiving void.

6

EDEN

THE SUBTLE HUM of voices from the infirmary had long since faded, drowned out by the rhythmic scrape of stone against metal. I moved the pestle in slow, methodical circles, grinding the dried leaves into a fine paste. Their sharp, elduven smells curled into the air, mingling with faint traces of linen bandages and aged wood. The motion was soothing and meditative—a quiet ritual I had perfected over the years.

Outside, the world reduced to muffled footsteps and the occasional murmur of a hushed conversation. The consistent motion of my work lulled me into a calm focus, threading my thoughts between the properties of each herb. *The balance of potency is needed to dull pain without dulling the mind.*

The fragile peace was shattered by a distant clamor. Voices rose with urgency. The heavy thud of boots echoed through the stone corridor, growing louder with each hurried step. My hands stilled, and my eyes darted to the door. The hinges of the infirmary door rattled when it slammed open.

A towering figure filled the doorway, blocking the light from the torches beyond. For a moment, I could only stare in silence. The dim glow illuminated his armor—black leather, dulled by streaks of fresh crimson. His dark tunic was soaked with a slow seepage on his shoulder.

My gaze snapped to his hands. One hand clutched his shoulder, fingers curled in rigid defiance against the pain wracking his body. The other, coated in red, dripped onto the floor. Moisture glistened on his brow as he clenched his jaw with grim determination. That look wasn't just pain or blood loss. It was a creeping, slow, and insidious poison that was eating him alive.

The intensity of his dark gaze was fixed on me, causing a jolt of awareness to pool deep in my belly. It felt raw, unsettling, and unfamiliar. A man whose life hung by a thread regarded me with a focus so intense that it left me breathless.

His steps faltered, and his weight shifted. Instinct took over as I surged forward. My hands caught his arm, and my fingers gripped the rigid muscle beneath the slickness of blood. His weight pressed into me as he leaned. He was heavy. The scent of leather, iron, and the faintest whisper of pine filled my senses, but the metallic tang of blood caused my pulse to spike. There was too much of it.

"Poison," he growled, the word edged with raw pain and dragged through clenched teeth. His voice was gruff, yet he remained unwilling to surrender to the agony.

"I know," I murmured, my voice steady despite the rapid thud of my heart. "It's okay now. Can you remove your—"

An abrupt intake of breath followed, accompanied by sudden tension in his body and the buckling of his knees. The full weight of him collapsed into me, and I staggered while my muscles strained to keep us both upright. His armor pressed against my chest, and the distinct smell of blood from his tunic flooded my senses. Panic clawed at my throat as I strained against his weight. "Calder! There's a man here! He's poisoned! I need help!"

Calder burst into the room with remnants of the tinctures she had brewed staining her apron, and the sharp smell of herbs lingering around her. Her eyes widened at the sight before her, and she wasted no time with questions. She rushed to my side, and helped lower him onto the cot. His body sagged into the coarse fabric, his limbs weighed down by exhaustion. His head lolled to the side, and his breath was shallow yet steady.

I stepped back, my hands trembling as I assessed the damage with clinical detachment.

Focus. Breathe. Work.

The wound on his shoulder was deep. The torn edges suggested a weapon that had done its work with vicious intent. Blood welled, pooling dark against his stained tunic. Worse still, the telltale signs of poison bloomed across his skin—a sticky, spreading discoloration that twisted through the wound like creeping ivy. It worked fast.

I swallowed hard and pushed aside the dread swirling in my stomach. There was no room for hesitation, no space for fear.

"Larkspur, I will prepare a rinse and an antidote," Calder ordered as he moved toward the workbench. "You will stitch him up and stop the bleeding."

I nodded and reached for the fastenings of his tunic, my fingers loosening the knots. Even through the haze of pain, his body tensed at my touch, muscles twitching as the poison coursed through him.

As I peeled back the fabric, I revealed scarred skin. A battlefield was etched across his body—silvered lines and deep-healed wounds, each one narrating a story of his past. My throat tightened. Whoever he was, he had endured.

His breath hitched and shuddered as his body waged war against the slow crawl of death pressing in on him. I couldn't let it win. I reached for a clean cloth, my hands steady as muscle memory took control.

Breathe.

Work.

Save him.

His face drew my attention again as I tied off the last stitch. He was lethal—sharp cheekbones and a strong jawline. His skin, tanned from time spent beneath the sun, contrasted with the stark pallor of the poison. His lips, set in a firm, grim line, twitched as if he battled between pain and defiance.

His thick, wild black hair spiraled at the tips, tousled as if he had spent days in battle without rest. A single cut trailed along his temple, dark against his skin. His features were not only handsome but also dangerous and untamed. However, the faint point of his ears startled me.

Who was he?

Warm, thick blood smeared my hands while I worked and stained my fingers with the burden of how close he was to death. I maintained pressure on the wound, feeling the sluggish pulse of his life beneath my palms. His body's labored movements struggled against the poison that was tearing through him.

My eyes returned to his attire. The cut of his tunic and the reinforced bracers were not standard knight's armor, unlike the men who passed through the infirmary in their polished, ceremonial breastplates and plumed helms. His gear facilitated movement and blended into the shadows rather than catching the light. It was purposeful and covert.

Calder's hurried steps caught my attention. She returned with a rinsing pot and a small bowl of antidote. The acrid smell of herbs and crushed roots filled the room. She knelt beside him, working quickly as she rinsed the wound with steady hands. The bitter concoction darkened the torn flesh as she pressed the antidote onto it, and its thick paste absorbed into his skin.

She raised his head to pour the remaining liquid between his lips. "Drink," she commanded.

His throat strained as he swallowed the liquid. His body jerked, and a loud, shuddering cough wracked through him, a strangled sound caught between a groan and a gasp. His fingers twitched, and his muscles tensed as his body resisted. He stilled again. The only sound left was his breathing. Though ragged and uneven, his breaths grew steadier with each passing moment. The antidote was working.

I settled back, willing my thoughts to settle. But my gaze betrayed me, drawn back to the movement of his chest. Beneath the streaks of blood and grime, the defined lines of muscle became undeniable. His body was built for combat and endurance. My fingers had felt his strength and the burning of his fevered skin beneath my touch, but the curve of his abdomen, with taut skin stretched over powerful muscle, had become visible.

Gods.

My cheeks flushed with heat.

"Damn," Calder muttered.

I flinched and glanced up at her; my pulse spiked as if she had caught me, but Calder didn't look my way. She wiped her hands on her apron. Her frown deepened as she studied him. "Sinclaire is always getting hurt, but this isn't like him."

Sinclaire.

I savored the name's unfamiliarity before finding my voice. "Sinclaire?"

Calder stiffened. Her frown smoothed, and her tone shifted into something too even.

"Sir Oberon Sinclaire," she clarified briskly. "A knight of the castle. The one who brought you here upon your arrival." She waved a hand dismissively. "Reckless, that one. He constantly puts himself in danger. It must have been another skirmish near the border."

The words sounded overly polished and rehearsed. My gaze returned to him as the name clung to the man before me: Oberon Sinclaire. A knight. Yet, he was different not only because of the armor that didn't conform to the standard, but also because of how Calder spoke about him.

Mystery lingered below his surface, concealed beneath scars and silence.

7

OBERON

MY EYES CRACKED open with a groan. The infirmary was dark and quiet, save for the faint rustle of leaves outside the arched windows and the distant echo of footsteps in the castle halls. The silence settled deep into the bones of a place untouched by the chaos of the waking world. The air was fragrant with dried herbs and a subtle medicinal tang.

I tilted my head back to glance out the window above me, where the stars blazed in the sky. I still had time to report to the prince before the sun rose over the horizon.

Grimacing, I sat up, flexed my hands, and rolled my shoulders to test the tension in the muscles beneath the bandages. It wasn't terrible. I had survived worse. However, the tight wrappings were a damn nuisance. I tugged at them, unwinding the linen and tossing it aside.

The wound was healing, though more slowly than I would have preferred. I didn't need to be coddled like a novice recruit. The office door creaked open when I was halfway through pulling my shirt over my head.

Calder paused in the doorway with her arms crossed. Her eyes scanned me with the exasperation I had grown accustomed to from her. "I knew you would do that," she sighed, shaking her head.

Ignoring the sting of movement, I finished fastening the ties at my wrists. "Then you should have saved yourself the effort of wasting bandages."

She scoffed and brushed past me to the table where the discarded bandages lay. "That's why I sent Quinn to her quarters." She flicked a loose thread from the table. "I knew you would get up the moment you had the chance."

I grunted. "Quinn?"

Calder sighed and turned to the infirmary desk, picking up a small, worn leather-bound book. My eyes flicked to it, and my brow twitched in recognition. The image of that young woman clutching a leather journal with white knuckles at the garden archway came to mind. That meant she had passed Calder's examinations that night.

How long had it been since then?

Weeks?

Maybe more.

"Quinn Larkspur. She keeps records," Calder explained, leafing through the pages, "regarding the patients she treats. But the beginning... It's different."

I crossed my arms. "How does this concern me, Calder?"

"She has suffered." Calder's voice dropped. Her eyes roamed the pages, brow furrowed. "It's in her writing. Hesitant. As though she expects someone to be reading over her shoulder."

I leaned back against the infirmary wall, unimpressed. "You know what I do. We both know that people have suffered at my hands, no less. Stop being cryptic and explain why you think this is my problem."

Calder closed the book with a soft thump and glanced at me. "Perhaps it's not," she said, tilting her head. "But I think it might be."

Lacking patience, I huffed. "Just get to the fucking point, Calder. I have to report to Alric."

She held my gaze for a moment longer, then handed me the journal. "Look through it. The beginning. I believe she can help beyond healing. Her competence stems from experience. We might need her more than you realize, Sinclaire." She paused. "Hells, *you* may need her."

I snatched it from her hand with a grunt, prepared to dismiss whatever horseshit she was pushing this time. But as I flipped open the worn cover, my gaze fell upon the first few lines, and my brows furrowed.

It was overly cautious. Her words lingered on the page as if she had rewritten them several times before permitting them to remain. She omitted certain details, leaving gaps where explanations were needed. Calder was right: they weren't just the notes of an herbalist or healer.

The still parchment crackled beneath my fingers as I flipped through a few more pages. Initially, the entries were ordinary:

ingredient lists, dosages, and descriptions of effects. Yet, the way she wrote them gnawed at me.

The ointments and salves were standard enough, though the sheer number of pain-relieving mixtures stood out. Some were for muscle aches; others addressed wounds, burns, and bruising. I frowned and turned another page. Then came the poisons. A slow breath left me as I gripped the book tighter. Not just poisons.

Antidotes.

Many were common and well-documented. However, for others, the agony reflected in their listed symptoms extended beyond clinical observation. The descriptions were not detached; they weren't authored by a healer who studied their patient from afar. They were too precise, too visceral.

They weren't symptoms she had seen; they were symptoms she had felt. Certain toxins had notes scribbled in the margins—how long they took to set in, how the pain felt at each stage, and which body part seized first. The handwriting became tighter there, more frantic.

My jaw locked.

Had someone tested these on her?

A bitter taste rose in my throat. Poison was *not* a casual interest by any means. It wasn't something one could experiment with lightly. The notes weren't just a healer's curiosity, but a matter of survival.

I shut the book and drummed my fingers against the leather before curling them around the edges.

Calder observed me with a stoic expression. "You see it now," she murmured. It wasn't a question.

Running my fingers through my hair, I tucked the book under my arm. "I don't know what I'm looking at," I admitted.

Calder tilted her head. "No?"

I shot her a glare. "I sense someone who is concealing something. Someone more knowledgeable than she admits." My arm flexed against the leather binding. "Someone who has endured more than she will reveal."

Calder nodded, as if that was what she expected to hear. "And?"

"And what? You expect me to fix it?"

"I expect you to take notice," she corrected, her voice sharp but kind. "You're not as blind as you pretend to be, Sinclaire. You have selective vision. You see things and choose not to care."

"You think this changes that?"

A small, perceptive smile tugged at her lips. "I think it already has."

I turned away before she could say more, pushing the infirmary door open with more force than necessary. This wasn't something I had time for. I had a report to make, a job to do. But as I stalked through the castle halls, the journal's weight under my arm bore an unexpected significance.

Quickening my pace, I walked faster as if it would shake the damn thing from my mind. The words and symptoms clawed at my thoughts, refusing to let go.

First sixty seconds: Numbness spreads from the fingertips. A slow, creeping chill. Lips tingle. Breathing remains unaffected.

It was vivid in my mind. Her fingers trembling as she gripped her charcoal, the stick pressing too hard into the page, causing her letters to appear sharp and frantic.

Two minutes: The numbness deepens, spreading up the arms and to the chest. Muscles twitch involuntarily. Heat rises in the throat but lacks actual fever.

I exhaled slowly, ignoring the rising burn in my chest.

Five minutes: Fingers curl inward. Clenching is impossible. The chill becomes fire. A paradox. Pain radiates through the limbs.

Had she experienced this? Was it something inflicted upon her? Was it intentional? A test? Punishment?

Fourteen minutes: The chest tightens—not from asphyxiation, but from the pull of the ribs being peeled apart from the inside.

My teeth ached from the intensity of my clamped jaw. Only someone familiar with those descriptions and the brutally precise pain mapping could articulate that, unless they had endured it themselves, breath by breath.

Ten minutes: Vision blurs. Ears ring. The body is now frozen, yet the pain persists. The mind stays awake. The heart stutters, but it does not stop.

I struggled against the knot in my throat. I had witnessed death, had tortured and killed, enough to know the pain in her notes was neither swift nor merciful. It was a prolonged and agonizing torment.

Fifteen minutes: Consciousness flickers. Limbs heavy. Heartbeat irregular. Lungs no longer responsive. There is nothing left to do but wait.

Then there was the last note, so dark it looked angry, scrawled beneath the entry: *Doesn't kill at once. Leaves them aware. A cruel way to die, but not the most vicious.*

The pounding in my ears was so loud that I couldn't hear my footsteps when I turned a corner. I wasn't fond of the sensations winding through my chest; I didn't enjoy caring, yet something told me I had little choice.

The prince's chambers were as lavish as ever, featuring polished marble floors, heavy velvet drapes that absorbed the moonlight, and a fireplace crackling in the corner, casting flickering shadows across the room's gold accents. A large mahogany desk stood against the far wall, topped with neat piles of parchment, maps, and an open inkwell. Alric stood near the hearth, clad in loose-fitting nightclothes; the pale linen tunic hung open at the collar. His sharp green eyes caught the firelight, and his golden hair was tousled, likely from running his hands through it. He appeared more like a young noble lounging before bed than a ruler burdened by the responsibilities of a kingdom.

He turned as I entered, and a smirk danced on his lips. "You look like death, Oberon."

The guards closed the doors behind me, and I scoffed. "You should have seen me yesterday."

He chuckled, his arms stretched above his head. "I take it your mission was... eventful?"

I sank into a chair by the fire, winced as my shoulder collided with the back, and stretched my legs out in front of me. "Carrow talked."

Alric's smirk faded, and his expression sharpened with interest. "And?"

Sighing, I ran a hand over my jaw. "The Blacksmiths' guild. They're the ones planning the rebellion." Alric remained silent. His gaze was distant, and his fingers tapped against the arm of his chair. So, I raised another concern. "The poison they used on me was different."

He sighed and rubbed his temples. "I'm not surprised."

I frowned. "Explain."

Alric leaned forward, resting his elbows on his knees. "The Blacksmiths' Guild is located in the forest to the east of the border, at its southernmost edge."

My eyes narrowed. "That's the Fae border."

Alric nodded. "That's why they had access to such a poison. Not because of you," he waved a hand, "but because they needed to adapt their survival tactics to their environment."

My fingers drummed against my thigh. It made sense, but it didn't sit right.

Alric looked unconcerned. He leaned back in his chair, a slow smile tugging at his lips. "Either way, they are no longer a threat if you cleared most of their camp, as I expect you did. A weak guild of blacksmiths is nothing to worry about."

I nodded, though the unease remained in my gut.

Silence lingered between us for several breaths until Alric's eyes glanced at the leather-bound book under my arm. He raised a brow. "Didn't take you for much of a reader."

Scoffing, I shook my head. The journal landed on the small table between us with a dull *thump*. "This one is different."

Alric tilted his head. "Different, how?"

Considering my words, I traced my thumb over the ridges of my knuckles. I avoided explaining things that didn't pertain to my missions or orders. But this had been bothering me more than I cared to admit. "It's Quinn Larkspur's. The new herbalist," I huffed.

His brows lifted. "Oh?"

I scowled at the accusations in his tone, but he only grinned. "I wasn't looking for it," I explained, ignoring his amusement. "But Calder handed it to me and told me to read the beginning."

My fingers intertwined in my lap. "It's not just notes on herbs; there are remedies, salves, and tinctures. And the poisons... the antidotes..." I frowned. "They are too detailed. Too personal."

Alric's smile disappeared, and his expression became more serious. "Personal how?"

It didn't seem appropriate to share her writings and past with someone she hadn't met, but Alric was the prince, her ruler, and her employer.

I knew him well enough to understand that he wouldn't use such knowledge with hostile intentions. The Count, who found me half-dead in a ditch and raised me to be a weapon, had sent me to kill the young crown prince. He said Alric wasn't fit to rule. Too weak. Too naïve.

Alric's guards caught me when I got close enough to prove him wrong. He could have had me executed, and perhaps he should have. However, he showed mercy by taking me into his service. He gave me the title of Knight on paper while still using me as an assassin in practice.

If Calder was correct and Quinn was useful for much more than we had realized, he needed to know.

Exhaling, I opened the journal and flipped to the section that had twisted my stomach. I turned it so he could see and tapped my finger on the hastily scribbled notes in the margins. "She wasn't writing about patients," I explained. "She was writing about herself."

Alric's gaze skimmed over the entries. His expression darkened as he scrutinized the frantic handwriting, the vivid descriptions of pain, and the precise timing of each symptom that revealed she had experienced them herself.

He sat back, rubbing his jaw. "So, what do you plan to do?"

I blinked and met his gaze. "What?"

He gestured to the journal. "You wouldn't be telling me this if you didn't care, Oberon."

"I don't care," I scoffed.

"Sure. And I'm a common foot soldier," Alric laughed.

I pressed my teeth together. "She's hiding something."

"No doubt."

"She's not my problem."

Alric sighed and stood from his seat. "No, but she's about to be."

My brows furrowed as he approached his desk. "I'm not sure I understand."

"We received letters from Silverfel while you were handling Carrow's bandits," he explained, picking up a paper from the desk. "Reports of an unknown sickness affecting the town have been received. Their healer is struggling, and they need assistance. I'm sure you know our border knights are there."

I rose from my seat as he handed me the letter written in hurried, uneven strokes, as if penned by someone exhausted or frantic. Near the edges, dried bloodstains and ink smudges disfigured the parchment.

To The Courts of Aurelith,

I write with urgency, as time is not on our side. A sickness has taken hold of Silverfel, spreading faster than our healer can combat it. Fever, convulsions, bleeding from the gums and nose. These are but the beginning. Those afflicted weaken within nights, slipping into a stupor before their bodies fail.

We have tried every known remedy, including poultices, tinctures, and even the oldest of Silverfel's herbal traditions, yet nothing halts its progression. This is no ordinary illness. It is relentless, and we are losing.

I have pleaded for aid before, but the men who oversee our forces refuse to trust the knowledge of women or herbalists, calling for a 'proper' physician. None have come, and none will.

Suppose the Courts do not send help soon, Silverfel will fall to this sickness, and whatever afflicts us may not stop here.

I beg you to send someone more knowledgeable. Someone who can help.

-T. Whitlow, Silverfel Healer

I traced a finger over the signature. "Why are you showing me this?"

Alric's expression remained neutral when I glanced up from the letter. "I believe you understand why," he sighed. "I spoke with Calder. She mentioned that Larkspur would be the best fit to handle it." He gestured toward the journal. "And now I understand why."

My fingers flexed against the parchment, and my expression darkened. "You're planning to send her there."

He nodded. "With you."

"You expect me to be a child minder?" I scoffed.

Alric smirked. "No, I expect you to keep her safe and ensure she doesn't get herself killed, Oberon."

"Of course you do. And you think she will go along with that?"

Alric smirked. "She won't be able to resist. You've seen her work. She won't turn her back on those in need. Not after surviving so much to reach this point."

I pursed my lips. It annoyed me he was right. The illness wasn't simple; it was new and unnatural.

The decision to send Quinn Larkspur was sensible. She differed from the other herbalists dispatched to treat soldiers with scraped knees and upset stomachs. She understood things that others did not. She had experienced them. She knew exactly what they needed.

My tongue traced the inside of my lip before I looked back at Alric. "You're sure about this?"

"You don't think she is capable?"

"No. That isn't the problem. I think Calder is right."

Alric's lips twitched. "Then, what is it that bothers you?"

I didn't have a straightforward answer, just a feeling—a sense of wrongness that lingered in a corner of my mind. Something about her, about Silverfel, about it all.

"I'll go," I muttered, returning the letter to him. "When do we leave?"

Ease washed over Alric's features. "Tomorrow. At first light. Calder is preparing what Larkspur will need, but it requires the sun's time." I picked up the journal from the table and moved toward the door. "Oberon."

He folded his arms across his chest when I glanced over my shoulder. "Don't remain oblivious to it. If magic is involved... You need to be prepared."

I held his gaze for a moment. "Get some sleep, Alric."

8

EDEN

WHEN I PUSHED the infirmary doors open, I expected to find him where I had left him the previous night. Instead, I stood in the doorway, dumbfounded as I stared at the empty cot. *Why did I care?*

Perhaps it was curiosity. He was frustrating, impossible, and far too obstinate. I couldn't shake the image of him from last night—pale, drenched in sweat, struggling to remain conscious. No ordinary man could have walked away from that in just a few hours. No typical man could have survived.

My feet carried me toward Calder's office. I hesitated before knocking, then pushed the door open. She glanced up from her work. "Looking for something?" She continued searching through the papers scattered across her desk, frowning at one before setting it aside. Next, she moved on to the bulky book that lay open in front of her.

"Not something. Someone." I crossed my arms. "The knight, Sir Sinclaire. He's gone."

Calder hummed as if it were the most unremarkable thing in the world. "Of course he is."

My lips parted as I stared at her, my arms lowering in defeat. "He was poisoned."

She met my gaze with an arched brow. "And?"

I opened my mouth to speak, but the words caught in my throat. He shouldn't have been able to move. He shouldn't have left. I wanted to understand how he managed it.

Calder rubbed her hands on her apron. "He always acts like that. He stumbles in, half alive, and is gone before regaining his health." She shrugged. "I would bet quince that he's already back to work." She cocked her head as she watched me. "If you're so curious, then watch him when you see him. He reopens his wounds with that stubbornness of his."

I forced a smile. "I'm not curious. I'm just concerned for his safety, as an herbalist."

She smirked.

I turned to leave and rolled my eyes when she could no longer see my face. It wasn't my problem. I wasn't his keeper. If he wanted to throw himself into a fight and reopen his wounds, that was his business. Still, the thought persisted. If he collapsed during training or bled out somewhere because he was too damn proud to rest... I had to tend to him. That was it. That was the only reason I cared.

"Wait, Quinn." The sound of a heavy book closing and papers rustling in the wind filled the hush between us.

I turned back to face her.

"Go to the greenhouse; an herb appears to be out of place. Its roots may be strangling the others." She rubbed the bridge of her nose. "You are much better suited for this task than the other two."

Caring for the plants had been more appealing than dealing with stubborn, deathly ill knights who vanished into the night. I nodded and left her office. With a frustrated sigh, I took my tools and gloves from the infirmary desk and walked out.

The morning air brought a slight chill against my skin, a coolness that did little to ease my deep fatigue. My limbs still felt heavy from lack of sleep, compounded by the weight of unanswered questions on my conscience. The cot had been empty. He had left. But how?

Soft shades of lavender and gold still painted the sky as the last traces of dawn clung to the horizon. I focus on the gravelly texture beneath my boots, allowing it to soothe me after the long night I spent battling the memories that clawed at me.

The instructions from Calder were straightforward—a simple task designed to give me a break from the stuffy infirmary air. I spent several days and nights cooped up there before the knight arrived. Perhaps I could have convinced him to stay and heal if I had been there when he woke.

The distinct clang of steel-on-steel cut through the quiet morning. My steps slowed when I approached the courtyard, captivated by the sparring match unfolding before me. Two figures moved with practiced motions, but my focus narrowed to just one of them.

Oberon Sinclaire moved with a grace that seemed impossible. It stunned me. His movements were precise and controlled. It wasn't just skill; it was instinct. It was as if battle was not something he did, but something he was. Even when injured, he didn't hesitate or falter. There was a recklessness in his movements, a quiet defiance that made it clear this was the only place he felt alive.

He was up and already moving. Already fighting. Less than a day ago, he had been half-dead in the infirmary. His fever was too high for him to stay conscious for more than a few breaths. But there he stood, swinging a sword as if he hadn't been lying on a cot, bleeding out just hours ago.

But that wasn't the source of the feeling that stirred in my chest. It was the distinct contours of his face, the way his dark hair fell across his forehead, damp with sweat. With his sleeves rolled up, the taut muscles in his forearms flexed as he gripped the hilt of his sword. The slight parting of his lips as he exhaled, his chest rising and falling with steady, measured breaths.

It was the way he carried himself, as if he held the weight of the world on his shoulders and refused to let it break him. He had witnessed things no one else could comprehend. He fought even when there was no battle to be won. Gods help me, that was far more dangerous. Far more thrilling.

I've known it since I first saw him, scowling in the infirmary with those onyx eyes. But seeing him in this state—alive, focused, and challenging his opponent with quiet intensity—evoked feelings it shouldn't have. He was rude, grumpy, and impossible to converse with without the urge to strangle him.

I should have walked away, gone straight to the greenhouse, as Calder requested, but my feet refused to budge.

His forearm muscles tensed as he gripped his sword, and his tunic clung to his body with every precise movement. It was absurd to stare. Yet, knowing that didn't stop me, nor did the heat creeping up my neck.

The other man was dark-haired and broad-shouldered and wore a shit-eating grin. He swung his blade in a quick arc. Sinclaire parried one-handed, his grip steady but lacking the force I imagined he should have had with both arms.

"You're slower today," the man taunted as he stepped back. "Thought Fae blood made you stronger, Sinclaire."

Fae blood?

Oberon huffed. "Stronger doesn't mean invincible."

The man smirked. "Right, right. We wouldn't want to strain your delicate Fae heritage too much."

Fae.

Oberon Sinclaire had Fae blood, and my mind struggled to comprehend it. Following the uprising, Prince Alric had exiled the Fae to Valeithwyn; they were powerful and dangerous beings, often regarded as cursed. Yet he was one of them, working under the man who had banished them. It shouldn't have surprised me. Even now, he moved with effortless grace, as if he were carved from legend.

Oberon lunged forward, driving the man back with a sharp clash of metal. "Say that again, asshole."

The teasing earned another chuckle. "Oh, you're still grumpy, don't worry. That part of you is all human."

Sinclaire huffed and shook his head. His lips twitched, and amusement flickered across his features before his expression hardened once more. When he adjusted his stance, my eyes darted to the sharp cut of his waist beneath his tunic, noting how his belt sat low and the muscles of his abdomen were visible through the fabric.

What was wrong with me? I didn't know him, but he was a frustrating and irritable jerk and... not entirely a man. But gods help me, he was handsome.

I didn't like the way I was drawn to him.

"Do you plan to talk all morning, Garrick? Or are you going to fight?"

Garrick.

They exchanged another sharp remark when I averted my gaze. I had actual work to do—plants to tend and things that mattered. Not this. Not him. The problem with looking away was that it only made me more aware of how badly I had been staring to begin with.

The greenhouse was enchanting, untouched by the weight of the castle's stone walls and the people within them. Sunlight streamed through the high glass ceiling, casting golden patches over the rows of plants stretching along the wooden tables and raised garden beds. The air was warm and humid, thick with the crisp bite of mint, the soft floral sweetness of lavender, and the sharp, medicinal tang of rosemary.

I inhaled, letting the familiar scents settle my nerves.

Focus, Eden. You're here for a reason.

Calder mentioned a misplaced herb causing trouble. This indicated that it was worth addressing if she had sent me instead of one of the other herbalists. Alternatively, she might have wanted me out of the way. Either scenario was plausible.

My gaze swept over the vibrant greenery, my fingers brushing against the leaves as I walked. The plants here were robust, untouched by the blight that crept through the castle halls. But something else stirred among them.

A vine slithered through the soil, its dark green leaves curling over the edge of a planter. Frostmoths clung to the stems of nearby herbs, their wings edged with ice crystals and their fragile bodies still as stone. An ice beetle skittered away, its iridescent shell reflecting the light in a pale, wintry sheen. The surrounding herbs sagged, their colors faded, and their energy drained.

My stomach clenched.

Bellthorn.

The cursed plant drained life from everything it touched, thriving where it shouldn't. A frost spider with brittle legs hovered nearby, its web spun into a delicate lace of frost, strands trembling as if sensing the creeping corruption. Even the windwhispers, those tiny creatures that flitted like breath against winter glass, avoided the planter.

This wasn't just an overgrown weed. It was a warning. But for what?

Kneeling beside the flowerbed, I traced the vine's path with narrowed eyes. Bellthorn was stubborn and parasitic. It wrapped around other roots, stealing nutrients and choking out weaker plants. While it had its uses in specific remedies, it could be dangerous if left unchecked.

My fingers ran through the soil, feeling the depth of the roots and how they spread beneath the surface. If I weren't careful, removing it could cause it to regrow. That was the nature of bellthorn. It clung. It endured, even when you thought you had eradicated it.

The thought left a bitter taste in my mouth.

This wasn't an accident. It didn't just happen. Someone placed it here, knowing exactly what it could do. The greenhouse was a space for growth and cultivation, but the individual who did this opted for destruction instead. Why? If someone poisoned the plants on which we relied, how long would it be before they turned their attention to something or someone else?

A slow, controlled breath left me as I pushed the thought aside, needing to eliminate it before it caused further damage.

I loosened the soil with my fingers, feeling how the roots wove deep and tangled around those of the struggling herbs. Bellthorn didn't just grow; it invaded. If I pulled too hard, I risked snapping the root system, leaving parts behind to fester and grow stronger. I carved around the largest vine with my dagger, digging into the soil beneath it.

Freeing the plant was challenging; its roots resisted my efforts. But with one final tug, the vine came loose. I tossed it onto the stone path beside me and wiped the sweat from my forehead with my wrist. The herbs left behind still appeared weak, but they should recover now that the threat is gone. Reaching into my satchel, I retrieved a small bundle of sagebrush and mint, crumbling the leaves between my fingers before scattering them over the soil. Their properties helped cleanse any lingering damage the bellthorn inflicted.

Sitting back on my heels, I gazed at the space where the vine had been. Bellthorn was a survivor. It dug deep, spread wide, and made itself unnoticeable until it was too late. It was familiar. I swallowed hard and shook the thought away as a breeze blew in from the greenhouse doors, carrying the distant clash of swords from the courtyard.

After disposing of the bellthorn, I dusted the dirt from my hands and returned to the infirmary, stealing one last glance at Sinclaire and Garrick, who were still sparring as I passed. Calder would still be there, hunched over her worktable as she muttered regarding the incompetence of men who thought they could treat sword wounds with whiskey and good intentions.

Sure enough, she stood at the desk, sorting through a bundle of dried herbs. Her eyes flicked up when I entered. "You're back sooner than I expected," she said, tying a string around a bundle before setting it aside. "Found the problem?"

"Bellthorn," I reply, cutting straight to the point.

Her hands froze for a moment before she turned to face me. "Are you sure?"

I nodded and crossed my arms. "It wasn't growing wild. Someone must have planted it there. The roots were deep, and the placement was intentional. It choked the weaker plants."

Calder sighed "Damn fools," she muttered under her breath, rubbing at her temple. That reaction told me more than I had expected.

My eyes narrowed. "This isn't the first time, is it?"

She gave me an intense look and sighed. "No, it's not. This has happened before, but not for some time. Last time, it was nightshade mixed in with the mint beds. Before that, a fungal rot had spread through the thyme. I had my suspicions then, but I couldn't prove anything."

A slow unease pooled in my stomach. "Who would do this?"

"That's the question, isn't it? Not everyone values healing. Some would rather let things rot."

Frowning, I rolled the thought over in my mind. *Someone wanted to weaken the Courts' supplies.* "Whoever it is, they know plants," I drawled. "They knew where to place the bellthorn to do the most damage."

Calder hummed in agreement, then shook her head. "Keep an eye out. We will handle this quietly for now."

I nodded, but remaining silent caused part of me to bristle. It hadn't been mere sabotage, and it wouldn't end there. Not if it had been occurring for so long.

My hand rested on the door handle when Calder spoke again. "Quinn." I turned back and noticed the thoughtful crease in Calder's brow. She crossed her arms and tapped her fingers against her sleeve. "We've received letters from Silverfel," she announced. "Requests for aid."

My pulse stuttered. Silverfel was one of the kingdom's oldest settlements, tucked away in the dense forest to the south of the capital's border. "What aid?" I asked.

Calder huffed and pushed off from the edge of her desk. "They're vague. The healer is requesting more supplies. There's also mention of something... strange. An illness that isn't responding to any of their treatments. They have requested a male physician."

"Not a healer?"

She gave me a knowing look. "Not a *woman* or a healer."

Of course.

Older settlements still clung to outdated beliefs, favoring male physicians over women or trained herbalists, regardless of their skills.

"They don't have time to be picky," Calder continued. "Whatever is happening in Silverfel is spreading."

I shifted my weight. "Are you sending someone?"

"Yes. I am."

Her hesitation and her expression implied that she was urging me to go. Although I had never ridden a horse before, it couldn't be all that bad.

But why me?

Others under Calder's guidance had seniority. Was it because of the bellthorn? Because of what I had uncovered? That made little sense. It bore no relation to the greenhouse.

I shifted on my feet. "Why me?"

"Because you are the best suited for this." She must have seen the doubt written on my face because she sighed and rubbed her temple. "They are asking for a male physician, but we both know that's not what they need. You have the knowledge and the skills. Hells, you are more meticulous in your notes than half of the royal scholars. If anyone can sort this out, it is you."

Swallowing, I looked down at my hands. "What if it's beyond me? What if I fail?"

"I wouldn't send you if I didn't find you capable. Besides, you won't be alone. A knight will accompany you," she replied, returning to her seat.

"A knight?" I echoed. A flicker of unease crept into my voice. "Which knight?"

9

Oberon

THE MORNING LIGHT slanted through the high-arched windows, gilding the dust motes that swirled in the draft. The hush of dawn still cloaked the corridor. Beyond the walls, distant birds chirped, their sound a counterpoint to the steady echo of my boots.

The castle was waking, though sluggish. The guards shifted at their posts, murmuring among themselves. Their voices were a quiet undercurrent beneath the occasional rustle of servants moving through the halls. None of it demanded my attention.

With each step, a dull, persistent throb pulsed through my shoulder, serving as an irritating reminder of my former carelessness. I rolled it to test the stiffness, feeling the sharp and persistent tension pulling. It was possibly still bleeding, too. My jaw tightened, and I bit back a grimace.

The damned wound had been slow to heal. Now, I had torn it open again.

Calder would have forced me to go to the infirmary if she had seen me favoring it. The thought of enduring her inevitable lecture—her exasperated sighs, her pointed remarks about how I never let myself heal properly—was enough to steer me elsewhere.

I had no interest in dealing with the new herbalist any sooner than necessary; the forced pleasantries and her ability to conceal whatever thoughts ran through her mind were off-putting.

Calder and Alric spoke of her as if she were rare and trustworthy. They didn't see what I did: the controlled and careful nature of her actions, the way she guarded her words. A darkness lurked beneath her surface that she wasn't willing to show. She wasn't just here to help or for the quince. Whatever motives she had for coming to this castle, I would uncover them.

My fingers flexed around the worn leather of her journal. I should have returned it to her the previous night. I should have closed it the moment I finished reading. But I had lingered, flipping through the pages long after I had memorized the parts that disturbed me. The words had sunk deep into my thoughts, a warning whispered too late.

As I approached the stables, the scent of hay and leather wafted through the crisp morning air. The aroma of damp soil and manure blended with the faint smell of rain. Sparrows flitted among the rafters, their tiny wings stirring up dust while a barn cat stretched atop a hay bale. Its tail flicked in irritation at the commotion of the awakening grounds. The familiar sounds of shifting hooves, the murmur of stable hands attending to their tasks, and the occasional snort of a restless mare filled the space.

I had readied Neryth earlier, tightened the girth strap, checked the bridle, and ensured the saddlebags were secure. The massive black destrier stood fully geared just outside the stable doors, his coat gleaming in the slanting light. His ears flicked, and his nostrils flared as he sensed my approach. He shifted his weight, and his muscles rippled beneath his dark hide, exuding the quiet power that had made him my only trusted companion.

A flash of movement beyond him caught my attention.

The herbalist stood at the edge of the stable doors, eyeing Neryth as though he were an insurmountable beast. Her fingers twitched at the hem of her uniform before she caught herself and curled them into fists. She didn't know how to ride. It almost made me smirk.

Almost.

"Dilthen Doe." My voice carried with my approach.

Her eyes snapped toward me, and the corner of her mouth pulled into a tight, forced smile. A flicker of irritation crossed her face, subtle yet satisfying.

Oh, good. She enjoyed this as much as I did.

The moment her eyes landed on the journal in my hand, her smile faltered, a brief crack in the mask she wore so well. Her shoulders stiffened, and her chin tilted higher, as if it could disguise the unease rolling through her. She met my gaze when I stopped a few paces in front of her. Her expression smoothed into glass. "Sir Sinclaire," she greeted. She displayed a practiced steadiness but remained guarded.

I extended the journal to her. Her firm grasp suggested that she believed I might snatch it away. "Calder didn't ask for permission before she handed over your notes." It was a statement meant to convey that I could read her.

Her jaw tensed before she responded, "She told me Prince Alric needed evidence of my competence before she sent me to Silverfel."

An indirect way to say no.

"Welcome to the Capital," I scoffed. She didn't know how things worked here if she thought this was an overstep. The sooner she learned, the better.

She had taken long enough to arrive, and standing around exchanging pleasantries was just wasting more time. I had no patience for unnecessary delays. I nodded toward Neryth. "I assume you can ride."

I already knew the answer, but I relished the anticipation of watching that forced smile break.

"Yes." Her response was immediate.

I narrowed my eyes and tilted my head, feigning consideration. "Alright then," I said, gesturing to the horse. "Get on."

Her lips parted as a flicker of hesitation crossed her face. I thought she might argue, but she squared her shoulders and stepped forward with stiff determination. She lifted her foot to the stirrup, her fingers gripping the saddle's pommel with white-knuckled resolve. She hesitated for a breath, a moment of uncertainty.

She was hopeless.

Without giving her time to reconsider, I stepped behind her. My hands gripped her waist and lifted her onto the horse with little effort. Her layers of fabric concealed most of her form, but she was thinner than expected. There was strength, but not enough for someone accustomed to hard travel.

Neryth snorted beneath her as she shifted, adjusting in the saddle. I stepped back to observe how she settled, working to compose herself after the brief shock of being manhandled.

She released a startled sound, somewhere between a gasp and a curse, as Neryth stomped his hoof. There was no protest or immediate retort, only the gasp and the quick way she braced herself.

She wasn't used to being handled, then.

She went rigid when I swung myself into the saddle behind her, as straight as a damn spear. She straightened, and her spine locked in place as if sheer stubbornness alone could prevent her from acknowledging our proximity.

"Hold on tight," I said firmly. "If you think you might fall, lean into me. I'd prefer not to hear an earful from Calder because of your stubbornness."

Her head turned, revealing the tension in her jaw. She likely wanted to deliver a sharp retort meant to create distance where there was none. But I didn't give her the opportunity. With a flick of the reins, I urged Neryth forward.

The rhythmic pounding of hooves shattered the early morning silence as the deep, steady beats of Neryth's stride echoed through the ground. The scent of wet leaves and turned soil was cool, carrying the lingering bite of dawn. Around us, the forest enveloped the world. Towering oaks and slender birches swayed in the wind, their golden-green canopy rippling like silk.

A soft mist clung to the ground in the shaded hollows where the sun had yet to reach, curling around the undergrowth. Birds stirred in the branches, their wings rustling against the leaves as they took flight. A frost hare darted across the path ahead, a blur before vanishing into the brambles. Somewhere in the distance, a raven's low, throaty call echoed through the trees.

Quinn remained unmoved. She was still rigid. Too proud.

I huffed loudly enough for her to hear. "You ride as if you're waiting for a blade in your back."

The tension in her shoulders tightened even further.

She had gone silent. Her breaths were steady yet restrained, focusing on maintaining her composure. This was how she held herself, despite the fluid motion of the horse beneath us. It was control. She refused to let herself slip and insisted on not relying on anyone else to keep her upright.

Her stubborn independence would have amused me had I not been grappling with my own growing discomfort. I was accustomed to riding, to the speed, the rush of wind through the trees, and the ground's pulse beneath thundering hooves. I lived for the thrill. However, I wasn't used to sitting behind someone, feeling each shift, each breath, and every subtle movement of the person in front of me.

Her thighs pressed against mine with each stride. The proximity was unavoidable, but that didn't make it any easier. Every bounce of Neryth's gait rocked our bodies together, and no matter how much I tried to focus on the ride, the awareness settled deep in my bones. Unwelcome heat curled up my spine.

Quinn, of course, was oblivious to my distress.

She leaned forward and adjusted to the horse's rhythm. Her hips swayed in time with Neryth's movements, a gesture that was graceful in a way she probably didn't even realize. I gripped the reins tighter, forcing myself to look ahead, only to glance back at her a second later. The gentle curve of her back, the way the fabric of her uniform molded against her frame, and how the strands of her hair whipped against my cheek with the wind were cool and silken. I shifted, cleared my throat, and adjusted the reins to keep myself occupied.

The faintest trace of herbs and the elduven tang of the infirmary still clung to her, mixed with that floral smell that was unique to her. The lingering chill of the morning air sharpened it and weaved it into the damp smell of the forest floor, of moss and fallen leaves. It was an oddly soothing combination.

Until she started talking.

Or rather, *yelling* over the pounding of hooves against the dirt path. "Are you always so pleasant in the morning, or is it just me?"

Hoping she would take the hint, I remained focused on the path ahead. At the very least, her constant chatter relieved the tension that had settled between us.

But I should have known better.

She interpreted my silence as a sign of encouragement. "I understand. You're a big, brooding knight. You have to maintain that image." She shifted her position. "But you could at least pretend to be friendly. Maybe even smile. Have you ever tried that? Smiling, I mean."

My fingers flexed against the worn leather as I tightened my grip on the reins. *She couldn't sustain this forever. Her voice would eventually give out from yelling.*

She kept proving me wrong.

"I bet you're grumpy because you didn't get enough sleep. You should take a nap when we arrive. Oh, wait. You probably sleep with one eye open, considering the whole perception thing and all."

The corner of my eye twitched.

"Farn."

Enough.

With a subtle flick of the reins, I urged Neryth forward in a sudden burst of speed. Quinn released a startled yelp, and her hands scrambled to grip the saddle.

For a blissful, perfect moment, there was silence.

"How rude!" Her head whipped to the side, eyes flashing as she scowled at me. I hissed through my teeth and bit back a groan as she twisted in the saddle to glare at me over her shoulder. "I'm sure most people have conversations while traveling; it could help pass the time."

"I don't need conversation," I warned. "I need silence."

"Well, I do."

Of course, she did.

And judging by the smug, slight tilt in her voice, she knew how much she had grated on my nerves. She relished every damned second of it. A slow sigh escaped me, meant to ensure she heard my annoyance. If she continued to run her mouth, I had to steer the conversation to a more tolerable topic.

"Fine," I grumbled. "Why?"

She twisted in the saddle as if she couldn't believe I had responded. Then came that irritating, triumphant curve of her lips. "Oh, so you do engage in conversation," she teased.

I shot her a look.

She cleared her throat. "Right. Why do I talk so much? It's simple. I don't like silence."

I arched a brow. "Why?"

She shrugged, but it was too casual a gesture. "Because when it's quiet, I overthink." She sounded sincere. It was less that she wanted to provoke me and more that she revealed something she hadn't meant to admit.

I should have left it at that and let the conversation die, just as I had with others I had cut short over the years. But I added it to the ever-growing list of things I should have done around her.

"Thinking about what?"

She hesitated, scrambling to push the information back behind whatever armor she wore, and sighed. "Oh, you know. Life. Death. The possibility that I could be thrown off this horse at any moment and break my neck."

"Not if you hold on properly," I scoffed

"So, you do care if I fall off."

"I care about getting to Silverfel without having to scrape you off the ground halfway there."

She snorted but didn't press further. Tilting her head back, she gazed up at the treetops as we rode beneath them. Sunlight filtered through the leaves, dappling her freckled face in shifting gold. "Well, what about you?"

"What about me?"

"Why do you dislike conversation?" she ventured.

I huffed, redirecting my focus to the path. "People talk too damn much."

She let out a hearty laugh. "I can't argue with that!"

Neryth chose that moment to leap over a fallen branch. His powerful muscles contracted and released in one fluid motion. The impact of landing sent a jolt through us both. Quinn rocked against me, and her head collided with my shoulder.

A vicious pain lanced through me. I clenched my teeth, willing myself to stifle any reaction and breathe through it as I had a thousand times before. But it was too late. She turned her head, undoubtedly ready to make another witty remark. Except her eyes darted across my face, catching that breath of pain before I masked it. Her expression soured.

Damn it.

I groaned.

"Are you—"

"I'm fine."

"Like hells you are," she hissed. Her brows creased, and her lips formed a tight line. The expression warned of an impending argument that didn't interest me. But it felt different this time—less irritation, more... concern.

Hearing her curse stirred unwelcome feelings within me, and I despised how unguarded it sounded coming from her, slipping past her lips without a second thought. The way it settled into my skin was an irritant I couldn't shake. It grated against me in ways I didn't comprehend. I had heard women swear before and was accustomed to it, thanks to Calder. But hearing it from her unsettled me, and I had no explanation for why.

She became rigid again and sank into a blissful silence.

The sun dipped lower in the sky, streaking the clouds in molten gold and ember-red. The light fractured through the canopy, dancing shadows along the path ahead. The air cooled, the smell of damp soil thickening as dusk crept in. Before us stood the uprooted tree, it was massive and gnarled, its roots twisting toward the sky and dense with dirt and stone. The trunk sprawled across the path, its bark weathered and stripped bare where rain and wind had battered it. Moss and fungi crept along its surface, evidence of its long slumber.

Quinn shifted in the saddle, breaking the silence. "Whoa." Her voice carried a note of fascination as she took in the sight. "Did something knock it over? Or has it always been like this?"

"Storm took it down a long time ago." I pulled the reins as I guided Neryth around the obstacle.

She hummed thoughtfully. Her eyes lingered on the fallen giant as she attempted to piece together a story from the way the bark had peeled and split. Silence settled again, heavier this time, until the skeletal remains of a village emerged through the trees.

Quinn pointed. "What is that?"

"Our midpoint," I said tersely. "Emberhollow."

"What happened there?"

I flicked a glance at her. *Was her village under a damned rock? Was she even from Aurelith?* "The uprising."

Her posture shifted, the tension in her shoulders clear, and her fingers curled. "They didn't talk about that back home," she murmured. "If I could even call it that now."

The way she said that didn't sit well with me. I narrowed my eyes. "Most have seen it while traveling."

"I didn't leave the village until I left for the castle."

That disarmed me. Her words bore a peculiar weight, not only in their expression but also in what remained unspoken. "Never?" I pried.

She shook her head, her eyes still fixed on the town's skeletal remains. The last of the sun bled across the horizon, its dying light painting the ruins in deep hues of orange and violet. The jagged remnants of rooftops jutted into the darkening sky like broken ribs, while the crumbling chimneys served as gravestones, unmoving guards of a place long lost to time.

I shouldn't have been curious. I should have let the silence stretch between us while it lasted.

Unfortunately, I included that on the list of should-haves.

"Where are you from, then?"

The change was subtle: a slight tilt of her chin and a shift in her posture.

"It's just a small village; you wouldn't recognize it."

Evasion.

I let the silence settle this time. Her fingers toyed restlessly with the edge of the saddle as if she needed to keep occupied. Naturally, she didn't let the quiet linger with us long.

"Stop here," she demanded.

My grip on the reins tightened. "We're halfway to Silverfel. If we keep going, we'll arrive by mid-morning. I'm not stopping."

Quinn shot me a glare, and damn her, the heat of it curled straight into my gut. "If you won't stop so I can assess the damage to your bleeding wound, at least stop because I need to piss, and my butt hurts," she clipped.

I swept a hand across my face, inhaling sharply to stifle the growl in my throat.

Stubborn adaneth.

"Fine." I pulled the reins and steered Neryth toward the river bordering the village's outskirts. He huffed as I dismounted and reached up to help Quinn. She was anything but graceful about it. The moment her feet touched the ground, she stretched her legs and let out a murderous groan.

I tied Neryth's reins to a low-hanging branch before her eyes burned into my back. When I turned, her hands gripped her hips, her chin lifted, and her eyes were full of intent. Ready for war.

"Oh, for fuck's sake," I groaned.

"You split it open while you were sparring with Garrick, didn't you?" Her brows furrowed, and her lips pressed into a firm line. That stormy, relentless look was back. She was prepared to pry me apart piece by piece.

My brows pulled together, and my eyes narrowed while I studied her face. That was a remarkable guess. As if she could read my thoughts, she continued. "I saw you on my way to the greenhouse. As if your vanishing into the night wasn't enough."

Of course, she noticed. Her eyes darted around, taking in her surroundings like a trained scout, when I found her at the castle garden. I shouldn't have expected anything less.

Shifting my weight to my good side, I scoffed. "I didn't have time to sit around a miserable infirmary."

Quinn closed her eyes and took a slow, deliberate breath, as if *I* were the one testing *her* patience. When she opened them again, they appeared calm and calculating. She wouldn't let it go. "Why didn't you go before we left?"

Because I didn't want Calder prying into my business, and I wanted to avoid seeing her there before I had to see her every day. I rolled my shoulders with feigned indifference. "I didn't want to deal with Calder nagging me."

Her lips pursed before she muttered, "A lot of good that did you." I expected more arguing, for her to keep digging, pushing, and demanding. Instead, she stepped around me and moved toward Neryth. Her fingers brushed against the buckles of the saddlebag, grazing the leather with deliberate intent, before she turned and glared at me. "Take it off."

I scowled. "Excuse me?"

She raised an unimpressed brow. "Your shirt, Sir Oberon Sinclaire," she articulated.

"I'm fine."

She stepped closer. "You're bleeding through it." I glanced at my aching shoulder. Small, undeniable dark blotches seeped through the fabric.

Quinn crossed her arms and shifted her weight to one side, watching me with an expectancy that made my blood heat. "You can either remove it yourself, or I can remove it for you."

I huffed a quiet, bitter breath. "You're insufferable."

She smiled sweetly. "And *you* are terrible at hiding injuries. Take. It. Off."

10

EDEN

THE EVENING AIR carried a crisp bite, a quiet warning of the creeping night. Gold and crimson stretched in molten threads over the river's surface. The dying sun spilled fire across the slow-moving current. Damp soil mingled with distant brine, thickened by the murmur of insects. Emberwings flickered in and out of sight, pulsing with amber light. Shadows lengthened through the underbrush where unseen creatures stirred, their rustling drowned beneath the rhythmic croak of dusk-born toads.

Oberon shifted his weight. His jaw ticked, a muscle twitched in his cheek, and his brow drew. "What?"

"Are you obstinate *and* deaf?" I shot back, my voice edged with command. "Take your shirt off, Sinclaire. I'm not asking. If it's bleeding enough for me to see through black fabric, it needs to be restitched and wrapped."

He stared at me, unreadable. For a heartbeat, I expected refusal—a sharp retort, the usual pushback. But his shoulders lifted in a slow, resigned sigh, and his fingers moved to the laces of his tunic. The knot came undone with a single pull.

"Fine."

I gestured to a fallen log along the riverbank, its bark worn smooth by time and the elements. "Sit. I'll be unsteady if I have to stitch like this."

He scoffed but obeyed, moving with the signature fluid grace of a predator, always ready to strike. As he pulled the tunic over his head, the last light of the sun caught along the contours of his body, gilding him in gold. I swallowed hard as the glow painted him in shades of copper and ember. His back resembled a battlefield—each scar a silvered thread woven across otherwise unmarred strength. Broad shoulders, muscles shaped by discipline rather than vanity, tapered into a lean, dangerous frame. He looked forged, elemental. A force contained within skin.

My gaze dragged lower.

Focus.

Fingers tightening around my satchel strap, I forced my attention away, pulling free a needle, thread, and rag. The motions steadied me until my eyes landed on the wound. The torn flesh, the blood, the iron in the air. It felt too close, too known. The past curled its fingers into the present. Phantom pain rose from scars that never faded.

Oberon shifted behind me, breaking the spell. I took a deep breath and dipped the rag into the river. The water swirled red as I wrung it out. His jaw tightened when I pressed it to his side, and his shoulders flexed, restrained beneath my touch.

"Try not to move," I murmured.

He exhaled a slow, deliberate breath. "Not my first wound, Dilthen Doe."

That slur again. He wouldn't find satisfaction in my reaction. Acknowledging the name would only encourage him. Perhaps if I ignored it, he would let it go.

Silence settled between us as I cleaned the wound, carefully assessing the damage. The cut had split open again. Its jagged edges gaped to expose raw, pink flesh. The skin around it was flushed and swollen, an angry red that made me wince. It hadn't become infected yet, but it had grown close. It needed fresh stitches and ointment to stop it from worsening.

I steadied my hands and threaded the needle.

Oberon sat unnervingly still. His eyes observed me, but I didn't dare look back. If I met his gaze, I might lose track of what I was doing. I needed to concentrate.

I pressed my lips together and made the first stitch. His muscles tensed beneath my fingers, but he didn't flinch. Calder's voice echoed in my mind: *He always acts like that. He stumbles in half alive and is gone before regaining his health.* He must have been accustomed to pain. The thought unsettled me more than I wanted to admit.

My shoulders relaxed when I tied the last knot. My hands ached from the tension, my fingers stiff from gripping the needle, but it was done. The wound was closed. When I pulled back, my gaze caught his. I should have looked away, tended to the salve, or the bloodied cloth in my lap. But for one breathless moment, his dark eyes held me.

He tried to unravel me, making the space between us feel too small. His warmth still lingered on my fingertips, even though I wasn't touching him anymore. A slow flush crept up my neck and across my cheeks before I looked away. Whatever he sought, he wouldn't find it.

After reaching for the cloth, I dipped it in the river, and gently smoothed a thin layer of salve over the wound. Crushed herbs and beeswax wafted into the cooling air, steadying me.

"Be more careful," I murmured, a soft chide. He didn't have time to reply before I snatched the tunic from his hand.

"What are you doing?"

"Cleaning it."

Kneeling at the river's edge, I scrubbed the blood from the fabric. The water ran red before the current swept it away, carrying the evidence downstream. I had done this countless times. It had nothing to do with him. It was the wound, the risk of infection if he wore that filthy thing again.

When I returned, the tunic wrung out and dripping, his eyes remained fixed on me. His expression revealed nothing, but his gaze felt critical and angry.

I frowned and held the damp shirt out to him. "You can't wear a bloodied tunic over a clean wound. It'll get infected, which means more problems for both of us."

He remained still.

His silence made my chest tighten. "I didn't think you would bother cleaning it yourself," I added, lifting my arm and nudging the tunic toward him. "So, here." His jaw ticked. I braced for another sharp remark, but he simply took the tunic from my hand.

Turning away, I sank back to my knees at the river's edge. Night had settled in. The last remnants of twilight had vanished, leaving only the fractured glow of the half-moon rippling across the dark water. The trees loomed as towering shadows, their branches tangled against the starry sky. In the underbrush, unseen creatures stirred: the rustle of wings, the skitter of something small, and the distant cry of an owl swallowed by the darkness.

I would sooner have drowned myself than endure another tension-filled staring contest with an angry Fae. Cupping my hands, I dipped them into the river, a shiver racing up my arms from the cold. It tasted of stone and soil.

Clean enough.

Behind me, there was the rustle of fabric. "I thought you needed to—"

"I didn't," I interrupted, wiping a stray droplet from my chin. "It was an excuse."

Silence followed, punctuated by a sharp, brooding huff. "You just lectured me about wearing a dirty shirt over a healing wound, and now you're drinking from the same river you washed it in?"

Lowering my hands, I glanced back over my shoulder. He stood there, arms crossed, tunic still clutched in one hand. His expression teetered between irritation and disbelief.

I shrugged. "What, worried about me now?"

A faint scowl ghosted across his moonlit features before his eyes narrowed. "It's my job to keep you safe," he gritted out, "as infuriating as that may be. And your logic is flawed. I don't need you getting sick before you've had a chance to heal anyone in the village. Did you not bring a flask?"

With a sigh, I shook my head. "I never needed one, so I didn't have one to bring. The river is clean enough. It's flowing, not stagnant. Don't you drink from rivers, Sinclaire?"

"Not after I just saw someone scrub blood-soaked fabric in there," he scoffed.

I rolled my eyes and turned back to the water. Coolness seeped through my fingers as I flicked a few droplets in his direction. "Relax. You're acting like I'm about to drop dead."

His glare burned into my back as he tried to dissect my reasoning... or me. "You're reckless," he muttered.

A short, dry laugh escaped me, and I wiped my hands dry on my uniform. "And you're paranoid. Guess we—"

A sharp, wet crack shattered the night, reverberating through the trees. Then another. The sound was the unmistakable resonance of bones cracking under immense pressure.

I rose to my feet. Every muscle in my body tensed, and my blood ran cold. That wasn't the forest settling; it certainly wasn't a harmless animal rustling through the underbrush.

Oberon's hand flew to the hilt of his sword, his entire body becoming still. Rigid. Alert. His ears, pointed beneath the tousled edges of his dark hair, twitched as he listened. A breeze stirred the trees, subtle at first, and then it intensified.

A putrid stench rode the wind.

My hands flew up to cover my nose. "Oh, gods. What is that?"

"We need to go." His voice was tight and clipped with urgency while he yanked the damp tunic over himself.

Emberhollow had been consumed by twilight. The skeletal ruins and crooked chimneys lay in wait, shrouded in shadows.

The sound returned, closer this time. It was a deep, wet crunch of sinew tearing and bones breaking under something heavy. Then, silence so profound that it rang in my ears.

My stomach turned to stone. The air felt wrong. Dense. The forest itself had stopped breathing.

"What is that?" I whispered, my throat dry.

"We don't have time to find out." He grabbed my arm and pulled. His hands gripped my waist, lifting me onto the saddle as if I weighed nothing. Untying the reins with practiced speed, he swung up behind me. The heat of his chest pressed against my back, solid and grounding even through the damp fabric of his shirt.

"Hold on tight," he warned.

He snapped the reins, and the horse lunged forward. The wind tore past my ears as we plunged into the woods, with branches and shadows blurring around us. My knuckles whitened against the saddle. I struggled to think or breathe over the thunder of hoofbeats and the pounding in my chest. *What was that sound? What thing made a noise like that?*

I turned my head to glance at him. "What was that?!"

His arms caged me with a tense posture. "You said you never left your home village," he shouted. "Do they ever talk about other villages there?"

"I was too busy surviving to listen much. Why?" Another sickening crack echoed behind us, followed by a guttural growl. My muscles grew so taut that they ached.

Oberon leaned in closer, his breath warm against my ear. "Welcome to Emberhollow," he growled. "Where the dead don't always stay buried."

11

OBERON

MY GRIP TIGHTENED on the reins while I guided Neryth along the dense, uneven path. The distant snap of twigs and low, guttural growls echoed through the forest behind us. The air was thick with an unnatural presence that made me wary.

Every noise tugged at my awareness. The slightest movement in the trees made me reach for my sword. Ashenmaws didn't easily give up a chase. I didn't know if they had followed us this far, but I didn't assume we were safe. That mistake could have cost us our lives.

Quinn tensed before she spoke. "Sinclaire, what—"

"Quiet," I muttered, knowing I couldn't afford the distraction, especially when her voice might have attracted them.

Thankfully, she listened, straightening her posture and facing ahead again.

Smart.

The breeze rustled the branches, causing a sudden surge of unease in my stomach. Silverfel was close, but the horrors of Emberhollow still consumed my thoughts. It unsettled me that Quinn had never even heard of it. She mentioned the Gods, which meant she believed in the Veilborn faith, a religion that remained mostly within small rural villages. *What small, isolated village had she come from that no one spoke of it? Or did they discuss other villages' pasts and superstitions, but she simply missed it?*

Her words from earlier echoed in my mind: *'too busy surviving.'* The matter-of-fact way she said it made it clear that whatever she had experienced was grave enough to make her ignore fear and legends in favor of survival. I didn't like what that implied, especially after what I read in her journal.

As Silverfel came into view, I eased Neryth to a slower pace. Quinn shifted her weight until her back pressed against my chest. Her body was no longer tense, but my muscles became rigid in response.

"What are you doing?"

"Being a fool," she sighed.

My head tilted as I waited for a proper explanation.

She hummed, then muttered, "I would be more than stubborn not to admit that was terrifying." Throughout the night, she acted sharp-tongued and quick-witted, never revealing her shaken state. But now, with the worst of it behind us, she let herself lean into me. "You will survive," she added.

I scoffed, but I didn't push her away. The Ashenmaws continued to crackle and growl in my mind. If she needed a moment to catch her breath, so be it. *Why didn't I mind it as much as I should have?*

Maybe it was the fatigue.

Quinn straightened abruptly, breaking the strange moment that had settled between us. She pointed to the dense thicket just off the path. "Do you think it's safe to piss there?"

I gazed at her, bewildered. "Are you serious?"

"Would I joke about something like this?" she said, her expression blank.

After everything we had just endured, her primary concern was relieving herself. "Make it quick," I muttered, scanning the trees. "And don't wander."

She slid off the horse with a groan and stretched her legs before making her way to the thicket. I kept my eyes on the forest, listening for anything unusual. When she returned, she seemed far more at ease than she had any right to be after the night we had. She stretched her arms overhead and groaned. "I can't sit on that horse any longer," she announced. "I'm walking."

Albeit frustrating, it didn't surprise me. "We're almost there."

"And?" She raised an eyebrow. "Your decision to stay on doesn't mean I have to."

My leg swung over the saddle before I dropped beside her. "Fine."

The sun had begun its slow ascent, spilling pale gold through the dense canopy. The thick morning fog fractured its light, rendering it weak. It should have brought warmth and stirred the forest awake with birdsong and the rustle of unseen creatures in the underbrush.

But there was no flutter of wings, no chittering of dusk hares bounding through the grass, nor the distant howl of a morning silver wolf calling its pack. There was nothing, and that unsettled me.

The closer we walked to Silverfel, the thicker the fog became. The mist enveloped the village, making the buildings hazy.

Quinn glanced over a few times. I waited for her to express whatever was on her mind. After the fifth glance, she shot me a look with furrowed brows, and I could no longer hold my tongue. "What?"

"Nothing."

I raised an eyebrow. "That was too much nothing, Dilthen Doe."

She pursed her lips, and her eyes narrowed. "Are you going to explain what that was back there, or do I have to guess?"

She wouldn't let it go. If her journal revealed anything, it was that she needed answers to everything that piqued her curiosity and challenged her. "Ashenmaws."

"Ashenmaws," she echoed, rolling the word over her tongue. "That's a name that doesn't inspire confidence."

My gaze stayed fixed on the path ahead. "It shouldn't."

She stole another glance at me. "You've seen them before."

For several strides, I ignored her relentless badgering.

"Are you going to tell me?" she pressed. "Or do I have to keep guessing and talking your ear off?"

I should have known better.

"They are the result of a Fae bargain gone wrong."

After a few steps, I noticed she had stopped walking. I turned, my brows furrowed in irritation. "What now?"

"You say that as if you know," she wondered, searching my eyes for something I was determined not to let her find.

"I do."

Her brows furrowed, but she didn't respond. Whatever she thought of could remain in her head this time. I wasn't just familiar with the Ashenmaws; I understood them, which was unsettling for a human.

As we approached Silverfel, the fog thickened, curling around the buildings like creeping fingers. Smoke spiraled from chimneys, but no voices or movement greeted us—only the muted sound of our boots against the damp road. The village felt unnaturally still. Once we reached the town square, I tied Neryth to the Village well in the center.

"Stay here," I commanded, turning to Quinn.

She scoffed. "Why?"

"Because it was an order."

She rolled her eyes. "That's not a valid reason."

"I need to find the village healer," I gritted.

"Need I remind you, Sir Knight, that *you* are accompanying *me*? The sooner I see the sick, the sooner I can help them."

Damn it. She was right. "The healer will—"

"I don't need the healer to hold my hand, Sinclaire." Her voice was firm, her chin lifted in stubborn defiance. "I'm going with you."

She wasn't budging. And I didn't enjoy the idea of leaving her alone, even if she was a nuisance.

"Fine," I muttered and strode ahead. "Stay close."

As we walked through the village, a tavern sat to the left. Its sign swayed in the mist. The place was silent. The smell of stale ale still lingered in the air. Across from it stood an inn, its shutters closed tightly, as if that could keep illness from seeping through the cracks. Quinn's footsteps were steady beside me, her fingers twisted in her skirt. Despite her bravado, she remained affected by the eerie stillness that hung over Silverfel.

We continued past several homes with shut doors and dark windows. At the far end of the village, we came to a sign hanging above a modest wooden building that read, "Village Healer and Apothecary." I knocked and glanced at Quinn. She still looked determined, but her grip on her dress hadn't loosened.

The door creaked open, and an older man peered through, glancing between us. His gaze settled on Quinn. He squinted at her uniform before recognition flickered in his weary eyes. She lifted her identification tag by the tassel, holding it up as if to convey, '*You can trust me.*'

His gaze lingered on it for a few breaths until he exhaled, and his shoulders slumped with relief. "Thank the gods," he muttered as he opened the door wider. "Please, come in."

Quinn stepped through first. I followed, ducking under the low door frame. The interior was infused with the scent of dried herbs and a bitter, medicinal undertone reminiscent of the castle infirmary. An underlying staleness hinted at the sickness that had settled in and refused to leave.

The healer shut the door behind us and skipped introductions. "They finally sent someone who knows what they're doing." His eyes flicked to me and then back to Quinn. "I assume they briefed you since they sent a guard with you?"

My eyes narrowed at the comment. Alric sent me to ensure she was prudent and to detect any signs of magic. What justified her need for protection?

Quinn tucked her tag away and adjusted her satchel. "We were informed of the illness spreading through the village, but I need to know everything you have observed, including when it started, the symptoms, and how quickly it spreads."

The man ran a hand across his face. "I'll tell you everything I know, but first, you should see them for yourselves."

The healer hesitated outside the door to the knights' quarters. His hands tightened around the latch while his eyes darted between us. A tautness stretched across his features as he chose each word carefully. "Were you told of their... demands?" he asked, his tone hushed. "It may be better if- "

Quinn cut him off with a bright smile. "Stubborn men won't stop me from doing my job. I am here because of their demands."

The image of the desperate letter flashed in my mind. The knights demanded a physician. A man, more specifically. They asked not to receive an herbalist. Quinn didn't come from a prestigious academy, nor had the courts trained her.

She was everything they *didn't* want. I knew how knights were. Their disdain never needed words.

The healer gave her a long, searching look. Then he sighed and scratched the back of his neck before turning to push the door open. "If you're sure," he muttered.

Inside, the indistinct murmur of voices cut off abruptly. Several rows of knights lay on cots while others sat slouched against the walls. Their armor was piled between beds and leaned carelessly in heaps against the far side of the room. A fire burned in the hearth at the back, casting a flickering light over the worn faces that watched us as we entered.

One knight stood in the middle of the room. Relief spread over his features when he locked eyes with me. "Oh, thank the gods. They sent a man who knows what they're—"

The healer interrupted him. "The young woman here is an herbalist sent by the courts."

The knight's gaze flicked to Quinn. His face darkened, his shoulders squared, and he scowled. "Then send her back."

Silence lingered between us, palpable with tension.

My jaw tightened, and I willed myself not to glare at the man outright. I yearned to grip the handle of my blade, a desperate itch in my fingers. Men like him were arrogant bastards who thought their rank made them untouchable, that their expectations were law. The way he looked at Quinn as though she was less or unworthy sent a slow burn of irritation slithering through my chest.

Why did it bother me?

Quinn ignored him. Her sharp amber eyes flicked across the room, scanning every inch of space. Even as she stood still, with squared shoulders and hands clasped together, there was tension in her stance. Her lack of reaction was a choice.

The knight waited for her to shrink back, to let his presence weigh on her. But determination flickered in her eyes when she focused on the arrogant man before her. She stepped forward, stopping toe-to-toe with him. My hand landed on the hilt of my sword in a casual warning.

Quinn tilted her head back to look at him, meeting his glare with her composed expression. Then she smiled. It wasn't soft or innocent. No. It was a knife-edge smile that didn't soothe a soul but unsettled it.

"I understand your concerns and requests," she stated. "However, the courts found me the most suitable due to my methods for discovering and creating new cures." She let her words linger, her tone friendly. "I don't want to be here any more than you want me to be. I suggest you cooperate, so you won't have to see my face for more than a few days."

A few knights behind them coughed, stifling their laughs.

The arrogant knight's lips pressed into a thin line. A muscle in his jaw twitched, and his gaze darted to the hand on my sword, my stony expression, and then to Quinn. He huffed and stepped back. "Fine."

Coward.

Quinn gave a curt nod. She was adept at hiding her fear and stress. She stepped back, scanning the room and noting every detail, before retrieving her journal and charcoal. "Who got sick first?" she asked, skipping the pleasantries.

The knights judged her, several bristling at her presence. But she remained patient. The longer the silence stretched, the more it became clear she wouldn't yield.

One of the older men, pale and drawn, gestured toward the rear of the room, where the hearth burned. "Them," he muttered. "They were the first to fall ill."

Quinn's attention turned to the knights closest to the fire. I followed her gaze to the men slumped against their cots. They appeared worse than the others. Their skin glistened with sweat, and their breaths were shallow.

She pressed on. "And their symptoms?"

One of the younger knights shifted his weight and glanced at the others before replying. "It started with fatigue. Then came fevers and coughing. They... they say their limbs feel heavy, like lead."

Another person spoke up. "Sometimes, they talk in their sleep, saying things that make little sense."

Quinn nodded and scribbled notes in her journal. "So, you have all been sharing space, using the same water source, and eating the same food?"

A chorus of agreement.

She tapped the end of the charcoal against the page. Her eyes flicked back to the sick men huddled by the hearth. "And they've been sleeping by the fire this whole time?"

Another knight chuckled. "Those were the cots they claimed when we arrived."

Quinn hummed, clearly piecing things together and following a trail visible only to her. I couldn't detect any magic in the room, yet they were the first villagers to fall ill. If magic were at play, I would sense it around these men. Her brow furrowed, and her lips pressed together as she flipped back a few pages in her journal—something wasn't adding up. The way she squeezed the journal's spine indicated she felt it, too.

The healer led us from house to house, each door revealing the same grim scene, the same symptoms, the same slow decay. The stench of sickness hung heavily in the air—herbs and stale sweat, fever-warmed sheets, and the faint, sour tang of something rotting beneath it all.

Outside, the village should have felt alive. Stray dogs should have lounged near doorsteps, waiting for scraps to fall. Barn cats—thick-furred and sharp-eyed—should have prowled through alleyways, hunting whatever the night disturbed. There should have been moss sparrows, small, gray-feathered birds that nested in the eaves of homes, their songs light and scratchy.

But there was nothing.

Even the animals sensed the creeping fear that had settled over the village with the fog. The villagers wore it on their faces, in furtive glances, hunched shoulders, and the way their hands twitched toward the door latches as we passed.

By the fourth house, Quinn's posture had shifted. Her shoulders bore a new tension that settled deep and felt brittle at the edges. She gripped her journal too tightly; her knuckles paled under the pressure. *Had she noticed yet?* A sense of unease permeated every interaction and whispered conversation as the village watched her.

As we stepped out of the last house, dusky shadows stretched long across the dirt roads, swallowing the spaces between buildings and pooling in the alleyways, waiting for the sun to set. Quinn stood still for a long moment, her hands clenched at her sides, before rubbing her temples. *She wasn't just troubled; she was angry... But why?*

"It's not the water," she whispered quietly.

I gazed down at her. "Then why instruct them to boil it?"

Her eyes locked with mine. "I don't know what else to tell them yet. They need reassurance while I figure this out."

As we stepped back into the village healer's building, Quinn cast the healer a quick glance before speaking. "Do you have any notes or books on local ailments? Are there any stories about past outbreaks, superstitions, myths, or legends?" She paused. "And I mean anything, no matter how ridiculous it seems."

12

EDEN

THE HEALER FROWNED and rubbed his beard while he pondered my question. "Superstitions?"

"Yes," I asserted. "Even if you think it's nonsense."

He sighed and moved toward a shelf. His fingers brushed against the spines of old books as if he were searching for a memory rather than a title. "Ailments I can help with, but superstitions..." He hesitated, then shook his head. "Most of that was abandoned years ago."

Something in his tone disturbed me. "What do you mean?"

The healer waved a dismissive hand. "The village used to have certain... practices. Old customs meant to ward off magic. But people stopped bothering with the magic that was outlawed, and the kingdom quelling anything remotely suspicious. They figured there was no point."

My head turned toward Oberon, and our eyes locked in silent understanding. *A place steeped in fear and quiet rituals upheld for generations had abandoned its ways just as the people fell ill?* It gave me goosebumps.

The healer shifted beneath my scrutiny, wearing a wary expression.

"What customs?" I pressed.

He shrugged. "Simple things: symbols carved into doorways, salt scattered across thresholds, and leaving offerings outside the village when the seasons changed. Nothing that should matter." He hesitated before adding, "Nothing that should have caused this."

Pulling out my journal, I flipped to an empty page. As I noted the details, my fingers tightened around the charcoal, and my brows furrowed in concentration. These weren't just superstitions; they were protective measures—ones the village had relied on for years. It wasn't a coincidence. It was calculated. Or worse—coerced.

Oberon's discerning voice cut through my thoughts. "You don't believe in coincidences." He didn't ask; he noted.

My charcoal scraped against the parchment. "Not when people are dying."

The healer guided us to the inn, pausing briefly to share a few quiet words with the innkeeper before handing over a single key.

"Shared room," he said cautiously. "It's all we can afford."

The weight of the books and notes in my arms captured my focus. Their knowledge was more important than our sleeping arrangements. I nodded and adjusted my grip as he departed down the dim corridor.

Oberon opened the door and stepped inside first. The room was modest, with wooden floors creaking beneath our boots and a single narrow window allowing a sliver of night. A lone candle flickered on the bedside table, casting a faint golden light against the walls.

I walked past him without a glance, heading straight for the desk. The books landed with a solid thud, parchment rustling while I spread them out. The chair groaned under my weight. There was much to sift through—histories of past plagues, theories on cursed lands, and recipes for tinctures that promised relief. It was enough to keep me awake for several nights. The sooner I began, the sooner I would find what cured the villagers' suffering.

Behind me, Oberon released a heavy sigh. "You take the bed. I'll take the floor." My attention stayed on the faded ink before me. Sleep wasn't in my plans for the night.

His footsteps grew nearer. "Herbalist." There was a pause. "Did you hear me?"

Sighing, I waved him off, skimming a paragraph on warding salts. "I heard you."

"And?"

I turned the page. "And I'm sitting here."

Silence lingered between us for a moment.

"That wasn't an option," he gritted out.

A slow hum escaped my lips in response. I was disinterested in entertaining him. He could remain frustrated. I had more pressing concerns than a bed neither of us would use.

The gentle clinking of buckles filled the space, followed by a metal clatter and a heavy thump against the floor. I sighed through my nose, refusing to face him. He wanted to be tenacious? Fine. But I had a job to complete.

The notes were messy—pages filled with symptoms, scattered observations, and half-formed theories. My fingers smudged the ink while I sifted through them, cross-referencing everything I had collected throughout the day.

Frowning, I tapped my charcoal against the page, the rhythmic motion grounding my thoughts. The healer mentioned the village had once practiced protective customs—warding symbols, salt barriers, offerings—but had since abandoned them.

What changed?

Prince Alric had long banned magic. What would change if someone were secretly using it? Why would people only start falling ill after the traditions ended?

I flipped the page, staring at my scrawled notes until the words blurred together in my vision. My limbs ached with exhaustion, and the multitude of possibilities alongside the scarcity of answers weighed heavily on my mind.

The candle's flame flickered, casting restless shadows over the pages. Another night blurred into dawn, and the pieces still refused to fall into place.

My palm pressed against my temple and I dug my fingers into my scalp as if I might extract the answers from my skull. The symptoms didn't match any known illness. No common element linked the afflicted. The village had been here for decades, maybe centuries. So, why now? Why did abandoning the old customs lead to this?

Sniffling, I flexed my fingers, stained with charcoal and ink. My pouch of nuts and seeds rested beside my notes. I chewed on a few, my mind too tangled to care. Sleep wasn't an option. Not when I still hadn't anything.

Another page turned. More notes. More theories. More of the same.

The floor creaked.

Oberon's presence was a constant, silent force in the room. He came and went with the same unspoken routine—leaving in the morning and returning late at night. He never inquired about what I had discovered or why I remained at this desk, but his gaze felt weighty as he passed by.

The chair creaked as I shifted, easing the stiffness from my shoulders. The sky beyond the narrow window had darkened, with orange and crimson hues of sunset creeping in.

A scoff emerged from behind me, low and unimpressed.

I ignored it and flipped to the next page.

Oberon let out a humorless laugh. I envisioned the shake of his head and the clench of his jaw as he bit back a remark.

His footsteps approached the bed, the familiar jingle of buckles resonating in the space as he loosened his armor. Metal clattered against the floor, followed by the familiar, heavy thud of his sword being set down.

He remained silent for a long moment.

"How long?" His voice was hoarse from exhaustion.

I turned to look at him. "How long what?"

His eyes flicked toward the mess of parchment spread across the desk. "How long were you planning to do this?"

Bristling, I turned back to the desk. "Until I have answers."

He grunted. "And if they don't come?"

My charcoal rested on the desk with a light *tap*. "They will."

Another silence stretched, broken by the sound of fabric shifting and the faint creak of the mattress.

"You won't be of any use to them if you're dead."

I scoffed. "I'm fine."

MY EYES BLINKED open to the candle's sputtering flame. Groaning, I stretched my stiff fingers and rubbed my tired eyes. I had dozed off again. The dim light of dawn filtered through the window, casting a pale glow over the desk. The notes before me blurred together until I forced myself to focus again.

I was so close. The patterns were there, but the pieces refused to align. The symptoms—their spread—followed no logic of an ordinary illness. It wasn't the water, the grain, the livestock, or a common ailment. The healer had ruled out the usual suspects.

So what was it?

I rubbed my temples.

If the illness had been airborne, it would have spread differently. If it had originated from contact, families living together would have fallen ill simultaneously, but that wasn't the case. The infection pattern was uneven and scattered. The disease affected a few households while leaving their neighbors untouched. Others had one sick individual while the rest of the family remained healthy.

It seemed rather illogical.

Unless it wasn't natural.

A chill crawled over me as the thought settled.

Magic.

My pulse ticked faster.

Leaning forward, I skimmed my notes again with sharper eyes. If it were magic, it would explain the inconsistencies. If someone had woven something into the land, something bound to the old customs, then breaking those traditions could have shattered whatever protection was keeping it away.

The healer had mentioned that they once followed warding customs—salt barriers, symbols carved into doorways, and offerings left at the village's edge. They had abandoned these practices. If those traditions protected the town, and someone had removed them, then maybe this wasn't an illness; maybe it was a consequence.

My stomach churned, and I glanced at my pouch. It was empty. A dull ache gnawed at me as my stomach protested, but I had been through worse.

Rising from the desk, I stretched my stiff limbs and neck before moving toward my satchel, rummaging through what little I had left. If I were right, if this sickness were caused by magic, I could test it. Various plants responded when exposed to magic. A few amplified it, several dulled it, and others outright rejected it. If I triggered a response, I could find the source.

Across the room, Oberon lay on the floor, his back pressed against the wooden planks. Strands of dark hair fell over his forehead. One arm rested on his stomach while the other sprawled beside him. His long legs were bent at the knee, and his boots sat discarded at his side as if he hadn't decided whether to sleep or keep watch. The dying embers of the hearth cast flickering shadows over him that highlighted the strong angles of his features and the scars on his exposed skin.

His breathing was deep and steady, but not at ease. Even in sleep, tension was clear in his jaw, and his fingers twitched restlessly as they reached for a blade. He was a predator forced into stillness, waiting for the moment he needed to strike.

He wouldn't be there to shadow me, like a storm cloud poised to break. Careful not to make a sound, I grabbed my journal and herbs and quietly slipped out of the inn.

The fog clung to the buildings, curled over rooftops, and slithered through the narrow streets, swirling in thick, damp tendrils around my boots. The scent of damp soil and aged wood lingered in the air, a smell that followed rain but offered no promise of renewal. The silence was overwhelming. It pressed against my ears and made every step too loud, too noticeable.

Oberon's horse appeared through the haze as I approached the village center, still tied to the well. The beast stood near a large bucket of water, filled to the brim. My steps slowed, and unease prickled at the edges of my mind.

Oberon must have tended to him.

The horse huffed, its breath curling in the frigid air. It flicked its tail and stomped its hoof—small, cautious movements that hinted at irritation or warning. Its dark eyes met mine for a moment. "You and I both," I muttered.

The strange feeling lingered in my gut, an itch I couldn't scratch, but I pushed forward. The knights' quarters stood ahead, its wooden frame worn by time and weather. Its iron reinforcements, dark with rust, attested to its long resistance against the elements. I knocked, not bothering to wait for an invitation before entering.

The knight, who behaved as if my presence were a personal insult, stood. His scowl deepened at the sight of me, and irritation hung thick in the dim room. The glow of a single lantern cast jagged shadows against the walls, illuminating the hard lines of his face as he appraised me. His gaze flicked past me, his lips twisting into a smirk, and he folded his arms across his chest. "Where's your dog?"

A slow breath steadied me. The words shouldn't have bothered me; I shouldn't have cared. Yet, they irritated me.

I straightened my back and met his gaze without hesitation. "Mind your tone." His smirk widened, but I pressed on. "Sir Sinclaire is here on the prince's orders. I suggest you consider your behavior, as I am unaware of what those orders entail."

That wiped the smirk from his face.

My gaze drifted past him as I scanned the room. Exhaustion kept most from paying attention. A few watched with eyes gleaming in the low light, filled with curiosity. My focus returned to the arrogant knight before me when he stepped forward, closing the distance. He was tall, like most knights, but I refused to shrink back. If I had survived Marcus, I could handle him.

His smirk was slow and curling, dripping with condescension. "Bold of you," he mused, tilting his head to look down at me. "Walking into a room full of men alone. Makes a man wonder..." His lingering gaze dragged over me as he stripped me bare with nothing but his eyes. "If you came here hoping to be handled a little rough. Can't say you're my usual taste, but I enjoy breaking in something new."

A chill unfurled within me. With a raised brow, I smirked back. "Should I be afraid of you?"

For a moment, his expression wavered, but then he schooled his features into an air of smug amusement. "A clever girl would be."

With a sigh, I tilted my head with feigned disinterest. "Good thing I'm more than just clever, then." My voice dropped. "I'm here to do my job, not stroke your fragile ego. Your opinion of me is irrelevant."

The smirk on his face widened. His hand shot out, and my breath hitched with anger. His grip on my jaw bruised, fingers sinking into my skin as if to make a point. "Bravery only gets you so far, Herbalist," he hissed, his breath too close.

Fighting back a wince, I locked my jaw when his fingers squeezed. I had faced worse than an arrogant knight with a power complex. I oscillated between violence and insults before another voice intervened.

"Let her go."

A second knight positioned himself behind him, arms crossed, and a heavy warning evident in his eyes. His words conveyed irritation rather than concern. "You're being child-ish, Valdier. The rest of us would prefer to keep our heads."

Valdier held his grip for a moment longer, his fingers flexing as he debated whether I was worth the effort. With a scoff, he shoved me back. His lip curled. "Not even worth dirtying my hands over."

I straightened, refusing to reveal the ache blooming along my jaw as I smirked. "Miracles do happen. You managed to form a coherent thought." His eyes flashed, but he didn't reach for me again. Smart choice. I wouldn't have played nice a second time.

Turning away, I retrieved the herbs from my satchel. "Now, if you're finished sulking like a child denied his favorite toy, I have proper work to do."

The mortar emitted a dull crack as I ground the herbs, let-ting my frustration seep into the motion. I mixed them with warm water from Oberon's flask, disregarding the whispering knights. Their egotistical skepticism pressed against my back, but I had no patience for it.

The first dose poured into a small cup and I turned to the nearest knight, extending it toward him. "Drink." He hesitated, glancing at me and the mixture as if it might kill him. My expression, or perhaps the way his breath still rattled in his chest, compelled him to take it.

Then another knight. And another.

Time passed, and the change was undeniable. Their pallid complexions brightened with color. Clammy skin dried out. The rattling in their breaths transformed into steady inhales.

By mid-morning, they stood, stretched, and tested their limbs as if they hadn't just been on death's doorstep.

A grin tugged at my lips as I watched them move, but the realization pulled it away.

Magic.

It wasn't just the herbs. The illness, the sudden decline, and their rapid recovery suggested that it was unnatural.

Valdier grunted and crossed his arms, his face contorting into a scowling frown.

I huffed, glancing at the knights who had been gifted new bodies. "You're not just going to linger, are you?" They exchanged hesitant glances. I gathered the remaining mixtures and handed them to the men. "Take these to the villagers. Follow my instructions, or you will waste everyone's time."

They grabbed the doses with the written instructions and left. The remaining knights, especially those closest to the hearth, weren't improving. Their condition had deteriorated. While the others stood, these men remained motionless. Stubborn fevers clung to them, and their breathing was shallow, rattling like rusted hinges.

A chill slithered through me.

It was the fire.

My pulse quickened as my mind raced through the details. Perhaps not the fire itself, but every house had a hearth. Each sick villager had relied on theirs for warmth. Those who had recovered were no longer near open flames, while those still suffering hadn't moved away from theirs.

So, what was different?

Why were they still sick when the others had returned to normal?

I stepped closer to the fire. The heat of the fire on my skin didn't hold my attention. It was the burn, the smell, the crackling, spitting embers of the flames, and their flickering dance of red and gold.

The timber.

Or rather, something on it that released dust or fumes into the air, something they inhaled every time they stoked the flames. A slow-acting poison. Not strong enough to kill quickly, but sufficient to leave them burning with fever and their lungs clouded by illness.

I threw the door open and rushed out of the knights' quarters.

The world outside was different. The heavy, suffocating stillness had lifted, replaced by the first true stirrings of life I had heard since our arrival. Muffled conversations drifted from the tavern, boots scraped against the cobblestone, children played outside their homes, and there was a distant metallic clang as people moved once more.

I did that.

The thought struck unexpectedly, accompanied by a fleeting sense of satisfaction, but there was no time to indulge in it. The illness would return if I didn't identify the source.

"Hey, little herbalist."

The voice pulled me from my thoughts, tinged with irritation and a hint of reluctant respect. I halted mid-stride to glance over my shoulder. Valdier stood with his arms crossed, regarding me as if I were a riddle he couldn't solve. He must have despised the fact that I had succeeded.

"Why don't you join us in celebrating?" he said, his voice strained as if the words tasted bitter on his tongue. "You did great work."

"No time," I blurted, returning to the path ahead.

Wait.

I turned back to grasp his arm. "Where do you find the firewood?"

He stiffened, his eyes widened, and his brows shot up in alarm. "Uh... There's a location in the woods east of the village, near the ridge."

Without another word, I turned and sprinted.

13

OBERON

The tavern pulsed with restless energy, thick with the aroma of ale, roasting meat, and damp wool. Laughter and drunken boasts clashed against the steady clatter of tankards slamming onto wooden tables, each impact a heartbeat in the tavern's fevered rhythm. Shadows flickered along the walls, cast by the dancing flames of lanterns swinging above.

She healed the village while I was still asleep.

Sneakui dilthen adaneth.

Sneaky little woman.

My eyes scanned the crowded room, searching. She had to be here somewhere—drained and exhausted from everything she had done, with little sleep. But there was no sign of her.

A slow tension curled beneath my skin before movement near the far end of the tavern caught my attention. A younger knight, one of the few who had dared to speak when she questioned them, sat hunched over his drink. His fingers traced the rim of his mug, his eyes distant, as if he were still grappling with the weight of what had occurred.

I strode toward him, my voice laced with impatience. "Where is the herbalist?"

His head snapped up, and his posture stiffened. Under my gaze, he shifted uncomfortably, tightening his grip around the handle of his cup. "She stayed," he admitted. His eyes darted to his fellow knights, hoping one would answer on his behalf. When no one did, he exhaled heavily. "She made medicine for the villagers and stayed by the hearth to tend to the knights who weren't improving." His brows furrowed.

Of course, she did.

A muscle in my jaw twitched. I raked a hand through my hair, gripping the strands at the base of my skull. I should have expected nothing less.

Conversations dwindled, and voices faded into an uneasy silence as I passed. The knights' gazes pressed against my back, burdened by unspoken questions. The heavy slam of the door behind me pierced through the tavern's din.

Three steps into the square, movement caught my eye along a narrow path leading into the woods. A blurred flash of a cloak whipped behind a figure. An instinctual, bone-deep ache pulsed in my chest. My teeth clenched, and my boot sunk into the gravel path, propelling me forward.

"Herbalist!" My voice pierced through the trees, but she didn't stop. She didn't hesitate or waver.

A snap cracked through my ribs. An aching, splintering sensation unfurled into something wilder. Heat surged through my veins, searing through reason. It wasn't just concern that drove me forward; it was something deeper, raw, and unshackled. It had nothing to do with duty and everything to do with her.

The forest blurred past me. Shadows twisted in the fog, and bare, skeletal branches clawed at the sky. My pulse, a steady war drum, thundered in my ears.

The chase set me alight.

Every stride and sharp pivot she made drew me closer. Her movements were fast, controlled, and fluid—born of instinct and necessity. She ran as though she belonged to the wild, as though Elduvaris itself yielded beneath her steps, undisturbed.

She had learned this. Had honed it. The knowledge of escape was etched into her bones, polished over time.

It was breathtaking. Dark. Addictive.

My heart pounded.

Why did it excite me?

Hunting was in my nature. To move unseen, to close the distance before my prey knew I was there, was instinctual. But chasing her wasn't about the hunt. It was how she ran. She must have learned what it meant to be prey from experience.

The thought of someone else chasing her—hunting her with cruel intent—sent a dark sensation slithering through my gut. A sudden, unique, and unwelcome feeling dug in deep and wound tight around my bones.

My mind flickered back to the journal, to the ink-stained pages filled with precise agony, the remedies, poisons, and wounds described in depth. Each word had been deliberate and clinical, yet beneath them, it was raw and shaped by experience. My body tensed. My boots slammed against the damp soil, pushing harder, faster. But she was too quick. Too fucking fast, even for me.

Phantom hands of mist curled through the trees, swirling as we tore through them. The scent of wet leaves, overturned soil, and damp rock filled my senses. A nightbird cried somewhere above us; the wind swallowed its lonely, warbling call. Insects scattered, their tiny wings clicking in startled chaos as we passed. A golden-banded moth flickered too close but vanished into the fog before I could swat it away.

She pivoted in a sudden, flawless movement. Her body twisted, knee bent, as she dropped low, sliding across slick grass and damp leaves in a motion so fluid it seemed inhuman and left me breathless.

It was perfect—no missteps or hesitation. It wasn't the frantic, desperate scrambling of prey trying to escape a predator. No, it was control, adaptation, a honed skill.

And it was enthralling.

An intense, unwelcome hunger coursed down my spine. I craved the thrill of the chase, the way she moved and ran.

I wanted *more*.

I wanted to *keep* chasing her.

I *needed* to catch her.

My boots skidded across the damp soil as I pivoted, mirroring her. When we slowed, the bitter air seared my lungs, and my chest heaved with ragged breaths.

"Herbalist."

She stood before me, heaving, her cheeks flushed and lips parted. Wild, untamed strands of dark hair clung to her face. The smudges beneath her amber eyes did nothing to dull the fire within them. She was still immersed in it, still exhilarated as I was, caught up in the thrill of the chase, as if she hadn't just guided me through the most maddening pursuit of my life. My gaze dropped, and my breath hitched for an entirely different reason.

Her skirts lifted as she adjusted her stance, and for the briefest moment, there was a flash of skin. The smooth curve of her thigh, the taut muscle beneath pale flesh, flexed. Molten heat slammed through me in a violent, gut-wrenching pulse of desire. A need so intense and sudden it had my cock twitching, straining uncomfortably against my pants. The reaction was instant and visceral as my body betrayed me before my mind could suppress it.

In one swift motion, a dagger was unsheathed from its holster against her thigh as she suddenly dropped to her knees. *Saints.* It was effortless, strikingly graceful, and precise. Every movement was controlled. Heat licked up my spine. My pulse stuttered, and my teeth ground together as I sucked in a sharp breath, trying and failing to wrestle my thoughts back into focus.

The iron-laced smell of blood hit the air when a dark line split across her palm, glistening under the moonlight.

The world tilted.

My focus snapped, and my vision turned red. Everything inside me coiled as I braced against the force of the new sensation crashing through me. I inhaled sharply through my nose, but it did nothing to stop the twisting in my gut.

The words tore from me, angry and desperate. "What the hells are you doing?" She didn't flinch. Blood dripped from her clenched fist, sizzling as it hit the vine at her feet. The muscle in my jaw locked so tightly it ached.

I focused on how the plant reacted to her blood, on her. Alric had been right. It was magic. And I had utterly fucking missed it.

"Magic," she murmured, as if she had plucked the realization straight from my mind. Her bright, steady eyes met mine. "This is what has been poisoning them." A pause. The weight of the truth settled between us. "They have been burning this in their wood."

A smoldering fury washed over me.

"How the fuck did you know that?" I glowered, stepping closer.

Her eyes narrowed. "Oh, I don't know, Sinclaire," she mocked. "Maybe it's because I pay attention?"

Heat flared across my skin, my pulse still hammering. She was bleeding, crimson streaks marring the pale canvas of her skin, and instead of tending to it, she merely glared at me.

My jaw ticked as I took another step. "That doesn't answer my damn question." She must have placed it there. There was no way I could have overlooked this. There was no way she had found a solution while I had found nothing. She knew more than she was letting on. And I was determined to make her explain herself.

She scoffed and crossed her arms, letting her injured hand dangle carelessly. Blood dripped from her fingertips, dark and glistening. "Solving this is my job. I consider everything, not just what's in front of me. Unlike you, who glares and threatens until everything falls into place."

A slow breath dragged through my teeth.

She was challenging. Exasperating. Maddening.

Yet, the blood on her skin, the flush in her cheeks, the sharp snap of her voice... The frustration, that dark, twisting hunger, created an unbearable heat pooling in my stomach. I dragged a hand through my hair as my control continued to wane. My pulse was a deafening drumbeat in my ears, overwhelming reason. My vision narrowed until the world became nothing but the stark red of her blood against her skin.

I had killed men without hesitation. I had made them beg for death, drawn out their suffering until the only mercy left was the blade in my hand. But seeing her blood sent a rush of aggravation through me. Made my hands itch and my restraint fray.

It shouldn't have.

My job was to protect her and ensure she completed this mission. That's why it bothered me and why I was so damn close to losing control. I failed to protect her. That must have been it.

She managed one step before my hand shot out, locked around her wrist, and yanked her back hard. Her spine hit the tree with a dull thud, an impact that rattled through both of us. My grip secured her wrists, pinning them above her head. A sharp, pained gasp escaped her lips. My pulse quickened, and my breathing became rough. Quinn twisted against my hold, her amber eyes flashing. "What in the five hells is your problem?"

My free hand pressed against the tree beside her head, fingers curled around the rough bark as I enclosed her. "You knew what to look for," I growled. "You recognized it before I did."

She scoffed and tugged at her wrists again in a futile struggle against my grip. "I'm an herbalist," she hissed through gritted teeth. "It's my job to know. That's why they sent me here, not just you."

I leaned in closer, close enough to convey the weight of my presence and the unspoken threat. "No, Dilthen Doe." My voice was a whisper of steel.

Her breath hitched.

"You ran straight to it," I continued, my words a slow, deliberate blade. "You were faster than me. And you didn't hesitate before cutting your hand to test it."

When my words struck, her throat bobbed. Her pulse fluttered at the base of her neck, and Saints help me, I longed to feel it beneath my teeth. Quinn rolled her eyes, but a flicker of her pulse, a quick jump beneath her skin, betrayed her. "Oh, I'm sorry." Her voice dripped with mockery. "Should I have waited for you to scowl at it first, Sir Knight?"

My cheek twitched. "You put it there, didn't you?"

She let out a laugh of disbelief. "Are you serious?"

The accusation thickened the atmosphere between us, making the space suffocating. Her eyes searched my face. She knew I wasn't just suspicious. I was pushing her too far. Testing her. Watching for the slightest crack.

Her lips parted with a shallow breath as her expression shifted. Her brow arched, and her smirk deepened. "You think I orchestrated an entire curse?" Her voice dropped lower, rich with mock amusement. "For what? To frolic in the woods with you?"

The tension inside me frayed, unraveled, and became dangerous.

I was still hard, still aching from the chase and how she moved and ran as if made to be pursued. And with her wrists still locked in my grip, her body pinned against mine, I felt her. The heat of her. The shape of her pressing into me.

My control was tenuous.

I let the silence stretch between us as I absorbed the way her pulse thrummed beneath my fingers. We locked eyes, and I could taste the challenge in the air. "No," I admitted, my voice rougher. "But I know you're hiding more than you're saying."

Quinn's smirk was a blade sliding from its sheath. "Funny," she murmured, "I was about to say the same about you."

My eyes burned with the warning that flickered in my gaze. I should have intimidated her. She should have shrank back, swallowed her words, and looked away. But her chin tipped up, daring me to push harder.

Audaçi—o hi adaneth.

The audacity of this woman.

My grip tightened before I forced myself to release her. The instant my fingers left her skin, she pushed off the tree, shot me a glare, and then turned to stalk away.

Damn her.

I huffed a harsh breath, raking a hand through my hair. I had to find answers, which meant I needed to read her notes, search for clues that indicated she had been hiding something, and discover what the hells had concealed it.

Once there was ample space between us, I headed toward the village. By the time I returned, the streets were empty. The villagers still crowded the tavern, exhaustion weighing on the night in a thick shroud.

Low in the town square, a fire's embers crackled quietly.

Quinn hefted an armful of logs toward the pit. The orange glow painted flickering shadows across her face. Soot streaked her cheeks, her skin glistened with sweat, and wisps of dark red hair curled at her temples. She grunted as she dropped the logs into place, stepping back to brush her hands against the rough fabric of her apron.

An unfamiliar tightness coiled in my chest.

Regret?

I scoffed inwardly. *No.*

Neryth strained against the rope at the well beside her. His muscles flexed as his hooves scraped against the stone, pawing for balance. His ears flicked toward her, and his nostrils flared as if he sensed a disturbance I hadn't yet deciphered.

Pushing forward, I shouldered through the inn's door. The heavy wooden slab thudded shut behind me, sealing out the night. I strode toward the table, spun the chair around, and dropped into it, straddling the worn wood. Quinn's notes lay scattered across the surface. With every page, every scribbled formula, and every hastily drawn rune, the weight in my stomach sank lower.

She had unraveled it.

Every part.

My teeth ground together as another page turned, the parchment rasping under my fingers. She hadn't just been guessing; she had proof and discovered connections I hadn't even considered. She was right.

A curse escaped my lips as the book slammed shut. My fingers drummed against the leather cover of her journal. My thoughts spiraled back through every missed clue and overlooked sign.

Why had I not seen it?

I ran through it again, this time at a slower pace: the beliefs and traditions the village had abandoned, the symptoms, the patterns, the color, and smell of the logs, and the magic beneath them. Magic was present in the forest. Right in front of me, she sliced her palm and allowed her blood to drip onto the vine. I stood beside her, watching. But I missed it.

How?

Magic always left a mark. Even when concealed, dulled, or buried beneath layers of deception, it left traces: a shift in the air, a pull in the wrong direction, the weight of the unseen pressing against reality.

And I hadn't sensed a damn thing. My stomach twisted. Someone had concealed the magic so well that even my Fae blood hadn't detected it.

The implications set my instincts on edge and made the nape of my neck prickle. I sighed, rubbing my face before returning to Quinn's notes. She had pieced it together without magic, without knowing what to look for—just her relentless, maddening logic and refusal to let anything slip past her.

I despised relying on others. I didn't trust it.

Relying on others signifies weakness and vulnerability, and grants someone the power to let you down or betray you. I learned early on that trusting the wrong person could cost everything.

Heat licked beneath my skin as I pushed away from the desk. Crossing the room, I braced my hands against the window ledge. Quinn was still outside, hauling another armful of firewood. The firelight flickered around her, reminding me of the soot smudged across her cheek and the damp strands of hair clinging to her temples. Ash streaked her apron, dirt scuffed her boots, and quiet determination set on her features.

She was reckless, headstrong, and exceedingly clever.

And I needed her.

I pushed the door open, stepping into the cool night air. The scent of damp soil and lingering smoke clung to the square, mingling with the distant murmur of laughter spilling from the tavern.

Neryth's hooves scraped against the stone. His ears flicked back, nostrils flaring as he stretched his neck toward Quinn. Above us, a cluster of crows perched along the rooftops, watching without a single chirp.

Quinn stacked logs with a steady rhythm, her movements precise but stiff. The fire crackled beside her, casting flickering shadows across the dirt. I stood a short distance away, arms crossed over my chest. "Why didn't you make the others help?"

She lifted another log onto the pile. "I don't need another arrogant man telling me what to do."

My brow twitched.

Another?

I huffed, prepared to snap back, but the slight tremor in her hands halted me. The soot smeared across her fingers concealed the fresh burns, the raw patches where her skin had turned red. And she still hadn't wrapped her stupid, cut palm.

A sharp pang of irritation flared in my chest.

"Do you only care about everyone else?" I bit out. "Or do you just enjoy being a hypocrite?"

That made her pause. She turned to me with furrowed brows. "Excuse me?"

Nodding toward her hands, I stepped forward. "You nagged me about my shoulder getting infected, yet here you are—burned, bleeding, and toiling while the men you healed are off drinking."

Neryth stomped his hoof, and a crow ruffled its feathers above us as the rooftop watchers shifted.

Quinn scowled, flexing her fingers as if she had just realized how raw they were. "I'm fine."

"Oh, you're fine. Of course. Silly me."

Her glare intensified as she curled her fingers to hide the worst of it. I couldn't decide what infuriated me more—the reckless self-neglect or the realization that I actually cared.

Quinn's eyes flashed, and her shoulders squared as if she were ready for a fight. "I said I'm fine. It won't hinder my work."

I tipped my head back, searching for the patience that had been lost to her. A sigh escaped me as I locked eyes with her again. "Oh, well, if it won't hinder your work," I gestured to the wood, "by all means, go ahead. Bleed all over the firewood."

She stepped closer, jabbing a grimy finger at my chest. "If you were truly concerned, perhaps you should have offered help earlier instead of throwing accusations at me."

I had half a mind to toss her over my shoulder just to silence her. A muscle in my jaw twitched. I forced a slow breath through my nose, attempting to ease the sharp edge of my temper. "This isn't about that," I gritted.

Quinn scoffed, brushing past me as though the conversation was over. She bent down to pick up another log, but her hands trembled under the weight. Red skin stretched tightly over her knuckles, and the burns contrasted sharply with the smudges of soot.

Stubborn, reckless adaneth.

I reached out and caught her wrist before she could lift it. She tensed but didn't pull away. Her gaze flicked to mine, wary yet steady. Despite her exhaustion, the fire in her eyes remained undimmed. She set her jaw, her posture defiant, even as her body betrayed its limits.

Damn it.

"I was wrong."

Quinn froze. Her lips parted. My chest tightened, and I let her go.

She blinked once and tilted her head. "What?"

"You heard me." I resisted the urge to grind my teeth.

A beat of silence stretched between us before she lifted the log, walked past me, and let it fall onto the burning pile with a dull thud.

"Is that all? Nothing else?"

She dusted her hands on her skirts. "You expect me to what? Say thank you?"

My fists clenched at my sides. "Most people recognize an apology when they hear it."

She looked at me with a raised brow. "You didn't apologize."

I scowled. "It was implied."

Quinn chuckled softly, shaking her head as she returned to the logs. "Go to the tavern, Sinclaire."

My irritation spiked again. "I am not—"

She cut me off. "You're better off gathering information. Drunk men say foolish things. If something is wrong in this village, you'll hear it there." I hesitated, watching her pick up another log. The slight, unmistakable wince on her face revealed her pain as her burnt hand gripped it.

My jaw flexed as I fought the urge to argue, to force her to stop before she tore her hands apart completely. I knew better. Nothing I said would have prevented her from working. A slow breath escaped my lips. "Fine."

The tavern keeper served me a steaming bowl of spiced venison stew, with dark rye bread and a tankard of honeyed mead. Roasted juniper, smoked meat, warm spices, ale, and sweat mingled in the heavy air. Laughter and slurred conversations rumbled through the packed room, voices rising and falling in a drunken cadence.

My stomach twisted with restless unease as I stared at the food. Had the herbalist eaten anything other than the nuts and seeds on the desk? Had she even slept beyond those brief, unintentional naps since our arrival?

My chest burned.

Why did I care? She was stubborn. She had made that abundantly clear. I didn't owe her.

But the image of her face when I had pinned her against that tree refused to leave my mind. Her wrists were too delicate in my grip, and deep, exhausted shadows rested beneath her eyes. My jaw clenched tighter as I forced myself to cut into the meat, grounding my focus in the sharp tang of juniper and smoke, the slight burn of spice.

Focus.

Information.

The tavern swelled with carefree voices, men deep in their cups. My gaze drifted across the room, settling on a group of knights at the far end. Young. Intoxicated. Speaking too freely. I dismissed them.

Until I heard her name.

My grip on the knife tightened.

"...She's got that look, y'know?" one of them laughed, downing his ale. "All prim n' proper, actin' like she's too good for any of us."

"She's an herbalist, not a noble," another scoffed. "Bet she's just waiting for the right man to put her in her place."

A slow, dark, heat knotted in my gut.

"The way she looked when Valdier had her by the jaw?" A low whistle pierced the tavern's murmur. "I bet she's feisty in bed."

The world narrowed.

He what?

My mind went blank, then burned. One of them had touched her, and I hadn't noticed.

I should have been more aware.

She should have informed me.

My thoughts clawed through every moment and every interaction. *Did she flinch? Did her voice waver? Had I missed the signs?*

I had pushed her, taunted her, and questioned her intentions. I hadn't seen it. I hadn't thought, even for a moment, that one of them might have touched her.

It pissed me off.

She had healed them, walked into their quarters alone, tended to their wounds, and hadn't considered the danger. The thought never crossed my mind. My suspicions had occupied my thoughts, my damn arrogance had blinded me, and those bastards were laughing. They didn't even realize how close they were to losing their teeth.

Why did it eat at me?

Because I knew what could have happened.

Or what already had.

She had recklessly walked into a chamber filled with knights, unaware of the weight of her vulnerability. *Did she think they honored an unspoken code of decency? That men, hardened by war and raised in violence, saw her as more than an opportunity?*

It was too vivid: the shift in their stance, the way they closed in, testing her nerves, hands brushing too closely under the guise of jest, one of them reaching, gripping, and the startled intake of her breath. A glance passed between them, unspoken but understood.

How far did it go?

The sickening thought burrowed, slithered, and spread in my mind.

She hadn't mentioned it, hadn't even hinted at it. But that didn't mean it hadn't happened.

Fuck.

My jaw popped.

Forcing my fingers to relax, I drove the knife into my meal, slicing through the meat with deliberate precision. One wrong move, one slip, and I would lose control. I couldn't make a scene here, but if he had done more, if any of them had, there wouldn't be enough left of them to bury. The slow burn of my drink did little to dull the sharpness of my thoughts.

One of them laughed. "She's got them big, pretty eyes, y'know? The kind that look up at ya all soft—"

"—or wild," another chuckled. A violent heat gripped my spine. My fingers curled against the table, nails pressing into the wood.

I was going to fucking kill them.

"Healer's hands are always nice. But hers? Soft. Even with all that work she does."

"Did ya' see how small her wrists are? Could pro'lly wrap a whole hand around 'em."

"Bet she likes that."

A new surge of anger ignited within me and settled deeply in my bones. The tavern blurred, and voices twisted into static against the throbbing in my skull.

"Not sure what the fuss is about," one of them scoffed. "She'd be pretty if it weren't for her face looking like a dirty canvas." I rolled my knife methodically between my fingers, my pulse steady but loud. My body knew better than to react too soon, but I was dancing on the thin line of self-control.

The man across from him smirked and leaned in. "But imagine her tied up. Held down. The look she gave Valdier, but it's your hand on her jaw." He released a low groan. "The way her eyes would roll back?"

My hand released the blade before my mind caught up. Steel whispered through the air, sliced past the bastard's ear so close it severed a few strands of hair, and buried deep into the wooden beam behind him. Suffocating silence followed. The kind that thickened the air, pressed against the ribs, and squeezed the breath from lungs.

Chairs scraped against the floor as they rose to their feet, hands gripping the edges of the table. The casual arrogance they had displayed moments ago cracked and crumbled into a far more satisfying fear—anger. I met their eyes while my fingers tapped against the wood. Each *thunk* against the table served as a warning. Their chests heaved rapidly and shallowly while mine remained steady.

The heat in my blood cooled and intensified, becoming focused and quieter. A searing sting burned through my vision as silver blurred my peripherals. Their eyes widened, and their jaws slackened as recognition dawned on their faces.

They realized they hadn't been speaking in the presence of another knight. Not a man who would let their words pass as harmless filth, nor another brute who laughed it off, shrugged it off, or sat by idly.

No.

They realized that I wasn't a man at all.

14

EDEN

THE DOOR CREAKED shut behind me, sealing me in under the weight of my exhaustion. The inn room was dimly lit, and the single candle on the wooden table flickered against the walls, casting shadows that danced in my peripheral vision. The smell of charred wood and smoke clung to my clothes, becoming woven into my skin and hair. It reminded me of the fires I had spent the night battling. The contaminated logs had burned fast, taking with them any remnants of the ailment that had been festering within them. I had made sure of it.

My lungs ached, each breath shallow and stinging as if the embers still smoldered in my chest. I wiggled my fingers, wincing at the sharp bite of pain. The burns on my hands and forearms were raw, the skin swollen and red where the logs had been too hot, too close. They should heal. Pain was a temporary thing, an inconvenience. It only hindered my work if I let it.

'*Do you only care about everyone else?*'

Of course, I did. It was my responsibility.

But that wasn't the point.

I had sent him to the tavern to gather information he couldn't get elsewhere. The men in metal costumes were fools. They were puppets dressed in gilded armor, who pretended to hold authority. They knew nothing of the sickness that had been ravaging Silverfel. It was a lie, an excuse to remove him from the smoke, away from the rot and ruin. The thought of him breathing it in, with his lungs blackened by the same filth I had willingly inhaled, was unbearable.

Meanwhile, I was scorched, exhausted, sore, and foolish for enduring it. I suppressed the thought before it could take root and turn dangerous.

The room was empty. He wasn't back yet.

Good.

I needed a moment to breathe, to let the tremor in my hands fade, and to push away whatever had burrowed into my core since our argument. It was his expression in the woods. The way his eyes flickered silver so suddenly, so unnaturally, that I froze in place, caught in the shift for the briefest moment.

It was unprecedented. The silver wasn't a trick of the light, a reflection, or a fleeting illusion. It had consumed his irises, swallowing the dark in an instant. The air had changed, becoming heavy and charged with an invisible pressure against my skin.

It should have scared me. Something in me expected it to unnerve me, but it intrigued me.

Despite the warning in his gaze and the sharp edge of his demeanor, I pushed closer instead of pulling away. The emotionless gleam in his eyes should have felt threatening, yet I couldn't look away. I grinned, though nervously. I stood at the precipice of the vast and unknowable, a realm that was both dangerous and fascinating.

I was too tired to wrestle with whatever had shifted between us and too tired to ignore it.

My fingers found the open cut on my palm and traced over it, pressing just hard enough to sting. It was the same cut he had used to accuse me, the one I hadn't bothered to heal. Oberon regarded me as if I were reckless. Maybe I was. Maybe I wanted to be. The pain was grounding, tangible amid the exhaustion that weighed on me. I couldn't let myself dwell on those thoughts.

I had a job to finish.

Dragging my heavy limbs, I crossed the room to the basin in the corner. Age clouded the mirror above it; its glass was warped and streaked, but that didn't soften my reflection. My face was hollow-eyed and worn, with smudges of soot clinging to my skin. Beneath the grime, my complexion was pallid, dark circles heavy beneath my eyes, and strands of damp hair stuck to my forehead.

I appeared as if I had walked through the Veil.

Focusing on the basin, my hands dipped in the icy water. The sting was immediate. I bit my cheek and scrubbed, watching as the water darkened and swirled with remnants of fire and blood.

The burns were severe. They weren't the worst I had ever experienced, but they were serious enough that I should have treated them hours earlier.

Searching through my satchel, I took out a small tin and flipped it open with my thumb. The familiar smell of comfrey and beeswax filled the air. I scooped out a small amount and spread it over the burns on my palms. The moment it touched the rawest burns, an involuntary hiss escaped my lips. The balm worked quickly, sinking into my skin and soothing the worst of the sting. But it hadn't eased the deeper ache.

Next was the cut on my hand. It had stopped bleeding, but the surrounding skin still throbbed, hot and angry. I doused it with the last of my tincture, biting my cheek as the sting shot up my arm. The pain settled into a dull throb as I wrapped a clean strip of linen around each palm and secured the bandage in place.

The linen stretched as I moved my fingers, but it held firm. It had to be enough. Exhaustion tugged at my limbs, dulling my senses. My body begged for rest and food, but there was too much left to do.

I sat back on the bed and flexed my fingers. The ache lingered, a deep, pulsing throb beneath the bandages, but the sharper sting had faded to a more tolerable level.

It was fine.

I was fine.

I had to be.

The door slammed open so violently that the walls shuddered. My muscles seized, and a wave of awareness surged through me, but I had no time to flinch before his gaze met mine. Oberon's eyes blazed like tempered steel. Silver shimmered at the edges of his irises while his stare raked over me, as if noting every inch, wound, and breath. His nostrils flared, but he remained silent. He stood there, staring, his jaw clenched so tightly that it seemed he might break it.

A heavy, ragged exhale tore from his chest. He shut the door with more restraint than he had used to open it, but the tension radiating from him filled every inch of the room. I half-expected him to storm toward me, to lash out at me with whatever had provoked him this time. Instead, he pressed himself against the door as if he needed its solid weight to keep him grounded. His fingers tangled in his hair, his shoulders coiled, and his entire body was wound tight.

The silence stretched, heavy with an unfamiliar tension, until his gravelly voice sliced through it. "Why the hells didn't you tell me?"

I gathered the scattered bandages and supplies around me, my fingers moving on instinct. I was too tired for this. For him. "Tell you what, Sinclaire?"

His voice was sharper this time, its edges worn. "Valdier."

I frowned. "Who?"

Oberon pressed his tongue against his canine, angling his jaw. He pushed off the door and stalked toward me.

My breath hitched, my heart raced, and I sprang to my feet before he reached me, squaring my shoulders as if that would make me fiercer.

He stopped just short, close enough to see the tension in his throat when he swallowed. His gaze scanned my face before settling on my jaw. His expression darkened. His voice dropped to a lower, more restrained tone when he spoke again, the quiet tip of a dagger before the strike.

"The knight that left those bruises."

I blinked at him. The exhaustion in my bones clashed with the irritation sparking in my chest.

Bruises. Right.

I had forgotten.

Lifting my chin, I fought the urge to sigh. "I'm fine." His jaw twitched, and his hands balled into fists at his sides. "I handled it." My voice remained steady while I crossed my arms over my chest, dismissing the dull sting from my burned and cut hands. The linen bandages pressed tightly against my skin, but I held my ground. "It wasn't a big deal."

Oberon's eyes flashed, a warning before the storm. "Not a big—" He cut himself off, his chest rising and falling in a harsh rhythm. His fingers curled, and his knuckles cracked as if he were restraining himself from breaking something.

Or *someone.*

He stepped closer. "You handled it?" His voice was quieter, but that made it worse. More dangerous. "Is that what you call letting that bastard put his hands on you?"

My irritation flared, burning even hotter than the throbbing in my palms. "I didn't let him do anything."

"Then why the fuck am I only hearing about this now?"

"Because it wasn't your problem." The words slipped out before I could halt them. Too harsh. Too weary.

Oberon's eyes narrowed. "Not my problem?" His tone was subdued once more, yet it carried an unmistakable bite. "I am here to ensure your safety. To protect you."

My jaw muscles tensed, regretting that I had ever spoken. "I *am* safe."

A flicker of calculation crossed his face, a crack in his rage. He studied me, his searching gaze attempting to unravel every thread I had sewn into place. I hated how easily he could do it. He straightened. "Right," he said, his expression schooling. "Because you're always fine. Always handling everything on your own."

I disliked how he said that, like he was privy to something I wasn't, as if he saw through me. I refused to let him see more.

"So glad we agree," I mumbled, pulling away to the desk for some distance. My fingers skimmed the pages of my journal, and I frowned. The desk wasn't how I had left it. Someone had shifted the papers and moved the books. Smudges of charcoal marked the edges of pages I hadn't touched.

I turned, narrowing my eyes at Oberon. "This isn't how I left it." I glanced between him and my notes. "You were tampering with my things."

He didn't even have the decency to look guilty. "I was reading them... And organizing them better than you did."

I scoffed, muttering under my breath before leafing through the pages. "Why? What did you expect to find?"

Oberon sighed. "It's the magic." My stomach twisted. With a grim expression, he approached the desk, his presence looming over me. "I didn't sense it, and that's been bothering me."

A slow, creeping unease settled in my chest. "Magic leaves traces," he continued. "Even if it's subtle, I should have felt it. But I didn't."

He could sense magic? Did he use Fae magic?

Pressing my fingers into the leather, I squeezed the journal. "So, are you saying something was hiding it?"

He nodded once, the movement stiff and jerky. "That's the only explanation. This means that whoever, or whatever, is behind this didn't just enchant the bellthorn; they knew how to cover their tracks."

"Then how do we stop it?"

Oberon pressed his hands against the desk. His gaze fixed on mine. "It's not just the plants, Dilthen Doe." His tone lowered, heavier than before. "It's what they were feeding."

I swallowed hard. "What do you mean?"

"This isn't merely a cursed vine poisoning the village—it's a curse that spreads through the woods and takes root. The firewood was simply the catalyst."

My blood ran cold.

"Then what do we do?"

He stepped closer, the gap between us disappearing as his fingers pressed against the desk, his gaze holding me in place. "We find the heart of it," he declared, his tone gravelly and resolute. His eyes burned into mine. "And we scorch it."

THE AIR IN the forest was heavy with more than just humidity. Although the fires had been extinguished, the odor of charred wood lingered, mingling with the repulsive scent of decomposition. It wasn't merely decay; it went deeper than that. Something ancient and festering lay waiting beneath the surface.

My hands tightened around the satchel strap as I adjusted it. Oberon walked ahead, his posture rigid and his movements precise. He seemed more on edge than usual, and that worried me. "Do you feel anything now?" I whispered.

He inclined his head, his eyes scanning the trees with the patience of a predator. The muscles in his jaw contracted, and he muttered, "No." I wanted to ask what it would feel like and what he was searching for, but I wasn't sure if I wanted the answer.

The further we walked, the worse it became.

The trees were wrong. Their trunks were gnarled, their hands frozen in agony. Dark veins ran up their bark, pulsing beneath the surface as though alive and feeding. The leaves overhead weren't green but sickly yellow-gray, curling inward as if retreating from the air.

The suffocating silence pressed against my ears. There were no birds, no rustling creatures in the underbrush, not even the chirp of insects. Except—

My gaze shifted to the side, and I came to a standstill. A creature moved along the bark of a nearby tree, a shimmering, translucent being with an excessive number of legs and an elongated body that rippled as it crawled with unnatural movements. It was something that shouldn't exist. My stomach twisted, and I stepped back. It made no sound. None of them did.

My feet sank into the soft ground, worse than moss or damp soil. I crouched, brushed my fingers against the dirt, and pulled back with a grimace. It was wet and blackened—tainted. The same dark rot that had clung to the bellthorn vine and reacted to my blood coated the forest floor like a disease.

The ground pulsed under my fingers. "This is it," I murmured, glancing up at Oberon. "This is where it's coming from."

He gave a curt nod and unsheathed his blade. The whisper of steel sent a shiver through the air. "Stay close." I rolled my eyes and sighed, earning a sharp look in response.

As we moved forward, the trees closed in around us. Their branches twisted together above, forming a tunnel that funneled us toward the unseen. The hairs on my arms stood up. The air thickened, infused with more than simple magic. It felt sentient, as if it were watching.

A massive, withered tree stood in the clearing, its bark split open with a gaping wound, oozing blackened sap that reeked of death. Its roots stretched across the ground like skeletal fingers, curling around stones and pulling them as if they were being swallowed whole.

Grotesque bone ornaments hung, woven among its branches.

Human bones dangled from sinewy strands, swaying despite the lack of wind. Cleaned, blanched, and stark against the dark bark, skulls, ribcages, and shattered femurs hung. The air around the tree crackled. The rot was thickest here, seeping into the ground and poisoning the air.

My eyes widened. Beside me, Oberon muttered a curse under his breath, muffled by the roar of my pulse. My hands clenched into fists to steady myself against the ache in my palm, but the air had grown heavier. A pair of hollow eyes blinked from the tree's hollowed trunk.

Not human... Not animal... Something ancient. Hungry.

A twisted figure, its limbs overly long, its movements disconcerting in a way my mind couldn't reconcile. The elongated, sinewy frame dragged itself from the tree's hollow, and its mouth pulled back into a grotesque, knowing grin that ignited every nerve in my body with dread. The bones from the tree rattled with its movements, clicking together in a manner that resembled a summons.

A call to the dead.

I inched backward, my heart in my throat. Oberon issued a hushed command, keeping his focus on the creature. "Stay behind me."

The creature uncurled from the hollow. Its spindly limbs scraped against the bark as it pulled itself free. Its skin was the color of decay, stretched thin and torn over its elongated frame. Its fingers, clawed with too many joints, dragged along the ground as it straightened to its full, unnatural height.

The bones dangling from the branches above clattered together, as if whispering in response to its presence. Oberon positioned himself between me and the creature, his sword gleaming even in the dim, corrupted light filtering through the twisted canopy.

"That's not a Fae," I murmured. "Is it?"

"No," Oberon replied through clenched teeth. "It's worse."

The creature tilted its head. It had no lips, only a stretched maw filled with jagged teeth. The sound was unsettling when it spoke in a rasping, hollow voice that resembled wind rattling through dead trees.

"*What do you seek?*" The sound wrapped around my ribs.

Oberon didn't flinch. "We're here to end this curse."

A deep, throaty noise rumbled from the thing's chest. *Was it laughing?* It lifted one elongated finger and pointed at me. "*The herbalist must bleed.*"

My stomach dropped.

Oberon shifted his stance to block me. "Not happening."

One moment, the creature stood beneath the cursed tree; the next, it loomed before us, a twisted horror of gnarled limbs and malevolence. Its form shifted as if the land itself rejected its presence. I gasped, stumbling back as blackened, bony talons lashed toward me. A flash of steel intercepted them. Sparks exploded in the dark as Oberon's sword absorbed the impact of the strike. The force sent him skidding back, boots gouging into the decayed soil.

"Damn it, move!" he barked.

I forced my feet to obey, scrambling back as my mind raced. The bellthorn held the curse. The land was poisoned by something ancient, crafted to fester and spread. The air reeked of rot and magic. *But how could we sever it? How would we*—

The ground shifted beneath me, and a sickening crack split the silence. A root shot up, and I twisted away, tripping and rolling to the side as another lashed toward my legs. Oberon's booming voice resonated through the chaos, commanding as he slashed through the writhing wood. "Herbalist!" Another strike, another severed root. "Whatever you're thinking, think faster!"

I bit back a curse.

It watched me. Not Oberon, who stood slashing and fighting it, but *me*. Was it because I could end this or because it had tasted my blood on the bellthorn and wanted more?

Oberon's movements were fluid, precise, and relentless. His sword extended his body, slicing through sinew and bark. He severed limbs and vines with inhuman speed, but the wounds healed before my eyes. The curse refused to let them fall.

"It's healing too quickly!" I shouted, dodging back as a twisted limb slammed into the ground where I had stood just a breath before. Oberon shifted his stance, his fingers curling tighter around his blade. The land cracked beneath his boots, and power thrummed in the air.

The beast lunged. Its massive, gnarled limb arced toward me. I braced for the impact. There was a sickening crunch and then silence.

Oberon stood before me, a storm given form. His grip locked around the beast's gnarled limb. Black veins burst across his skin, crawling up his arm in jagged, pulsing lines. I watched in horror as the sickness burrowed deep, threading into his flesh in hungry roots, spreading beneath his skin to rot him from the inside out.

My stomach lurched.

It halted.

The air shuddered. An unseen pulse rippled outward, warping the surrounding space. Silver-blue light bled from his veins, fierce and untamed, crackling in strokes of lightning beneath the surface. The darkness recoiled and peeled away as if it had never intended to touch him. The cursed veins shattered, brittle as ink on glass, burning away into nothing.

The creature shrieked, producing a raw, unnatural sound that grated on my skull. It twisted, recoiling—not from pain, but from recognition. *It feared him.*

Oberon exhaled, slow and controlled. His breath misted in the unnatural chill that had descended upon us. When he spoke, his voice was no longer entirely human. The heavy, resonant words slithered through the air, vibrating my bones. They were a forgotten language, older than the kingdom itself. Each syllable hummed with a power that warped at the edges of reality, bending it to his will.

The silvery gleam in his eyes burned brighter. With calculated precision, he drove his sword into the ground. An alarming pulse rippled through the soil. The beast screamed, its limbs fracturing and splintering like dry wood. The air became suffocating under the weight of Oberon's power.

The land trembled in his wake.

But it wasn't enough. The roots pulsed, empowered by him, not diminished. Magic was the key: a force as ancient as the curse itself.

'The herbalist must bleed.'

A sacrifice.

My throat tightened. Not just blood. It wanted an offering.

I fumbled through my satchel, fingers scrambling over dried herbs: hallowroot, duskthistle, veilthorn. My hand closed around my dagger.

Oberon's head snapped in my direction. His expression darkened when he noticed the blade in my hand. "Dilthen Doe," he warned.

There was no time.

The bandage around my palm unraveled. I held my breath as the dagger pressed into the wound, slicing it open once more. The blood welled, dark and glistening in the cursed light. With my other hand, I crushed the herbs, mixing them into a thick, magical paste rich in iron.

One opportunity. One possibility.

I surged forward, pressing my bloodied palm against the cursed bark.

The effect was immediate.

A scream split the air, not just sound but something more profound that scraped against my spine, clawed through my skull, and rattled the marrow of my bones. The trees groaned under its force, their branches shuddering as if the roots themselves were trying to recoil. Overhead, the skeletal remains tangled in the canopy clattered together, disturbed by the shift in magic. The ground trembled beneath me, pulsing with the intensity of the curse's death throes.

The creature convulsed. Its grotesque form twisted, and limbs contorted as if unseen hands gripped it from within, wrenching it apart piece by piece. Shadows recoiled as the air split with unnatural cracks.

Oberon's sword carved a silver arc, piercing the creature's skull in one brutal, final stroke. The steel sank deep, and the surrounding sounds shattered into a deep hum.

A shockwave rippled outward, racing over the ground, splitting through the decay, and burning away the lingering corruption. The curse shattered with a violent pulse. The sheer force of its impact against my skin threatened to knock the breath from my lungs.

The beast emitted one last strangled cry before its limbs buckled. Bark and sinew fractured as its monstrous form collapsed inward. Cracks splintered through its body, leaving only crumbling bone and blackened ash.

A deafening silence followed. It was not the heavy, stifling kind that had settled when the curse loomed, but a genuine silence. The air changed, no longer laden with decay.

The burden had been lifted.

My pulse thrummed in my ears as I took a ragged breath. Every muscle in my body trembled, drained from the magic and the intensity of what we had just survived. But my eyes remained fixed on Oberon.

He stood in the clearing, his sword once again buried in the ground, his fingers clenched around the hilt. His chest rose and fell in sharp, uneven breaths. His other hand clutched the arm that the curse had attempted to claim. His knuckles were white, and his fingers trembled.

I took a nervous step toward him. "You..." My voice quivered. Swallowing hard against my tight throat, I searched his face and the shadows cast across his sharp features. "You knew this would work, didn't you?"

A muscle in Oberon's face twitched. He didn't look at me or speak for a moment. In a voice quieter than I expected, he admitted, "No." His hands disturbed me more than his answer, the way he couldn't stop them from shaking.

And the fact he didn't try to hide it.

15

EDEN

WHEN WE RETURNED to the village, I headed to the knights' quarters, ignoring the protest of my aching limbs and the bone-deep weariness clawing at my skull. Every part of me screamed for rest—my muscles burned, my fingers trembled from overuse, and a dull ache pulsed at the base of my spine. But I couldn't stop. Not yet. Not when knights still needed to wake up, and fevers required watching.

I had long since learned to push through exhaustion. It was a lesson carved into me through nights spent curled on chilly tiles, shivering beneath threadbare blankets. Through the sting of untreated wounds, skin cracked and raw, left to mend on its own, and through the hollow ache of a body forced to endure what no one wanted to repair.

I learned because no one was ever there to heal me.

Fatigue was a luxury I had never been allowed. My parents taught me that. Marcus reinforced it. Pain became my instructor, my reality.

If I stopped, I lost. If I faltered, I suffered. If I slowed, I paid the price. So, I adapted. I trained my body to move when it wanted to collapse, to work when exhaustion blurred my vision. I learned to ignore the slow, creeping drag of fatigue, to push past the limits that others acknowledged. I kept going because even if it was just one more patient, one more person, I could help them.

Because no one had done it for me.

Behind me, Oberon huffed. The sound sliced through the silence, a wordless statement in itself. Yet he didn't stop me. Of course, he wouldn't. He knew better. He understood that no matter how often he urged me to rest, I wouldn't listen. Not when people were still suffering.

The knights' quarters smelled of sweat, aged herbs, and the acrid bite of alcohol. The hearth burned with clean wood, the fire brighter, casting jagged shadows across the wooden beams.

I adjusted my satchel, squared my shoulders, and entered.

Soft murmurs filled the air—restless knights shifting in their cots, the rustle of blankets as bodies turned in fitful sleep, and the groggy mutterings of men caught in that fragile space between wakefulness and oblivion. The smell of sweat, stale ale, and lingering herbs thickened the atmosphere, pressing against my senses. Several knights had succumbed to unconsciousness after drowning themselves in celebration until they could take no more. Others stirred as I passed, blinking sluggishly, their gazes unfocused and their minds still clouded by exhaustion and drink.

I moved through the room in silence, my hands working on instinct—pressing the backs of my fingers to fevered foreheads, checking pulses that thudded too weakly, and smoothing blankets that feverish patients had kicked aside. A few knights murmured quiet thanks, but most were too far gone to notice my presence. That was fine; I didn't need gratitude.

But my body slowed down. My thoughts dragged; each movement required more effort, and every breath felt heavier. I had pushed myself too far again, but stopping wasn't an option.

There was a sudden shift in the air, a ripple of tension so thick it felt suffocating, that unmistakable prickle of being watched.

I pushed myself to keep moving, my fingers steady as I completed the examination of the knight before me, but my senses expanded outward, searching. My heartbeat quickened.

I lifted my gaze and scanned the room.

Oberon stood near the entrance, motionless—too motionless. Rigid tension gripped his broad shoulders, and his chest rose and fell with slow, measured breaths. He clenched his jaw, and I half expected to hear his teeth grinding together.

A knot formed in my stomach when I followed his line of sight.

Valdier.

The arrogant knight who had gripped my face stood at the back of the room, speaking to two younger knights in hushed tones. His stance was casual, and his expression relaxed. He didn't even glance our way.

Dark bruises marred his jaw and cheekbone in unsightly shades of purple and blue. Those bruises hadn't been there before. My gaze flicked back to Oberon.

His expression was a facade of stony indifference. Yet, fury burned in his eyes.

Whatever had happened to Valdier, it hadn't been enough. He contemplated completing what he had begun. A tense sigh escaped my lips, softened by the crackling hearth and the restless whispers of the surrounding knights.

I returned my attention to my work, moving to the next cot and willing myself to ignore the storm brewing behind me—the unspoken violence, the slow, simmering aggression rolling off Oberon in waves. I didn't have time to mull over his temper or analyze how those bruises on Valdier's face sent a strange, unsettling heat curling low in my stomach; a feeling I couldn't put into words and couldn't push away.

There was no time to reflect on the fact that he had done that because of me. I had spent far too much time trying to understand Oberon Sinclaire.

The cots nearest to the hearth flickered in the firelight, with the warmth casting long, wavering shadows along the stone walls. A slow inhale broke the silence as I approached the knight in the worst condition. There was a shift beneath the blankets. His chest rose and fell in steady, even breaths.

His eyelids fluttered. His gaze was unfocused, still caught in the haze of sleep, but when he noticed me, his expression changed. His breath hitched, and his lips parted as if he had forgotten how to speak. His eyes widened, filling with raw wonder.

I faltered.

No one had ever gazed at me like that.

Not my parents, who viewed me as a burden, a nuisance, ugly in both form and presence—an obligation rather than a daughter. They looked at me with unsympathetic detachment, as if I were nothing more than a weight chained to their lives.

Not Marcus, who had treated me like a possession. A thing to own, to break, to control. A lie in the shape of a human, meant to be erased in private but paraded in public when it suited his image.

For as long as I could remember, I had been too much and never enough. Overly stubborn. Excessively plain. Quite inconvenient. I learned that my usefulness measured my worth; that my hands could heal, but my face could never inspire softness. My presence was tolerated at best and ignored at worst.

Yet this knight regarded me as though I were worthy of being noticed, as if I were more than merely my purpose.

"You're awake!" I exclaimed. My fingers reached for his wrist, searching for his pulse and clinging to the comfort of routine. His gaze dropped to my hands, taking in the burns, the bruises, the raw, reddened skin that still throbbed and needed bandaging again after the fight in the woods. His brows furrowed when he reached out, grasping my hands.

I froze.

His grip was careful and reverent. His thumbs glided over my knuckles, brushing against the wounds as if he could erase them with the lightest touch. His hands were warm, rough with calluses, yet gentle.

As if I were something fragile.

Precious.

My heart stuttered, creating a sharp, uneven rhythm against my breast. I swallowed hard and forced a shaky laugh. "It's nothing," I blurted. "Just a little..."

His grip shifted, holding me still. He reached up with his other hand, his fingertips brushing my temple as he tucked a loose strand of hair behind my ear. The touch was achingly soft.

I wanted to say something—anything. But all I managed was a breathless, startled "oh", and my body went rigid. Heat bloomed across my cheeks.

What is happening?

"You're beautiful," he murmured, his voice soft yet confident. The words pierced me, leaving me fragile and brittle, like a wounded animal trying to protect itself.

Beautiful?

That word didn't belong to me. "Beautiful" was meant for delicate things, for things that mattered. It wasn't for the girl who learned that love was conditional, who discovered that affection was a trick, dangled out of reach, a prize she had never been good enough to earn. The girl who knew, with quiet certainty, that he wouldn't have said that if he had seen beneath her sleeves, if he had truly seen her from the inside.

No.

Beautiful wasn't a word meant for people like me.

But his hands were so warm, his voice was steady, and he spoke as though he saw what I couldn't. His thumb traced over the backs of my fingers, avoiding the most profound injuries marring my skin.

"Oh, love," he murmured, as if he had sensed every fractured thought in my mind. "If only you could see yourself as I see you."

I couldn't breathe. I should have distanced myself and responded dismissively to push the moment away before it could harm me. However, for a brief, disorienting moment, I let it overwhelm me: the comforting warmth of his touch, the strangeness of his words, and the dangerous, unfamiliar spark of longing curling in my chest.

A scoff shattered the growing tension. "Oh, cut it out, Heartwell," another knight mused. Heartwell sighed, his fingers relaxing, and the warmth faded away. With it, the fragile haze that had enveloped me disappeared.

Shaking my head, I reached for something to say to fill the awkward, gaping silence and to mend how foolish I must have appeared. "I— I don't..." The words tangled in my throat, emerging softly- uncertain. Heartwell's gaze softened as if he could perceive the battle raging behind my eyes.

He pitied me.

Gods, that made it so much worse.

I took a clumsy step back, desperate to create space between us, but my boot caught on the uneven floor, and the room tilted. A familiar, sharp inhale pierced my senses as steady hands gripped my biceps, arresting my fall. My back met solid, warm muscle. My breath trembled.

His grip was firm. His fingers pressed hard enough to anchor me. I tilted my head back, but Oberon didn't look at me; he watched Hartwell. The knight's expression was weary yet watchful, a subtle hardness seeping into his features. He must have known he had overstepped. He must have understood too late that his words had unsettled more than just me.

The muscles in Oberon's jaw tightened before his piercing onyx eyes met mine. "You've done enough, Herbalist," he insisted, voice firm yet devoid of anger. "The knights will live. You must rest."

"I'm fine," I whispered.

His fingers flexed. "No."

The single word held weight, resting between us in an unspoken vow. His voice didn't rise or sharpen. It conveyed a finality that was impossible to defy. "Enough."

Oberon's hands relaxed and then fell away. He stepped aside, gesturing for me to go first. I hesitated, my gaze flicking back to Heartwell. Exhaustion still clung to his features, shadowing his eyes, but his expression softened when I met his gaze, as if I had become a quiet moment in the storm, a presence worth holding onto.

"I'm glad you're awake," I whispered. A small smile tugged at his lips, but he didn't respond. My gaze shifted back to Oberon, who continued to stare at him. He was merely being cautious. After what had happened with Valdier, he had his reasons. It was his duty to protect me.

So why did I feel as if I was missing something?

Heavy footsteps trailed behind me as I stepped into the chilly night air. "He was lying." Oberon walked beside me, his expression as unyielding as stone. His usual stoic mask hid a sharp edge beneath it.

I blinked. "I... What?"

"That knight. He was lying."

I let out an incredulous breath. "About what? His ability to hold a conversation?"

Oberon ignored the quip, his gaze fixed ahead. "Men like him will say whatever you want to hear to get you under them."

I scoffed, crossing my arms. "What makes you think I wanted to be under him?"

The muscle below his eye twitched. "I noticed the way you looked at him, Dilthen Doe." He gritted his teeth as if it pained him to say those words.

My steps wavered.

The way I looked at him? Like what? That I felt heard? Seen?

Fiery heat pooled in my chest. "Perhaps," I clipped, "he would make better company than you."

Oberon stopped.

His nostrils flared, and his eyes flickered silver, reminding me of how his arm had appeared in the forest as it expelled the black magic seeping through his veins. The way the air shimmered around him, and how he seemed—heaving and cradling his arm after the creature crumbled before us—weighed on my mind. Regret washed over me. He must have been exhausted and sore. Yet he followed me to ensure I stayed safe in a room full of arrogant men. I was too stubborn to consider anything beyond checking on the men who had spent an entire day celebrating at the tavern.

The innkeeper called out to him, but he didn't slow his pace as he climbed the stairs. I walked over to the counter in his stead. "You have a letter," she said. "It appears to be from the castle. The postman mentioned it was urgent."

I forced a gentle smile. "Thank you," I murmured, accepting the letter with steady hands despite the fatigue weighing on my limbs. With a practiced motion, I slid my dagger under the wax seal, slicing it open with a quick flick of my wrist. Another formality. Another task. Another demand.

The words blurred together until my eyes landed on "Vaelwick". My breath hitched, and my fingers gripped the parchment tightly. Exhaustion melted away as I reread the message, scanning over the words as if they could change, as if they would rearrange themselves into something less impossible.

The Courts summoned us to Vaelwick.

A creeping pressure coiled around my ribs. My boots thudded against the floor as I marched down the hall. The letter crumpled in my grip.

Oberon stood in the center of the room, his eyes snapping to mine as I entered with my arms crossed. The moment he opened his mouth, I interrupted him. "We have orders." I marched past him and slammed the letter onto the table, my voice harsher than I intended. "We're going to Vaelwick."

16

EDEN

CANDLE SMOKE FILLED the air, mingling with the cloying scent of perfume. It enveloped me in a dense, suffocating fog. My dress was too tight; the corset dug into my ribs, making each breath feel stolen rather than given.

I sat stiff-backed at the dining table, my hands folded neatly in my lap and my nails digging into my palms. Across from me, my father swirled his glass of amber liquid while he scrutinized me with sharp, assessing eyes. My mother's fingers rested on my shoulder, a gentle weight that felt like a shackle.

Stay still. Stay quiet. Be what they require you to be.

"You're lovely," Marcus murmured, his voice silken and sweet, poison in honey. I tensed when he reached for my hand. His fingers ghosted over mine before curling around them. He *held me as if I were something delicate or breakable—a thing to be cherished.*

I couldn't move. Couldn't breathe.

"Like something crafted," he continued, his grip tightening. "Sculpted. Almost too perfect to be real."

My stomach twisted. Gods, I wanted to pull away, but I knew better. I understood what would happen if I embarrassed them, so I remained still and quiet.

Somewhere behind me, the faint crack of a whip rang out in the silence, and I flinched.

Marcus chuckled, and his voice curled around me like a noose. "Nothing to say? No need to be shy, Darling. A girl like you," the whip cracked again. My throat tightened as I dug my nails deeper into my palm. "—was made to be adored."

My breath hitched, and my pulse hammered into my skull. Liar.

My father sighed with annoyance. "Don't be ungrateful, Eden."

My mother's nails dragged along my arm. "Smile. Please, just smile."

I tried, but it felt like swallowing glass.

Marcus lifted a hand to brush the hair behind my ear so soft and slow, like the knight had. I flinched harder this time. His expression darkened, and the room suddenly felt wrong. The candlelight flickered, casting a warped glow over his features, and shadows twisted across his face.

The whip cracked again, closer now. The walls curled inward. Marcus's grip on my hand became iron. The shadows behind him stretched, turning monstrous.

"Why do you look so scared?" Amusement played at the edges of his insensitivity. "Don't you know? You are mine, Eden." The darkness swarmed and swallowed everything but his emotionless, hungry eyes.

"You should be grateful," my father's voice rasped from beyond the abyss.

"You should be honored," my mother whispered. The sound was ice against my ear.

No. No, no, no.

The whip cracked and split the air as if it had struck my skin. My mouth opened in a scream.

I woke up with a gasp. My body trembled, and my wrists ached. My chest heaved as my lungs strained for air that felt too heavy for them to hold.

The room came into focus. Dim candlelight illuminated wooden beams, and the air carried the scent of smoke and old parchment. Not that dining room or that mansion. *I was at the inn, far from Wickloe, far from them.*

My eyes landed on Oberon's.

He sat on the floor beside the bed, his dark eyes searching my face with furrowed brows. His fingers pressed against my arm.

Had he been trying to wake me?

I swallowed hard. My heart throbbed in my chest, and my throat was dry and raw. I tried to look away, grounding myself in the candlelight, the worn blanket tangled around my legs, and the distant sound of footsteps. Not on the crack of a whip or the sound of his voice that replayed in my mind.

Oberon remained still and silent. He simply waited. I clenched my hands against the sheets. I needed to say something to reassure us both that I was present. But I could only muster a raspy whisper when I finally spoke. "I'm okay."

We made eye contact again, and his eyes narrowed. He didn't look the least bit convinced. "I'm fine," I said, unsure if I was trying to convince myself or him. "It's fine."

It wasn't fine.

It was anything but fine.

The echoes of the nightmare still gripped me. The faint crack of the whip continued to resonate in my mind, and the scars on my back had reopened into fresh wounds. The weight of Marcus's hand against my skin remained palpable. His way of always calling me "Darling" suggested that he believed I belonged to him—a possession, a prize to display on his shelf.

A shudder ran through me, urging the memories to fade. Oberon's fingers flexed. I had been trembling. His voice was hushed and cautious. "Liar." I pushed myself upright with a shaky breath.

My cheeks were damp.

I froze.

When did I cry?

A laugh bubbled up, sounding forced. "Gods," I muttered, dragging the heel of my palm across my face to wipe away the evidence. "That must have looked dramatic."

I hated the way Oberon looked at me. It stripped me bare and made me feel exposed, as though he could dissect everything I didn't say—everything I wanted to bury. I took another deep breath and released a lighter laugh. "You can let go now. I'm awake, see?" I waved my hand in the air, attempting to appear nonchalant and conceal that I had crumbled in my sleep.

My jaw slackened as I stared at my hand, and I frowned. The cuts and burns had been bandaged. I didn't do that. I intended to, but fell asleep when my head touched the bed. I didn't even remember dozing off.

My eyes darted to Oberon's, and the breath I hadn't realized I was holding collapsed in my chest. The intensity of his gaze and how he saw through me was overwhelming. A fresh wave of tears welled up in my eyes. I gritted my teeth, but the more I tried to suppress it, the worse it became.

Shit.

I ripped my gaze away from his with a sharp inhale, blinking at the wall, the floor, anywhere but him. "Can you do anything besides stare at me?"

Oberon made a sound just short of a scoff. His grip on my arm tightened briefly before he let go and leaned back. "Forgive me for ensuring that you were still breathing," he muttered.

A weak laugh escaped me, but it didn't hide the tremor in my voice. "I'm fine."

THE FRESH MORNING air nipped at my skin as I rolled my shoulders, stretching my arms overhead to shake off the lingering stiffness of sleep. My breath fogged in the pre-dawn light as I exhaled, pretending to breathe smoke to mask my unease. Beside me, the horse's hooves scuffed against the dirt as Oberon secured the last of our supplies. The sounds of leather straps tightening and buckles fastening filled the quiet between us.

"How far is Vaelwick?" I asked, rubbing the horse's neck. Its warmth seeped into my fingertips, providing a grounding sensation against the morning chill.

Oberon gave the strap one final tug before answering. "Close," he grumbled, his voice rough from the early morning air. "But it's across the river. We should arrive by sunrise."

I nodded. A small wave of relief eased the tightness in my shoulders. At least we didn't have to pass through Emberhollow again—no monstrous Ashenmaws lurking in the mist as they called for blood. The memory still clung to me, the phantom sensation of their piercing shrieks reverberating in my bones.

That had passed.

The nightmare had ended.

Oberon noticed the change in my expression and gave me a pointed look. "Don't get too comfortable," he warned, his tone laced with unspoken caution. He didn't elaborate. He would have said more if it had been important... *wouldn't he?*

I relaxed my grip on the saddle as we crossed the main path. The dirt road winding through the trees was a ribbon of shadow in the dim light. I took one last glance at Silverfel.

The heavy, stifling fog that covered the village when we arrived had lifted. The air was clearer now, lighter, as if the land had been holding its breath and could finally release it. A hollow stillness remained, the quiet after something dark had passed, leaving only memories. The thing we faced, the illness that had clawed through the village, had become insignificant. A memory. A nightmare that would fade with time.

Whatever lay ahead for us in Vaelwick was unlikely to be more dreadful than that. Blighted harvests and creatures disappearing into the forest were problems we could manage. Such issues didn't seize your mind and linger long after your safety. They were commonplace enough.

NIGHTFALL DRAPED OVER the woods in deep blues and grays as we drew closer to the river. Silhouettes of trees reached toward the sky. The distant rush of water filled the silence, a whisper that only intensified the quiet between us. The air carried the scent of the river mixed with moss, wet leaves, and an unfamiliar metallic tang beneath.

I shifted in the saddle, my fingers wrapping around the worn leather reins. The unease that had settled in my stomach churned, making it impossible to sit still. My body remained tense, every muscle bracing for danger.

"So," I broke the silence, my voice sounding too loud in the hush of the woods. "How big is Vaelwick? Is it bigger than Silverfel or smaller? Do they have an inn, or are we—"

"Herbalist," Oberon warned quietly. The alert set my nerves on edge. He dismounted in one fluid motion. His boots touched the ground silently, his movements precise and deliberate. He crouched low, fingers skimming the dirt, and his sharp gaze flicked over the underbrush.

"What—"

He silenced me with a single glance, and my pulse quickened. I followed his line of sight but only saw the tangled undergrowth, the dark shapes of branches shifting in the faint breeze. A threat lurked nearby that he sensed, but I didn't.

A lump formed in my throat.

Oberon's jaw tightened when his fingers brushed against the ground again. Then, with casual efficiency, he pulled a dagger from his belt and slashed downward. A sharp snap echoed as a thin, invisible cord recoiled into the brush, disappearing into the darkness. A trap. My grip on the saddle tightened as tension filled the air.

We weren't alone.

A hiss pierced the night.

The arrow whispered through the air and brushed against my skin, the only warning before it zipped past my ear, narrowly avoiding my shoulder. The world lurched. I flinched, ducking, my breath caught between my ribs. My heartbeat throbbed in my skull.

Oberon shoved himself onto the horse behind me in one smooth, hurried motion, the warmth of his presence searing through my back. My breath turned shallow. Whoever had set the trap and watched us from the shadows had closed in.

Oberon's voice rang out above the thunderous sound of hoofbeats. "Take the reins!" he barked, capturing my attention. The demand surprised me, but I focused on the gleaming knives fanned between his fingers, which I hadn't seen him draw.

My pulse faltered. My voice was muffled by the wind and the pounding of hooves. "Where did those come from?" I shouted.

The muscle in his jaw jumped, irritation flashing in his silver-flecked gaze. "Take the damned reins, Herbalist!"

"I don't know how to—"

"Then learn!"

Another arrow flew past. Oberon twisted at the last second, and the tip grazed his cheek, leaving a thin line of crimson behind. He held my wide gaze without flinching.

Panic gripped me as I scrambled for the reins and almost missed them due to the trembling in my hands. The leather straps felt foreign in my grip, slick with sweat. I didn't know how to sit on a horse, let alone steer one. *But if I lost control, we would die.*

The horse jolted beneath us, spurred on by the chaos. The sudden lurch sent me rocking sideways, my grip slipping. Behind me, Oberon became a living weapon, his knives striking true. The pained groans of our pursuers blended with the sickening *thunk* of metal meeting flesh. The sound caused my stomach to lurch.

Gods.

We hadn't outrun them.

We barreled straight for the river.

A flicker of movement ahead made my breath seize in my throat. The dark water stretched before us, glassy and endless, with no sign of a bridge or way across it.

We were trapped.

My stomach plummeted. "Sinclaire!" I choked out. "There's no bridge!"

"Jump it!"

"What?" My voice pitched in panic. "Are you out of your mind?"

We rode too fast, and the river was too wide. Our chances of making that jump were slim to none.

Oberon stirred behind me, pressing forward until his chest pressed against my back. His arms ensnared mine, anchoring me in place. His warm breath brushed my ear as he growled, "Brace yourself."

He snapped the reins.

The horse let out a fierce cry and surged forward. The force yanked me from the saddle and threw me against Oberon as the warhorse dug its hooves into the ground, propelling us toward the edge with terrifying speed. The wind lashed against my face, and my lungs felt constricted in my chest.

The ground disappeared.

Weightlessness enveloped us.

For a moment, no sound or movement lay beneath us—only the vast expanse and the dark maw of the river. My stomach flipped, my breath halted, and my whole body tensed as we soared through the air.

The far bank loomed closer.

Hooves struck the soil near the riverbank. The force rattled through me, snapping my teeth together. The horse skidded, sliding in the mud, as the weight of two riders threw it off balance. My heart lurched, and my fingers clenched the reins in a death grip. When we crashed to the ground, the destrier quickly recovered. Its muscles convulsed as it heaved itself forward and regained its footing.

We made it.

The shaking rattled my bones. My breaths came in sharp, uneven gasps. My eyes were glued to the river, as if staring too long might rewind time and reveal that we had plunged into the water and drowned.

Oberon's hands still covered mine on the reins. His grip remained firm, his warmth the only thing anchoring me here. He pulled back first, gazing at the tree line and scanning for movement. He stayed ever-vigilant and ready to fight.

My voice rose above a whisper. "How did we make that?" My heart pounded in my ears. "Gods, you are truly deranged."

Oberon tore his gaze away from the trees and met mine. "Any other horse would have landed us in the river—or left us stranded, fighting off bandits. But Neryth isn't just any horse."

I blinked.

Neryth. The name was unfamiliar, yet fitting.

When my gaze shifted to his face, I was drawn to a thin, fresh line of red streaked just above his temple. Another cut I hadn't even noticed occurring. A frustrated breath escaped from me. I should have been aware. His injuries were a consequence of my hesitation.

Oberon turned his gaze to me, his brows furrowed. "What?"

I sighed and shook my head. "You're collecting injuries at this point."

His expression settled into that familiar deadpan stare. "You're one to talk."

A breathless chuckle escaped me, easing the tension in my chest. "I suppose so."

Without another word, Oberon leaned forward again, reclaiming the reins. His hands brushed against mine, his calloused fingers grazing my knuckles as he flicked them, guiding Neryth into the woods. His movements seemed effortless, and his composure remained unshaken.

I was captivated by the way he wielded those knives as if they belonged in his hands. The blades fanned between his knuckles with effortless precision, not a man holding a weapon but a man extending his fingers.

The knights didn't carry ranged weapons, did they?

And the trap... he hadn't hesitated or second-guessed. He knew what to look for. Drills and honor-bound battles didn't teach that awareness. Did they?

I turned enough to glance back at his uniform. The dark fabric blended with the night, shifting alongside the flickering shadows. Such armor was unlike any knight's armor I had ever seen—too flexible, too subtle, designed for movement rather than defense. It allowed him to vanish into the darkness as if it were a part of him.

It wasn't the armor he wore while escorting me to the infirmary on my first night at the castle. That armor had been ornate, designed to intimidate—obsidian plates, pauldrons etched with gilded vines, and a helmet crowned with horns that made him appear more beast than man. It had been a performance, a deception of power, as if the elaborate design allowed him to look the part well enough to distract.

But now, the gilded façade had vanished. There was no unnecessary weight. Practicality drove every piece, designed for function rather than spectacle. This armor's purpose wasn't visibility but survival—moving low and making the first strike.

It didn't resemble a knight's gear but that of a hunter.

And his horse. The damned creature was massive. *Did knights ride such beasts?* Warhorses demonstrated strength, yet Neryth surpassed that. He embodied a being crafted for endurance, speed, and battle. He carried Oberon as if the weight of armor and weapons were negligible. As though his training had gone far beyond mere battlefield charges.

A low rumble echoed in the distance, pulling me from my thoughts. I lifted my gaze to the sky. Thick clouds obscured most of the stars, a heavy curtain blocking the moon's glow. The sky had been clear earlier.

Oberon must have sensed my shift in tension. "Great. As if tonight weren't miserable enough," he muttered.

Though I agreed, someone had to keep up morale. "I think the night has been rather... exciting." Oberon groaned as if I had spoiled his evening. I held back a grin. "Do you think we'll reach Vaelwick before it rains?"

A pause long enough for me to know he was considering something. "I doubt it. There are several abandoned buildings in the area. We can stop at one until the storm passes."

I frowned. *Abandoned buildings?* The density of the trees concealed the path ahead. How did he know that? I turned in the saddle to peer back at him again, narrowing my eyes. "And how do you know that?"

His focus remained ahead, but his jaw tightened. "I know things."

"Oh, how reassuring, Sinclaire. That clears up everything," I scoffed.

This time, he glanced at me, allowing me to catch the scowl in his now onyx eyes before he looked away. "I scouted the area once. A long time ago."

I gazed at him, unimpressed. That might have meant anything coming from him.

When? Why? With whom?

I wanted to press further, to dissect the vagueness of his answer, but exhaustion weighed more heavily on me than curiosity. Investigating would have to wait until my head no longer ached and I wasn't drenched in sweat from yet another near-death experience.

Tilting my head, I studied him with a smirk. "Do you have any other emotions, or is being grumpy your entire personality?"

Oberon expelled air through his nose, burdened by a deep sense of impatience. "Do you ever let people think in peace?"

I gasped. "Oh, I'm sorry. Am I interrupting your deep, brooding reflection? Perhaps you're having an existential crisis?"

His grip tightened on the reins. "Just keep your eyes ahead, Herbalist." With a huff, I shifted my focus to watch the darkened road stretch endlessly before us. The strain between us had settled into the familiar rhythm we fell into when the silence made me wary: me needling him with questions and him gritting his teeth through it.

17

OBERON

THOUGH SMALL AND resilient, the abandoned building withstood the passage of time and encroaching decay. Unlike most forgotten places I've seen, it still held an air of defiance; its frame refused to bow to ruin. The warped slats of the walls allowed the wind to slip through in ghostly whispers, scattering brittle leaves across the frozen dirt.

My boots landed with a heavy thump, the weight of the moment pressing down on my shoulders. There was no rot, no prominent weak spots, and, more importantly, no traps. A few moths clung to the splintered beams, their wings fluttering against the icy draft like dying embers.

I tracked their fragile movements until my attention shifted to the shadows stretching long against the warped walls. An

unnatural silence lingered in the space, making my instincts
bristle, as if something had claimed the place.

My knuckles recognized the familiar spin of my dagger,
a habitual gesture. The steel caught the moonlight filtering
through the fractured roof, with brief reflections flickering
in the dust-laden air. The blade felt heavy in the silence, a
reminder that I was present, breathing, and upright.

A scoff broke the eerie stillness.

"Show-off."

My eyes darted to Quinn. She leaned against the doorway
with her arms crossed, unimpressed as always. I shot her a
pointed look, warning her to remain silent. She rolled her eyes
in response, dismissing my unspoken order with a defiance
that only she could muster.

'The way her eyes would roll back...'

My fingers tightened around my dagger, pressing into the
leather. The knight's words from the tavern echoed in my
mind—the jeers, the implications, the truths concealed beneath them.

I scowled and shoved the memory to where it belonged:
buried and forgotten.

The wood groaned beneath my boot as I kicked the door
open harder than necessary. The sound split through the
night, serving as a warning against the dark, yet nothing
stirred. Even the usual chittering of night insects had dulled
as if Elduvaris were holding its breath.

Dagger in hand, I entered, my eyes scanning the room.
It was empty. No movement or life was visible except for a

single frost-limbed spider that skittered across the floor before vanishing into the cracks.

At least, *something* had gone right.

Quinn's voice echoed in the space. "Can I go in now?" The sound lingered, absorbed by the void, but there was no response.

She moved past me as I stepped aside. Her shoulder brushed against mine in a fleeting warmth against the cool night air before she set her satchel on the floor by the hearth. Her movements remained steady and controlled, yet her fingers trembled. The ambush had rattled her more than she wanted to admit. Her knuckles turned white on the reins; her gasp when the arrows flew by, and her widened eyes upon realizing our disadvantage in numbers spoke volumes.

'What? Are you out of your mind?'

Yes.

It was absurd.

The jump had been blind and desperate, with the river churning below like the gaping maw of a beast. I wasn't even sure we would survive, but staying was worse. Darkness obscured her view of the dense canopy. It would have been difficult to distinguish the moving shapes among the trees and the glint of metal reflecting the sparse moonlight that filtered through the leaves.

Killing them was within my capabilities. That wasn't the doubt. I had faced worse odds and walked away, bathed in the blood of those foolish enough to stand in my way. But to fend them off while ensuring she emerged unharmed? That had been the risk. Not the jump or the river.

Her.

My mission was to keep her safe, and, regardless of whether I liked it, I needed her.

Whoever cursed Silverfel was aware of the Fae residing in Aurelith. They concealed the magic from me, causing it to escape my perception. It was a deliberate act, a warning, a challenge, and a silent dare.

And I needed her to unravel it. Her wits, her talents, and her knowledge were essential. She had dedicated her life to studying poisons, herbs, and how magic intertwined with nature, even if she refused to acknowledge it. If anyone could decipher the curse's origin, it was her.

Outside, the wind howled through the trees, rattling the building's loose beams. Distant thunder rumbled in the night, creating a static-charged atmosphere. A few drafts slipped through the crevices of the walls, carrying the aroma of damp elduvaris and distant rain.

Quinn kneeled by the hearth, inspecting the logs that someone had left behind long ago. Her fingers brushed against them, testing before reaching for the striking tools. She struck them together—once, twice—and nothing happened. A spark flickered, feeble and fleeting, but it extinguished in the kindling. She huffed and readjusted the bundle of dry twigs.

Another attempt.

Another failure.

The entire hearth would have roared to life with a single spark had I ignited it, but my curiosity held me back. Frustration did not dissuade her determination. Her jaw remained set while the fire became an adversary she refused to lose to. She didn't ask for help, even when she should have.

Had she always been so self-reliant?

The wind slammed against the walls. The lantern light flickered, casting long, restless shadows across the room. One of them danced over her bandaged hand, a reminder that her wound had yet to heal. Fumbling with the tools as if she had something to prove would only worsen it.

She made one last attempt before I spoke. "If you can't start a fire, just say so."

Quinn flinched, her head whipping around to face me. Her wide pupils struggled to constrict as darkness swallowed the edges of her irises. Her gaze remained distant and unfocused while my voice pulled her from her reverie.

Unease pulsed through me.

For a moment, she stared. Uneven breaths escaped her when her lips parted, a sign that she had forgotten her words. Then she blinked, scoffed, and pulled herself out of it, except that her practiced and seamless reaction lacked the proper speed. "I know how to light a fire," she muttered. "I just—" She cut herself off with a shake of her head and stood.

Then winced.

My eyes narrowed.

Pushing off the wall, I crossed the room in a few strides, kneeled, and picked up the kindling where she had left it. The tools felt cool in my hands, smooth from years of use. With a practiced flick, I struck them together. A breath of ember curled through the thirsty kindling before flames licked up the dry twigs. The logs followed, crackling as they yielded to the heat. The golden glow stretched outward, pushing back the restless darkness and chasing away the chill lingering in the room's corners.

Quinn crossed her arms over her chest. "Of course, you would do it on the first try," she sighed, watching the fire as if it had betrayed her.

I tossed the flint aside as the flames grew stronger.

She tilted her head, studying me with an intensity that sent goosebumps down my spine. Not mocking. Not challenging. Just... considering. The dazed look had vanished, but its ghost still lingered between us. "Is there anything you can't do?" she asked.

I met her gaze, holding it as I deadpanned, "Make you stop talking."

A startled snort escaped her. "I suppose so."

The wind howled outside, rattling the walls with a restless energy. The wood groaned beneath me when I dropped into the chair, testing its strength before allowing my weight to settle into it. The tension in the room eased, growing quieter and allowing for easier breathing.

Quinn rubbed her arm, her fingers gliding over the bandages on her palm. Her gaze remained distant, lost in thought. *Silverfel.*

Was that what occupied her thoughts? The moment she reopened the cut on her palm, despite my warning?

Her fingers flexed as though testing for pain. She wouldn't speak unless she wanted to, so I shifted my attention to the fire and its shadows. Anywhere but her.

The glow vanished when she stepped in front of the hearth, her silhouette obstructing the faint light. I blinked, and my gaze lifted upward to the rag and a tin of salve in her hand.

A deep groan rumbled from my chest.

"Take it off," she demanded.

She must have noticed the slashes in my tunic. Knives and arrows flew toward me as we left the ambush. They missed their mark, yet several had made a slice. Nothing deep. Nothing that required fussing over.

Rather than for her being hit or grazed by them, it had been the preferable outcome.

"I don't need it."

"I might as well check your stitches," she insisted.

My muscles tensed. I had forgotten about those—the ones she restitched on our way to Silverfel, which nearly killed us because she insisted we stop. She distracted me; her gentle hands touched my skin, and I forgot how to think.

She reached for my sleeve.

I sighed and grabbed the hem of my tunic, yanking it over my head. A tingling sensation slid up my spine as the fabric brushed against my skin. It had become a peculiar habit: she insisted I remove my clothes, and I complied with her.

My focus centered on Quinn when she kneeled before me.

'She's got those big, pretty eyes. The kind that looks up at you all soft.'

My teeth ground together, and I averted my gaze from her. I shouldn't have felt that searing, twisting anger in my chest, that possessiveness curling low and vicious within me. It wasn't my place.

Not after what I had done.

Or what I *hadn't* done to protect her.

I wasn't meant for this. I wasn't built to protect anyone. I was a predator, a murderer, a torturer.

Her fingertips grazed my shoulder, featherlight, tracing the line where the stitches had once been. I went rigid at the touch.

Soft.

So damned soft.

"It shouldn't have healed that fast," she murmured, frowning. "That's not humanly possible."

"Well, I'm not human." The words came out clipped and harsher than I intended. I wasn't angry with her; it made sense that she felt confused. I loathed how she made me feel. She stirred my Fae instincts, a part of me I had forced into dormancy, awakening them with her mere presence.

'The herbalist must bleed.'

The words crept through my mind. My jaw tightened again as the memory surfaced—the beast in Silverfel lunging for her, its gnarled roots snapping, and the way my vision had tunneled. My instincts took control before I considered a response. It was pure reaction, pure rage, pure possession.

I hated she made me care enough to follow it.

Her brows knitted together, and her body became tense.

Good. She should be wary of me. She should keep her distance like everyone else. It was safer that way.

Except... she didn't.

Her familiar, forced smile reappeared, a feeble attempt to dissipate the heavy, charged silence between us. She made a light, meaningless joke, yet the words fell flat. My thoughts tangled with the sensation of her presence being too close, too warm, too overwhelming.

Her hands found purchase on my jaw as she stood, her gentle fingers cool against my heated skin. She tilted my face toward the firelight, her lips parting as she assessed the damage. I should have pulled away. There were a few scrapes that would heal by morning. I didn't need her fussing over them.

The bandage wrapped around her palm brushed against my skin, causing a dark sensation to curl deep in my chest. The memory of her slicing her palm open without hesitation, blood welling crimson against pale skin, resurfaced. My anger wound and unraveled inside me.

She trembled in her sleep. Her voice sounded fragile and broken as she begged someone to stop. I shook her arm to wake her from whatever horror had gripped her in rest. Her eyes glistened when she realized I had re-bandaged her hand. The heat of her body against mine, the way she tensed but didn't pull away as my hands covered hers on the reins, and I steadied her when fear threatened to overwhelm her. Yet she stood before me, touching me as though I were the one who required care.

I swallowed hard, my throat as dry as sand. I should have moved or done something, but her face held me captive. The firelight flickered across her skin, painting gold along her cheekbones and tracing the curve of her parted lips. She wiped the blood from my cheek with careful fingers, gentle despite the faint tremor in her hands.

She said something—another joke, another desperate attempt to shatter whatever new tension had rooted itself between us. She met my gaze and faltered. A sharp current surged through my spine, searing hot in my gut, as color bloomed high on her cheeks, deepening into a warm breathlessness. She looked as though I had caught her doing something she shouldn't have.

'You're beautiful.'

The words acted like a slow-burning ember, smoldering beneath my skin. A low, simmering irritation coiled in my gut, tightening with every breath and replacing the energy that had flowed through me. She *was* beautiful, bewitching in a way that defied reason. But that hadn't been what irritated me. It was the way she blushed, how another man's words had captured that reaction from her, causing her skin to flush with a delicate shade of pink.

Why did that bother me?

She wasn't mine.

The thought hit hard, a harsh truth that should have been comforting. Yet something within me growled in protest- a deep, primal instinct I had spent my whole life suppressing.

Mine.

No.

She *could* never be mine. She *would* never be mine.

The laws prohibited Fae from loving humans. They were obsessed with their flawless, untainted lineages. That was why they abandoned me; I became a mistake, a blemish they wanted to forget.

So, what triggered such a visceral reaction from it?

From me?

Why did she torment me in ways that no one else ever had?

A stillness lingered between us, stretched tight. Her soft voice shattered it. "Are you..." She hesitated, her brow furrowing. My entire body went rigid, hyper-aware of her every movement. "Are you an assassin?"

My thoughts blanked.

I blinked. Her words took a moment to register. She had rendered me speechless once again. My brows furrowed. "What?"

She crossed her arms, the warmth of her touch a fading memory. I hated losing it more than I wanted to acknowledge. "Is that why you're so grumpy, dark, and mysterious? It all makes sense now."

I should have seen this coming. After Silverfel, after the way she pieced together every puzzle with her clever, infuriating mind, I found it surprising that it took her so long to uncover the truth.

"Your armor when I first arrived at the castle. Your uniform." She waved a finger at me, gesturing to my appearance. "Your dark and mysterious aura, your throwing knives, and the way you discovered that trap before the ambush." She rattled them off with excitement, as if thrilled by her discovery.

Then, with a sharp gasp, her lips curled into an overly pleased grin. "Oh, gods. You thought I might be a sinister assassin or something, too, didn't you?" She barked a laugh, her eyes gleaming with amusement. "That's why you slammed me against that tree. You give me too much credit, Sinclaire... I think I like it."

My stomach twisted.

Hi fucking insufferable adaneth.

This fucking insufferable adaneth.

My tongue pressed to my canine, eyes narrowing. "What?"
Her expression dulled. "Did I get it wrong?"

I huffed. "Aren't you afraid?" Rising to my feet, I grabbed
my tunic and slipped it over my head.

She blinked. "Of what?"

My teeth ground together as I stepped forward, closing the
distance between us. The firelight flickered, casting dancing
shadows across her face as I glared at her. "Of me, Dilthen
Doe," I snarled. "Because if you aren't, you should be."

Her brows furrowed, but she didn't back down. She didn't
flinch. Instead, her shoulders squared, and her gaze met mine
with unwavering resolve. "You don't scare me." The words
struck deep in my chest.

"If you harbor death within you," she continued, "then I
shall dance with him. Your darkness is what draws me in. Like
a moth to a flame, you captivate my soul, and I am drawn to
you in ways I cannot explain. So no, Oberon Sinclaire, I am
not afraid of you."

A sharp breath escaped my lungs. My heartbeat drummed
in my ears, mirroring the slow, burning tension that vibrated
between us. It wrapped around my ribs with an unspoken
force, drawing me toward her when I should have stepped
away.

She remained still and unflinching.

And that just made it worse.

"You don't know what I have done, Dilthen Doe," I warned, my voice low, almost guttural. The weight of my past hung between us, intensifying with every breath. "The people I have hunted. The ones I have silenced. The things I have had to do to survive."

Her eyes searched mine. I waited for the unavoidable flicker of fear, for the moment she would understand and see my true nature.

Yet she didn't recoil or tremble.

Her expression softened. "I understand what it means to be hunted," she countered. "I understand what it means to do whatever is necessary to survive."

I stepped forward, narrowing the space between us until only heat and shadow remained. My fingers lifted to brush over the area on her jaw where the bruises still lingered, dark reminders of that bastard knight's touch. A slow, aching pull twisted inside me as my thumb ghosted over the bruised skin, light as a breath.

She shivered.

"You should be afraid," I murmured, my voice dangerously soft. "I've killed men for less than what that bastard did to you in Silverfel." My gaze fell to the mark, the ugly proof of his touch, and my chest tightened. "For much less."

She scoffed. "Do you think I haven't figured that out?"

My fingers curled against her skin, just enough to feel the warmth beneath the bruises, the proof of her presence. "I don't regret it," I admitted. The words, though soft-spoken, pierced the thick air between us with the threat they carried. "Not a single one."

Her lips parted as if she intended to challenge me, perhaps to pry more from me. After a moment, she enunciated, "I am not afraid of you, Oberon Sinclaire." The words sent a painful sensation ripping through my ribs.

My thumb traced over the bruise one last time as my pulse throbbed beneath my skin.

"You will be."

18

EDEN

THE THICK, DAMP air pressed against my skin while the walls closed in on me. The aroma of wet stone and iron overwhelmed my senses. My wrists burned from the old shackles that bit into my flesh. Somewhere behind me, chains rattled just before—

Crack.

White-hot, searing pain ignited across my back. My body jerked, and my breath caught in my throat. I squeezed my eyes shut, but it didn't matter. I knew where I was. I knew what came next.

"Again."

Marcus's voice stayed calm and patient, as if instructing a servant rather than ordering my suffering. The whip sliced through the air. **Crack.** Fire exploded along my spine. My jaw *ached from clenching my teeth. Don't make a sound. Don't give him the satisfaction.*

Another lash.

And another.

The pain blended. Heat and agony coursed through me until I could no longer tell one strike from the next. My breathing was shallow. Every inhale prickled against my lungs. The coppery, thick smell of blood lingered.

A hand gripped my chin and forced my head up. I tried to twist away, but his fingers pressed harder, and his nails dug in. His eyes gleamed with a dark intention that set my skin crawling.

"You're shaking, Darling," Marcus murmured, tilting his head. "Why fight it? We both know you belong here."

No.

I wanted to spit in his face—to tear him apart. But I remained frozen, unable to move as if still shackled, still his.

Another crack.

I flinched as the pain ricocheted through me. The walls around me blurred, shifted, warped—

Then I fell.

My heart hammered in my chest, and the chilled air bit at my sweat-damp skin when I gasped awake. The scent of rain enveloped me. The room had changed. The wooden floor beneath me felt real. The hearth crackled, casting a dim glow across the room.

The crack of thunder that rolled through the night caused me to flinch as I sat up. The sound was too close- too similar to a whip splitting the air. My fingers clawed at my back before

I realized there was no blood, no fresh wounds—just scars, just ghosts.

I slowed my breathing, grounding myself in the present. *The storm raged beyond these old walls, and I sat here—not there, but here.*

A shadow shifted near the hearth, and I flinched.

Oberon sat in the chair with his back against the far wall, arms crossed and gaze dark. He must have heard me again. Shame coiled in my gut. I swallowed hard against my raw throat and pushed myself upright, refusing to meet his eyes. "It was just a dream," I murmured, more to myself than to him.

Silence stretched between us until he responded. His voice was quiet. "I know." He didn't push or pry; he simply sat there as he had last time. Somehow, that was enough.

THE QUIET RIDE into Vaelwick made my skin crawl, a sensation that settled deep in my bones as a warning. I tried to recall the last time I had heard a bird, a rustle in the trees, or any other sign of life, but nothing came to mind. Maybe it was just my nerves, but even Neryth's steps felt heavier, as Elduvaris itself resisted us, swallowing the sound before it could reach the air.

Fields stretched in lifeless patches along the roadside, the land hollowed of its former vibrance. Blackened husks of crops lay shriveled, collapsed into the soil like broken ribs in an unmarked grave. The sight twisted deep in my gut. It wasn't just a poor harvest; it represented devastation—a blight. The land hadn't just failed; it had been ruined.

As we approached the entrance, a breeze stirred, rolling over us. The dense, foul stench that hit me clung to the back of my throat—an unnatural rot worse than the decay of plants. My stomach lurched, and I pulled my sleeve up over my nose, muffling my gag.

"Gods," I wheezed, my voice muffled by the fabric. "That's foul."

The air itself was contaminated. Whatever had settled here didn't affect only the crops; it was pervasive.

Oberon remained silent during the ride, lost in his brooding thoughts. He offered no sharp comments, exasperated sighs, or even an attempt to silence me, which only heightened my unease.

Things were far worse than I had realized.

I slid off Neryth's side, landing on the damp ground with a *thud* and a grunt. My muscles ached from the long ride, and the dull, pulsing throb in my palm reminded me of my bandaged wound. I flexed my fingers, pressing them against the rough fabric before letting my hand fall back to my side. The ground beneath my boots radiated warmth, an oddly high temperature for the location and time of year.

Oberon dismounted silently. I sighed, brushing aside stray strands of hair from my face as I turned to take in the village.

The silence felt suffocating.

No candlelight flickered through the windows, nor did distant voices murmur behind the doors. The houses stood hollow and dark, their wooden frames worn by time and neglect. From their eaves, trinkets dangled, swaying in the decaying breeze. Their delicate chimes pierced the stillness, creating an eerie melody of death.

Wards? Warnings? My brow furrowed as I examined them. The craftsmanship appeared deliberate. Someone had positioned them for a reason, but whether they kept something out or contained it was another matter.

I glanced at Oberon, searching for any sign of unease, but his face remained impassive. His sharp gaze swept over the village like a predator waiting for movement in the brush. If he felt unsettled, he didn't show it.

"This isn't normal," I whispered.

He remained silent while he knocked on the nearest door. The sound resonated, piercing the wood and echoing in the unnatural silence. We waited, but there was nothing. No footsteps approaching, no creak of shifting floorboards, not even the whisper of breath behind a curtain.

I tried the next house. Then another.

Nothing.

The stillness stretched, unlike the emptiness of an abandoned village. A prickle arose at the back of my neck, the unmistakable sensation of being watched. Hidden eyes peered from the darkness, held back by fear.

"They're hiding," I murmured, stepping closer to Oberon, seeking the quiet reassurance of his presence. He didn't react, but his jaw set tight, and his gaze remained fixed on the looming mansion at the village's center, an ominous figure against the darkening sky. The grand architecture contrasted with the modest homes, its dark stone and iron-trimmed windows setting it apart—untouched by the sickness seeping into the land. If anyone would answer, it ought to be the person who lived there.

Oberon strode up the path, his boots crunching on the gravel with a purposeful tread. When he reached the heavy wooden doors, he rapped his knuckles against them.

A lengthy moment passed before the door creaked open.

The man who greeted us was older, with blonde hair and deep lines etched into his weary face. He carried himself like someone who had spent years bearing burdens too heavy to mention. His sharp gaze landed on Oberon first, scanning him from top to bottom. His shoulders tensed, and his spine straightened with the slightest flicker of recognition before he inclined his head.

"Sir Sinclaire," he greeted. I waited for his attention to turn to me, but it never did. Not a single glance or acknowledgment was given.

Right.

Like the knights in Silverfel and the nobles in the courts, he wouldn't regard me the same way he regarded Oberon. I didn't possess a knight's title or noble rank. I was a woman—an herbalist clad in travel-worn linens, bearing the marks of battle. In his eyes, I meant nothing.

A specter of remembrance stirred. An additional house, another door, another pair of unreadable eyes.

Blue and white walls, as pristine as porcelain, stretched toward a vaulted ceiling adorned with shimmering chandeliers. I had once stood in a grand entryway much like this one, the polished marble beneath my feet so smooth that it made my steps feel weightless. I was younger then, still foolish enough to believe I could create something for myself.

Marcus greeted me at the top of the staircase, a vision of gold and ivory with a warm smile and honeyed voice. "You look stunning, Darling." I felt small beneath his gaze, burdened by the weight of those words that dripped with a suffocating tone of manipulation. He offered me a hand, expecting me to accept it. He adorned the walls of his house with paintings of men who shared his sharp, aristocratic features—men who took what they wanted and left ruin in their wake.

I didn't know then how deeply those walls would become my prison.

I clenched my fingers into my dress. *That time had passed. The fragrance in the air wasn't Marcus's cologne. The man before me wasn't him.*

Lord Everette stepped back. "Come in. There is much to discuss."

The heavy doors closed behind us with a resounding thud, shutting out the night.

"I'm Lord Everette. I oversee Vaelwick," he announced, the flickering glow of a candle casting long shadows across his face. The entryway soared high, its grand archways embellished with dark wood and aging tapestries. The scents of damp stone and parchment hung heavily, mingling with the subtle smoke from the hearth's smoldering embers. Despite the fire's warmth, a chill descended upon my skin.

Lord Everette lifted his candle, gesturing toward the symbols carved into the doors and the small trinkets strung along the archways.

"These are protection wards," he murmured.

Oberon tilted his head, examining the markings. "Protection from what?"

The lord hesitated.

My pulse thrummed, each beat pounding in my ears. I forced myself to focus on the candlelight as it flickered across Lord Everette's face, deepening the weary lines etched into his skin. Shadows stretched behind him, reaching toward the corners of the room.

"From whatever lurks in the fields," he said, his voice lowered. "Whatever has cursed our crops and driven away our animals. Some believe it to be the work of the Fae. Others..." He trailed off, stroking his beard, his gaze shifting toward the darkened windows.

"Others?" I prompted.

The lord exhaled, his fingers tapping a slow, measured rhythm against the wooden banister. "There are rumors-whispers from travelers who claim to have seen figures in the mist. A sickness that does not behave like any ordinary plague. People waking in the night, standing outside their homes, staring at the fields, without remembering how they got there. It's as if something called for them."

The room felt smaller and the candlelight dimmer. Beside me, Oberon shifted his posture just enough for me to notice and sense the tension coiling in his shoulders.

I swallowed hard. "Have there been any deaths?"

Lord Everette's gaze fell. The silence before his reply carried a weighty dread. Then he nodded. "Two. Both young men had strayed too far into the fields. When we found them, their eyes looked... unsettling."

"Wrong, how?" I asked, bracing for the reply. Lord Everette hesitated again, carefully choosing his words as if voicing them might imbue them with power.

Oberon took a step forward. "What did their eyes look like?"

The lord's gaze shifted between us, contemplating whether to speak. At last, he murmured, "They were black. Completely. As if the night had engulfed them."

A shiver crept down my spine, leaving goosebumps in its wake. *Breathe. Think.* "Why are there no candles or torches lit throughout the village?"

Lord Everette studied me before responding. "The people of Vaelwick are... cautious," he explained. "They keep their lights dim at night to avoid attracting unwanted attention."

Unwanted attention.

My fingers curled into the bandages on my palm, the rough fabric grounding me before I dug my nails into my skin. The place felt wrong. It seeped into the walls, slithered between the floorboards, and coiled around my ankles like the mist in Silverfel, making me believe I wasn't alone, even when I was.

"And the healers you sent for?" Oberon asked.

Lord Everette pursed his lips and rubbed his temples. "The last one arrived a week ago," he admitted. "He left the same night."

I frowned. "Why?"

He glanced at me, then looked away, as if still hesitant to meet my gaze. "He claimed to have seen something outside his window."

The crackling fire in the hearth was the only sound in the suffocating quiet.

"Did he say what?" I pressed.

Lord Everette's mouth tightened, and the look in his eyes showed regret for having said so much. Something had frightened that healer enough to flee in the middle of the night. "He wouldn't speak of it," he murmured.

My stomach churned.

Oberon narrowed his gaze as though considering his next words. "What about the animals?"

I blinked, glancing at him, but his gaze remained fixed on the lord.

"Gone," the Lord admitted. "At first, we thought thieves had taken them. Yet, no tracks existed—no sign of a struggle, no broken gates. They vanished. One by one."

"How long ago?" I asked.

"The first few went missing over a month ago. Then, it became more frequent. By the time the sickness reached the crops, none were left." His fingers drummed against the banister, restless. "Even the dogs disappeared. The ones that remained..." He hesitated.

My brows furrowed. "What?"

"They refused to go near the fields. They would cower. Snarl at nothing. Then, one morning, they vanished as well."

Oberon's expression remained the same, though his hands twitched at his sides while the candlelight cast shadows along the sharp planes of his face. He wasn't pleased by the situation either. "Have you seen it yourself? Whatever is lurking out there?"

Lord Everette's eyes flickered toward the covered windows. "No," he admitted. "But I have heard it."

A pause.

Oberon exhaled, stroking his jaw before speaking again. "Is there an inn in the village?"

Lord Everette's expression revealed the answer before he even spoke. "There are two rooms prepared for you in my home," he offered.

I stiffened.

Two rooms.

The manor walls closed in, thick with dust and oppressive with my discomfort. A draft moved through the corridor, carrying the smells of old parchment and damp wood.

Staying somewhere with locked doors, warmth, and accessible answers felt safer. Yet, I couldn't shake the unease that settled in my gut, the sense that accepting his hospitality meant stepping deeper into something we might not escape.

Before Silverfel, the idea of traveling with Oberon had been intolerable and sharing a space seemed unthinkable. He embodied jagged edges and bitter silence, a storm under careful restraint, and I hadn't been interested in being caught in it. But as I stood in the grand, suffocating halls of Lord Everette's estate, my skin prickled with apprehension. The air felt too still, too clean-scrubbed of life and warmth until only emptiness remained. The polished floors reflected the candlelight in an eerie, sterile glow. The towering walls, lined with aging portraits and tapestries, loomed like silent sentinels, watching.

It was too similar.

Too much like *him.*

I forced my jaw to unclench, fingers twitching toward my sleeve before restraining myself. I managed a stiff but acceptable smile. "Thank you."

Had Oberon noticed?

His eyes flickered silver when he glanced at me before turning back to Everette. Then, he inclined his head. "Lead the way."

After Lord Everette showed us our rooms, I turned to Oberon, folding my arms across my chest. "We should investigate and see what the travelers experienced."

He huffed. "At sunrise. We'll get a better view then."

"No. If the sightings occur at night, then we need to observe them at night."

He swept a hand across his face as though I had drained the energy from his body. "You're impossible, you know that?"

I shrugged. "I've heard worse."

For a moment, he stared at me. He muttered something under his breath, likely a curse aimed at me, before gesturing toward the stairs. "Fine. But if you end up dead, I'm leaving your body for the crows."

I grinned and started walking through the hall. "I wouldn't expect anything less." I had to escape this place. The mansion's walls loomed over me with old secrets and silent judgment. Waiting until morning wasn't the choice I wanted to make when the answers we needed might be waiting outside.

THE NIGHT UNFOLDED at a sluggish pace until the faintest glow of dawn crept over the horizon. I squinted at my notes, struggling to interpret the symbols and trinkets we had encountered. A few felt familiar, protective wards and charms designed to ward off sickness or spirits, but others...

Others made little sense.

I turned the page, jotting quick notes beside rough sketches of the carvings we had discovered near the village perimeter. Other symbols seemed too intricate and deliberate to be mere superstition. Someone had placed them there for a reason.

Oberon let out a long sigh behind me. "We should have just waited. Rested."

"And miss all this fun?" I muttered, jotting down another note.

A breeze stirred, crawling through the air with a thick, cloying scent that made me stiffen. My stomach twisted. The stench intensified, permeating my flesh and clinging to the back of my throat, reminiscent of something decaying in the sun. I gagged, pressing my sleeve against my nose. "Seriously, what *is* that?"

Oberon turned toward the field. The wind shifted his cloak as he turned his head. His jaw muscles tensed before he gestured for me to follow. "Let's find out."

19

EDEN

RESTLESSNESS SANK DEEPER into my stomach with each step toward the crop field. A thick decay filled the air, its putrid stench clinging to the back of my mouth and burning my nostrils. It surpassed the smell of dead plants. The rot didn't stem from the failed harvest, but from something far worse. The damp soil beneath us felt unstable, ready to give way at any moment. My mind attempted to reason through it, seeking a logical explanation, but instinct screamed louder. This place exhibited more than mere abandonment; it had been tainted.

I hesitated before stepping forward, but just as I moved toward the gap in the broken fence, an arm shot out, blocking my path. I blinked up at Oberon in confusion. His stance remained rigid, with his shoulders wound tight. "Don't walk through it," he commanded. It was worse than I wished to know if he was being this careful. I frowned but didn't argue.

Could he sense magic here? Or was he heeding the Lord's warnings?

"What if it's a body?"

He scanned the field with intense focus, as if he noticed something I couldn't. Silver flickered in his eyes like a glimmer of storm light in the darkness. "It is," he said.

"What?"

"But it's not in the field." His posture grew tense and wary. "Stay close." His tone made me roll my eyes before I could stop myself. He was so protective for someone who pretended not to care.

His head whipped toward me so fast that it spilled adrenaline through my veins. "Dilthen Doe," his voice curled low and lethal. "Roll your eyes one more time, and I will make them roll back into your fucking skull."

Goosebumps prickled along my arms. The words should have unnerved me, perhaps even scared me, but they sent a thrill through me—a reckless exhilaration that compelled me to push him further.

Fighting the smirk that threatened to break free, I concealed it behind my sleeve and murmured, "Alright, alright." Then, more quietly, "So dramatic." His gaze burned into me, yet he didn't take the bait. I stepped behind him, wrapping my arm around myself to quell the gnawing unease. I remained silent after that—not out of discipline, but because my stomach twisted in knots.

We hadn't eaten, which was a good thing because—

I halted.

A young man's body lay twisted in the dirt, discarded with limbs bent at unnatural angles. His skin had become a sickly pale, creeping in a slow, insidious decay. His mouth gaped as if he had died mid-scream, with his lips cracked and frozen in eternal terror. His eyes struck me cold—the void-black pits that stared up at nothing, endless and empty. Dried blood stiffened his clothes, dark patches spreading in shadows across his chest and arms. His fingers curled inward, claw-like, as if he had tried to grasp, fight, and hold on to life.

A lump formed in my throat.

"Oh, gods." The words were a breathless whisper, lost in the early morning. Oberon moved around the body with precision, his stance that of a predator, his boots pressing into the dirt with confidence. Though his expression remained unchanged, his focus sharpened, and tension coiled beneath his skin.

My arm tightened around my waist. *What was he thinking?* "Is there any trace of magic?" My sleeve muffled my voice as I pressed it harder against my face, trying to block out the stench of death.

Oberon crouched next to the corpse, examining every detail with clinical precision. He didn't rush, blink, or breathe for a long time. Without looking up, he answered simply, "No."

A pit formed in my stomach. No magic meant no explanation. *Then what was he looking at? How had he known it was a body? Or where it had been lying?*

I shifted my weight. "How do you think he died?"

A hollow, shrill screech ripped through the silence. It curled through my ears, drilled into my skull, and scraped against my ribs. The marrow in my bones felt scooped out and left hollow and brittle under the pressure of the sound. My body locked up, my muscles tensed, and my breath was strangled in my throat.

Oberon grabbed my wrist, yanking me behind him with a forceful tug. His other hand hovered near his sword, fingers poised and ready. His irises burned silver, flickering as he gazed toward the trees—the dark, endless expanse of them, the void between the trunks—searching. Hunting.

My heartbeat thumped in my ears, echoing the disjointed rhythm of my breath. The sound emanated from everywhere and nowhere, winding around us and disappearing as quickly as it had arrived. The lifeless body at our feet was insignificant compared to whatever was alive out there.

Movement.

A shadow flickered between the trees, yet the branches remained still. The underbrush lay motionless. It glided through the mist, a presence that didn't belong in this world. Oberon's grip on my wrist tightened, his fingers digging into my skin in silent warning: stay close.

A second screech split the air closer than before.

Then silence. Thick, suffocating silence.

My shaking hands curled into fists, nails biting into my palms.

Where was it?

My body shifted closer to Oberon, the warmth of his presence steadying me. I lifted the hem of my skirt to free my dagger from the sheath against my thigh. The blade felt cool and solid in my grasp, a slight comfort against the eeriness that surrounded us. I parted my lips to say something, but my breath hitched.

A swaying figure stood in the field. My fingers clamped around Oberon's forearm. "What is that?" I squinted, trying to comprehend the shape and how it rocked.

A violent twist clenched my gut, a profound, primal warning. "That's not... that's not human, is it?" Each syllable was wrapped in a held breath. The thing in the field swayed, its movements fragmented and jerky—a puppet controlled by unsteady hands.

Oberon's voice was guttural, sending a curl of instinctive unease swirling in my stomach. "No."

The answer didn't surprise me, but hearing the horror of it confirmed rooted a sickening dread in my chest.

I choked against the rot coating my throat, but the drumming in my ears was too loud to focus. "Is it getting closer?" I whispered. Oberon shifted to my front again, maintaining a loose yet cautious stance, his body blocking me from the grotesque creature beyond the broken fence. His fingers twitched near the pommel of his sword, but his posture remained unwavering.

If the thing noticed, it didn't care. It staggered forward, a single step. Then it lurched. Its joints moved at unnatural angles, as if it was unfamiliar with how bodies should move. A long, drawn-out pause lingered between each step.

Then it paused, observed, and probed. The weight of its attention crawled over my skin, an unsettling presence that shouldn't have existed. It had no eyes and no discernible features, yet I felt its gaze as it scrutinized me. A shiver ran down my spine, and I tightened my grip on the dagger clutched in my trembling hands.

The figure vanished, breaking apart in the wind. I blinked hard, as my mind raced to make sense of the absence. Oberon turned rigid. The line of his shoulders stiffened as he tightened his grip on his sword. The faintest creak of leather echoed in the silence.

The emptiness was tangible. My pulse pounded harder. "Where did it—"

The temperature plummeted. The air became frigid, seeping into my bones. Every muscle tensed as my breath hitched with an inhale I couldn't expel. A blackened, leathery face emerged from the air beside me, twisting into existence where nothing had been a moment ago. The thing's mouth split open, flesh ripping apart, exposing rows upon rows of jagged teeth, stained yellow and red. A hollow, ear-piercing screech tore from its gaping maw, rattling through my skull in shards of ice.

A strangled noise ripped from my throat when panic lurched hot and fast through me. I stumbled backward, instinct overriding thought. My boot caught on something solid. The world tilted. A wet, squelching noise filled my ears when my hands landed against the decomposing corpse behind me. The sickening give of rotting flesh compressed beneath my weight, and a *gloopy plop* followed, like an overripe fruit bursting underfoot.

A putrid gas exploded around me, creating a thick, noxious cloud that scratched my throat, stung my eyes, and burned my nostrils. I gagged, pulling my sleeve up to cover my nose. My stomach lurched.

Oberon's blade cut through the creature.

Steel met what should have been flesh, but the impact didn't bring resistance. It brought nothing. The blade sliced through its charred face, but the moment it struck, the head dissipated, the mist unraveling in the wind. The body followed, misting into nothingness.

I scrambled to my feet, breath heaving, and hand trembling on the handle of my dagger. "Did it... did you...?"

Oberon's torso moved rhythmically, yet tension wove through every muscle, his silver irises glinting in the dim light. His tone was as inevitable as death itself. "No. My sword won't kill it."

His words made my stomach knot. He didn't say *I missed* or *needed to strike harder*. He said it *won't kill it*.

"Dilthen Doe." Oberon's hand seized my arm. "Run." Dry, wilted wheat whipped at my ankles as we tore through the field. My lungs burned, but I didn't dare slow down. The only thing more terrifying than the creature was the fact that Oberon was running.

The force of being shoved inside slammed my shoulder into the doorframe, causing a sharp jolt to rattle through my bones. The impact sent me stumbling. My feet dragged against the tile, and my arms flailed to keep me upright. Pain lashed through my hand when my palm caught the floor to stop me. The cut split open again. A fresh warmth seeped through the bandages, sticky against my skin.

Hard tile beneath me. The bite of reopened wounds. The echo of boots closing in behind me.

"Run again, and I'll make sure you can't."

The voice wasn't Oberon's. The moment wasn't then.

But my chest tightened as if it was, as if the past had reached through the thin veil of time and curled its fingers around my throat.

My eyes shut tight.

Breathe.

Breathe.

Breathe.

My lungs burned as though they could no longer draw in air. I unclenched my fingers. But the damage had been done. The sharp crescents of my nails marked my palms, pressing deep enough to sting.

"Herbalist."

Oberon's voice sliced through the fog, pulling me back to the moment. The entryway was empty except for us. The vast space swallowed the echo of his words, making them heavier than they should have been.

He didn't know. He didn't mean it.

My breaths shuddered through me, uneven, but I made myself move. I pulled my shoulders back, straightened, and curled my fingers into the fabric of my dress to conceal the fresh bloom of blood soaking through the bandages.

Oberon watched me with an intensity that peeled back layers I didn't want him to see. I took a deep breath and forced a smile, tilting my chin enough to make it convincing. "I tripped, but I'm fine." The dim morning light filtered through the tall windows, highlighting his face. The muscles there flickered taut beneath his skin.

He didn't call me on the lie. But it was clear he didn't believe it.

His gaze shifted toward the dark staircase ahead of him. His body remained tense, with a restrained energy thrumming beneath the surface, though I wasn't sure whether it resulted from frustration, caution, or something else. "Don't go back out there alone," he ordered. A flicker of warmth brushed against the chill in my bones. Not because of his words, but because of how he said them. No anger, no irritation. Just command.

I pressed the moment deep into the recesses of my mind, where it could fester in silence. If I ignored it long enough, the tremor in my hands might fade. Maybe the past wouldn't claw its way to the surface. Maybe. The laugh escaped me, thinner than I intended, brittle at the edges. "Oh? And here I thought it was safe."

Oberon didn't share my humor.

His expression remained impassive, carved from stone, as he positioned himself in front of me in one swift motion. The shift was so sudden and decisive that my feet stopped. My pulse quickened as a wall of solid muscle and unwavering will stood between me and my way forward. His onyx eyes fixated on me. Oberon's expression had always been unreadable, but there was an unfamiliar weight to it, a quiet intensity that held me in place. He didn't just gaze at me.

He saw me.

"Dilthen Doe." The words were soft. The low timbre of his voice sent goosebumps along my spine, but the plea beneath it unsettled me. *Don't.* No elaboration, no demand.

My fingers dug deeper into my skirt, and the rough fabric pressed against my palm, the sticky warmth of my blood seeping through the bandages. He wouldn't move until I acknowledged him. So, I lifted my chin enough to shift the balance. "I wasn't planning on it." It wasn't a lie. Not entirely.

Oberon's gaze raked over me. His lips parted as if he hadn't decided what to say, but knew he wanted to respond. A tense pause settled between us before he exhaled sharply through his nose, signifying restraint. His jaw tightened, and he stepped aside. I moved past him before he could see any deeper, before his perceptive eyes could peel back the layers I wasn't ready to expose. I kept my steps even, my shoulders straight, willing my heart to return to its proper rhythm.

I wasn't sure what he'd find if he looked deeper into me, and I wasn't ready to find out.

THE MORNING IN Vaelwick was a stark contrast to the night we arrived. The village stirred awake with the rhythm of daily life. Vendors arranged their wares, and the smell of fresh bread drifted through the narrow streets. Children darted between legs, their high-pitched laughter filling the air. On the surface, it was ordinary, familiar, and just like any other place. But beneath the hum of routine, wary eyes observed.

It wasn't the idle curiosity of strangers passing through or the grudging acknowledgment of outsiders. This was different, more deliberate. Conversations tapered off as we passed. Voices dropped into hushed murmurs as if lingering too long on our presence might summon something worse. Heads turned, only for glances to flick away just as quickly, as though we carried misfortune in our wake.

It was as if *we* were the ones stalking the night.

I slowed near a group of villagers gathered outside a weathered stall, their fingers knotting dried herbs into bundles. The smell of rosemary and sage lingered in the damp air, masking a more acrid smell. The five of them—three women and two men—worked in silence, their hands never still even as they exchanged glances at my approach.

I wasn't welcome. That much was clear.

"Excuse me," I said, forcing a polite smile that I hoped wouldn't betray my unease. "I was wondering about the trinkets around town that hang from the eaves and posts. What are they made of?" For a moment, only the rustling of herbs answered me. Then, an older woman with silver streaks in her thick braid met my gaze with a measured look. Her fingers worked on a small, carved figure between them.

"Bones. Wood. Twine," She said with a voice rough as worn river stones.

Nodding, my eyes followed the contours of the tiny effigy. It was humanoid, but only just. Its features were too distorted, its limbs too thin. "And they symbolize...?"

A younger woman, just out of her teens, spoke up. "Protection, warnings. Prayers, sometimes."

I followed her gaze to a nearby doorway where someone had drawn a sigil in what I hoped was chalk. Darker streaks bled into the wood grooves, resisting the rain that ought to have washed them away. "And the markings?" I asked.

The older woman's hands stilled for a moment. "The same," she said. The hair on my arms stood on end. She spoke those words as if they carried immense weight, as though voicing them could unravel something best left undisturbed.

The younger woman hesitated, then added, "Each family has its signs, some older than the village itself."

Something unsettled twisted in my gut. Older than the village? The black wheat swaying in the mist, untouched by the wind, refusing to rot. "And the field?" I asked carefully. "The black wheat?"

The shift was immediate.

Their fingers stilled. The air thickened with an unspoken tension. The younger woman swallowed, her lips parting. The older one shot her a quick look. "It's cursed," the girl muttered, ignoring the warning.

A muscle feathered in the older woman's jaw. One man, broad-shouldered and lined with age, looked at me. His expression was stern. But his voice was taut, a rope stretched too thin. "You don' belong here, Herbalist."

The quiet that followed was suffocating.

I held his gaze, even as my gut twisted, instinct telling me to retreat. To leave it alone. "I only want to understand," I said.

His jaw tightened. He shook his head once. "Understandin' won't save you."

Oberon stepped closer, creating a subtle change in the air, accompanied by the quiet pull that followed him. Tension settled over his frame, winding. His voice was steady and low. "What do you mean?"

The man's gaze flicked to him. Beside him, the women kept their eyes lowered, busying their hands as they twisted herbs into tight, intricate knots. The sharp scent of rosemary curled through the air, but it did little to mask the unease that pressed in on each of us.

The man exhaled sharply through his nose, issuing a warning. "Means you should leave before you find out."

Oberon didn't move. Not a single shift of his weight, not a flicker of reaction. But his presence changed in a way that was impossible to ignore. The surrounding air became heavier and pressed in further, daring the man to try again.

The villager shifted on his feet. His wariness deepened, but he held firm. "Things in Vaelwick don't take kindly to outsiders askin' questions." His calculating gaze flicked to me. To my hands, still dusted with remnants of crushed herbs from the market. To the bandages wrapped around my fingers.

His lips parted, hesitated, then set in a thin, grim line. "'Specially ones who think they can fix what's been decided."

A slow, insidious chill unfurled in my gut. "Decided by who?" I asked.

The reaction was immediate. The women moved with quick, efficient hands, gathering their things in silence. The man stepped back, his expression set into stone.

Oberon didn't press further. His fingers brushed against my wrist. The message was definite: *We're done here.* I turned with him as my feet carried me away from the stall, but my thoughts lingered and unsettled me.

As we walked, I flipped through my journal, scanning the pages and searching for answers. But the words blurred, the notes I had taken lost shape and meaning, and fragments refused to align. The pieces lay scattered as bones in the dirt, but they didn't fit together as they should have.

Frowning, I lifted my gaze, allowing my eyes to adapt to the bright midday sun. It was too hot.

Vaelwick sat northwest of Silverfel. It shouldn't be much warmer, if any. Silverfel's dense canopy might have lowered the temperature, its shadows sheltering the village. Vaelwick was different. Exposed.

Sprawling fields stretched toward the horizon. Golden and black waves of dead wheat and brittle grass rolled with the lazy whisper of the wind. The only trees were on the other side of the fields, opposite from the town. No shade. Nowhere to hide from the relentless press of the sun overhead.

My eyes followed the slow ripple of movement across the fields. It should have been soothing, but it wasn't. The wheat swayed out of time with the wind, as if moving to an unseen rhythm.

I swallowed against the dryness in my throat. My uniform was too thick, designed for the freezing, damp castle corridors, and long nights wrapped in stone walls, not for the relentless heat turning me into a seared prime filet—or maybe steamed. My fingers flexed, feeling the dampness gathering beneath my bandages and the prickle of sweat on my skin. I wanted to roll my sleeves up to let the air touch my arms and cool the discomfort.

The thought lingered, an old weight I thought I had shed. The past never left. It only settled beneath my skin and sleeves, waiting for these moments to remind me it was still there.

Oberon stood at the mansion door with arms crossed. He didn't just wait. He made sure I entered. I slowed as I passed him, readjusting my grip on my journal.

Why did he do that? He just stood there, still as stone, watching. Waiting. It made ignoring his presence impossible.

"I'm going to the room... I mean, *my* room," I corrected, the words fumbling off my tongue. My grip tightened on the journal as if it might anchor me. I felt self-conscious under his gaze, and I hated that I did.

"I have too much to figure out," I added, lifting the journal as if that explained everything. He furrowed his brows, but he didn't respond.

Maybe he felt the shift between us, the unspoken weight that had settled into the spaces where silence once felt normal. Now, it only felt thick. Heavy.

I paused, then shook my head at myself. Enough. I stepped past him into the mansion's threshold, and a chill swept over me. The air was cooler inside, but no less suffocating.

At the bottom of the stairs, I hesitated again. The ceilings loomed overhead, and the silence stretched more than it should have. Even the flickering candlelight became distant, swallowed by shadows that gathered in the high corners of the hall. A whisper of unease trailed through me.

Marcus's mansion had been that way. It was too large, too empty. The emptiness turned every creak into footsteps and every shifting shadow into watching eyes. There were too many doors, places for someone to be lurking just out of sight.

My pulse stuttered fast.

We weren't in Wickloe. I wasn't there anymore.

Clearing my throat, I pushed myself forward, step by step, until the memory loosened its grip, and I reached my door. The journal dropped on the table with a dull *thud,* pages fluttering before settling. With a groan, I sank into the chair and pressed my fingers to my temple.

Focus.

The notes I had taken throughout Vaelwick were a mess of half-scrawled observations, fragmented warnings, and scrawled sigils. It was there, but disjointed, scattered, a puzzle with pieces missing their edges.

I rewrote everything with a clean sheet of parchment, breaking it apart piece by piece.

First, the trinkets. Bones, wood, twine. Carved with intent. Symbols of protection, warnings, prayers. But against what?

Second, the sigils. Crude but deliberate markings on doors. The older woman said each family had its own, passed down through generations. It wasn't just superstition, but something rooted in history, in survival.

Third, the field. The black wheat. *Cursed*, they had called it. No one said why. No one explained what it meant. But one villager had let a detail slip, quiet, half-muttered, before silencing herself.

'The crops feed on it.'

Feed on what?

I frowned, tapping the quill against the table. My gaze swept over the notes, retracing the words as I searched for the missing link. The trinkets, the sigils, the field—protection, warnings, a curse, a secret they refused to name.

Something didn't make sense.

Or maybe I was just too late to see the pattern.

Maybe the roots of the field held the answer I sought, the truth Vaelwick concealed.

Waiting. Growing. Feeding.

Tearing off a small piece of the black wheat loaf, I absently chewed as I sketched a rough map of the village. The bread was dense, heavier than I expected, with a bitter aftertaste that lingered on my tongue. It didn't taste spoiled but had an unpleasant aftertaste—an elduven sharpness, damp soil after rain, but darker. Stranger.

I ignored it and pressed on, marking the locations of the sigils I had seen, the houses with more trinkets than others, the general layout of the field. The quill followed the patterns I had traced throughout the day, but my restless and jagged thoughts churned beneath the surface.

Straightening, I scanned my messy scrawl.

People protected the houses closest to the fields the most, carving more sigils, trinkets, and desperate prayers into their walls. It wasn't random or tradition. It was defense. They weren't just superstitions or old customs. They were *barriers*.

The bite of bread I had been chewing went down dry, sticking in my throat like dust. My hand gripped the charcoal tighter. The man's warning echoed back to me, creeping through the cracks in my mind in a whispered omen.

"You don't belong here, Herbalist."

Not *us*. Not Oberon.

Me.

A heavy pounding started in my chest.

Why?

Herbalists weren't threats. We worked with plants, studied the land, and healed the sick. We helped. So why did a withering village—its crops struggling, its land sickly, its people desperate—see me as something that didn't belong?

The charcoal stilled between my fingers.

Unless... it wasn't wilting.

I sat up straighter, my breath unsteady. *What if they weren't afraid of me being useless here? What if they were worried I would interfere?*

Tearing off another piece of the loaf and chewing, my gaze fixed on my notes, though I wasn't seeing them anymore. The creatures that the travelers spoke of in whispers, the ones Oberon and I had seen, were in the fields where animals refused to venture. Where the deaths happened and where people vanished if they ventured too far into the wheat. Everything was connected to that field.

Setting aside the charcoal, I exhaled and swept my hair back.

But why? When I looked at it earlier, it had seemed... normal. Strange in its endlessness, eerie in how the wind moved through it with breaths, but otherwise, it was just a field. Or at least, it was on the surface.

A sharp chill crawled up my spine.

On the surface.

I stared at the half-eaten loaf in my hand with unease. The wheat thrived. The grain grew thick and tall while everything else around it struggled to survive, its roots starved of whatever life remained in the soil. That's why the villagers muttered about the wheat feeding on something. Because whatever it was...

It was buried.

20

OBERON

MY BOOTS DRAGGED against the aged wooden floor while I paced the length of my room. My thoughts should have been on the creature in the fields, the rot, the decay, and the strange symbols carved into every damned door in this rancid village. But my mind circled back, drawn to her instead.

The pained whimpers. Her fingers clawed at her back as desperation twisted her features, making her appear unguarded. She had gasped awake, drenched in sweat, as if she had surfaced from drowning. Her choked sobs were half-swallowed, and my name slipped past her lips in breathless panic before she even realized where she was.

I had sat there in hesitation.

Why did she call for me?

'I am not afraid of you, Oberon Sinclaire.'

She should have been. She knew what I was. What I was capable of. Yet she had looked me dead in the eye and said it without a flicker of doubt. But whatever haunted her nights terrified her. Enough that in that moment of blind, gut-wrenching terror, she had called for *me*.

I had never been good with things that required comfort or softness. My hands knew how to wield a blade, break bone, and silence a threat. *But what did you do when the battle wasn't before you? When the enemy had already seeped into her being?*

She flinched when I shook her awake in Silverfel before her eyes focused. Then she had brushed it off, thrown up her walls as if I hadn't watched her unravel. Her composure slid back into place like armor, though her hands trembled as she suppressed her emotions. And I had let her.

I should have pressed, should have forced her to talk, but I wanted to see if something would slip. If she would say a name, a place, some sliver of truth to tell me who plagued her sleep, who had carved those invisible wounds into her. Instead, I only received silence.

The way she carried herself when we entered the mansion. The air had shifted the moment she stepped inside. Tension gripped my ribs, and my Fae senses hummed with unease. It was how her shoulders had tensed ever so slightly and her fingers had curled before she forced them to relax. It was how she had smiled when the lord mentioned our separate rooms and how it hadn't reached her eyes.

That fleeting moment of hesitation. Of discomfort. *Why?*

Why had she reacted as though being alone was the more significant threat? What was she so afraid of that sharing a room with me—a man, an assassin, a half-Fae—seemed like the safer option?

I combed through the memories of notes in her journal, searching for a thread to pull, a connection to make sense of it. But there was none.

Groaning, I dropped into the chair by the table, pulled off my gloves, and let my head fall back against the wooden frame. My fingers flexed against my palms. I was restless. My Fae was agitated. It prowled around the fringes of my thoughts, demanding answers. A novel feeling that she alone had pulled from it.

How the hells was I supposed to fight a ghost from her past? A tormentor I couldn't name?

And now, whatever was in the field had targeted her.

I grit my teeth. My restless fingers flexed in my lap as the memory resurfaced. The strangled noise she made when she stumbled and her boots snagged on the decayed corpse at our feet. The way her breath hitched, her chest rising and falling in shallow, frantic gasps. Her eyes widened, pupils dilated, as the thing before her rose, its grotesque, jagged, unnatural maw splitting open.

The sound it made wasn't meant for human ears. A high, ear-piercing shriek that sent bile crawling up my throat. Terror froze her. Locked every muscle in place. She was trapped, helpless, as the thing lunged at her. I had moved without thought when my blade cut through its form. The steel met resistance before the creature dissolved into nothing but mist.

It wasn't just that creature.

I pressed my palms into my thighs to ground myself against the worn fabric of my trousers and the leather of my belts. My gaze fixed on the floorboards, but I only saw Silverfel. The dense, suffocating trees. The thing in the woods. The way it had fixated on her then, too. Not me, the one wielding the sword, the one it recognized and feared.

Her.

That couldn't be a coincidence.

I sighed and dragged a hand through my hair. My thoughts were tangled as I retraced every detail, every clue. There had to be something that connected them—Silverfel, Vaelwick, the rot that had spread in the villages, the creatures that moved through the dark. *Was it because she was an herbalist?*

The people of Silverfel had been desperate for a cure. They had whispered of sickness but ignored the curses. And here, in Vaelwick, they weren't ignoring them. They knew. They carved symbols into their doors, strung charms over their homes, and muttered about rituals meant to ward off the evil.

Had her knowledge drawn these creatures to her? Had they come because of what she was?

My jaw tightened.

No.

It didn't sit right. The pieces were too scattered, and the logic was too thin. *If they hunted herbalists, why her? Why had the thing in Silverfel fixated on her? Why had the creature in the fields lunged for her instead of me?*

It wasn't just because an herbalist meddled with forces beyond her control. There had to be a connection I couldn't see yet.

What I saw was that they hunted her.

And she hadn't even realized it.

WHEN MORNING CAME, I still hadn't slept. Not for lack of trying. I had laid there, staring at the ceiling, waiting for exhaustion to take hold. I willed my mind to be quiet, but it didn't. My thoughts churned, picking apart every detail, every inconsistency, and every damned thing that didn't sit right with me. I dragged a hand down my face, irritation bristling beneath my skin. None of it made sense.

Eventually, I gave up. Sleep had eluded me, and waiting for it to arrive did nothing to change that.

With a deep sigh, I pushed to my feet and ran a hand through my hair, the strands sticking up in every direction. Quinn's room sat next to mine. She hadn't said a word to me since we had parted for the night, which wasn't unusual. But after Silverfel, I had minimal trust in her ability to stay put.

I rapped my knuckles against the door.

No answer.

I waited a beat. Then another. Still nothing.

If she had slipped off without telling me again, so help me—

The door swung open when my fingers wrapped around the knob, and Quinn barreled into me. "No time!" she clipped, slipping past my grip.

"For fuck's sake, Herbalist, not again!" I snapped, spinning on my heel and taking off after her. She was ahead of me, dodging around corners as if she had planned this.

I cursed under my breath as I bolted down the winding staircase, my boots slamming against the wood. Quinn, however, had made my life even more difficult. Instead of running like a normal person, she launched herself onto the handrail and slid down it with infuriating ease. I gaped for a moment, then moved faster, my frustration boiling over. She landed at the bottom with the practiced grace that told me she had done it more times than I cared to know.

Saints fucking preserve me.

"Dilthen Doe!" My voice thundered through the vast mansion. "At least tell me where you're headed this time!"

She nearly crashed into Lord Everette. With infuriating nonchalance, Quinn recovered with a half-hearted bow before slipping past him as if he were furniture. Lord Everette's brows shot up in surprise as I stormed after her, bracing myself for whatever madness she dragged me into this time.

Quinn skidded to a halt when we reached the stables, where Neryth stood behind a gate. His ears flicked as if even he knew something reckless was going to happen. I hadn't even caught my breath when Quinn spun on me, her eyes gleaming with wild, exhilarated intensity. She heaved, her chest rising and falling in frantic bursts. Sweat clung to her brow, and strands of hair stuck to the flushed skin of her cheeks and neck.

Despite Vaelwick's warm weather, she wore excessive layers, pulling her sleeves down to her wrists for extra protection. It should have been obvious by now. *How had I not noticed?*

I pushed the thought aside and opened my mouth to demand what in the five hells she had been thinking, but she didn't give me the chance. "I figured it out!" she blurted, throwing a shovel at me. Its weight felt like an omen in my grasp. I couldn't even properly scowl at the damn thing before she gripped another, ready to march forward, her eyes burning with that reckless, unshakable fire. "There's something buried in the crop field."

Saints, help me.

Pinching the bridge of my nose, I steeled myself against the frustration that clawed at me. Naturally, she had figured something out, and it had led to this.

I didn't doubt her. Quinn didn't charge headfirst into chaos without reason. She was sharper than most, quicker, and annoyingly perceptive. But she had no sense of self-preservation. No hesitation or fear. She threw herself into the unknown with nothing but sheer willpower and the unspoken expectation that I was right behind her.

The problem was that her expectations had been correct. I would have followed Quinn Larkspur through the Veil if it meant I could have kept her safe. Alive. With or without Alric's command.

And that unsettled me more than I cared to admit.

My jaw rolled as I glanced at the shovel in my hand, feeling the weight of inevitability. With a resigned sigh, I hoisted the damned thing over my shoulder and met her eager, determined stare.

"Then let's go dig up some nightmares."

21

EDEN

THE GRAVEYARD OF blackened stalks swayed despite the unnatural stillness in the air. The field hadn't just withered. It had been drained of vitality. The silence was as if elduvaris itself was holding its breath. The closer we got, the heavier the air became. It was dense with an unseen weight, a presence that lingered beneath the soil.

I halted at the edge.

Oberon's boots crunched against the brittle remains of wheat as he strode ahead. A few paces in, he stopped and turned when he realized I hadn't followed. His piercing gaze locked onto me, stripping away any chance of pretense. "Where?"

I blinked, my pulse stumbling. "What?"

"Where are we supposed to be digging?" He gestured to the endless stretch of decayed wheat, the landscape that offered nothing but desolation. "Or do you even know what we're digging for?"

My throat tightened. I gripped my journal harder, and my fingers pressed deep into the leather as if I could wring the answer from its pages. I knew... or at least I thought I did. The crops had been fed, but not by sunlight or soil. They had drawn from something buried beneath them.

But what if I was wrong? What if we uncovered something that wasn't meant to be disturbed?

"I—" My voice faltered.

Oberon didn't move, but there was a shift in his patience. The silent expectation. I forced my breath steady as my mind raced through the sigils, the warnings, the unmarked graves, and the deaths.

They led here.

Swallowing my hesitation, I stepped forward. "The center," I said, forcing certainty into my voice. "We dig in the center."

His gaze lingered, weighing my words, but he didn't argue. Didn't scoff, sigh, or call this a waste of time. He planted his feet, adjusted his grip on the shovel, and drove the blade into the ground.

The first thrust sent a dull, wet sound through the silence. The second was harsher; the resistance in the soil was more than just compacted dirt. My breath hitched as he worked. Each rhythmic thrust and scrape peeled away layers of soil, chipping into whatever lay beneath.

The eerie, smothering silence of the field pressed in around us, but my focus had shifted. It wasn't the unnatural hush that froze me. It was him. It was the way he had given no sharp remarks, and there was no hesitation. Just a relentless, unquestioning effort.

The rhythmic scrape of the shovel biting into the ground filled the space between us. My gaze drifted, almost absently at first, to follow the precise motion of his arms as he rolled his sleeves up to his elbows. The fabric dragged against his skin before falling away, revealing the sharp definition of his forearms, muscles flexing with every controlled movement. A thin sheen of sweat clung to him, catching in the dim light and accentuating the taut lines of his build.

The heat of Vaelwick had gotten to him. His dark hair was damp, and a few errant strands fell loose across his forehead. He parted his lips. His breath was even but heavier from exertion.

I swallowed, too aware of the warmth creeping over my skin. Oberon drove the shovel deeper into the ground, then stilled and lifted his head. His dark, unreadable gaze collided with mine. His grip on the handle tightened, and the muscles in his shoulders tensed as if he were bracing himself for something. The shovel remained planted in the dirt, forgotten for a beat too long. The air between us shifted into a slow, crackling tension that curled around my spine, making my pulse kick against my throat. I forced myself to look away.

"I should…" I cleared my throat. "I should help."

Desperate for something to focus on, I shoved my shovel into the dirt. The movement was clumsy, my grip too tight, and I didn't register the impact. His stare continued to linger on me. "Doesn't all that fabric get heavy in this heat?" His voice was smooth. *Was he... teasing?* "I didn't realize modesty was a survival skill."

My hands clenched around the shovel. I willed myself to keep my eyes fixed on the dirt and ignore the way my skin prickled under the weight of his attention.

Of course, he noticed.

I forced out a dry, unimpressed laugh, shoving the shovel's blade deeper into the ground. "You wouldn't last a day in a dress like this."

He let out a quiet, amused sound. "I would sooner die." I glanced up, expecting his usual scowl, the ever-present glower that made it impossible to tell what he thought. But there was no frustration, no blank, indifferent stare. A subtle but unmistakable smirk curved just enough to soften the sharpness of his features. And his eyes held a dangerous glint, an amusement that made my stomach tighten and my breath catch.

My face went up in flames.

I dropped my gaze back to the dirt, gripping the shovel harder as if I could will the heat from my skin. But it was too late. It spread up my neck and burned beneath the thick layers of my uniform. Oberon's low chuckle curled around me, making the heat unbearable. I took a deep breath before driving the shovel into the dirt with unnecessary force.

Focus. Focus on the field.

Not on him or on how attractive he looks.

I huffed, and my grip tightened as I forced my gaze away from the man beside me, who should not have been smirking. Who should not have set my face ablaze with his deep, unexpected chuckle.

After some time, the shovel struck something solid.

My whole body ached, and my muscles had grown sluggish from the heat. My dress clung to my skin, damp with sweat, and the fabric stuck in places it shouldn't. I only noticed how severe it was when I swiped at my forehead, meaning to wipe away the dampness—only for my sleeve to smear against my skin instead. I grimaced, ready to say something to break the tension with another joke, another distraction, but the words died on my tongue.

Oberon watched me.

The air lodged in my throat, and my stomach twisted. His gaze was heavy in a way that made my skin prickle.

Judging?

No.

The way his eyes dragged over me made me shrink, hyper-aware of how I must have looked, sweaty, disheveled, dirt-smudged along my arms and collarbone. I looked awful.

Since when did I care?

Oberon extended a flask toward me, halting that thought. He said nothing as he held it there in an unspoken offer. I hesitated before my fingers brushed against the cool metal. The contrast to my overheated skin sent a shiver up my spine. I chewed my lip, disregarding how my body reacted.

"Why won't you roll up your sleeves?" His tone was softer, less teasing. More... curious.

My throat tightened, and I forced a shrug. "Sweat helps cool the body. If I roll up my sleeves, the sun will dry it too fast." I tipped the flask against my lips. The chilled water was a shocking contrast to the heat in my chest. "Excessive sun exposure can lead to dehydration and heat exhaustion."

Oberon's gaze flicked to my arms before trailing back to my face. He peeled back the layers of my words and searched for the truth beneath them. It was a logical fact. Yet, beneath the weight of his silence, it was thin. I swallowed, pretended not to notice, and took another sip before returning the flask. His fingers brushed mine as he took it. It was a fleeting touch, but my pulse jumped regardless, and my skin burned in a way that was unrelated to the sun.

I forced my attention downward, willing my heart to steady as my eyes landed on the exposed ground between us. The dirt had shifted enough to reveal something hard beneath it. It wasn't stone. It was smooth yet jagged in places, brittle bone wrapped in withered roots.

"What do you think that is?" I asked, lowering to my knees as I brushed away more soil. My fingers skimmed the surface of the uncovered shape, and an unsettling give met my touch. It wasn't quite solid, but not fully decayed.

"You're asking me?" Oberon's voice held a trace of amusement.

"Sigils."

That got his attention. "What?"

He crouched beside me. His presence sparked against my senses, his body too close. I fixed my gaze on the object in front of us, but the heat radiated from him, as did the shift of his breath and the slow, steady way he studied the shape.

I knew he was handsome—anyone with working eyes would. But sitting this close, the heat of the Vaelwick sun clinging to both of us, I was suddenly aware of every detail. The way sweat glistened on his skin, tracing the sharp angles of his forearms. The way his dark hair, damp from exertion, clung to his forehead in loose strands, curling just where it dried.

His forearm's strong, corded muscle flexed as he braced a hand on his knee. A sheen of sweat clung to his collarbone, and his shirt was damp where it clung to his chest. And there was the way he smelled of iron, leather, and cedar, tinged with the faintest trace of salt from the effort.

Gods.

I swallowed hard.

The heat must have affected my thoughts.

"It's... sigils," I muttered, half-distracted, still tracing the carved markings with my fingers. Deep, careful cuts scored the surface of jagged runes etched into what appeared to be twisted bark. The more I brushed away, the less it resembled wood. *No, this was something else.* The ridges and contours beneath the soil formed a shape too structured, too unnatural. The bones curled inward to form a ribcage but were too long and thin.

Oberon leaned closer. His shoulder brushed mine, and his breath fanned against my cheek. The air between us became tense in a way I had no words to explain.

I dared a glance at him, and we locked eyes.

He had been staring at me.

The thought sent a bolt of heat straight through me, curling low in my stomach. My lips parted, and Oberon's expression flickered. His brows furrowed, and the corners of his eyes twitched. His gaze drifted to my lips. His breathing changed, and his fingers flexed against his knee.

Then his eyes turned silver with a slow shift, gleaming in the dimming light. His pupils dilated and constricted as if something inside him was fighting to surface. The tension became palpable. A tingling heat pooled low in my belly, my breath caught, and my pulse became frantic and uneven.

What did it mean when his eyes turned silver? What was it tied to?

A foul, cloying, meaty stench slammed into me, curling in the back of my throat. I gagged, and my hand shot up to cover my nose.

The dirt beneath my hands crumbled. Something inside the effigy moved as a deep, wet pop echoed from beneath the sigil-carved surface. I recoiled, and my fingers dug into the dirt behind me as though it could steady me. Oberon's hand shot out and wrapped around my arm, yanking me back just as a sliver of black goop oozed through the cracks in the sigils.

The air shuddered.

A long, unnatural groan rumbled from the thing buried before us, reverberating through the ground. The runes along its surface pulsed a sickly, blue-green glow that flickered like the afterimage of a flame in the dark.

The thing breathed a rattling, hollow breath.

No.

Oberon was on his feet, sword drawn, his body rigid in an unfamiliar way. "We need to go." His voice was fierce, low, and steady. His silver-lit gaze never left the shifting soil.

I could only stare at the thing lying half-uncovered. My mind struggled to make sense of it. I had expected bones. Roots. Something dead. But this wasn't old. This wasn't dead. Someone had put this here, had carved those sigils to keep it buried, and now we had disturbed it.

The ground shuddered, the withered crops trembled, and the stench of rot swelled around us, wrapping tight and winding down my throat. A sudden, jerking spasm from the thing sent a spray of dirt flying as a shape lurched from the pit. It had once been a hand. Tendons knotted where flesh had withered away, stretched too tight over elongated bones. The fingers curled, each one tipped with broken nails.

It twitched.

And twitched again.

My stomach lurched. I took a slow, unsteady step back. "Sinclaire." The hand snapped toward me before Oberon's sword sliced through the wrist. A spray of inky black liquid spattered the dirt, and the stench of decay thickened. The severed hand writhed where it landed, fingers still flexing—still reaching for me.

My pulse pounded against my skull.

The ground split, and a wet, sucking noise filled the air as the thing dragged itself free.

Oberon grabbed my wrist. "Run!"

The field lurched beneath us. The once-dry soil turned damp as it began to shift and breathe. The stench of rot thickened, curling in the back of my throat and coating my tongue in something sour.

A horrid, rattling shriek split the air.

I stumbled, but Oberon's grip tightened. His firm hand was burning hot around my wrist. He yanked me forward before I could hit the ground. My lungs burned. My legs ached. But if we stopped, we were dead.

The shriek turned into laughter. Twisted. Gurgling. Inhuman. My stomach dropped as I risked a glance over my shoulder and immediately regretted it.

It stood, unfolding limb by limb.

It had once been human or close to it. The thing that clawed its way from the dirt had no right to move. The tight skin stretched over its frame, splitting its flesh at the joints and exposing blackened sinew.

Where there should have been eyes, there were only hollow sockets, writhing with something wet and moving. The skin around its mouth had rotted away. The lips stripped back to reveal a jagged grin of broken, splintered teeth.

And it laughed. The noise crawled through the air, a dry, rattling rasp that burrowed into my ears, into my skull. I choked on my breath. It didn't just come from the thing in the field. It came from beneath us.

Oberon muttered something in another language before yelling, "Move, Herbalist!" The ground split, and dozens of blackened fingers shot from the ground that clawed at our boots, grasped at our legs, and pulled. I faltered as cold, dead hands wrapped around my ankle. Oberon's blade flashed in my vision with a spray of black ichor. The hands fell away, twitching.

He yanked me forward. "Don't stop!" We broke free of the field just as the ground buckled inward, collapsing beneath the weight of whatever lay beneath. A pit. A mass grave. A burial ground that should have never been disturbed.

The laughter followed us into the trees, which swallowed us whole. Branches tore at my sleeves, whipping across my skin as we hurtled forward, our footfalls uneven against the gnarled roots beneath us. A fire burned in my lungs; every breath was like swallowing embers.

Oberon was a creature built for the hunt ahead of me, traversing the trees with ease. But this time, we were the prey. The laughter grew, slithered between the trunks, and twisted as if it were alive.

I forced my focus ahead. We needed to get out of the damned trees.

Whispers began, faint at first, rustling through the leaves. But they grew louder and clearer.

"You shouldn't have come."

"You don't belong here."

"Leave. Leave. Leave."

My breath hitched. It was the same voice as the man at the village market. I snapped my head toward Oberon. "Do you hear that?" His stride didn't falter, but his jaw tightened. He must have heard it, too.

"Turn back."

"They're waiting."

"You were never meant to leave."

Something shifted in my periphery, but there was nothing there: only trees, shadows, and a suffocating force pressing too closely.

Oberon grasped my arm, bringing me to a halt. His chest heaved as his silver eyes searched the woods in front of us and then behind. Tension coiled through him.

We weren't alone.

A low, rattling breath stirred the branches just behind me. When I turned my head, a figure stood too close—half in shadow, half in the dim slant of evening light. It was worse than the thing from the field.

Taller. Gaunt. Its limbs were too long, its neck crooked and twitching. Its mouth hung parted, revealing jagged, brittle, splintered shards. There weren't any eye sockets, only empty, cavernous voids—a depth that stretched on forever.

Oberon shoved me. "Damn ha adaneth, run!"

The air burned my lungs. My boots found purchase as I tore through the trees, branches snapping beneath my weight. Oberon stayed beside me, the creature keeping pace behind us. A wet, rattling sound. Not a growl or a breath, but something trying to remember how to be human.

The ground trembled, and the trees shuddered.

I stumbled, catching myself just before my knee hit the dirt. Oberon grabbed my arm and yanked me forward before I lost momentum. The laughter had stopped, replaced with a deep, guttural clicking and a pulse in the air. I felt it in my bones and teeth.

Oberon cursed under his breath. "Veilbound."

The word made little sense, but there was no time to ask. There was cracking through the trees behind us, too fast, too heavy.

The trees thinned ahead, a clearing. "We need to—" The moment we hit the tree line, something slammed into us. The force sent me sprawling across the ground. The breath ripped from my chest as I hit the dirt and rolled until my back slammed against something solid. My vision blurred, and my ears rang.

Oberon sprang to his feet mid-roll and pivoted with his blade drawn.

A shadow loomed just beyond the clearing. It was hulking with twisted limbs and exposed sinew. Its mouth was a maw stretched too wide, splitting its chest.

Inside were more faces that were contorted in silent screams, shifting beneath the torn flesh. My stomach lurched again. Oberon stepped forward, separating me from the creature, and slipped into an unprecedented stance.

Fae.

The thing snapped its head toward me. A blur of glowing silver and steel flashed across my vision as Oberon's blade severed flesh.

The air shattered and rippled, forcing me to cover my ears.

A deafening screech split through the clearing, high and raw, like rusted metal scraping against bone. The thing lurched. Its grotesque jaw split wider, and the faces beneath its skin writhed as if they were alive.

Oberon's blade tore through its side, but it didn't fall. It didn't even bleed. I scrambled back when the thing jerked toward me. Its limbs spasmed as too many joints bent the wrong way. Oberon slammed his body into it with a fierce growl, pushing the creature back. His silvered eyes gleamed cruel and feral. The grip on his sword tightened before he drove it straight into its gaping maw.

For a moment, everything froze.

The creature's body twitched. The faces beneath its skin screamed in unison. Black bile erupted from its mouth, splattering across the ground.

I flinched as the smell of rot and charred meat filled the air. My stomach twisted, but I had to stay upright. I had to move. Oberon wrenched his blade free as the thing collapsed. A sickening, wet crack filled the air while its body hit the ground, twitching, its grotesque mouth still stretched open in its final, soundless shriek.

The surrounding air hummed in the silence.

Oberon's chest heaved. His knuckles were white around the hilt of his sword. He didn't move or take his eyes off the corpse.

I swallowed hard. My fingers trembled as I wiped the sweat from my brow. My skin felt too tight, and my voice was unrecognizable when I spoke. "What was that?"

Oberon let out a frustrated breath. "Veilbound," he muttered. He yanked a cloth from his belt to clean his blade. "Or something close enough to it."

His voice was steady, but tension rolled off him in waves. I willed myself to breathe, to comprehend the thing in the field, the laughter, and the symbols carved into the doors. The thing looked at me the same way the one in Silverfel had. It wasn't a coincidence. "What does it want?"

Oberon looked at me, his silvered irises still glowing. "I think it wants *you*."

22

EDEN

MY THROAT FELT tight, parched from the heat, the run, and the tension. The eerie silver gleam in Oberon's eyes hadn't faded. His fingers remained curled around the hilt of his sword, knuckles taut, his entire body braced as if he expected another attack.

I shook my head, forcing my voice to stay steady.

Think.

Focus.

"That thing came after us both. You were standing right there."

His jaw tightened. "It only looked at *you*."

A chill scraped along my spine, and I wrapped my arms around myself. My gaze drifted back to the twisted corpse sprawled on the ground. It was unnatural in a way that made my stomach churn. The flesh was withering, skin sloughing away in patches as black bile oozed from its slackened mouth. The stench of decay clung to the air.

The sigils beneath the body, carved deep into the dirt, were obscured by the foul sludge coating them. But beneath it, something moved.

A sudden crack split the silence. The ground beneath the corpse shuddered.

I flinched and stumbled back. Oberon's arm caught my waist, yanking me away just while the ground beneath the Veilbound collapsed. A sharp gasp stuck in my throat as the corpse sank and dragged downward. The ground gaped open, bile bubbling as the land itself came to life, swallowing the body whole.

My pulse pounded, the scene unfolding before me feeling too surreal, too impossible. "That's—"

"Not normal." Oberon hadn't let go of me. His voice was a deadly calm, despite his tension, a slow-burning energy in the way his muscles remained rigid. His firm grip on my waist lingered, as if he were trying to ground himself in the aftermath.

The tremors stilled, the bile ceased bubbling, and the ground settled as if nothing had happened. But the sigils remained, glistening beneath the grime.

Oberon's chest relaxed before he eased his arm from around me. Losing his warmth left my skin tingling. He crouched, ran a hand over a carving, and smeared away the remaining filth. His brow furrowed as his eyes traced the symbols with unnerving focus.

"These aren't just warding sigils," he muttered. His voice was low and distant. "They're binding marks."

Binding.

"You think something was trapped here?"

Oberon remained still, fingers pressed against the soil, before he lifted his gaze to mine. "Not something," he corrected. "Someone."

"Someone?"

Oberon's gaze drifted back to the sigils, his fingers tracing the grooves with reverence, as if the mere act of touching them might awaken what lay beneath us. The way he moved with such caution sent a fresh wave of unease coursing through my veins. He didn't just read the symbols. He *felt* them. "These marks don't just bind." His silver eyes flicked up and locked onto mine with quiet intensity. "They consume."

A chill slithered through me.

He sat back on his heels and gestured toward the etched stone. "Warding sigils repel. Binding sigils imprison. But these?" His voice darkened, laced with restrained fury. "These are meant to *drain*. To strip something, or someone, of everything until nothing remains."

The bile in my stomach churned. I turned back toward the collapsed soil, to the thick, sludgy remnants of whatever foul magic had been at work. The ground still bore the scars of what had just happened, yet it looked undisturbed. It had swallowed its secrets whole.

"Then whoever was buried here—"

"—is long gone," Oberon clipped, his voice hard. The tension in his shoulders hadn't eased. He wiped his gloved hand on his trousers, stiff and measured, as if trying to rid himself of something unseen.

A lump formed in my throat. "If someone was buried here, then this wasn't just a grave." I turned to him. "This was a sacrifice."

Oberon went still, but a muscle in his jaw twitched. His gaze lingered on the sigils for a long, weighted moment before he spoke. "Yes."

That single word sent a pulse of dread rippling through me. I swallowed hard, my eyes trailing over the crude symbols carved into the stone. They weren't failed protections nor remnants of a forgotten ward. They were far worse. Someone hadn't just died here. They had been bled dry. Erased.

This wasn't just a desperate offering to unseen gods, an ill-conceived ritual lost to time. It had been calculated and purposeful. Someone had buried a body beneath this field for a reason. I fought the urge to retreat into instinct—to take notes, document every detail, and make sense of the horror we had just uncovered. The twist in my gut told me there was more to it.

A low, pulsing hum resonated just beneath the threshold of hearing.

The air shifted as a ripple of unseen magic crawled over my skin, raising every hair on my arms. Unseen fingers dragged through the air, scraping the ends of my awareness.

Oberon pushed to his feet, moving beside me while his gloved hand wrapped around the hilt of his sword.

The sigils ignited with a pulse of raw energy, surging up from the ground. Dust and debris exploded into the air. The wind howled as if the ground itself had exhaled. The force sent me stumbling, my boots sliding against the loose dirt.

Whispers, low and urgent, slithered through the wind in a language I didn't recognize but felt. The sound didn't just echo, it sank into me, curled through my ribs, and seeped into my bones. They were pleading.

A choked noise clawed up my throat as I lurched back. Oberon's hand clamped around my wrist and hauled me away.

The whispers twisted into raw, shattered, and endless screams. Their agony split the air apart, tearing through the unnatural wind—through me.

I had heard suffering in the dying, in the grieving, in *myself*. But this wasn't just grief, it was rage. Whatever had woken up was furious.

The ground heaved beneath us. A deep, resonant crack ripped through the clearing when the sigil-covered stone fractured. A fissure tore through the dirt, gaping wide, and from its depths poured a wave of pure rot. The smell of death, ruin, and power buried too long beneath the ground crashed over me.

Oberon's grip on my wrist tightened. "Move!" A hand erupted from the ground. My stomach lurched at the blackened flesh, peeling in ragged sheets, clung to exposed, gleaming bone. The fingers twitched, curled, and searched.

I couldn't move.

Couldn't breathe.

Another hand punched through the dirt. A wet, sickening rip followed as the ground split apart. The ground convulsed and cracked wider as bodies spilled forth from the gash in the ground. One after another, they clawed their way free, limbs tangled, movements jerky and unnatural. The dirt heaved them up from a wound that had split open.

A shallow breath escaped me as my eyes locked onto their hollowed faces—jaws slack, sockets empty. The stench coated my tongue. The decay was so strong that it blurred my peripheral vision. I wanted to scream, but the sound stuck, trapped beneath the weight of horror that pressed against my chest as it sank its claws into my lungs.

The metallic *shhiiing* of Oberon's sword carved through the air as he drew it from its sheath, the blade gleaming in the dim, shifting light. I forced myself to swallow against the bile that rose in my throat. My chest tightened. My skin crawled.

"Sinclaire, what is this?" I rasped.

Oberon's silver-flecked gaze flicked between the writhing corpses and the glowing sigils beneath them. "Necromancy." Quiet fury edged his tone. His grip on his sword tightened. "And it's old."

This hadn't been a fresh summoning. It had brewed and festered beneath the field for Gods knew how long.

The dead had been waiting.

And we had just woken them.

The tallest of them—a woman—let out a rattling, gurgling shriek. Her head lolled, her jaw hung too wide, her bones cracked and popped as she turned toward me.

I swayed as my legs threatened to give out beneath me. She looked at me. Not Oberon. Not the field around us. Just me.

My mouth ran dry. The horror in my chest twisted and became colder, crueler.

Why?

Why me?

Oberon's deep voice cut through the rising panic. "Dilthen Doe." I tore my eyes away from the corpse and found his. That silver gaze was steady and waiting.

I sucked in a sharp breath, ignoring the way my hands trembled as I gripped my dagger and ran. My boots tore across the loosened soil as I bolted, dagger clenched in my fist so hard my knuckles ached. The corpses pulled themselves free. Dirt and rotted flesh sloughed off their bones as they staggered to their feet.

Oberon stayed close behind me. His sword swung through the air as he cut through the first one that lunged at me. The sickening sound of metal splitting flesh and bone rang in my ears, but the damn thing didn't falter. It just shuddered, gurgled, and kept going.

"Move!" Oberon barked.

I twisted away just as the corpse's rotted fingers swiped for my throat. I felt the rush of air as it missed, the icy grasp of decay shy of my pulse.

More of them had risen, one after another, clawing out of the shattered soil, their sunken faces twisted in expressions of torment and hunger. The woman—the tallest of them—staggered forward. That guttural, wet shriek tore from her throat once more. Her arms twitched at her sides, fingers flexing, curling, and reaching.

Still focused on me.

Panic sank into me. *Think. Move.* "The sigils!" I gasped, skidding to a stop just outside the bodies. "They're what's keeping them alive!"

Oberon's gaze snapped to the markings that glowed beneath the corpses' feet, their symbols pulsating with a sickly, unnatural light. "Then we break them," he gritted. He moved again, blade flashing, carving a path through the undead.

Dagger in hand, I dropped to my knees and dug into the first sigil I could reach. The moment the metal tore through the carved lines, the air shifted. The shrieking stopped. The corpses froze. Then they screamed. A death wail—a guttural, unreal sound that sent my skull splitting open with pain.

I clamped my hands over my ears, gritting my teeth against the burn in my skull, and reached for the next sigil. Then the next. Each time I carved through one, another corpse collapsed into a pile of rot and dust.

Oberon was a whirlwind of steel beside me, slicing any that got too close. But even he was wavering. His movements were slower, and his expression was tight with strain. The magic fought back. The air buzzed, vibrated, and pressed in with a physical weight as it tried to suffocate us.

One more.

Just one more.

My blade slammed into the final sigil. The surrounding sound shattered as a wave of dark energy erupted from the broken circle, rippling outward in a shockwave. Every corpse convulsed, their skeletal jaws gaping in silent agony as they crumbled to dust. The moment the last body fell apart, the air went still.

The weight had left. The magic had died. My ragged breathing was the only sound left. Oberon stood next to me with his sword lowered, staring at the wreckage around us.

I sucked in a shaky breath and lifted my gaze to where the tall woman had stood. The only thing left of her was a tattered scrap of fabric, half-buried in the broken soil. I swallowed. My pulse refused to slow. "Necromancy," I rasped in a whisper.

Oberon ran a bloodied hand through his hair. "And not just any necromancy," he said. "This was a warning."

OBERON SAT AT the rickety wooden table in my room, flipping through the pages of my notes with an intensity that made my skin prickle. His jaw was tight, his fingers tense where they gripped the parchment, but he said nothing. Not yet. He did that thing again, where he stared too long and let the silence stretch until it became uncomfortable.

I paced near the window, arms crossed tight against my chest. My mind spun like a wheel caught in the mud. My body still felt wrung out, with muscles that ached from the fight, but exhaustion wasn't enough to prevent the unease that curled deep in my gut.

A warning. That's what he'd said. That necromantic ritual—those things in the field—weren't random. They weren't a forgotten relic of dark magic buried beneath the crops.

Someone put them there. Someone wanted us to find them.

But why?

I stopped pacing long enough to rub at my temples, trying to drown out the echoes of that horrible shrieking still lodged in my skull. The smell of decay clung to my clothes, no matter how many times I had scrubbed my skin raw in the basin.

Oberon sighed and shut my journal with a decisive snap. "It's deliberate," he muttered, more to himself than to me.

I frowned. "What do you mean?"

He gestured toward the notes, tapping a gloved finger over the sketched sigils I had copied earlier. "This kind of necromancy isn't just for show. It's layered, complex, and meant to sustain itself until something breaks the cycle. We saw that firsthand." His silver eyes flicked up, locking onto mine. "But it wasn't meant to last forever. It was decaying before we even touched it."

The unpleasant thought slithered through me. "You're saying... it was set to fail?"

Oberon nodded.

A chill coasted my spine. "Then what was the point?"

His expression darkened. "To send a message."

I swallowed against the tightness in my throat. "To whom?"

Oberon's gaze drifted past me toward the window, where the moon was nothing more than a sliver against the inky sky. "You," he murmured.

My stomach twisted. I shook my head. "That doesn't make any sense. Why would—"

"Because it's not the first time," he cut in, standing from the chair. He loomed closer now, broad shoulders casting a shadow over the table.

My breath caught. "What are you talking about?"

"The creature in Silverfel," he said. "It went for you. It could've targeted anyone, but it didn't. And now this." His unwavering eyes searched mine. "This magic—it wasn't an attack. It was a spectacle. A warning. And it was meant for *you*."

The words sat heavy between us, thick with implication. I took a step back. Oberon's gaze flicked over me, catching the movement. His expression darkened.

I hated he saw it, that my body betrayed me. But more than the lingering adrenaline and the unease clawing its way up my throat, one thought pushed its way to the front of my mind. It was so stark and sudden that it made my stomach drop.

Why me?

I crossed my arms over my chest. "I don't," I stammered, my voice quieter than intended. "I don't understand. Why me?"

Oberon sighed again and dragged his hand down his face. His silver eyes flicked up to meet mine. I felt exposed under that gaze. He had been dissecting every inch of me, peeling back my layers in a way that made my pulse quicken for different reasons than fear.

"You're an herbalist," he said at last.

I blinked. "So?"

His fist clenched. "*So,* herbalists handle matters that others overlook: curses, poisons, remedies, and wards. Perhaps someone doesn't want you to look too closely at what's happening here."

I opened my mouth, ready to protest, but the words died in my throat. He was right. I had been asking too many questions, pushing too hard, digging too deep, and someone, or something, wanted me to stop. My fingers curled into my arms.

Oberon leaned forward, close enough to see the subtle glow in his irises, the faint pulse of something other beneath his skin. "You don't have to understand it yet," he said. "But you need to start accepting that this—" he gestured between us, to the journal, to the remnants of that damned ritual still lingering in the air "—isn't a coincidence."

23

OBERON

Quinn curled in on herself, and her arms tightened over her ribs. She processed and pieced things together just as I did. Quinn didn't let fear dictate her thoughts. She was logical, methodical, and stubborn as sin. If she was shaken, it meant she knew I was right.

The chair creaked beneath my weight when I sat down again. My thoughts churned as I worked through the connections, staring at the sigils in her notes. They still gnawed at me, just out of reach. The mist. How the thing in the field had dissolved, vanishing as if it had never been there. It hadn't just disappeared. It had turned to mist, dissipating into the fog that clung to this cursed land, a sickness.

Something that shouldn't have been able to cross over from the Veil. Something summoned... *a tether*.

My gaze flicked back to the journal, reopening it to the scrawled markings of the sigils we had uncovered. Sigils represented intent and purpose, serving as protection or binding, but something had corrupted them. Turned them into the bones, and the thing buried beneath the dirt. I flexed my fingers as I leaned forward. That was the connection. The thing in the field wasn't just a cursed beast; it was connected to what was buried, drawn to it, and feeding off it. Which meant the body was the anchor.

If this thing was from the Veil, it couldn't exist without being held here. That's why the creature hadn't fully manifested and had dissolved instead of dying. It wasn't just being summoned. It was being sustained.

The sigils didn't protect against the entity of the field. They kept whatever was buried bound to this place. A slow, sick feeling churned within me. "Shit," I muttered under my breath.

Quinn glanced at me. "What?"

I met her gaze, feeling its weight settle in my chest. "That thing isn't just a curse. It's a manifestation, and that means it has rules. Something made it and is keeping it here." I tapped the sketch of the sigils. "And I think it's that body we dug up."

Her brows pulled together. "You think it's tied to it?"

"I think it's more than that. I think it needs it. It's not just a body. It's a fucking beacon. A bridge between here and whatever is bleeding through from the Veil."

Her throat bobbed. "So, what do we do?"

The answer settled in my bones the moment the pieces fell into place. "We burn it."

"You said that last time," she muttered under her breath. There was a beat of silence. "We go at first light."

I shook my head. "I go. Now."

"Like hells you are."

"Dilthen Doe, if that thing comes back while we're out there..." I paused. "I need you alive. You're the one it's hunting." She chewed her lip as I leaned forward. "We need to find out why it's targeting you. Until we do, you aren't just a target. You're bait."

Quinn's eyes darkened. Her jaw clenched so tightly that I could hear her teeth grind together. "I'm not staying behind," she said, unwavering. "If that thing comes back, it will be after me. Do you think I'll just sit here and wait for you?"

I exhaled hard through my nose, determined to keep my voice lowered. "Yes. That is *exactly* what you are going to do."

The firelight carved sharp angles into her face, turning the frustration in her eyes into defiance. Determination. A challenge I didn't have time for. "No, Sinclaire. I can handle myself."

I stared at her, trying to suppress the frustration in my chest, but it wasn't just that. It was something more profound—the feeling I had since that creature in the field had waited for her, hunted her—the same feeling I had when she threw herself at the nightmare in Silverfel without hesitation.

I hated it.

It made my pulse quicken and made me want to reach for her, to anchor her here where I knew she was safe. "This isn't about whether or not you can handle yourself," I said, lowering my voice. "It's about what will happen if you don't."

Her lips parted.

"If that thing comes back while we're out there, we won't be able to kill it. Not yet. You *know* that." My hand curled into a fist on the table. "And if it gets to you before we figure this out, we lose everything."

I lose everything.

She swallowed, but she didn't relent. Of course, she didn't. She never did. I could see the war in her eyes—pride and fury clashing with reason, logic battling the undeniable truth that she wasn't in control. And I wasn't willing to gamble with her life to appease her stubbornness.

"I'm not some delicate thing you must protect," she muttered. Her voice was quieter, but just as fierce.

I huffed a bitter laugh. "Believe me, I know." *Saints, did I know.* There was nothing delicate about Quinn. She was sharp edges and fire, unyielding in a way that made people underestimate her. But I didn't. I had seen how she fought. How she was always three steps ahead, always calculating her next move. She was quick, resourceful, and fucking brilliant.

And none of that mattered if the thing in that field got to her first.

The thought sent a rush of discomfort through me. My mind conjured images I didn't want—her eyes going wide in shock, her body crumpling, her blood soaking the soil beneath her feet. I shoved my chair back, stood to meet her again, and though I didn't close the space between us, I made sure she felt the weight of my presence.

The finality of my words.

"Let me do this, Herbalist," I said, softer but no less severe. "Let me end it."

Her fingers twitched at her sides. The rise and fall of her chest measured the weight of her words to follow. She sighed, tilting her head back to meet my gaze again.

"Fine," she muttered. Her voice was firm but hesitant, wavering just enough to betray what she refused to say out loud: *Don't go. Stay.*

"But if you don't come back—"

"I will."

She searched my face. "You better."

Despite the tension still wound in my gut, I smirked. And she froze. Her eyes flicked to my mouth before she caught herself, tearing her gaze away. A faint blush crept up her neck and traced her skin.

Back in the field, she stared at me that way, her eyes fixed on my mouth.

When I realized she had been staring, my body went rigid, betraying me. It sent a pulse of heat through my gut when I realized she hadn't just *looked* at me; she had raked her eyes over me. Gazed at me. And she blushed from what she saw. She had tried to play it off then, just as she tried to do now.

There was a shift between us, the way the air stretched thin, pulled taut between what we would and wouldn't say.

The way she avoided my eyes and the way she looked at me when she thought I wasn't looking told me she pondered about it. About me. About what it meant that I stood so close, smirked at her, with a darkness pulling at the borders of my lips. Because I hadn't before. And the way she had to force herself to look away, to swallow whatever had surfaced in that moment. It sent a satisfied sensation snaking through my chest.

I moved close enough to watch the flush creep higher. To watch her react. "Are you worried about me, Dilthen Doe?"

She scoffed, rolling her eyes too hastily. It was defensive. Flustered. "Shut up, Sinclaire."

I huffed a quiet laugh, but I knew her well enough now. If I took too long, she would follow. I just had to burn that thing before she had the chance.

THE FIELD WAS quiet without Quinn. The unnatural silence descended, as though the land had stilled in her absence. I should have focused, listened for the faintest shift of wheat stalks, the near-imperceptible rustle of something moving through the dense, stagnant air, and searched for the smell of rot or any sign that the ground had been disturbed by more than just our hands. But I couldn't concentrate. My thoughts continued to wind their way back to her, to how her breath caught, the way a blush rose high on her cheeks, crept down her neck, and disappeared beneath the collar of her shirt, how her lips had parted, her pupils dilated, and the sweat had clung to her, dampening the delicate strands of hair at her temples, trailing the curve of her throat. I had been close enough to see it. Close enough to reach out, to touch.

I wanted to.

I wanted to trace the sharp edge of her jaw and press my thumb against her bottom lip to see if it was as soft as it looked. To tilt her chin up and—

Flexing my fingers at my sides, I forced the thought away. Maybe it was the heat. It had gotten to her first, warped her senses, and made her look at me in that way.

Or maybe it had gotten to *me*.

Because I had smirked and hadn't even tried to stop it. I *hated* it. I loathed how it had happened so fast and how she made it so easy, as if she had peeled back layers I hadn't meant to lose. I couldn't remember the last time I had smiled that way. I had with Garrick, long ago, when the world was simpler. But that was different.

And then the moment had shattered.

Her eyes widened in horror when she realized what was moving beneath her. The instant of stillness before the hand shot up from the dirt, fingers reaching, grasping, and searching for her. The same feeling that had torn through me in Silverfel came rushing back with jagged, splintered edges, embedding itself within my chest.

I clenched my teeth and forced the thought back.

Focus.

I kept moving, each step deliberate as I drew closer to the center of the field. The shovels were still there, discarded where we had left them. The ground remained raw, its edges broken and disturbed from when we had uncovered it.

An unexpected onset of unease settled over me as I wracked my brain, combing through everything Lord Everette had told us, everything the villagers had whispered with fear thick in their voices, and everything Quinn and I had seen first-hand. The things we had fought, the bodies, the sickness, the thin veil of air that made my skin crawl, and the one thing we hadn't considered: if that thing was moving, it wasn't tethering those creatures from the Veil to the crops anymore.

The field had been a gatekeeper. It was a tether between whatever unnatural force lingered and the village itself. And without its anchor, what stopped those things from the Veil from spilling further into Vaelwick?

What stopped them from reaching Quinn?

Lord Everette's warning surfaced unbidden in my mind. The way his face had paled when he said it. His voice had dropped above a whisper as if he risked summoning whatever it was. The villagers had seen something lurking outside their windows. Standing just beyond the glass, watching them.

This was what it wanted. The necromancy hadn't been just a warning. It wasn't a mindless display of power. No—this had been deliberate. A lure. A trap to draw me out and separate me from Quinn.

My pulse pounded in my ears, and I took a slow step back, my fingers curling at my sides. I had walked right into it, right into its design. And now, Quinn was back at the mansion, unaware. Vulnerable.

The air was oppressive as unseen hands grabbed at my skin. My breath became sharper. Every instinct screamed that I was being watched, that whatever had crawled free from this grave hadn't left. It was waiting.

There was a rustle behind me, a whisper in the dead wheat. My focus snapped toward the sound with my muscles coiled. The silence stretched taut. My senses strained against the unnatural stillness, trying to catch what my eyes couldn't see. Then, the air bent. It was deeper than wind or a shift in temperature. A ripple pressed against my back, warping the space behind me, and pulling at the edges of reality itself.

I twisted. The creature stood tall, gaunt, and smiling. The dead wheat remained still around it as if Elduvaris had been reluctant to acknowledge its presence. I met its hollow gaze without flinching, my fingers steady as they curled around the hilt of my sword.

The voice scraped against my skull. It was hollow and grating, brittle bones dragged across rusted metal. Familiar in the way rot clung to memory. It held the same unnatural resonance as we had faced in Silverfel, but older.

"What do you seek, Fae?"

My jaw tightened. My instincts bristled at the weight of those words. It was a test. A challenge. I held its gaze, feeling the pulse of the ancient being staring back at me through the yawning abyss of its eyes. "Where is the body?" I demanded.

Its grin stretched unnaturally wide, splitting its face in two. The surrounding wheat shuddered in response.

"The dead do not linger where they are unwelcome."

I stepped forward. "Then where is it?"

Its head tilted further, its movement sharp and disjointed. It mimicked life without understanding how it worked. It was a grotesque parody of human motion, a puppet whose strings had been tangled and pulled at odd angles. Then it laughed—a dry, brittle sound that scraped against the night. It wasn't the laughter that came from amusement. There was no mirth, no warmth. It was hollow and soulless, like it remembered how laughter should sound but couldn't replicate it.

I didn't let my gaze waver. I didn't dare. But it didn't matter. There was no warning, no motion. It was there one moment and closer the next, as if the distance had unraveled between us. The space it occupied hadn't just shrunk; it bent and pressed against me with a weight that had nothing to do with its physical form.

The air grew dense with rot that was older than decay. The smell of something long past putrefaction that should no longer exist but refused to be forgotten seeped into my skin and bones, crawling up my spine and pressing into the gaps between my vertebrae. It didn't just stand before me—it *imposed* itself, warping the space between us until proximity became meaningless. It was toying with me. It knew, as well as I did, that I couldn't kill it, that I couldn't destroy it without its body. This was a game, and I had to play by its rules.

Its jaw creaked as it parted its lips—if they could even be called that. The voice that spilled into the night was hollow and jagged. *"Tell me, Fae,"* it crooned. *"What do you fear?"*

If it sensed my Fae blood with ease, what else did it sense?

The air between us throbbed with unnatural and probing energy—not physically, but more profoundly. the borders of my mind, testing and pressing as it searched for something to permeate.

Was that what fed it?

Fear?

That explained how it moved, spoke, and pressed closer, invading the space around it, a shifting shadow that refused to obey the world's laws. This thing wasn't just a mindless corpse-dweller.

It was a predator, and I was its prey.

"I don't feel fear," I deadpanned.

The thing laughed again, and the sound came from beneath me, risen from Elduvaris itself, something buried so deep that the weight of time couldn't smother it. It was an awful rattling, hollow chorus that came apart and reformed in the same breath. "*You lie.*"

"I am an assassin," I reasoned. "I have watched the light leave a man's eyes as he clutched his own throat. I have heard the final, gasping breaths of those who realized—too late—that death had claimed them. I have known fear. I have seen it. Smelled it. Felt it clinging to the air like a dying ember." I took a slow step forward, holding its hollow, shifting gaze. "But I do not feel it."

Its head tilted further. The movement was unnatural, as if its bones—if it had any—were barely held together. The laughter that followed was worse than before, a chorus of voices speaking at once. A dozen, maybe more, echoed from the void where its mouth should have been.

Her scream, high and raw, as if ripped from her throat and twisted, pierced the field. My entire body tensed. It wasn't real. It couldn't have been. But my instincts didn't care.

My body, my blood, screamed to run, to save her. I felt the shift in my veins and eyes as I forced myself to stay rooted where I stood. It was toying with me. It had seen the way I reacted. The thing made a sound between a chuckle and a rasping breath.

Mocking. Gloating.

"You have grown soft for a human, Fae."

My jaw clenched, and my teeth ground as I swallowed the instinct to lunge, to silence it. That was what it wanted. It tried to unravel me. Picked at the threads of my restraint to pull them apart. "What do you want?"

The air shook when its voice darkened, turning jagged and violent. *"The herbalist must bleed."*

24

OBERON

My heart slammed against my ribs hard enough to feel it in my throat. The laughter twisted and shifted into a soft and broken voice. *Her* voice.

The breath in my lungs burned, and the world around me narrowed. It mimicked the way she had sobbed in her sleep. How she cried as she gasped awake, clawed at her back, and her fingers curled against phantom wounds that never faded.

The air between us was stretched tight, a thread on the verge of snapping. The creature loomed, flickering between solid and unreal. It was on the edge of existence, shifting, fraying, and bending in ways my mind couldn't accept.

The echoes of Quinn's cries still clung to the surrounding space, hollow and taunting, and needled me in ways I refused to let show. I inhaled slowly through my nose, forcing my muscles to stay loose and my jaw to remain locked so the words I wanted to say wouldn't slip free. It wanted a reaction, a crack in my armor, a way to invade.

Beneath the shifting black mass that passed for a face, something moved. *Watched.* It didn't need eyes. The weight of its stare pressed against my skull.

"You have to do better than that," I said. "If you think I'll run back trembling, you don't know what I am."

Another whisper of laughter that was a layer of rusted metal dragging over stone. It tilted its head again, as though amused. *"I know what you are,"* it rasped. *"More than you do."*

A chill slithered along my spine, and my instincts tightened their grip on me. My fingers itched to reach for steel.

The creature shifted through. The space between us bent, folding around something unseen and older than the thing standing before me.

"She calls your name in the dark."

My pulse spiked.

"She dreams of you."

I clenched my teeth. *Ignore it.*

"She fears for you."

"And?"

It leaned forward with a grin in its voice.

"She will bleed for you, Fae."

For me?

My grip tightened, and my nails bit into my gloves hard enough to draw blood. There was a slow creep of feeling beyond rage, beyond control. An older, deeper, and darker burning pulsed in my veins. It was a warning, a threat. The creature's form trembled as it felt it, as if it recognized what stirred beneath my skin, and it hesitated.

Quinn's voice tore through the night with raw urgency in the stillness. "Sinclaire!" Her voice slammed through me.

Quinn. Real. Desperate. Alive.

My body wrenched away from the creature in a single breath. The wheat blurred past in streaks of gold and black, brittle stalks snapping under my boots. The mansion appeared in the distance, too far, too damned far.

Faster.

Behind me, the air bent. The creature was shifting again. It slipped between spaces and pulled the world apart at its seams. I felt it press against my back and heard the whisper just out of sight. A low, grating sound enveloped my skull. *"You will fail."* I pushed myself to move faster.

"You cannot fight what you do not understand." The voice slithered beneath my skin, needling into the cracks, but I shoved it away. Quinn's voice continued to ring in my ears. And that was the only thing that mattered. I pushed until my lungs burned and my legs ached. The mansion came into sharper focus. Light glowed in the upper windows of Quinn's room. I needed to reach her. To get there now.

A shape flickered ahead, just beyond the fields, between me and the mansion. It wasn't the thing from the field. No. It was a tall and staggering shadow.

It ripped toward me in a blur of jagged motion, faster than a beast that size had a right to be. A force of shattered stone and sheer malice slammed into my chest, knocking the air from my lungs. I hit the ground with a bone-rattling impact;

the dirt beneath me was still warm, as if it remembered the thing that had risen from it. Its form was solid and shifting, brittle bones held together by the absence of light. The smell of decay curled around me, clawing at my senses as it leaned in close. The shriek of scraping metal twisted through my skull.

I snarled against the pressure, gritting my teeth as I urged my mind to focus.

Through the haze, Quinn burst through the mansion doors, her wild strands of hair sticking to her sweat-slicked face. In one hand, she clutched a bundle of herbs; in the other, she held a torch.

My stomach dropped.

Saints, no.

The words ripped from my throat.

"Cin crazui adaneth!"

You crazy woman!

She didn't stop or falter. Her gaze locked onto mine, blazing with determination and fierce recklessness as she stormed forward, firelight dancing across her face. I snarled, shoving against the creature's crushing weight.

"I told you to stay put!"

She didn't slow. "You're welcome!" she shot back, voice taut between frustration and urgency. The thing lurched off me and twisted toward her with a hollow, rattling breath. Her eyes widened, but she ran faster. The creature *blinked*, becoming a mere distortion in the air before vanishing.

"HERBALIST!"

Forcing my body upright, I shoved through the pain in my back and ribs just as the thing reappeared before her. She skidded to a halt before the shifting mass of brittle limbs and clawing darkness. The torch wavered in her grip, the flickering light exposing the jagged edges of its form. The sound of grinding metal rattled around us, its voice a hollow echo that grated against my skull.

"The gods are waiting."

Quinn lifted the torch higher, her fingers curling tighter around the bundle of herbs in her other hand. She gripped the stems as her thumb rubbed the leaves with purpose.

Clever Dilthen Doe.

But not clever enough. The thing shifted in that same unnatural *blink,* and suddenly, it was behind her. Her body tensed with a gasp. I pushed off the ground and crossed the distance between us.

I slammed into it just as the thing reached for her. The impact vibrated through my bones. I grabbed at whatever I could—solid or shifting—and wrenched it away from her. The torchlight flared, casting deep, jagged shadows over its form as it screeched, a noise of splintering glass and torn metal. Quinn stumbled forward, spinning around with wide eyes. I shoved the creature back again, my voice a low snarl. "Run."

Her grip on the torch tightened, her knuckles white against the wood. To my vexation, she lifted her chin and said, "No."

Saints fucking damn me.

The laughter curdled the air, a twisted symphony of voices that didn't belong there. But they were different. Not the distorted mockery of my voice or the warped echoes of meaningless screams. The voices meant nothing to me.

I frowned, and my heart quivered in my ribs as the words snaked through the air. A man's voice spoke, low and coaxing, laced with a hint of sweetness. *"Playing hide and seek again?"* Then a woman's detached voice followed. *"You can't change what you are."* Confusion knotted in my gut as my mind scrambled to understand it.

My eyes landed on Quinn again.

She had gone rigid. Her face paled in the torchlight. The look in her eyes made my chest seize. Wide. Stricken. She no longer looked at the creature.

She watched *me,* gauging my reaction.

The voices weren't for me. It wasn't mocking *me.* They were hers. Her memories. Her nightmares were torn from the depths of her mind and laid bare between us, things I was never supposed to hear.

My veins pulsed as the silver-blue light crept along my skin. My instincts snarled at me to move, fight, and tear through whatever force this thing used to dig into her mind. "Herbalist!" I barked. The thing laughed in a low, rattling and pleased tone and then vanished. It was gone in an instant, as if it had never existed. I moved toward Quinn when I thought it was safe. When I assumed the creature got what it wanted or that it may have been another warning or mind game.

Her focus shifted behind me moments before her body crashed against mine, knocking the air from my lungs as her weight collided with my side. I twisted abruptly, and my boots dug into the dirt to catch my footing. My arm wrapped around her waist to steady us both. Her breath was hot against my chest, and her hands gripped my arms for balance as her body pressed flush against mine.

A sudden, blinding whoosh of flames erupted behind her, igniting the air into a searing blaze that licked up my face and cast everything in a golden-red haze. The creature was swallowed by its inferno. The fire devoured it with an unnatural hunger, crackling as if possessed. Shadows writhed and twisted around its form, contorting in agony as the flames curled over every inch of its being.

It screamed with thousands of voices within a cacophony of agony, loss, and damnation. An endless, wailing shriek rattled through my bones and tore through the night, filled with the voices of every soul sacrificed to it. The sound pressed into my skull, reverberated across my ribs, and dug into my marrow.

The fire became insatiable. Its body convulsed and writhed against the inferno, and its limbs twisted at unnatural angles, struggling against the flames that devoured its existence. The smell of charred rot burned my nose as a final, horrid screech split the air. The creature collapsed with one last violent convulsion. Its remnants crumbled into a heap of bones and ash, scattered by the wind as if they had never been there.

My heartbeat roared in my ears, my body still ran hot, and I still thrummed with the energy of the fight. The ancient and violent pulse through my veins itched for an outlet, and the sight of her defiance, the torch clenched in her trembling hand and her breath uneven yet unwavering, only stoked the fire that burned within me.

I grabbed Quinn's shoulders and shoved her back. "WHAT THE FUCK WERE YOU THINKING?!" I spat, my voice raw. My breath remained unsteady, and my chest heaved as adrenaline pulsed around us. "YOU WERE SUPPOSED TO STAY IN THE ROOM!"

Her head snapped up, eyes flashing with a reckless fury that exasperated me. "And let you die?!" she shot back.

"Die?!" I scoffed. "That thing was testing me, Herbalist! I had it handled!"

"Oh, of course, you did," she replied sarcastically, throwing her arms up as torchlight danced across the determined lines of her face.

My jaw set, grinding my teeth as I glared at her. "You—"

Her body went rigid with a sharp intake of breath. Maybe I had hit a nerve, pushed too hard, or pressed too far. Her scowl deepened. Her breathing became too fast, too shallow, and she swayed. A sick, ugly sensation twisted in me. I lunged forward just as her legs buckled, catching her before she hit the ground.

My hands clenched around her as I lowered us both, her weight slumping against me. "Herbalist." The word left my lips, more breath than sound. "Shit."

An unfamiliar feeling crawled up my throat.

She was still conscious, but barely. Her pulse fluttered when my fingers pressed into her skin. My heart thundered in my ears, silencing the world beyond *her*. "Dilthen Doe," my voice became quieter and filled with desperate urgency. "Hey, stay with me."

A warm, sticky wetness seeped against my palm that should *not* have been there. My stomach knotted, and a slow, creeping dread slithered through me as I shifted her to adjust my grip. My hand came away slick with blood.

"No." The guttural word ripped from my throat. In the chaos, when she collided with me, everything blurred. The fire, the screaming, the thing burning. I hadn't noticed, hadn't felt it happen despite her body being against mine.

My pulse roared when I pulled her closer. My hands moved fast, searching and pulling at the fabric. A dark stain bloomed across her back, spreading fast. When she crashed into me, she had taken the hit in my stead.

"Fuck." The rough and desperate word scraped from my chest. My fingers pressed against the wound as if I could staunch the bleeding. As if I could reverse time and undo the last few minutes. Her breath hitched again, and her body tensed weakly in my arms. I had been so damned distracted. So, fucking focused on its mind games, on its taunts, on the way it had echoed her past, that I hadn't seen the real danger. I hadn't seen it coming.

And she was bleeding out in my arms because of it.

25

EDEN

A FAMILIAR WHITE-HOT pain seared through my back. The pain throbbed, burning from the inside out, and every breath was a struggle against the tightness that twisted through my body. Voices murmured nearby, but were distant and muffled by the relentless ringing in my head. My heart thundered in my ears, drowning out everything else. I pried my eyes open and blinked while the dim candlelight above swam into view.

The voices sharpened into jagged edges against my skull, cutting through the thick haze in my mind. I tried to focus, to separate meaning from the noise, but the words were unintelligible. My body felt sluggish. Every muscle screamed in protest. Fire licked through my limbs, and pain seared through my back as I pushed up onto my elbows. A deep, pained groan clawed its way out of my chest.

Black spots wavered on the borders of my vision, creeping in like ink seeping through paper. I blinked hard, willing them away. The room came into focus in fractured pieces—the dark stone walls, the slanted ceiling, the heavy curtains suffocating the windows. The air was stale.

Dread split through me. My breath hitched, then quickened. Each inhale felt shallower, tighter, as though the walls were shrinking inward, as if the room was swallowing me whole. My arms snapped around me. My fingers dug into my shoulders hard enough to bruise, desperate to hold myself together. The air was too thin, too sharp. My ribs squeezed tighter.

I couldn't be there.

I couldn't—

Oberon was a stark presence against the backdrop of my unraveling senses. His lips moved and his brow furrowed with what might have been concern, but his voice reduced to a muffled echo beneath the rush of blood in my ears.

My eyes darted to the other man. His clothes were clean, crisp, and clinical. *Physician.* The breath in my chest turned to ice. Something metallic glinted in his hand when he stepped forward, and a searing wave of quick, brutal panic carved through me. My throat locked, and the walls of my mind folded in on themselves.

Every sound snapped into focus when he said, "She needs to remove her dress so I can—"

"No!" The word tore from me, scraping through my throat, broken as glass. A violent tremor ripped through my body, and my stomach lurched.

Oberon stiffened in my peripheral vision, his head snapping toward me, but I couldn't bring myself to look at him. My gaze remained locked on the physician. My hands clenched into fists around the sheets, gripping them until my knuckles ached. My skin felt too tight. My breath was too loud, too fast.

I couldn't let him touch me.

I couldn't let *anyone* touch me.

If they saw—

If they knew—

"I'll do it myself!" My voice wavered, but I forced steel into the words. "I don't need help! I don't need you!"

Oberon's jaw locked. His eyes darkened, and tension rippled through his frame. He took a single step forward, and I flinched back. My grip on the sheets tightened. His eyes darted to my hands.

He saw. Damn him—he saw.

"Herbalist," he urged. "You have to be treated."

"I'll handle it myself."

"You can't." His tone hardened. "Don't be fucking stubborn. You're bleeding out."

"I said I can handle it." My throat clenched around the words, strangling them.

His nostrils flared. Frustration bled into his stance, into the strain in his shoulders. "For fuck's sake, Herbalist," he pleaded, voice dipping lower. "Let him treat you."

"Fine!" The word flew out harsher than I intended. My whole body trembled from the effort to keep myself together. Oberon sighed and passed a hand over his face. His posture eased... Until I glared at the physician.

"Cut the back of my dress. I won't take it off."

The physician hesitated. "It would be better if—"

"I. Won't." I ground the words through clenched teeth, daring him to argue.

Oberon's brows furrowed deeper. His jaw set, and his arms folded over his chest. His eyes flicked between the physician and me, but I refused to meet his gaze. My breathing was still shallow. My pulse was still spiked.

"And don't say anything," I warned, voice trembling with quiet venom. "Either of you."

Silence draped over the room. Oberon's eyes narrowed. He looked at me too hard, as if he attempted to read something in my expression that I refused to give him.

My fingers tightened around the sheets again when the physician left, gripping so tight that my knuckles ached. I couldn't stop shaking.

Gods, Eden, get it together.

"Saints," Oberon sighed. The sound of buckles echoed through the room, followed by the clatter of his sword in its sheath and a soft *thunk* nearby. The bed shifted, and my head snapped up.

Oberon sat before me, legs bent and spread apart, with his back against the wall. He watched me for a long beat before lifting his arms in invitation. "Come here, Dilthen Doe."

The door opened, and I went rigid. My breath hitched, caught somewhere between my ribs, refusing to move.

The smell of wet stone and expensive cologne enveloped my senses. The flicker of candlelight cast long, stretching shadows. The soft scrape of boots over the floor echoed through my skull. A voice, low, smooth, and dangerous in its patience, slithered through my mind. "You keep fighting, Darling."

Marcus's fingers brushed over my shoulder, featherlight and deceptively gentle. A mockery of comfort. A reminder that he could take his time. I shuddered, but I couldn't move. I was caught.

Tight, leather-bound hands settled on my wrists.

"Be still." A command. A law.

My pulse throbbed low in my throat, but my body refused to obey me. My limbs remained locked, frozen beneath his hold. This was how he liked it. Not the screaming. Not the struggling. But when the fight drained out of me, leaving only resignation.

I wanted to claw my way out. To rip free, to run, but there was nowhere to go. There had never been. His fingers pressed just enough to make sure I knew he was in control. I pressed my eyes tight, my body burning with shame, with rage, with helplessness.

Move.

MOVE.

DO SOMETHING.

But I could only tremble.

Marcus hummed, pleased. "Much better." The pressure of his hands, the slow cadence of his breath, and the crushing reality that I was nothing more than a possession. "*You belong to me, Eden.*"

No.

No, no, no—

My shaking hands fisted in the sheets. My throat burned with the ghost of words I had never screamed.

I wasn't there.

I wasn't—

"Quinn."

A shudder ripped through me, my breathing shallow and uneven. The voice wasn't Marcus's. It wasn't one of *theirs*. It cut through the noise in my skull and brought me back to the present.

I blinked as my surroundings shifted back into place. Oberon was still facing me, still waiting. His forearms rested on his knees, his fingers curled into loose fists, tension coiled in every line of his body, and his gaze burned with intensity.

No.

He was angry.

He was angry at me.

I was a burden again. A problem to be fixed.

I wanted to shrink under its weight, under the frustration and scrutiny.

The physician's voice pulled me back again. "It may be best if you hold her in place." My body locked up, and my fingers twitched.

No.

No, no, no.

My hands weren't mine anymore. They were distant. Bruised wrists. Shackles. The cool bite of metal cut into my skin, chained me, and kept me still. The walls blurred. My pulse roared.

"Quinn, look at me." My eyes snapped to Oberon's. Keeping me here. That's what he was doing. He extended his arms again and waited. "Come here." It wasn't an order, but it left no room for argument.

My body refused at first. My instincts screamed to recoil, to curl inward, and to brace for impact, but I forced myself to move.

The first movement felt impossible, and the second was even more challenging. But I pressed forward until my forehead found his shoulder. His warmth seeped through the layers between us, a tether within the drowning void. I clutched at his tunic, desperate for something tangible, something real. His smell—leather, steel, and storm-soaked air—wrapped around me, a reminder that I wasn't there.

I was here. With him. His hands found my arms, keeping me in place without trapping me. I drew in a breath and held it as I braced myself for the inevitable.

"The fabric needs to be cut now," the physician announced. His voice was measured as if I were volatile. Like *I* was the danger in the room.

Oberon shifted beneath me, followed by a featherlight graze against the side of my neck. A whisper of sensation so delicate that it startled me. He gathered my hair, brushed it over my shoulder, and pulled it away from my back. I exhaled slowly and allowed my shoulders to loosen.

For a moment, just a moment, I wasn't drowning.

Cool metal touched the nape of my neck, and I flinched. Oberon's hands tightened on my arms enough to remind me he was still there. My grip on his shirt tightened in response, clinging to my sole connection in the present. Air rushed in, licking over raw, exposed skin as the fabric peeled away from my back. My knuckles turned white, and I winced as a sharp sting flared along the wound. A brief but heavy pause hung in the air, followed by a subtle shift of his frame as he leaned forward and pressed against me.

Then, every muscle in his body went rigid.

A deep, raw, and primal vibration rumbled through his chest. A low, quiet growl smothered by restraint. Anger in its most lethal form. The sound cut off when he inhaled, then exhaled in measured and forced breaths, as if he were shoving the rage back, caging it inside before it could tear free. But his body remained taut, locked in an unnatural stillness that felt more dangerous than any outburst.

He saw them.

My stomach twisted as a fresh wave of raw shame surged up, crashed against my ribs, and hollowed out my chest. My fists clenched against his shirt, desperate to anchor myself, to stop the spiral before it consumed me.

He must have been disgusted.

How could he not?

He must have realized that a court herbalist was too broken to tend to others, too damaged to stand at his side, to accompany him and cause him this. I was a burden. I had always been a burden. He must have felt it, too, just as *they* did. They all did. He must have regretted bringing me.

The clinking of metal cut off my thoughts. Followed by the soft pop of a bottle opening. "I'm going to clean and numb the area now," the physician announced.

Something cool touched my back, and I flinched. The contact jolted through me in a shockwave. Then came a sharp, searing bite that ripped me from the present. The past slammed into me. It bled through the walls, through my skin, sinking its claws into my mind and dragging me backward. I was drowning in it.

The stone floor was chilled beneath my knees. The air was filled with the stench of medicinal herbs, but they did nothing to mask the underlying smell of my blood.

Marcus stood before me, arms crossed, with amusement playing at the corners of his sharp mouth. "You should stop pretending, Eden," he mused, his voice smooth and indulgent. "You're no healer." I clenched my jaw. My breath was fast and uneven. I didn't look at him. I refused to grant him that satisfaction.

A gloved hand gripped my shoulder—the physician. "Hold still," he murmured, detached as if I were a mere experiment. An ointment was pressed into my lashings. It was cool at first, but it was a false relief. As the substance seeped into my wounds, the pain erupted into a firestorm spreading through my back.

Burning. Biting. Searing.

A ragged gasp escaped me, and my fingers clenched into fists against the stone, nails digging into my palms. Marcus's breath caressed my cheek as he crouched. Too close. "What is it, Darling?" His tone was sickly sweet. "I thought you liked remedies?"

STOP.

PLEASE JUST STOP.

Tears burned in my eyes, but I refused to let them fall. The walls of the past pressed in, crushing me.

I couldn't breathe.

I couldn't—

I shut my eyes tight.

Don't cry. Don't cry. Don't cry.

But my chest ached, and my throat burned. The pain, the memories and shame that penetrated my bones, was unbearable.

The physician sighed. "I'm going to start the stitches." There was a pause, followed by the faint rustling of fabric. He was readying the needle. "Try not to let her arch her back."

A sharp, grating sound filled the room, resonating from Oberon's teeth.

My jaw locked tight while I fought the instinct to brace for pain. *Find something else. Focus on anything else.* The steady, deep rise, and fall of Oberon's chest beneath me. The slow, deliberate rhythm of his breathing. I tried to match it, to anchor myself to it.

Inhale. Hold. Exhale.

It did little to keep the memories from ripping through the surface and dragging me under again.

A hand rested firmly on the small of my back. "You belong here, Darling." My breath hitched.

No. No, no, no.

The weight of Marcus's palm settled over my spine, fingers spreading, pressing—not painfully, not yet. Just enough.

Enough to let me know he was there, that he owned this moment, that he owned—

I stiffened. My stomach twisted.

Not real. Not now.

The phantom sensation was too much, too close.

My lungs burned with the need to escape, but my body betrayed me. I couldn't stop the slight hitch in my breath. I couldn't stop the way my shoulders drew inward, bracing for what would come next.

Marcus always felt those shifts. And he always loved them. A slow, pleased hum. "There it is." My pulse slammed in my throat, a frantic rhythm that did nothing to protect me. Don't move. Don't give him more.

His fingers traced the ridge of my spine, imitating tenderness. "You always try to run, Darling," he murmured. "Even when you're not moving." His grip tightened.

MAKE IT STOP!

Something touched my arm. It was a deliberate, firm stroke, but different. Oberon's calloused palm pressed over my elbow. "It's okay, Dilthen Doe." His tone was gruff, like he had to force himself to whisper. To make the words come out gently.

My chest ached.

"You're okay," he soothed. "I've got you."

Tears spilled and soaked into his tunic. I hadn't known I was holding my breath until my lungs burned from it. A tremor racked through me, then another. I shook so hard that my muscles throbbed from the strain.

I gritted my teeth, pushing back against the tremors that threatened me. *I couldn't let this happen. Not now. Not in front of him.* Oberon's scent enveloped me again.

Real. Present. Here.

I pushed myself to focus on it. Focus on *him*.

I hadn't noticed when the physician finished the stitches. I didn't even remember him saying he had. My body was locked in place. My mind was caught between the past and the present, drowning in the spaces between them.

"I will apply a salve to the wound to prevent infection. You should wrap it later when you can remove your dress."

I forced a slight nod against Oberon's shoulder before the cool sensation of the salve dragged me under again.

Footsteps clicked against the floor. Slow. Measured. Certain.

Marcus came to a halt behind me. I couldn't see him, but I could sense him. The insufferable presence that coiled around me like a snake waiting to strike. A gloved hand gripped my chin, tilting my head just enough to make my neck ache, reminding me I couldn't move unless he allowed it.

His breath brushed my ear, filled with amusement. "Were you out playing healer again?" My lungs hitched. The chains at my wrists felt heavier, the metal biting into raw, torn skin. Marcus sighed, shaking his head in mock disappointment. "You can't even save yourself."

The words cut deeper than any blade he had used on me.

I tried to pull away. I tried to twist my face from his grasp, but the pressure on my jaw only increased in a silent warning.

His fingers trailed lower.

The calloused hand slid up my arm and rested on the back of my head. "Come back to us." Oberon's body was still rigid, tense with anger, but I no longer understood who it was meant for. My heart pounded in my ears, drowning out the present. The walls felt too close, and unseen chains pulled at my limbs.

'It's my job to keep you safe.' I started shaking again. That's what it was. Duty. Another burden he had to bear. He was an assassin, a man who had killed countless people without hesitation. Yet there he was, forced to sit and keep someone like *me* calm.

The tears flowed uncontrollably again.

Why him? Why did he have to see this? Why did he have to hear it?

Oberon let out a deep, agonizing sigh when the door clicked shut, and an audible, raw sob wrenched free from my throat. I hated he was there to hear it.

26

EDEN

THE ROOM WAS tense when I woke. The kind that thickened the air and made every breath weighted. I shifted, and my breathing became uneven. His muscles stiffened beneath me. He was a storm pulling at the edges of restraint.

Oberon stared at me, unblinking. His piercing gaze twisted my stomach. *He read me.* The moment his stare pierced through the surface, past my defenses, he must have seen the panic lingering in the corners of my eyes and the fear still coiled tightly in my chest. His brows twitched.

It was too much. Blinding pain lanced through my back when I broke the contact too fast. My body screamed in protest, my vision swayed, but I buried it under my perfected mask.

"Herbalist."

I hesitated. My fingers wrapped into the sheets, and my gaze locked on my hands. I knew what I would see if I looked at him—the frustration, the anger that had been simmering beneath the surface since I woke up to the physician.

"We need to wrap—"

"No," I clipped.

There was a pause, a crackle in the silence.

"I will wrap it," I said.

With a sharp exhale, his hand raked through his hair, and his fingers gripped as if he were stopping himself from saying what he wanted to. "You shouldn't—"

"I will," I repeated, steel lining my voice.

The air between us shifted. Tensed. We glared at each other. His stare was threatening. The silver flickered just beneath the surface of his dark irises as he picked apart my reasoning, weighing every word I didn't say and searching for a crack, a way in. But I held firm.

"Fine," he conceded, his voice lower, rougher. "I'll be in my room." He turned before I could see whatever else lurked behind his gaze, and I let out the breath I didn't realize I had been holding. The moment the door shut behind him, my body betrayed me. My hands shook. My breath hitched.

Don't cry.

My jaw clenched, and my fingers tightened in the sheets. *Get it together.* The fact that someone had seen it was horrible enough. The fact that *he* had seen it made the situation unbearable.

I didn't know why it cut so deep, why it hurt worse than the wound itself. Maybe because he wasn't just anyone; he was Oberon Sinclaire, the heartless, unshakable assassin who had never looked at me with pity. Not when I stumbled, failed, or my past clawed its way to the surface. He teased me in the field, that smirk tugging at his lips, a flicker of something softer behind his sharp exterior. He did it again in the room—an almost imperceptible shift in his gaze, as if something had cracked, and a wall between us had fallen.

It was new, fragile, something I hadn't dared hope for.

And it was gone.

The wall was back up—thicker, heavier, and impenetrable. My fault. My stupid, reckless fault. I had overstepped, crossed an invisible line, and shown too much. I wasn't sure what I had seen in his eyes anymore.

Anger? Frustration? Disgust?

A lump lodged itself in my throat. I swallowed hard, but it didn't go away. *I should have known better. I should have stayed back and let him handle it. But when that creature lunged behind him, and I saw its claws poised to strike—*

A violent tremor shook me, shattering my thoughts. Pain flared through my back and forced a sharp breath from my lips. My fingers curled, and my nails bit into my palms as I forced myself to stay still. The wound was worse than I had thought. Sticky, warm blood seeped through the stitches, and a deep, pulsing ache radiated from it. I was more aware of the risks of infection than anyone. The deeper the wound, the greater the danger.

I needed to wrap it. To stop the bleeding. To breathe.

Gritting my teeth, I reached for the bandage roll. The stiff movement sent a lance of pain through my shoulder. I hissed, biting back a curse. My fingers curled around the rough fabric, knuckles white as I forced my body to obey.

"Steady breaths. You've been through worse."

The whisper was faint, but saying it aloud made it seem like I wasn't just sitting here, bleeding and breaking apart, but still had some semblance of control. My hands trembled as I wound the bandage around my shoulder, pressing the fabric against the raw, burning skin. *"Too tight. Loosen it."* The whisper came again, this time sharper, more forceful. I inhaled through my teeth and adjusted the wrap, fingers slipping against the warmth of my blood.

The room felt too quiet. Too empty.

The suffocating silence curled around me, amplifying every shallow breath and every rustle of fabric as I worked. I clenched my jaw. *"Stop shaking."* I wasn't cold, but my hands wouldn't listen.

It wasn't the wound that made me tremble. It was the way Oberon had looked at me. The stark fury in his eyes. The tension that had crackled in the space between us. It wasn't the usual irritation when I disobeyed, not the exasperation laced in his voice when I ignored his orders. It was harsher, colder.

And I had put it there.

The smirk he gave me before I ruined it. The soft edge in his voice when he called me "Dilthen Doe" made it sound like it meant something different, as if it wasn't just an insult and there was more to it. He made it sound warm.

It was gone.

I ruined it.

A bitter laugh threatened to slip past my lips, but I swallowed it. *Of course I did. That was what I did best, wasn't it? Destroyed things before they could hold any meaning.*

I shook my head and focused on the task at hand, grabbing the roll of bandages again. Layer after layer, my fingers pressed into each fold, ensuring it was tight, secure, and precise. The pressure helped. At least it gave me something else to focus on, other than the silence or the ache in my chest that had nothing to do with my wound.

Deep breaths, Eden.

It was done.

My arms fell limp at my sides, my muscles aching from the strain and exhaustion I couldn't shake. My body throbbed in dull, rhythmic pulses. The sting of my wound was indistinguishable from the more profound ache that settled in my bones. I needed rest. I needed to stop.

But my mind didn't let me, because I thought of him again. The way his jaw clenched as he held me, his teeth grinding as though the very act of touching me was a burden. I was something he had to tolerate and endure. The memory hit too hard. I swallowed, forcing down the lump in my throat as I gripped the torn fabric of my dress as if that alone could anchor me.

It shouldn't have mattered.

My hands shook as I lifted the ruined dress, the fabric feeling heavier than it should have, carrying the weight of everything I couldn't say, everything I wasn't strong enough to face. A ragged sob slipped out before I could stop it.

Damn it.

I bit the inside of my cheek hard enough to drag myself back, hard enough to keep the rest of the emotions clawing at my throat from spilling. I couldn't afford this. Not now. Not ever.

I had to fix this.

My fingers fumbled for the needle, but it was small and slippery with sweat. It kept slipping between my fingers. A sharp sting bit into the pad of my thumb, and I hissed, shaking my hand out before forcing myself to keep going.

One stitch at a time.

The thread pulled tight, drawing the fabric together in uneven, jagged lines. My hands shook, the needle trembling between my fingers, but I persevered. Stitch after stitch, the dress gradually came back together. It wasn't perfect or smooth, but it was wearable.

Good enough.

My fingers were stiff and aching when I set the dress aside. My body begged for rest, but my mind still returned to him. To the way he looked at me. To the way it felt to lose something I never had.

Oberon's tunic was stained with blood. He sat on the log at the river's edge, arms crossed, watching me scrub the fabric clean in the river. His gaze had been that usual sharp and unreadable look, but he hadn't stopped me. "You can't keep wearing a bloodied shirt over a clean, bandaged wound. It'll get infected. Which would only cause trouble for both of us."

A scoff tore from my lips as I flexed my fingers, trying to stop the trembling. My wrists ached from the tension, and the deep, raised scars on my arms caught my eye as I moved.

"Remember who you belong to, Darling."

The voice was a lingering serpent that slithered through my mind. My chest tightened, and my breath stalled as if my lungs had forgotten how to work. The room tilted, shadows pressing in on the periphery of my vision. I knew I was still here, but the past had its claws in me, dragging me under.

My knees hit the floor beside the bed, a sharp jolt rattled through me, and I sobbed. It tore through me in raw, uncontrollable waves, shaking my frame until I couldn't hold myself upright. My fingers clenched into the sheets, anchoring me, but it wasn't enough. I despised the overwhelming loss of control. I loathed it all.

I was used to the memories. I was used to waking in a panic and clawing my way back to reality. But I had never been so out of it. I had never felt so damn lost.

THE DOOR CREAKED open. Oberon's presence carried the way it always had, a pressure that settled into the air like a storm waiting to break. It was simply... him.

My eyes remained locked on the journal before me, flipping back through pages filled with cramped, hurried handwriting. My gaze skimmed over old notes. Had we missed something? Had I overlooked a detail that could have made a difference? The thought gnawed at me, a relentless, twisting thing. The corpse was never found, and I needed to be sure the village would be safe.

I *had* to be sure.

My fingers trembled as I traced over a half-written line, a thought I had meant to return to but never did. I couldn't make sense of my own words. Exhaustion was a stone on my shoulders, pressing heavier with each passing day. The nightmares kept me from resting. The stitches on my back kept me from forgetting.

Oberon's boots stopped just short of my table. His stare was palpable. "We received another letter." His voice was steady, but beneath it lay a tension woven into words.

My head lifted, blinking past the thick haze of sleeplessness. The room wavered around me, its dim candlelight casting everything in flickering shadows. Oberon. Stood still, unreadable as always, with the sealed parchment that dangled between two fingers, as if it were just another task, another duty to be carried out. But his posture told me it wasn't.

The golden light from the candle on my desk licked across the sharp planes of his face, catching in the hollows beneath his jaw and deepening the shadows that framed his ever-stoic expression. But there was a hesitation he wasn't voicing.

"Already?" My voice came out rough, strained from disuse. Oberon stepped forward and placed the letter on the table in front of me. The parchment made no sound, but it was heavier than it should have been. I swallowed hard, closed the journal, and pushed it aside.

"Where to?"

"Ruvenmere."

My brow creased as I studied him. "Where is that?"

"Fishing village on the Ruvenmere shore." Though it had a faint edge, his voice was as even as ever. He paused before adding, "How much *do* you know about the villages?"

That question gave me pause. Not just because of the fatigue and ache bouncing through my head, but because I wasn't sure myself. I only knew what the twins who ran the small baker's stall had told me, the vague warnings that were given under scrutiny by my parents, and the minor superstitions raised to my attention by gossiping patients at the village apothecary. I had been too busy surviving to listen well enough to any of it.

I must have pondered over it for too long. With a huff, Oberon continued. "We are being sent to investigate... disturbances."

That one word made my stomach drop. I stared at him, waiting for him to elaborate. When he didn't, I sighed. "Disturbances?"

Oberon dragged a hand down his face. "People are seeing and hearing things," he muttered, as though he didn't want to say it aloud. "Things that shouldn't be there."

A sick, familiar feeling curled through my gut. "Great," I muttered, leaning forward against the desk. "Because that's gone so well for us so far."

Oberon let out a humorless huff. "I'm glad we agree."

I pressed the heels of my palms into my eyes, rubbing hard as if I could wipe away the exhaustion, the weight that clung to me. "When?"

"First light."

I nodded, forcing my expression to be neutral. I should have known there would be no time to recover or catch one's breath. We never got that luxury, but Gods, I was tired. Not just the tiredness that settled in muscles and joints, but the kind that seeped into bones—a slow, sinking weight that no willpower shook.

Oberon stepped closer, setting the letter down with deliberate precision as if its weight mattered. His gaze flicked over my face, sharp and assessing, lingering just a little too long. The scrutiny was a blade, cutting through the last shreds of composure I had left.

He always saw too much. He could read the exhaustion in my features and see through the walls I had built as if they weren't even there. I hated that about him.

"You should sleep." It wasn't a suggestion. It was an order.

A quiet, humorless laugh slipped from my lips. "Right. Because that's working for me."

His jaw tensed, and the silver in his irises flickered.

He wanted to say something. It was in the slight shift of his stance and how his fingers curled at his sides. Maybe he wanted to discuss how I had woken up gasping the last two nights, breath stolen by things I couldn't escape. Perhaps he wanted to comment on how I guarded the stitches on my back or my inability to rest.

He huffed, rubbing a hand over his face as if to scrub something away.

Frustration? Exhaustion? Anger?

"Just be ready." His voice was clipped, final. I nodded once, gripping the edge of the table, watching as he turned for the door. But he hesitated at the threshold. His shoulders stiffened, tension running through him, something unsaid still lodged between his ribs.

"The nightmares." The words were low, quieter. "They're getting worse."

A lump formed in my throat. I hated he knew. Hated that he had noticed. No matter how much distance I tried to put between my suffering and his perception, it was never enough.

"Sinclaire—"

But he was already gone.

27

EDEN

I STRETCHED MY arms over my head and rolled my shoulders as I stepped onto the stable grounds. The crisp morning air was another layer of unsympathetic reality poured over me. Exhaustion clung to me, every muscle heavy and reluctant. The nightmares had kept me up again. Each time I closed my eyes, I was dragged back into that room where the phantom sting of old wounds mingled with the fresh ache in my back. Despite the days that had passed, I could still feel Oberon's hands on my arms, steadying me and keeping me tethered to this brutal world.

Now, he barely spoke to me. I yawned so hard that it turned into a groan, my hand rubbing my temples as I attempted to shake off the lingering remnants of sleep and sorrow. Something in the air shifted, a subtle change that made my skin prickle.

Oberon stood by Neryth, fastening the last of our bags to the saddle. His movements were precise—tightening straps, checking buckles—yet his stony gaze was fixed on me, as though I were nothing more than a fault line in his composure. The sting of his silence was tangible, a raw, gnawing ache that echoed my inner turmoil.

It was maddening how much it hurt.

Caught between exhaustion and a simmering sense of rejection, I blinked against the fatigue and frowned. I wanted to lash out, to demand he say whatever was festering behind that unreadable stare, but I swallowed the urge. I forced myself not to shrink beneath the weight of his assessment.

"You look like shit," he clipped.

I scoffed, managing a humorless chuckle as I ran a hand through my hair. "Thanks," I replied, the sarcasm thick enough to taste. In that brief exchange lay an entire conversation of unsaid words, of longing for closeness and the bitter acceptance of distance.

Oberon grunted and shook his head as he turned back to adjust the saddle. "You sure you won't pass out in the middle of this one?" His tone was dry, edged with the usual bite, but there was weight and hesitation beneath it. His knuckles were pale around the leather strap, and his movements lacked their usual effortless precision.

He was frustrated he was stuck with me for another assignment, wasn't he? Why wouldn't he be?

Rolling my shoulders, I forced a smirk. "If I do, just prop me up against a tree and keep going."

Oberon grunted as he secured the last strap and then patted Neryth's side. "Tempting."

I wanted to roll my eyes and toss a sharp remark back at him, which might ease the tension between us. But the words caught in my throat. It felt different; the banter seemed forced. Hollow. We both played a game neither of us wanted to admit had ended.

Stepping forward, I reached for the other saddlebag, my fingers moving through the contents, more out of restlessness than necessity. He shifted beside me, and the space between us felt vast—a divide neither of us dared to cross. I let the silence stretch before tilting my head. "If you keep staring at me like that, Sinclaire, I'll start to think you care."

His head snapped toward me, his onyx eyes flickering silver for a brief second. "Don't flatter yourself," he muttered, swinging onto Neryth's back as if the moment had never happened.

Pressure built in my chest. "Too late," I murmured, more to myself than to him, and I turned away before checking for his reaction, before I could make the mistake of searching for a truth in his expression that no longer existed.

Maybe it had never been.

TIME BLURRED, ESCAPING me as each moment bled into the next, lacking a distinct beginning or end. The steady rhythm of Neryth's hooves against the dirt should have anchored me in the present, but exhaustion had hollowed me out. It pressed behind my eyes, curled heavy in my skull, and settled deep within my bones.

The ache in my back pulsed in slow, rhythmic waves, a dull throb beneath the layers of bandages. I didn't remember mounting the horse, only Oberon's gruff warning to stay awake and not drift too far. I had tried, but the road was endless and unforgiving, and my body betrayed me. My eyelids felt heavier with each passing breath, and my thoughts drifted into a hazy, half-formed mess of memories and fragmented dreams.

"Herbalist." Oberon's voice sliced through the stillness, laced with irritation. I blinked hard. I had slumped forward, my balance wavering. I caught myself and gripped Neryth's side tighter to remain upright. "Still with me?" His tone was flat, but his grip on the reins tightened, and his shoulders squared even more.

I straightened my spine, biting back a wince as pain flared through my back. "If I weren't, you would have noticed."

Oberon grunted a quiet, wordless acknowledgment.

I let my gaze flick to him and observed as he scanned the horizon ahead of us. His posture seemed stiffer than usual. The set of his jaw was tight, tension taut in his frame, like a wire stretched too thin. Something flickered in his expression for a fleeting moment that I couldn't place before he schooled it back into his usual guarded neutrality.

I wanted to ask how much longer it would be. But what was the point? Time had lost its meaning. It could have been an hour or even a day. My body was running on pure stubbornness. The only thing keeping me upright was the sheer force of my will not to collapse in front of him.

The air felt cooler. Somewhere along the way, the landscape had changed. The damp scent of the coastline permeated the air, blending with the crisp, wet elduvaris. Ruvenmere wasn't far.

Oberon's gruff voice against me pulled me back again. My thoughts were blurred and sluggish, and I struggled to catch up as the steady rhythm of the ride threatened to lull me under again. His arm was wrapped around my chest, supporting me. I must have slumped back against him.

Shit.

A sharp pulse of pain jolted through me the moment I shifted, flaring along my ribs and igniting the stitched wound on my back. I winced, biting hard to keep from making a sound, but it was too late. Oberon knew. "You're awake," he said, his voice gruff.

Tension rippled through me. I forced myself to sit up straighter and ignored how his arm loosened just enough to let me move but not enough to let me go. "I wasn't asleep," I muttered, voice hoarse.

"Right."

I lacked the energy to argue. My back ached, my head was thick with fatigue, and the warmth of his body behind me was too much. It made it hard to focus, and my thoughts were slow and clouded. I needed to wake up, shake the lingering drowsiness, and push past the pain that gnawed at me.

Oberon's hand brushed against my side as he withdrew his arm. I shivered. He said nothing, but the heat of his assessing eyes was on me. He was watching.

I forced my muscles to stay rigid as I feigned control, pretending I hadn't just melted against him. "Keep yourself upright," he clipped. "We're almost there." I swallowed hard and nodded, locking my gaze ahead, willing myself to ignore how my skin still burned where his touch had been.

Ruvenmere emerged ahead, its outline faint through the thick fog curling along the shoreline. The mist clung to the village, shifting and pulsing as if it breathed. It was eerie and unnatural. I blinked hard, trying to shake the exhaustion that fogged my mind, but my vision remained heavy, and my thoughts felt sluggish. Shadows stretched between the buildings, shifting in the dense mist, and for a moment—just a flicker—I thought I saw...

No. That's not possible. I squinted at the tall, broad-shouldered, and familiar figure who stood near the village entrance. *Garrick?* I must have been seeing things.

Behind me, Oberon groaned, his voice dripping with annoyance. "Of course he's here."

My head jerked toward him, still deciding if I was hallucinating or if that was real. "That *is* Garrick, right?" I drawled, as if needing him to confirm reality itself.

Oberon huffed through his nose. "Unfortunately."

I frowned. What was he doing here? I had only seen Garrick once—when he and Oberon had been sparring outside the greenhouse. I had never spoken to him, but his reputation as a flirtatious, reckless knight preceded him.

As we rode closer, the figure stepped forward through the fog. The smug expression I remembered from their match was still plastered across his face as if it had never left. "Sinclaire!" Garrick's voice rang out, far too loud in the mist and far too cheerful for Oberon's liking. He spread his arms wide, grinning like they were old friends reunited. "Did you miss me, you grumpy bastard?"

Oberon groaned again. Louder this time.

Garrick's gaze flicked to me, his smirk deepening as if he had decided how this conversation would unfold. "And you must be the cute little herbalist."

I blinked. "Excuse me?"

The warning in my tone was sure, but Garrick only appeared amused. He ignored me and turned back to Oberon. "I must say, I'm shocked you managed to travel with someone this long without scaring them off."

Oberon muttered under his breath what sounded like "Saints fucking help me" before pulling Neryth to a stop.

Garrick, looking far too pleased with himself, leaned in. "You're fuming. You *did* miss me."

Oberon's glare could have set the entire village ablaze. "Why the fuck are you here?"

Garrick sighed dramatically, as though this were a significant burden to him. "Prince's orders." He let the words settle, watching Oberon's grip on the reins tighten with slow, dangerous intent before adding, "You know, considering your... *reputation*, Alric thought it best to have someone more *likable* accompany you."

Oberon's hands flexed so hard the leather reins groaned under the pressure. Garrick stifled a laugh and turned back to me with a wink. "And lucky for me, that means I get to meet the lovely herbalist."

I shook my head.

His demeanor shifted when I swung my leg over the saddle and slid off Neryth's back. The teasing glint in his eyes dimmed just enough for me to notice it. His smirk faltered for a moment, the edges of it turning unamused.

His gaze flicked over me, and his posture straightened. "What happened in Vaelwick?" The question was light, yet conveyed a subtle demand wrapped in a relaxed, careless tone.

I stiffened, unsure how to answer.

Oberon swung off Neryth behind me, his boots striking the dirt harder than necessary. The impact sent a small puff of dust curling into the cool air. At Garrick's question, his stance became rigid, tension snapping through him. His eyes darted toward Garrick in warning, but Garrick ignored him, keeping his focus locked on me.

I forced a neutral expression, concealing the exhaustion, the lingering ache, and the ghosts of Vaelwick that still clung to my skin. I had learned from Oberon how to control my features and wield silence as a weapon. I refused to reveal my trauma in the middle of a fog-drenched fishing village. "We handled it," I said, adjusting my satchel strap.

Garrick's brows lifted in skepticism, his gaze drifting over me again. Before he could probe further, Oberon intervened. "None of your damned business."

A beat of silence.

Garrick held my gaze a moment longer, attempting to discern something hidden within the cracks. "Right." The teasing glint returned to his tone, though it didn't reach his eyes. "Well, you look like shit."

A dry huff of laughter left me as I shook my head. "So, I've heard."

Oberon continued to glare daggers, while Garrick's infuriating grin only grew wider. "And you look just as angry as I remember," he said.

Oberon clenched his jaw, making it crack. "This is going to be a long fucking mission."

28

EDEN

I DISREGARDED OBERON and Garrick's bickering behind me. Their voices dissolved into a distant hum of irritation and amusement. Garrick was enjoying whatever nonsense he had wedged under Oberon's skin this time, and Oberon, despite himself, had taken the bait. Their energy felt misplaced against the stillness of Ruvenmere, but I didn't have the patience to care.

It had been over a week since we arrived. My stitches ached less. The village healer's teas helped me sleep, but exhaustion still clung to my bones. The missing piece, the thread that tied everything together, remained out of reach. It lurked beneath the surface, tangled in the fog, buried within the symbols and trinkets that clung to this place.

The trinkets swayed in the damp breeze, hollow bones clicked against carved wooden doorframes, and twine and shells rustled in whispers. I made quick sketches in my journal, noting the strange symbols etched into the thresholds of homes and shops. Some looked familiar—variations of warding sigils I had seen in Vaelwick, but distorted, altered in ways that made my gut twist. Protection magic, maybe. Or something else.

A crow perched on the thatched roof of a nearby house. Its dark eyes watched me with unsettling stillness. Another fluttered to a post beside it and ruffled its wings before making a low, croaking call. The birds had been watching since we arrived, lining rooftops and circling overhead. At first, I assumed it was a coincidence, but now I wasn't so sure. *Why were there so many crows in Aurelith?*

Then there was the fog.

It curled between the buildings, thickest near the shoreline, swallowing sound and movement. The villagers moved through it like ghosts, their heads bowed, their footsteps light, and their eyes averted. A stray dog slinked through an alleyway. Its ribs were visible beneath its dark coat, and its ears flicked at every distant creak of wood or hushed whisper. Even the animals here felt uneasy.

The hairs on my arms stood as a fisher stepped onto the dock, his lantern cutting through the mist. He paused, tilting his head as if listening for something beyond the waves before he turned abruptly and retreated into the village's safety.

The wrongness of this village was palpable, much like Vaelwick except... saltier. Beyond the superstitions, there was tension. A quiet, humming current beneath the surface wove itself into the air between the people, particularly between the elves and the humans. Their interactions were careful—two predators caught in a slow, circling dance, neither willing to strike first nor willing to turn their back.

I frowned, watching a human fisher speaking with an elven woman near the market stalls. His posture was rigid, his grip white-knuckled on the net handle. The elf's sharp features were carved into distance, but her eyes flicked toward him with a trace of suspicion. The space between them was measured as if an invisible barrier separated them. The weight of history, long-standing and unresolved.

Had it always been this way? Or was this new? A wound not yet scarred?

I chewed the inside of my cheek, my fingers tightening around my journal as I jotted a quick note. *If the people here didn't trust each other, how did they expect to survive?*

A gull screeched above, cutting through the uneasy silence. It dove low over the market and startled a merchant who swatted at it with a cloth. A stray cat, thin but quick, darted from beneath a cart, chasing the smell of fish scraps, only to hesitate near the elf and human, ears flicking as if sensing the same tension I did.

Despite my attempts to weave the threads together—the trinkets, the symbols, the stories whispered about the mist—I was still missing something. The villagers kept their distance from us. They answered my questions, but only just. I had to pull every ounce of information from them, and even then, I was being fed only what they wanted me to hear.

The mist thickened around the docks, swallowing shapes whole. A group of fishers gathered near the shoreline, murmuring amongst themselves. Their gazes shifted toward the sea, then toward us, as I pretended not to notice. I huffed out a breath as frustration curled tight in my chest. The pieces were scattered before me in a puzzle with missing edges, but they refused to fit no matter how I turned them.

"What am I not seeing?" The question hung in the damp air, swallowed by the ever-present mist.

"Freckles!" Garrick's voice jolted me from my thoughts. I turned just in time to see him grinning, mischief glinting in his ocean-blue eyes. Beside him, Oberon stood with his arms crossed, scowling as if he were contemplating a murder that ought to have brought him great satisfaction.

"What?" I asked, brows furrowing.

Garrick waggled his brows. "Are you even listening to us?"

"No," I snapped my journal shut. "I was working."

"She's ignoring you, Sinclaire. Guess that makes two of us." Garrick sighed dramatically, shaking his head. "Maybe one day you'll develop a pleasant personality like mine."

Oberon's growl was low and irritated, but I stepped between them and gave Garrick a warning look before I shifted my focus back to what mattered. "There's something off about this place," I said. "More than just the fog."

Oberon's petty feud with Garrick faded as his attention shifted to my words. His onyx eyes locked onto mine, intent and expectant. "Explain."

I gestured to the surrounding village—the narrow, damp streets, the way villagers passed each other without meeting eyes, how conversations ceased when another approached, and how the elves and humans coexisted, but not with one another. "They don't trust each other," I said. "Not fully."

Oberon's gaze shifted to scan the interactions I had been watching. At a market stall, a merchant placed change into an elven woman's hand, ensuring their fingers didn't brush. Near the docks, a group of human fishers spoke in hushed voices while casting wary glances toward a group of Elven hunters that passed by. In front of the bakery, a child feeding scraps to a stray dog was only yanked away by his mother when an elven man approached the stall beside them. "They live together, yet separately," I continued in a hushed tone. "It's subtle, but it exists."

Oberon's jaw tightened. "Then whatever is happening here is working against them."

I nodded, gripping my journal tighter. "We need to determine why." And we needed to do it soon.

A crow cawed overhead, its dark form gliding low between the rooftops before perching on a wooden post. *The same one? Or another?* It tilted its head as it watched.

Oberon huffed beside me as the tension rolled off him in waves. I didn't have to look at him to know his shoulders were taut; his jaw was clenched in a way that meant he was calculating.

Garrick, of course, was enjoying himself. "Trouble in paradise," he muttered under his breath, his gaze flitting between me and Oberon with unmistakable amusement. "Tensions are rising. Alliances are tested. Will they overcome the odds?"

He placed a dramatic hand over his chest. "The stakes have never been higher."

Oberon shot him a withering glare.

"Go ask the women about it, Garrick," I said, glancing up at him, hoping to channel his energy into something useful.

His mischievous smirk deepened, as if he had been expecting the invitation. "Are you suggesting that I'm a smooth talker?"

I rolled my eyes. "Might as well use it for the task at hand."

His gaze flicked over me- slow and appraising- his usual humor giving way to something unreadable. It lingered for just a moment too long, just enough to make my breath hitch. "Is that the only task at hand, Freckles?"

Damn him.

Heat rushed to my cheeks, and my fingers tightened around my journal. I shifted my weight under his gaze, regretting any reason I had given him to flirt. I knew better. Despite working with him for only over a week, I felt I knew him well enough not to fuel his flirtations. But he still flustered me, chipping away at my composure with nothing more than a well-timed look and a too-casual question.

The air between us stretched taut, and I felt Oberon's glare, a brand searing into the side of my head. Garrick's hum was smug, pleased with my reaction. I wanted to snap at him, to tell him to do his damn job.

Oberon took a deliberate step closer. "Go," he warned.

Garrick chuckled and held his hands up in mock surrender before stepping back. "Relax, Sinclaire. I'm going." He winked at me with unwavering confidence, turned on his heel, and strode toward the nearest group of women with the ease of a man who had never been denied an audience.

I let out a slow breath and shook my head, pretending to refocus on my journal. But my pulse was still uneven, and my skin was too warm. The man was unbearable.

I cleared my throat, forcing my voice to steady. "We should ask the fishers." It came out hoarse and weaker than I wanted. I clenched my jaw, frustrated with myself, with Garrick, and with the fact that I was still feeling the weight of his teasing and the simmering intensity of Oberon's silence.

That suffocating silence lingered. I didn't dare look at him, but his gaze burned into me. "Then let's go." His voice was calm and controlled, yet his irritation lay just beneath the surface. I nodded, jotting down "fishers—ask about sightings, voices in the fog" in my journal. I snapped the journal shut and stepped forward, Oberon's presence falling into step beside me.

Even as I walked, the tightness in my chest refused to ease. The unspoken weight between us pressed down on me. I needed to concentrate, to decipher this damn village, and to stop being so affected by them both.

The smell of salt and damp wood grew heavier as we neared the docks, the distant crash of waves filling the silence between us. The fishers watched warily, their expressions reflecting the apprehension of those who sensed trouble approaching. They looked at me as if I were the source of their problems. And they regarded Oberon as they would the elves.

A gull screeched overhead, piercing through the tension, yet the weight of their stares remained unyielding. Their hands stilled over their nets and crates, fingers curling around filet knives and rope as if bracing for a fight, not hostile but prepared. Their shoulders were taut, and their eyes darted between us.

The tension rippled through the air. The fishers weren't just suspicious. They were defensive. Their gazes darted to Oberon's ears and stance, and they watched how he moved. They didn't see a knight. They saw something other—someone of power.

Oberon's irritation was palpable in the space between us, in the stiffening of his shoulders and the sharp tick of his jaw. *Based on what he said before, he was used to this. So why did he react this way?*

The last thing I needed was for him to make this worse, so I forced a pleasant smile onto my face. "We hoped to ask a few questions," I started, my voice as warm as possible. "About the waters here."

One fisher, older than the rest, crossed his arms over his broad chest. His skin was weathered, and wind and time had carved deep creases into his face. "Ain't nothin' here for you knights." His eyes flicked to Oberon, lingering for a breath too long before snapping back to me.

Keep them talking.

"We're not here to cause trouble," I assured him. My voice was measured. "We just want to help."

A second man's face, etched by years of salt and sun, let out a rough chuckle. "Help?" He shook his head, producing a dry, humorless sound. "You want to help? Leave."

Oberon's patience wore thin. His arms crossed more tightly over his chest, and a slight ripple of tension was clear in his stance. He wouldn't act just yet, but he was ready.

I pressed on, maintaining a calm and careful tone. "We've heard the stories," I said, allowing my gaze to flick between them as I read their expressions. "The voices in the fog. The figures in the water."

The fishers didn't flinch.

"If the village is at risk," I continued, "don't you want it *gone*?"

Silence.

A few of them exchanged wary glances, shifting their weight from foot to foot as their hands flexed over the handles of their fishing knives and ropes. The elder fisher huffed through his nose, his jaw tightening like a rusted trap. "There are things in those waters you'd best not meddle with, girl." His tone was rough, but an edge of fear lay beneath it.

A prickle traced the back of my neck.

Oberon tilted his head, his dark eyes catching the dim, mist-filtered light. "What kind of things?"

The older man turned and spat into the dirt before meeting my gaze. "The kind that don't stay dead." A gull let out a shrill cry above us, its wings slicing through the air as it veered away from the shoreline. The elder fisher's lips pressed into a thin line, and his weathered hands clenched into fists at his sides. His gaze flickered toward the sea, toward the rolling fog creeping over the dark waves.

I studied him carefully, noting his stiffness and the twitching of his fingers at his sides. "What does that mean?" I asked, keeping my tone gentle but insistent.

The older man's mouth tightened. He shifted his weight, his boots scuffing against the damp dock. "It means what I said, girl," he muttered, voice rough as gravel.

I took a slow breath and forced my shoulders to stay relaxed. *Don't push. Keep him talking.* "So," I tried again, this time softer, letting just the right amount of curiosity and understanding seep into my words, "you've seen them, haven't you?"

A few of the fishers shifted, avoiding my eyes and glancing toward the water as if they wished they could turn and walk away. The older man hesitated. His mouth opened and then shut again. His fingers curled and then flexed. I watched as he ran a calloused hand over his face, wiping at the beads of sweat gathering on his brow despite the crisp air.

"Aye," he admitted, just above a whisper. "More than once."

Oberon straightened beside me. His presence *shifted*—not just alert, but heavier, weighted with understanding. "What did you see?"

The older man's gaze darted to Oberon, then back to me. His lips parted and pressed shut as though he might swallow the words again. But I saw the tension in his shoulders, the tremor in his fingers. He wanted to tell us. No. He *needed* to.

"They look like us," he rasped. "Like the ones we've lost."

A slow, creeping chill slid along my spine. "Lost?" I echoed, my voice quieter now, just above the lapping of the tide.

The fisher swallowed hard, his throat working as he nodded toward the sea. "The ones taken by the water."

I blinked. "You mean drowned?"

A muscle in his jaw twitched. "Some drowned," he said. "Others... they just vanished. Went out on their boats and never came back." His voice turned brittle. Each word was heavier than the last. "But sometimes—" His voice dropped to a whisper, as if the mist curling at our feet was listening. "Sometimes they do come back."

Oberon's tension coiled tighter beside. "What do you mean?" I asked, keeping my voice even despite the chill in my veins.

The older man met my eyes. His were dark and glassy, hollowed by things he had seen and wished he hadn't. "They come back wrong."

The other fishers had fallen silent, their gazes flickering, hands flexing over nets and knives. The younger man approaching us slowed, but the old fisher didn't acknowledge him. His attention remained fixed on me, his fingers curling against his palms as if anchoring himself.

"They don't speak," he muttered at last. "Not at first. They... stand there at the edge of the docks, starin' at us." A sharp prick of unease crawled along my arms. I could see it in my mind—the unmoving, silent figures lingering at the shoreline. "Like they don't know where they are," the fisher continued, his voice low and heavy. "Like they're tryin' to remember something."

"And then?"

The fisher's throat bobbed as he shook his head. "Then they start mimickin'"

My charcoal stilled mid-stroke.

"Mimicking?" Oberon pressed, his voice unreadable, the sharp edge of a blade hidden beneath the surface.

The fisher's weathered face paled. His breath came shallow, his fingers twitching at his sides. "They copy the way we move. The way we talk." He shook his head. "But it's never right."

"What do you mean?"

"The speech—it's delayed," the fisher said, his voice rough as if he were dragging each word through gravel. "Like they have to think about it. Like they're relearnin' somethin' they shouldn't have forgotten in the first place."

His eyes darkened, his gaze growing distant.

"And their voices..." He trailed off, his jaw tightening as if the words were dangerous.

A gust of wind rippled through the mist, shifting it in slow, curling tendrils around the docks.

He shook his head. "They don't sound human no more."

A shuffling sound broke through the thick silence, and my attention flicked toward the younger man who had dropped something earlier. He crouched, fingers brushing the damp wood as he retrieved whatever had slipped from his grasp. When he straightened, he turned to face us, his movements strangely deliberate.

My eyes locked onto his.

A polite smile curved his lips, but its form was wrong. His pointed ears caught the dim light as he squared his shoulders, mirroring the confident posture that Garrick often had. His gaze lingered too long, assessing me with an intensity that raised the fine hairs on my arms.

I redirected my attention to the fishers.

The older man's expression darkened. His eyes hardened. He stared at the dock planks beneath his feet as if the words he intended to say were ones he wished he could bury there. "They remember just enough to fool you," he mumbled. "But they aren't them no more."

A slow, sinking weight pressed against my chest. "That's awful," I murmured.

It was more than fear in his voice—it was grief. The kind that had settled into his bones lingered in the lines of his face. This wasn't just a fisher's tale. This had taken from him.

The silence that followed felt thick, filled with the things he wouldn't—or couldn't—say.

Footsteps approached from the village, breaking the tension. I looked up, spotting Garrick strolling toward us, that familiar smug smile tugging at his lips. I exhaled through my nose and flipped open my journal, trying to refocus as we turned away from the fishers, but the words blurred together, my thoughts still tangled in the conversation's weight.

"Hey, beautiful!"

After a few steps, a hand gripped my arm and spun me around. My heart kicked against my breast, my muscles stiffened, and my free hand twitched toward the dagger at my thigh.

The elf stood too close, his grin lazy and confident. Oberon stopped mid-step. His onyx eyes burned, and his entire body was taut, like a predator that caught the smell of something foul. The elf dared to laugh under the weight of that glare, raising his hands in mock surrender. "Apologies," he said, his grin never faltering. "I was just tryin' to catch up to you."

My pulse steadied as I adjusted my stance, shifting my weight back. He was taller than me, and there was an ease in his movement and confidence in his smile that irritated me. Oberon took another step toward us. I lifted my hand in his direction without looking at him, issuing a silent command. "Go find out what Garrick learned," I said, keeping my tone even. A heavy silence fell between us that carried the promise of violence.

He remained there, likely burning daggers into the elf's skull with a look that could have flayed him where he stood. I thought he might have ignored me for a long, stretched-out moment. That he would have stepped in, consequences be damned, until a sharp exhale cut through the air, carrying the weight of leashed restraint, followed by retreating footsteps.

Oberon had turned and stalked toward Garrick, but tension still rippled through his frame, tightening his shoulders and the way he moved. He was still listening.

I refocused my attention on the elf before me. "So," I said, tilting my head, watching him as closely as he watched me. "Who are you?"

"Fiery one, aye?" He chuckled, his smirk curling like smoke.

I folded my hands over my journal and turned to face him, keeping my expression neutral and giving him nothing to read. "Well, you *did* just grab me."

His lips twitched with amusement, but at least he had the decency to shove his hands into his pockets. "I *did* call out to you, but you didn't stop."

"I didn't think you were referring to me."

His gaze lingered on me as if he were trying to decide whether I was joking. "You are, though." His voice dipped, confidence wavering. "Beautiful, I mean." A brief, awkward chuckle followed as he glanced away.

My cheeks burned. *Was he blind? Why was I reacting?* I cleared my throat and grasped my journal tighter, feeling the familiar pressure of leather against my fingers. The elf shifted his weight, and his smirk faded.

"I heard you askin' questions."

29

OBERON

GARRICK RAMBLED ON beside me, filling me in on everything he had learned. At least half of the information was relevant to the rising tensions between the elves and humans and the power plays that shifted beneath the surface. The rest was just him boasting, spinning tales of his so-called exploits, and dropping the names of women he had flirted with as if any of it fucking mattered.

I wasn't listening. I couldn't. My focus was locked on the man in front of Quinn. He had the fucking nerve to touch her. To grab her arm and stop her from following me. And she let him, without so much as a glance my way, without giving me the chance to guard her.

My jaw clenched so tight I felt the tension crawl up my skull, winding through my bones, ready to snap. I took in every inch of the bastard—his stance, his grip, the casual ease with which he leaned into her space. He wasn't a threat in the way I had been trained to recognize one. He wasn't armed, wasn't calculating his next move like a predator, and wasn't exuding the danger I could carve through with steel. But none of that mattered.

My blood still burned.

Then she blushed.

The heat that curled through my chest was nothing short of violent. A sharp ache pulsed through my jaw as my teeth ground together, the pressure so intense it sent a dull throb up to my temple. This feeling, the twisting in my gut and simmering rage beneath my skin, was unpleasant.

I had felt it before. It has happened too many times. Every single time she interacted with others, they spoke to her, looked at her, and stood too close to her. It was there. This sharp, irrational possessiveness was coiled tight in my chest. It made no sense. It wasn't logical. It had nothing to do with strategy, survival, or anything I had spent my life training for.

And it only worsened after Vaelwick. After her blood soaked my hands. After she unraveled in my arms, and I saw—

Beside me, Garrick let out a low whistle, dragging my focus just long enough for me to register his presence again. I had almost forgotten he was there, too caught in the slow, simmering burn beneath my skin. "What has you brooding this time, Sinclaire?" he asked with amusement, thick with the insufferable arrogance he carried.

It made my fingers twitch, and my knuckles ache with the urge to plunge my fist into his smirking face. "Nothing," I clipped, the word more of a growl than a response.

He let out a slow, unconvinced hum. "Doesn't look like 'nothing'." His gaze flicked toward Quinn. And when I didn't respond, his smirk deepened. I hated the knowing look that crossed his face. "You're staring daggers into them."

I couldn't answer. If I had opened my mouth, I might have said things I wasn't ready to admit—words that laid too much bare and unraveled thoughts I hadn't untangled in my mind.

After a beat, he pressed further. "You look pissed, mate."

My knuckles cracked. The muscle in my jaw ached from clenching. "I don't like the way he looks at her. That's all."

Garrick's smirk widened, and his eyes gleamed with far too much enjoyment. "Like what?"

My glare flicked back toward Quinn and the bastard standing too close to her. I could *feel* the weight of that fucker's gaze, the slow drag of his eyes over her features, the hunger concealed beneath his measured expression. "Like he wants to eat her," I bit out, the words coated in bile.

Garrick laughed. That smug, irritating laugh made my fingers curl into fists. It was mockery—a pointed jab that sank right beneath my ribs, knowing which nerve to strike all too well. "You mean the way you look at her?"

I shot him a glare so fast that my neck popped. My pulse pounded in my skull. Garrick only grinned wider, leaning back as if he expected me to swing at him.

Saints help me; I almost did.

Quinn, unaware of the storm brewing inside me, flipped open her journal. Her focus shifted to the scratch of charcoal against the pages as she wrote.

Garrick hummed beside me, studying the scene with amusement before he stepped forward with an all-too-pleased grin. "Seems relative enough to go... *intervene*," he mused, far too entertained by whatever drama he believed was unfolding. I scowled, following behind him. I couldn't stand there watching them any longer.

"Made a new friend, Freckles?" Garrick's voice was casual, but the glint in his eyes was anything but. He stepped beside her, waiting for a reaction. Quinn ignored him, but her grip on the journal tightened. "And here I thought you only blushed for me." That earned him an elbow straight to the ribs.

Garrick coughed, laughing through a pained exhale, but my attention had snapped to Quinn. The corner of her eye narrowed. Her lips pressed together in that near-imperceptible wince, which she seemed to believe neither of us caught. I reached out and grazed her arm with a cautious touch. "Careful, Dilthen Doe," I warned.

The half-elf's attention shifted to me. His smile remained, but his eyes sharpened as he assessed me. He had understood Sindarin, had heard the warning in my tone, and had seen how my hand still rested against her arm, how I didn't move away.

Recognition flickered across his features. He wasn't as composed as he wanted to be for his smug posturing. His stance shifted with the slightest change in weight, revealing his discomfort.

Garrick let out a low chuckle. "Well, *this* is fun."

Quinn kept writing as though she hadn't been looked at as though she were a prize. Like she hadn't just fucking blushed for him. The muscles in my jaw clenched again, my teeth grinding together so hard that they ached.

Garrick had been right. And I loathed that.

Quinn looked up at me with steady, amber eyes that searched mine. I held her gaze for a breath, waiting for her to speak. She hesitated, tore her eyes away, and lifted her journal between us, cutting off whatever I might have seen in them.

My brows furrowed as I forced myself to focus on the page. The sketch of the trinkets dominated the space, drawn with the same precise detail she always put into her notes. But my focus landed on the small, scrawled words surrounding it.

More than warding charms?
Symbols match the ones in Vaelwick.
Fish bones. Protection or offering?
Why the docks? Why only there?

My eyes narrowed as I scanned the questions scribbled around the drawing, my mind circling her conclusions. She was right. The connection between Vaelwick and Ruvenmere wasn't just a coincidence. A pattern was forming in the shadows, threading through villages that whispered of ghosts.

Her focus was elsewhere when I glanced at her, as if she expected me to brush past it. That unsettled me more than it should have. I *should* have pushed her to rest instead of letting her run herself raw over a mission we weren't even halfway through solving, one that made little sense for us to be summoned in the first place, but I didn't because I understood now.

I didn't know what horrors awaited her when she let her guard fall, when she closed her eyes and let the silence creep in, but I knew they were wicked enough. Distressing enough that she would rather run herself ragged than be alone with them.

Feeling their weight, I dragged my knuckle over the words written at the bottom of the page. "The docks," I murmured. "We need to go there after sundown." Quinn's fingers tightened around the journal. She didn't meet my eyes, but she nodded.

Beside her, Garrick hummed, shifting his weight, his ever-present grin tugging at the corner of his mouth. "Are you guys done flirting?" he drawled in smug amusement. "Wanna fill me in on what's happening?"

Quinn tensed beside me. Her fingers twitched against the journal's worn cover, her shoulders straightened, and she looked like she wanted to throw the damn book at his head. I wanted her to do it.

The half-elf was still standing in front of us, watching and listening. His pointed ears twitched as his gaze flicked between Quinn and me, measuring what he saw. My jaw ticked. I relaxed my posture, but his stare irked me like an itch beneath my skin.

Dragging my gaze away from the journal, I huffed and shot Garrick a flat look. "We're going to the docks after sundown."

The half-elf perked up, tilting his head. "Why wait til' dark?"

Garrick mirrored his expression, crossing his arms. "Yeah, why wait? Wouldn't it be smarter to investigate now? While we can see whatever the hells we're looking for?"

Quinn spoke, her voice level but laced with exhaustion. "Because whatever is causing this isn't going to be standing in plain sight, waiting for us." She flipped the journal closed and tucked it under her arm. The movement was precise and too controlled. "The villagers only report seeing things at night—the voices, the figures on the water. The pattern matches Vaelwick. If we're to understand what is happening, we must witness it ourselves."

The half-elf folded his arms while he studied her. "You believe all that?"

A low whistle escaped Garrick's lips as he rocked back on his heels. "So, we're ghost hunting."

"Not ghosts," I corrected, sharper than I had intended.

Garrick's smirk widened, amusement glinting in his eyes. "Right. *Monsters.*"

Quinn rolled her eyes. "Are you coming or not?"

The half-elf tilted his head while he considered her. The corners of his mouth tipped up into a creeping smile. A smooth, deliberate expression. "You should be careful," he said, voice edged with a tone that peeved me. "The sea doesn't like outsiders poking around where they don't belong."

I don't like people poking around where they don't belong.

His eyes rested on Quinn, trailing over her to the point my blood hummed with irritation. He gave her the look he had earlier, which held far too much interest. He stepped back, turned without another word, and disappeared into the shifting crowd of the docks.

My hands flexed at my sides, my fingers clenching in and out of fists as he left. He knew more than he let show. He understood the significance of his warning, but didn't intend to share it.

Garrick, of course, wasted no time making himself a nuisance. He slung an arm around Quinn's shoulder, pulling her in with an exaggerated scoff. "Please," he said, unimpressed. "I wouldn't miss a romantic moonlit walk with my two favorite people."

Quinn elbowed him off. He emitted a sharp *oof* while she stepped out of reach. "Try that again," she warned, "and you won't make it to sundown."

Garrick clutched his chest as though she had just run him through. "Sinclaire, your lady is mean to me."

I glared at him. "She's not my lady."

Garrick looked between us, his grin stretching wider, eyes twinkling with mischief. "Sure, sure." He clapped his hands together. "So, docks at sundown. Until then, I'll be at the tavern, securing my place as the most charming man in Ruvenmere."

Quinn muttered under her breath as he strolled off, hands tucked in his coat, plotting his next round of debauchery.

I rolled my shoulders. "The docks. Be ready."

Her expression hardened. "I know."

The half-elf's words continued to stir in my mind when I stepped away. *The sea doesn't like outsiders poking around where they don't belong.*

MY KNUCKLES RAPPED against Quinn's door.

No answer.

I stood there for a beat, sighed harshly, and pushed the door open.

Empty.

A slow, simmering irritation turned in my gut. Saints, help me if she had headed to those damned docks alone.

She better have Garrick with her.

The cool salt-laced breeze rushed over me, carrying the smell of brine and damp wood. The air felt heavier. Beyond the dim glow of lanterns swaying on their rusted hooks, Ruvenmoths drifted in slow-moving embers, their pale wings pulsing with a ghostly luminescence as they flitted between the shadows, drawn to the light yet never quite touching it.

The streets were quiet, but not empty. A few stray cats prowled between crates and barrels, their eyes flashing when they caught the flicker of movement. A mangy dog stretched out beneath the awning of a market stall, lifting its head just enough to watch me with wary, half-lidded eyes before settling again. A rat scurried past down an alley as its nails clicked against the worn wooden planks of the dockside paths.

I swept my gaze over the street.

A movement in the market caught my eye.

Garrick was stretched out like a well-fed cat, his usual smug grin plastered across his face as a woman trailed her fingers down his chest. Garrick murmured something low, and his fingers brushed her arm. She leaned in, whispering against his jaw, her laughter a breathy lilt before she slipped back inside.

I groaned under my breath, regretting approaching him.

His eyes locked onto mine the moment I neared. That knowing smirk spread as he tilted his head. "Hey, Broody," he drawled, stretching his arms behind his head. "Where's our girl?"

Our girl.

My jaw ticked, and I glared at him. The words still landed deep and settled in a way I didn't care to explore. "You haven't seen her?" I clipped.

He hummed while his gaze swept over the street until his posture shifted. His smirk twitched, and he let out a sharp whistle. "Oh, boy." His tone had my muscles locked.

I followed his gaze, and my chest tightened. That bastard from earlier was leaning against a market stall, arms crossed, his posture easy and too relaxed. His expression was intentionally vague, but his gaze wasn't. It was locked on Quinn, watching her.

Quinn stood before him, flipping a bundle of herbs between her fingers, her journal tucked against her hip. Her expression was drawn and focused. Not wary or uneasy. She was listening. Taking in whatever bullshit he was feeding her.

She didn't look uncomfortable. But she didn't look aware, either.

A biting pressure built in my jaw.

Everything about it—about *him*—itched beneath my skin, needling at a part of me I couldn't name. He leaned into her space, and his gaze flickered over her with quiet calculation. The way she tilted her head to listen, unbothered.

Garrick hummed beside me, shoved his hands into his pockets, and exuded nothing but casual amusement.

My irritation flared hotter.

"You know," he mused, tilting his head, "what he said about the ocean seemed... off-putting."

I tore my gaze away from Quinn long enough to glare at him. "You think?"

He huffed a chuckle. "I mean, yeah, the whole 'the sea doesn't like outsiders poking around' bit isn't quite comforting. Not to mention, he seems awfully interested in her." His eyes flicked back to Quinn, and his smirk grew. "Can't say I blame him."

I could have responded to that. Could have said anything—a sharp retort, a cold dismissal, a warning.

But the half-elf had leaned in. Quinn didn't flinch or step back. She tilted her head closer again, as if what he was saying held any fucking value at all. A slow, simmering heat burned through my veins. Garrick let out an amused hum. "You could go over there, you know."

I ground my teeth. "She's not alone."

He snorted. "No, but she sure as hells isn't with us." He tilted his head toward me, watching, waiting for a reaction.

My expression remained flat.

"So," he continued, stretching the word, "are you going to do something about it? Or are you just going to stand here brooding like the jealous, overprotective—" I shot him a warning look so sharp it could have drawn blood. He raised his hands in mock surrender, but his smirk never faded. "Fine, fine," he said, clearly entertained by the situation. "But if she drowns because you let that half-elf sweet-talk her onto a boat, that's on you, Sinclaire."

My patience snapped. Garrick chuckled behind me as I strode toward her, my pulse hammering with violent and undeniable rage. The bastard was still speaking, still holding her attention as if he had any fucking right to it. She listened intently, nodding, her brows furrowed in thought as she rubbed a bundle of herbs between her fingers.

He was still looking at her.

And she was still letting him.

The half-elf's gaze flicked up and locked onto mine when I stopped beside her, lips curling at the edges, as though he knew something I didn't. He believed he had the right to stand there, talk to her, and look at her like that.

Quinn sighed when she felt my presence.

"You must stop doing this," I insisted.

She turned to me with a strained expression. "I don't have to wait for you, Sinclaire. The village is small enough that you would hear me from your room if I screamed out here."

I became rigid, my fingers twitching at my sides. She didn't know how those words affected me or how much they infuriated me. She thought it was a joke, just a throwaway statement to dismiss my concerns. She failed to realize that the thought of her voice cutting through the night in fear or pain made my blood run ice cold.

"I'm fine," she continued, brushing past me as if it was nothing.

"Horseshit."

Her eyes whipped to mine, filled with fire.

"At least keep Garrick with you if you refuse to let me guard you."

She scoffed and lifted her chin in defiance. "I don't need a guard."

My eyes locked on the half-elf as she spoke. A knowing gleam laced his features. His eyes, that smirk. It was a flicker of satisfaction that vexed me.

That bastard knew. He understood she was more than just an herbalist. He had been watching her, listening to her, and now he believed she was vulnerable. I wouldn't allow him to think that. I refused to let him believe she was unclaimed. Unprotected.

"Your back suggests otherwise," I ground out.

Quinn froze. Hurt flickered across her features before her mask snapped back into place, morphing into a pure, blistering rage. Her hand formed a fist at her side. "Fuck you," she snapped.

I stepped closer, leaning down and tilting my head as my voice lowered to a provocative tone. "Here?"

Her nostrils flared, and her eyes narrowed. My words sounded sensual to others—a challenge laden with implications. Only we recognized that the weight of those words had nothing to do with intimacy. The half-elf would hesitate before touching her again.

Quinn, however, appeared as if she wanted to punch me.

Good.

Do it.

Show him.

Garrick wedged between us with a chuckle and pushed me back. "Down, boy." His hand was firm against my chest, but I hardly felt it past the storm in my head. "The sun is about to set," he added. "We should head to the docks soon. And we can't do that if you two rip each other's throats out in front of the market stalls."

Quinn handed two bronze quince to the Elven woman behind the stall before shoving the herbs into her satchel with more force than necessary. "I wasn't—" She cut herself off, chewing her lip.

I rolled my shoulders back and compelled my muscles to relax. "Let's just go," I muttered.

She refused to look at me.

The piece-of-shit leaning against the stall still hadn't moved. Still had that same smug look in his eyes. But he had enough sense to keep his damn mouth shut. I gave him one last glare, walking away before I gave in to the urge to bash his skull into that stall and make him eat the gravel at my feet.

Quinn fell into step beside Garrick, maintaining just enough distance to make her point. Garrick, of course, was all too eager to break the tension. "Well, that was some unresolved energy," he drawled, loud enough for me to hear. I shot him a glare. He smirked. "Just saying, you two argue like lovers," he added. His grin widened when Quinn's face paled.

My pace quickened toward the docks. If I stayed near Garrick any longer, I *would* rip someone's throat out.

30

OBERON

THE SKY STRETCHED in dull orange and gold, casting the water in flickering, dying light. The sun had vanished, swallowed by the horizon, and the air had changed with it. The salt in the breeze felt heavier and thicker with moisture, and the mist creeping along the docks had grown denser. I stood at the edge of the furthest pier and stared out over the darkening waves, but I wasn't really looking at them.

Something was off.

The subtle unease slithered beneath my skin as I rolled my shoulders and flexed my fingers at my sides. The weight of my sword and the pressure of my belts were grounding, but the tension in my chest had nothing to do with a potential threat.

Not yet, at least.

Behind me, the soft rustle of pages turning mixed with the crash of waves. Quinn was still writing, chasing answers as the lanterns flickered around her. Her usual energy had dulled over the past few weeks. Her fire was muted, her words were softer, and her movements were slower and less decisive.

The stitches in her back had healed. It was in the way she moved. Her steps weren't as rigid, no longer careful to avoid pulling at the wounds. She no longer tensed when she reached for something or turned too fast. She still favored one side and adjusted the strap of her satchel to keep it from pressing against the worst of it, but she didn't wince as often.

I checked on her at night, sat with her when she woke, and waited for the haze of sleep to fade from her eyes before she inevitably sent me away, brushing it off with another muttered excuse.

I let her. Every time. But I wasn't blind.

She slept more, but not *better*. The sleep that dragged her under was heavy but never brought rest. She woke with the same tension in her shoulders and a guarded look that told me she had spent the entire night fighting off the demons that plagued her past.

Something had broken in her in Vaelwick...

And I didn't know how to fucking fix it.

"You know, Freckles, I could sit here and watch you work all night."

My tongue pressed against my canine.

Of course.

Garrick leaned back with his hands behind his head, watching her with that damn smirk. "It's fascinating, really," he continued. "The way you furrow your brows as if you're solving the kingdom's greatest mystery. Almost makes me believe you're thinking about me."

"I'm thinking about how best to poison your drink without anyone noticing." There was a smirk in her voice, but the way she said it made my hands curl into fists.

"Saints, you truly are cruel," Garrick sighed. "If I didn't know better, I'd say you were flirting with me."

My chest tightened.

"If that's flirting, I'm out of practice."

I resisted the urge to turn around.

"I would be more than happy to help you get back into it," Garrick teased.

She laughed.

An actual laugh. Not the strained amusement I had heard from her for days, the polite scoffs or the forced humor. A genuine, tired laugh that sent an intense and unfamiliar feeling through me. *I fucking hated it.*

I hated that I wanted to hear more of it, and that it wasn't me who pulled it from her. My fists tightened again. That wasn't how I was supposed to think. This shouldn't have mattered. *She* wasn't supposed to matter.

But she did.

Saints, *she did.*

I swallowed hard, blinking at the waves, but my mind refused to quiet. It drifted back, unbidden, to the field in Vaelwick—the heat, the smell of humid soil and crushed grass thick in the air. Sweat had clung to our skin as exhaustion settled into our limbs, and she had kneeled beside me. Her fingers glided across the dirt, tracing the sigils carved into the soil.

Her brows had furrowed in concentration, lips parted. Saints, the way she looked at me had sent heat pooling in my gut and licking up my spine.

The usual sharpness in her gaze had softened; her pupils were wide and dark, and her breath had become shallow. Hesitant. She had stammered. A rare crack in the wall she always kept in place.

It was unlike her, the hesitation, the flicker of uncertainty. And in that moment, it had undone me. She had been so close that I could feel the warmth radiating from her skin, see the delicate flush rising on her throat, and hear the unsteady hitch in her breath.

I wanted to close that distance. I nearly leaned in, almost let myself drown in that unbearable pull, losing the fight against the desires of my Fae blood. I was on the verge of discovering how those lips tasted, how she sounded when she didn't hold back every word. I hadn't let myself think of it much after that. It had been easier to shove it away, to drown myself in the anger instead. In the pain of her pulling back. How her walls went back up after that night.

With a steadying breath, I forced my hands to relax and stretched my fingers.

"There she is," Garrick murmured, his voice quieter now.

My muscles loosened. The tension should have faded, but the air shifted. It was subtle, like the tide pulling back before a wave, a second of stillness before impact. The breeze carried the sharp tang of salt, but a cloying and insidious rot lurked beneath it. It was a smell just on the edge of awareness that crept into my senses.

My shoulders turned rigid again.

The water lapped rhythmically against the pier as it had all evening. But now, the sound felt hollow. The trinkets hanging over the doorways clinked in the wind, their chimes fragile, whispered warnings carried on the breeze.

"You feel that?" Quinn's voice was quiet, but there was a weight behind it.

Garrick's crate creaked as he stood up straight. "Aye."

My fingers reached for the hilt of my sword as I stepped forward. The stench was the unmistakable odor of decaying flesh rotting beneath the waves—drowned and forgotten, bloated, waterlogged, and left to fester in the deep before washing onto shore. The smell clung to the mist, seeping into my lungs and coating my tongue with its vile density.

The fog was no longer just a veil over the village; it felt alive. It shifted, curled, and pressed in on us. One moment, it was still and silent; the next, the world tilted as if an unseen force had exhaled a deep breath from the Veil.

Stitched together from the darkest recesses of nightmares, a towering figure rose from the mist. Its limbs were too long. Its fingers—ragged claws—twitched in anticipation, as if the air were a meal for its hunger. The mist curled around it, clinging to its form, reluctant to release it. Even the fog feared what had emerged from the depths.

Its head was an animal skull, far too large for its skeletal body, bleached and cracked with age. Broken horns jutted from its crown, jagged and twisted, creating a cruel parody of something long dead. Where its eyes should have been, only dark, swirling voids observed us with intelligence beyond comprehension. The emptiness within those sockets seemed alive, swirling as if it recognized us.

A sickening gurgle rose from deep within its chest. It was a wet, choking sound, as if it were drowning in its own decay. Its jaw cracked wide, unhinging in a monstrous rift, and the noise twisted into a rattling, warbled laugh that chilled me to my core and tore at the fabric of reality.

The stench thickened as a rancid gust swept over us. The thing approached with every breath. In one fluid motion, it stepped forward, its shadow stretching over the pier.

Another step. And another.

Then it was gone.

The mist swallowed it whole, just as silently as it had come.

The dock beneath us groaned in protest, shuddering as it sensed the creature beneath its planks. A deep crack ran through the wood, splitting the pier as what lay below awakened. The air turned damp, thick with the stench of rotting seawater. Quinn gasped behind me, her breaths becoming shallow and jagged.

The fog curled around her. Its tendrils snaked up her legs as it breathed, moved, and desired.

"Sinclaire," her voice strained with a tremor of fear. I turned toward her, every instinct screaming at me as my body moved toward her.

The dock cracked underfoot as a blur of mist and bone lunged forward. I dove to the side, rolling across the slick planks just before it reached me. A jagged limb tore through the space I had just occupied with a spray of splinters.

Garrick pulled Quinn behind him with one arm, his sword drawn in the other. "Stay behind me, Freckles," he said over his shoulder, half-grinning. "I would rather not die by Sinclaire's hands later because I let you get hurt."

"No!" Quinn fought against him, her voice filled with panic. "Garrick, move!"

"Saints, Freckles, let him handle it!"

I pushed up from the dock and unsheathed my sword just as the creature lunged again. Bone met steel with a force that rattled my arms. The impact echoed across the water as I skidded backward on the damp wood.

It lashed at me faster this time. Clawed limbs struck in whips of movement, each one reforming the moment I cut it. It didn't bleed. Didn't wane. It just kept attacking.

Its eyes—or where they should have been—locked on mine with a hollow hunger as though it recognized me. Quinn's voice cut through the chaos, but I couldn't make out the words. I shoved my blade into the creature's side, forcing it back a step. The dock groaned under our weight before it stood still. The surrounding mist screamed with intention.

A sickening, wet gurgle filled the air.

Laughter that sounded as though it was choking on bile, the echoes of a thing that should not have been alive. The surrounding pressure tightened, and the mist constricted until it became tangible, heavier. It scraped down my spine and clung to the back of my mind.

H. L. RILLON

The dock beneath us creaked again as the wood strained, trying to pull away from whatever stirred beneath it. The mist, once drifting and passive, turned solid. Dense and damp, it pressed in from every side, breathing against my throat. It had weight now. Intention.

And it focused on her.

"You are soft, Fae." The voice coiled around me with malice. *"You fear for her."*

My grip tightened on the sword hilt, and the pulse in my jaw became a drumbeat of war. "No."

Another hollow, rotted, and triumphant laugh spilled from the mist. *"She will bleed for you."*

The words provoked. The fog pulsed around us with purpose, feeding off the moment—off me. It saw what I refused to acknowledge: that I thrived in battle. I embraced death. Yet the thought of *losing her* was too much to bear, and I didn't even understand why.

Her breathing was heavy nearby, close enough to feel through my heightened senses. There was a hint of salt in her hair and panic in her demeanor that she tried to conceal. And saints help this thing. If it ever laid a finger on her, I wouldn't just kill it.

I would fucking *unmake it.*

The beast stepped forward again, its sockets swirling with blood lust. "Sinclaire!" Her cry echoed in my chest and reverberated through the air. The surrounding mist shuddered as if it couldn't bear the sound of her voice. It knew what was coming. It screamed in recognition when a burning wave surged through me, flooding my veins and lighting every nerve on fire. My vision pulsed, and my veins burned with the fire that woke within me in Silverfel.

"Nia nin firn bodui," I growled, thrusting my sword into the dock. Silver-blue light shot down the blade and branched across the damp wood in strokes of lightning. The thing wailed, a guttural, high-pitched scream that raked across my skin before it vanished. The mist recoiled with a violent, visceral retreat, hissing and writhing as it crackled with the blue light. Only the lingering, sour smell of rotting seawater and the acrid stench of decay permeated the air. The silence that followed was unnatural.

Garrick stood in front of Quinn, his hand still on her arm as he braced her front, his mouth agape, confused by what had happened. His eyes narrowed on me. There was no smirk on his lips. No teasing glint in his gaze.

"What the fuck was that?" he muttered, his voice quieter than usual. My mind was still racing, and my senses heightened. The mist receded toward the ocean, slinking away as though it had been wounded and retreating into the dark waters from which it had come.

"A warning."

THE DIM ROOM held a single candle on the table that cast flickering shadows along the walls. The smell of roasted meat and herbs from the tavern lingered in the air, but it didn't settle the constriction in my chest. We sat in silence, the events at the docks still preying on my mind.

Garrick had no problem cutting through the thick tension with his usual lack of grace. "So, was Vaelwick like that too?" he asked, muffled by the food he was still chewing.

My gaze flicked to Quinn. Her fingers brushed the edge of her journal, organizing her notes as if she were somewhere else. I averted my eyes.

"Something like that," I muttered.

Garrick snorted. "Something like that? You mean to tell me you fought another mist-crawling, nightmare-breathing fucker and didn't think to warn me?"

I shot him a glare. "I didn't have the time to draft a letter, Garrick."

He shrugged, tearing a piece of bread with his teeth. "Still. It would have been nice to know we were walking into whatever that was." He gestured to the window with his bread. "You two have been incredibly cryptic."

Quinn sighed, flipping another page in her journal. "The creature in Vaelwick was different," she said. "That one was tethered to the fields. This one was more mobile. It chose its target."

Her.

It chose *her.*

I swallowed the growl in my throat and flexed my fingers as I leaned back in my chair. Garrick wiped his mouth with his sleeve. "Right. And it just *happened* to target you, Freckles?" He quirked a brow. "Like the thing in Vaelwick, I assume?"

Quinn went rigid for a moment. With a tight smile, she shook her head. "Probably just bad luck."

Garrick hummed, unconvinced, and flicked his gaze in my direction. I gritted my teeth. It wasn't bad luck, and she damn well knew it. Garrick propped his elbow on the table, rubbing his chin as he glanced between the two of us. "Alright," he drawled, breaking the silence. "What happened in Vaelwick?"

I leaned back in my chair with a sigh. "What do you think happened?"

Garrick raised a brow. "Well, judging by the way she looks like she's about to be sick, and you look ready to kill something, I'd say it wasn't a pleasant stroll through the wheat fields."

A wave of memories crashed into me. The way it slammed into us, sending Quinn barreling across the dirt, her body hitting the log with a thud, the frantic scramble. Running through the rotting wheat and woods as the ground lurched, bodies rose, each turning toward her. Ignoring me. How the thing in the field mimicked her scream.

How, for the first time in years, my chest seized.

Fear.

For her.

For the blood dripping from my hand, from her, warm and slick as I pulled her against me, as I tried to determine the severity of the wound. Fear for the way she reacted as her exhaustion and pain stole the fight out of her.

I forced myself to breathe while my fingers twitched against the grain of the table. Garrick's smirk faltered. "Hey," he said, gentler now. "I was just—"

"I don't want to talk about Vaelwick," Quinn cut in, her voice firm but quiet. Her hands trembled before she clenched them into fists.

Garrick's brows furrowed. His usual teasing demeanor dropped. His gaze flickered to me, waiting for an explanation. I pushed my tongue against the inside of my teeth and sighed. "It was worse than this," I muttered. "Much worse."

Quinn swallowed hard, shoving her chair back as she stood. "I need air."

Garrick stared after her until the door closed, then returned to me. "What happened to her, Sinclaire?"

GARRICK ECHOED ME in disbelief, "Necromancy?"

I nodded once. "It was something buried in the field." My voice sounded tight, strangled. I swept a hand through my hair. "They were giving sacrifices. It was... too much."

The weight of it pressed against me when the memories clawed their way to the surface. Every corpse had moved toward her as if they had known her, as though she were the reason they could move. I remember her eyes before she slammed into me. The thing in flames.

"And then Quinn..." The words caught in my throat. My hands curled into fists.

Her blood was on my hands. Her voice was hoarse with pain. The way she fucking looked at me, the way she flinched with her fists clenching the sheets as she yelled at me, at the physician—

"Fuck."

I shoved myself up from the chair, unable to sit still anymore. The room felt cramped. The air was too heavy. Garrick observed me, pondering whatever sarcastic comment he wanted to say. He let out a low breath. "Saints, Sinclaire..."

My heart was still hammering. My muscles coiled tight as my mind replayed every second. I tried to push it away. The wood creaked when I pressed my palms against the windowsill and angled my body, slowing my breaths. My head was spinning, tangled in anger, frustration, and helplessness.

Until I looked out at the street.

Quinn stood near the edge of the market, flipping through her journal as someone walked toward her from the docks.

"Sina fucking fíriel."

This fucking woman.

The words rumbled from my chest, burning through my teeth as I pushed off the window. Garrick's chair scraped against the floor behind me when I yanked the door open, but I didn't wait for him.

The hall blurred past me as I stormed down the stairs, boots striking the wooden planks with purpose. That bastard was too close. Too fucking confident. And Quinn wasn't paying attention. Or maybe she was. She might have thought he was another harmless flirt.

My fists curled tighter.

By the time I reached the tavern door, my blood pounded in my ears, drowning out the surrounding chatter. I shoved it open and stepped into the street, my eyes locked on them. The arrogant half-elf had stopped a few feet from her, hands tucked into his pockets, head tilted like he was playing some charming fucking game. Quinn hadn't looked up; she was too focused on her notes.

But he was staring at her as if he had every fucking right to. As if he knew something I didn't. He used her to taunt me—to test me. My gut twisted. *No.* I refused to give him the chance.

His lips curled at the edges, amusement flickering in his gaze when he turned his head to look at me.

I was going to wipe that fucking smirk off his face.

The half-elf pulled a hand out of his pocket and spoke in a casual tone. "Still scribbling away, beautiful?" His fingers brushed against the small of her back, and Quinn winced.

The world tunneled until there was no thought, just instinct—pure, seething, and unrelenting rage. My hand landed on her arm as I grabbed Quinn and yanked her aside, pulling her just out of reach of his filthy fucking hands before my fist collided with his face. Bone crunched beneath my knuckles with a sickly satisfying sound. The bastard stumbled back as blood dripped from his nose. His hand shot up to clutch his face, eyes wide with shock.

I hoped it was broken.

Hells, I hoped I had shattered his entire fucking face.

A few villagers gasped. The surrounding market froze, and the hum of conversation ceased.

I took a step forward, towering over him as he steadied himself and spat a mouthful of blood onto the cobblestones.

"Touch her again," I growled, my voice low, guttural, and deadly. "And I'll tear your fucking arm off." His stunned expression flickered. His eyes darted to Quinn, then to me.

The bastard let out a hoarse laugh, blood still dripping from his nose as he wiped at it with the back of his hand. Mocking. "Didn't think you'd be the jealous type, Fae," he mused. His grin returned, despite the pain etched on his features.

I didn't move. Didn't so much as blink.

Because I wasn't jealous, I was *pissed*. Pissed that he dared to touch her, that she had winced and still hadn't stepped away from him, and that she had even let him get that close. My fists clenched at my sides, aching to finish what I started. To drive another hit into his smug fucking face and guarantee he never touched her again.

31

EDEN

A SUDDEN CRACKLE of tension set my nerves on alert. "Still scribbling away, beautiful?" His hand brushed against my back. Dull pain radiated from where he touched, and I winced before a force yanked me aside. The elf was gone from my peripherals, replaced by a larger, aggressive mass.

The crack of bone echoed around us. I gasped, and the elf staggered back, blood gushing from his nose. His hands shot up to clutch his face as his expression shifted from shock to one of impressed surprise. The market went silent as conversations stopped and people watched.

Oberon took a step forward, looming over the man. His entire body was coiled tight, and his breathing was ragged with restrained violence. The shadows that clung to the sharp angles of his face made him appear less like a knight and more like the assassin he was. "Touch her again," he growled, his voice so low that it sent shivers down my spine. "And I will tear your fucking arm off."

My stomach dropped.

Garrick's stopped just behind me, panting. "Oh shit. Are you okay, Freckles?"

My fingers wrapped around Oberon's arm and gripped harder than I meant to, as if I could hold him back. "I'm fine," I murmured, trying to steady my breath and break through the tension that was wrapping around us like a noose. "Sinclaire, your eyes. You can't do this here." Heat radiated from him, and tension thrummed through his body. His breathing remained ragged but controlled.

"Didn't think you'd be the jealous type, Fae." The elf grinned. Not afraid or concerned. His lips twitched, wanting to smirk more, but he was holding back. He edged Oberon, testing him to see how far he could push. Seeing if he cared.

Gods.

My grip tightened on Oberon's sleeve. It was wrong. Something was amiss about this elven man from the moment he walked down the docks. The way the fishers had stared at him. The way he spoke of the sea, knowing yet uncaring.

The way he looked at me.

It hadn't just been arrogance. It had been calculated. A push. A test. A trap. Yet Oberon still dared him. His fingers twitched at his sides, and his body remained taut.

He was about to snap.

A slow whistle cut through the tension. "Well, this just got interesting," Garrick muttered behind us.

My grip tightened. "Let's just go." I stepped back. It took every ounce of effort and willpower to pull Oberon away. Even as I tugged him toward the tavern, the tension remained coiled inside him, waiting, seething, and ready to strike the moment I let go.

Garrick glared at the elf as we turned away—an expression that I hadn't seen from him before. Which meant he knew what Oberon's reaction meant too. If the elves had been wary of us before, they would become even more cautious now. The last thing we needed was Oberon—a Fae—giving them a reason to distrust us even more. The last thing *he* needed was to have even more eyes watching his every move, waiting for him to slip.

And if that elf was tied to the thing in the sea, if he wasn't just another man with too much confidence, then it knew how to rile him. It had seen his rage. It had seen his weakness.

Garrick exhaled when we stepped into the room and rubbed a hand over his face. "I've never seen you crack on someone except in battle," he muttered, leaning against the table. His usual lighthearted tone was gone, replaced by a more serious demeanor. "You held it together all day, Sinclaire. What made you snap?"

He just stood there, his back to us, shoulders rising and falling with the weight of whatever was still clawing at him. His fingers curled, then flexed at his sides. He still hadn't let go of the anger. It had rooted itself too deep beneath his skin.

I swallowed hard against my dry throat. It wasn't just because he had to protect me. It was how the man had looked at him, how he had smirked after he touched me, and how he had laughed when Oberon reacted. It wasn't just arrogance—it was baiting.

And Oberon took it.

His precious ironclad control had cracked. And for Oberon, that had to be maddening. Still, he didn't answer Garrick. He just pressed his hands against the wooden table. The tense silence lingered until I spoke. "It's done now. We need to focus on the mission."

Oberon huffed a bitter, humorless sound, and his knuckles turned white against the table.

Garrick, surprisingly, let the silence settle for a moment longer before pushing off from the wall. "Well," he sighed, "as much as I enjoyed watching you pummel that smug bastard, she's right." He grinned, though it didn't reach his eyes. "So, unless you want to put a leash on him, Freckles, I suggest we all find a way to cool off before we start another war in this cursed little town."

Oberon turned, his silver gaze flicking to Garrick. But he still didn't say a word. Garrick's smirk faded as he studied Oberon. His usual ease was still there, but his gaze sharpened as he tried to read him and make sense of what had happened. Oberon met his stare without flinching. The tension in his shoulders hadn't eased. He looked ready to strike again if given a reason.

I swallowed and spoke carefully, trying to shift the focus before another fight broke out. "I don't know if this is a good time," I muttered, flipping open my journal. "But he may be related to whatever's happening with the sea." I hesitated, then added, "Judging by the fact you just broke his nose, I assume you knew, too."

Oberon's jaw ticked as his gaze landed on me. He watched me with a deeper intensity than he had with Garrick, who hummed in thought and crossed his arms. "What he said about the sea is still bugging me," he admitted. "I don't see how he's connected, though."

I traced my fingers along the notes I had written earlier, scanning my frantic handwriting. The fisher's presence still lingered in the back of my mind, how he had looked at me and how the villagers had watched him, as if he were tolerated. The way he smirked when Oberon snapped showed that he wanted him to lose control.

"He knew something," I said, my voice quieter. "I just don't know what."

Oberon grunted, still rigid, his arms crossed over his chest. "I should have killed him," he muttered, more to himself than to us.

I stiffened.

Garrick let out a low whistle. "Damn, Sinclaire. I didn't know you could be so possessive." Oberon shot him a harsh warning glance. Which part had irritated him more? The teasing or the implication?

He was doing his job as my guard. And that man was a threat. It was the same as that knight in Silverfel.

Stay focused, Eden.

"What I'm saying is, if he *is* connected, then he knows more about you than he should now, Sinclaire." I gestured toward the window, toward the market where the half-elf had been. "That was a test, and you knew it."

Oberon's entire frame wound tighter. His fingers twitched, his muscles flexed, and the rise and fall of his chest became too slow. Too controlled.

I hesitated. "He knows how to pull your Fae instincts to the surface now. How to make you lose control. That's what he wanted."

Oberon took a step forward. Then another. My pulse quickened as he drew closer to me. The weight of his presence turned into a thunderstorm before the first strike. "You knew," he gritted out, his voice gravelly. "But you let him linger around you."

I flinched.

"You let him fucking touch you."

My breath hitched. "I didn't—"

"You care that he knows I want to rip him limb from fucking limb?" Oberon interrupted. His silver eyes burned into mine. "He knows you have fucking stitches in your back, Herbalist." His voice dipped to a lethal cadence. "He knows you're weak right now."

Weak?

The word dug into my ribs, cutting through whatever raw exhaustion had dulled my edges. I snapped my gaze to his, my glare sharp enough to rival him. "I can handle myself, Sin—"

"You mean like you did when you blushed at him?"

I scowled. Heat rushed through my veins. "I can't help that," I snapped, my voice rising. "Maybe it's just nice to feel wanted sometimes, Sinclaire. Like I'm more than a damaged liability!"

His nostrils flared, but I refused to yield. "What in the five hells does it matter to you if I blush anyway?" I argued, stepping closer. My hands shook at my sides, and my pulse thumped against my chest. "It isn't hurting the mission so long as I'm getting the information we need!"

Oberon's eyes narrowed. "Would you sleep with him for that information, too?"

I stared at him, eyes wide and jaw slack. The room felt smaller. Garrick pushed off the wall beside us before my vision tunneled to the man in front of me, to the sharp cut of his jaw and the heat still burning in his silver-rimmed glare.

The way he said it, the sharp bite behind it, wasn't just anger. It was ugly and aching. *But what for?*

My fists clenched at my sides.

Breathe. Don't react. Don't let him see how his words hit deeper than they should have.

A palpable silence rippled through the room as we glared at each other.

"You guys have serious sexual tension." Garrick's voice cut through the suffocating air, casual as ever. I whipped around and shot him a glare so sharp it could have skinned him alive. My heart was still pounding, and my blood was still boiling from Oberon's words. Garrick only smirked and leaned against the wall with his arms crossed over his chest.

"Gods," I dragged a hand through my hair. "This is not—"

"Oh, it is." He gestured between the two of us. "I mean, I was going to wait for the grand confession, but at this point, I might have to speed things along."

Oberon growled, a deep, guttural sound that made even Garrick hesitate for a breath before his smirk deepened. "Oh, you two are oblivious."

I gritted my teeth as Oberon continued to stare at me. The muscles in his arms clenched, and his veins pulsed with whatever Fae essence surged through him.

Snatching my journal off the table, I stormed out, slamming the door so hard behind me the walls shuddered. My hands shook. My breaths were shallow. I wasn't even sure where I was going, only that I needed to get out, needed space before I broke apart in front of them. Before Oberon saw any more from me.

Weak.

The word bounced around in my skull.

I pushed into my room and slammed that door, too. My fingers curled tight around my journal until my knuckles turned white. The argument replayed in my mind—his words, my words, the way his nostrils flared in restrained rage. The way his eyes had burned into me.

Like I had been wrong. Like *I* had wounded *him*.

My lips pressed together while I swallowed against the lump in my throat. I refused to cry over him again. I needed to focus, piece together what I knew and suspected, and stop ruminating over Oberon Sinclaire.

My palms pressed against the table, and I stared at the mess of ink and scattered thoughts before me. The connections were there, but something was still missing. The elf. The villagers. The sea. The trinkets. It circled back to the same damn thing, but I couldn't put my finger on what tied everything together.

I picked up my charcoal, ran my eyes over the notes again, and traced my steps from the beginning.

The fishers spoke of those taken by the sea, the ones who vanished beneath the waves only to return... changed. They weren't themselves when they came back. They only remembered enough to make their loved ones believe it was them. But it wasn't. *They* weren't. That detail clung to me, a sickness twisting in my stomach. *Not themselves.* That sounded unnatural.

Then there was that elf. The villagers looked at him as though he didn't belong, as if they were waiting for him to make a mistake. And the way he spoke of the ocean wasn't just passing knowledge. He knew more than he should. He was too smug, too certain. He had tested us, tested me. He wanted to see how much we knew.

Did the villagers suspect him? And if they did, why had they not done something about it? Unease crawled through my chest. What if it was because they couldn't? What if whatever came back from the ocean wasn't something they could fight?

The tension between the elves and humans was suffocating. The humans were wary, and the elves were resentful. The innkeeper's reaction to Oberon and how she flinched at his presence wasn't just hatred, it was fear.

Were they afraid because of what had happened here? Because of the ones taken? Or was it because they knew the truth?

My pulse pounded as the pieces shifted into place. The elves kept their distance, but the humans continued to fish. They continued to take their boats out to the sea and disappear. The elves weren't just angry, they were hiding something.

Then there were the trinkets. They weren't just for protection, nor were they just prayers. They weren't only meant to keep something out; they trapped something. They weren't simple warding charms but containment spells. The villagers weren't just trying to protect themselves from whatever haunted the sea; they were trying to contain it. They had been dealing with something.

And the ones who were taken... they didn't come back as themselves. I swallowed hard, my chest tightening. *If the things taken from the sea were returned, could they still be the same? Or were they something else that wore their faces?*

That elf felt off for a reason. The tension between the elves and humans had only worsened since this began. They were connected, but one piece was still missing. Something wasn't complete. I needed to go to the pier. To the docks where the missing villagers were last seen, from which they had returned, and where the water whispered its secrets.

32

OBERON

MY JAW TIGHTENED tight. The dull and simmering ache in it matched the one behind my ribs. I couldn't stop replaying what I had said to her or stop picking apart the way her expression had changed. How abruptly that fire in her eyes had become hollow.

The sharp edge of our argument kept cutting deeper, over and over, a rusted blade I couldn't pry loose. I shouldn't have let my anger get the better of me. I shouldn't have let my fear show. And that's what it was. Fear. That she would be hurt again.

But, *fuck*, she had blushed at that bastard, let him get close enough to touch her again as if he weren't a threat, and worse, she thought I saw her as damaged. As if she were just a burden that I had been saddled with, to be tolerated. She didn't know I saw the way she fought, the way she bled, the way she survived.

"Would you sleep with him for that information, too?"

The bitter, foul venom in the words still lingered on my tongue. My fists clenched on instinct, and my blood pulsed hot beneath my skin. The second they had left my mouth, I knew I had crossed a line I couldn't uncross. And then she was gone, storming out before I could chase the words and kill them myself.

Would she run?

No.

Not after Vaelwick. Not after...

A part of me still twisted with unease. Maybe it hadn't been me she didn't trust, but herself.

"Let's go spar in the woods or something, Sinclaire. You've been smoldering for hours." Garrick's voice halted my spiral. I blinked, not registering him at first. My gaze drifted to the window, where the trees bent in the wind.

Sparring sounded good. Hitting something sounded better. The floorboards creaked beneath each step. They, too, were tired of carrying my guilt. The words I had flung at her circled in my mind like birds. *Saints*, I had watched the light die in her eyes before a pained rage replaced it.

Quinn was likely still furious. I hadn't seen her since she stormed out, shoulders rigid and jaw trembling. But she hadn't run yet. I doubted she would go anywhere before I had the chance to make it worse.

I cinched my weapon belt tight, the leather biting into my hips in penance, and stepped out into the brittle morning.

Garrick waited, whistling an off-tune melody as we left the
tavern behind us. His cheer grated against my nerves. Too
bright. Too loud. Sunlight through shattered glass.

We crossed the main street, our boots striking the damp
stone, as we passed shuttered stalls and broken carts. A lean
cat watched us from beneath a crooked wheel, its eyes catching the light in twin embers. A few chickens pecked near
the old bakery, feathers ruffling in the breeze that swept in
from the shoreline. But even as they moved with caution,
something in the air warned them not to linger.

My thoughts still gnawed at me. Every muscle had drawn
tight. I needed the fight. Needed the snap of motion, the sting
of bone on bone. Needed to knock Garrick on his ass until
the storm in my chest bled dry.

I halted when we passed the last row of houses. The world
stilled, and my instincts roared to life. The breeze carried a
strange, syrupy sweetness beneath the salt. A smell of fruit left
to decay in a sealed jar that didn't belong.

No dogs barked. No gulls wheeled overhead. The fog became thicker than before, crawling low across the ground,
claiming it.

My gaze drifted toward the docks.

Mist smothered the piers and pressed with an unnatural
weight. It curled between the hulls of fishing boats, slipped
beneath abandoned nets, and coiled around wooden beams.
It was searching. And the sea listened in silence.

A rat darted across the street, then froze with its tiny chest
heaving, before vanishing back into shadow. A crow took
flight from a post, wings slicing the mist. A narrow and lean

fox stood at the mouth of an alley. Its fur shimmered with dew. Eyes of molten gold fixed on mine. Unmoving and un-blinking, it watched me.

The animals knew something was amiss.

Even the air held its breath.

Garrick continued to walk ahead of me, unaware of my unease. "Come on, Broody," he called, voice sharp in the hush. "It's been too damn long. I'm itching to get my ass kicked by you."

* * *

Garrick turned and pivoted on his heel, dodging my next strike with an ease that only made my grip on the hilt tighten. Bastard was toying with me, and he knew it.

"Oh, don't flatter yourself, Sinclaire," he said, his breath steady, his eyes gleaming with amusement. "I do enjoy the occasional battle of blades, but let's be honest—right now, you're about as distracted as a drunk in a brothel."

A raw growl built in my throat, and I lunged. The crack of our swords clashing echoed through the trees with a burst of sparks. "And you thought *talking* would help with that?" I stepped back.

"Hey, it's working, isn't it?" he shot back, grinning as he deflected my next strike, angling his sword to throw off my momentum. "At least you're *moving* instead of brooding in that damned window like a tragic ghost."

I clenched my jaw, eyes narrowing.

He wasn't wrong. I had agreed to this because I needed the release, the break in the noise, and the burn in my lungs. I needed to lose myself in movement, in muscle and instinct, rather than letting that sick, relentless rage take hold in my chest. Since last night, it had been simmering beneath my skin, a storm begging to break. I hadn't slept. Every time I closed my eyes, I saw the way her expression crumpled when the words left my mouth. The way she glared back.

Guilt had festered into something worse. Into fear. Fury.

With each strike I landed, each block, and each breathless clash, I made another attempt to outrun it. But it didn't work when the bitter words had been carved behind my teeth, when I still saw the way she walked away.

The clang of metal rang out again as Garrick forced me to pivot, his smirk widening. "You know," he panted, "for someone who claims not to care, you fight like a possessed man."

"I *don't* care," I snapped. My blade hissed, missing his shoulder by a hair.

"Right," he said, ducking. "And I'm a chaste saint."

Breathing hard, I bit back another retort. The wind stirred the trees, and their bony branches creaked. Somewhere above, a varrock shrieked—a lean, hook-beaked creature with ragged wings and cruel, gleaming eyes—circling like it could smell blood in the air.

I didn't want to talk. I wanted to forget. But Garrick persisted. The bastard had always been as relentless as a hound on a smell, especially when he sensed weakness, and even more so when it was me who bled it.

He danced back, cocky as ever, rolling his shoulders. It had been just another game to him. "So, what was it then?" His eyes gleamed beneath the canopy, his usual mischief lurking within them. He feinted left.

I didn't fall for it. I knew his movements too well, read the shift in his hips, the slight pause before he lunged. I caught him mid-motion, steel meeting steel with a harsh screech. My blade locked against his, and I twisted, grinding hard enough to wrench his grip. He grunted, boots skidding against the damp earth, but held his ground. He bared his teeth and pushed back with equal force.

"Did you say something *stupid*?" he asked, his voice too casual, strained beneath the pressure.

Pressing harder, I forced him lower. Our blades trembled where they met, vibrating with the tension between us. Not just steel—but emotion. Anger. Regret. The things I hadn't said. The things I *had*.

"Drop it," I growled with venom.

Garrick's smirk lingered at the corner of his mouth, even as sweat traced along his temple. "Hit a nerve, did I?"

Of course, he tried to bait me. He knew where to dig. And he was infuriatingly right. I shoved him back, snapping the lock with a snarl, and swung again. The brutal clash of metal rang out through the trees. He caught the strike in time, the impact rattling through both our arms in a thunderclap.

"You always overreact with her," he added. "That's how I know you're scared."

I froze for a breath. His weight slammed into mine with calculated force, twisting our blades apart. I stumbled back a few paces, boots digging into the dirt as I hissed through my teeth. My grip on my sword tightened until my knuckles went white.

Garrick stood tall, his chest rising and falling fast, but his gaze had lost its usual teasing edge. Now it was sharper. Focused. He was trying to peer straight through me.

"See?" he murmured. "You *are* scared. And I don't mean *of* her."

Forcing my stance steady again, I scowled. "You don't know what the fuck you're talking about." But the words tasted bitter. Hollow.

His grin widened. "Oh, but I do, Sinclaire." He spun his sword in a lazy arc as if he weren't standing at the edge of danger. "You're scared of losing her."

The words hit harder than any blade could have. My chest seized, lungs tightening around the fury that flared hot. I lunged, steel singing through the air with a scream.

Garrick knew what he was doing. That glint in his eyes was no longer smug. It was deliberate. Calculated. Pushing just hard enough to see if I had broken it again. And saints, I was close. Every inch of me vibrated with tension that curled like a beast beneath my skin.

My knuckles went white on the hilt. My breathing deepened, grew too measured. If I didn't control it, if I didn't cling to the edge of the discipline that I had lived my whole damn life by, I would break.

I wanted to tell him to shut the fuck up, to shove the words down his throat with the point of my blade. But the words caught behind my teeth. Because he knew, and that infuriated me the most. I rolled my shoulders, trying to shake the tension. "This isn't about her."

"Isn't it?" Garrick countered, shifting his stance, a predator circling wounded prey. He studied me as if I had already lost. "From where I'm standing, it sure as hells looks like it is." He twirled his sword again and locked his gaze on mine. "I've seen you kill for less, Sinclaire. I've seen you colder than the grave. And I've seen you control your temper better than that."

My eyes narrowed as I stepped forward, driving my blade against his. Sparks flared between us as steel met steel. He held his ground, eyes never leaving mine.

"I never saw your eyes turn silver like that before," he said, quieter now. Penetrating deeper. "Much less over a man touching a woman."

My jaw rolled. He was right. Quinn had awakened my Fae blood, and I detested it. Despised that the moment that bastard laid a hand on her, something primal inside me rose like a tide. That I had moved without calculation, without the indifferent logic that had kept me alive for years. The assassin—the part of me trained to observe and wait—had been set aside.

The Fae in me had claimed her, and that terrified me.

Garrick saw the change in my expression. His smirk curled again, triumphant. "There it is." I slammed his blade aside, hard enough to send him stumbling. He caught himself, boots dragging through the dirt.

My mask snapped back into place with a glare. "This conversation is over."

He steadied himself, the grin widening into a smile of pride. "Oh, I bet it is." The next clash was fast and violent. "The way you reacted at the docks was something," he continued, tone slick with amusement. "Like you've done it a dozen times."

Our blades collided with a shrill *clang* and a force that sang up my arms. Garrick circled. His eyes burned bright with intent. "Not to mention your veins glowed, you little Faerie," he added with a mocking lilt. "And I know for a damned fact that doesn't happen unless something calls it out."

My jaw clenched so hard it ached.

Her blood.

On my hands.

The heat of it. The metallic tang. The way it spilled between my fingers, as if it belonged there. The soft gasp of pain when my arms caught her, the tremble in her body.

I lunged harder than I meant to. Garrick blocked. His boots slid back a step in the dirt. His grin widened. He knew he had hit a raw spot.

Bastard.

White-hot, primal fury rose. That same nauseating fear I had felt the moment her body went limp in my arms settled into my bones and whispered, "*You weren't enough to stop it.*"

I huffed, forcing the thoughts loose before they took root too deeply. But they lurked in my subconscious. "Are you finished?" I gritted out, my voice low and scraped raw, my blade pressing harder against his.

Garrick leaned in enough for the following words to land harder. "That depends," he said, the amusement still unshaken in his voice. "Are you ready to admit I'm right?"

Part of me was tempted to answer. The other side of me yearned to break his jaw. I shoved him off, the clash of our blades tearing apart with a burst of force that sent him stumbling back a few paces. I stepped away, chest heaving, jaw locked tight as I fought to regain the control I never should have lost. The fury in my veins hadn't cooled—it pulsed beneath my skin, demanding release. Violence.

"There's nothing to admit," I muttered, turning away from him before I succumbed to the urge to strike again. My voice was rough, frayed at the edges. I slid my blade back into its sheath with a sharp *snap*. My fingers curled into fists, hands still itching from everything I repressed: Guilt. Fear. That dark, possessive protectiveness that knotted in my stomach every time I thought of her bleeding.

"Sure, Sinclaire," Garrick drawled behind me, his voice loose and casual, but there was weight in it. "Keep telling yourself that." He adjusted his stance behind me, boots shifting in the dirt, the familiar scrape of his blade readying again. Preparing for another round.

I didn't turn back. If I did, I wouldn't fight to spar.

I would fight to feel nothing at all.

33

EDEN

THE SOUND OF my knocking was dull and muffled against the thick wood of the door, swallowed by the stillness that hung in the corridor. Holding my breath, I waited for any sign of movement, yet the silence on the other side lingered. I drew in a slow, steady breath and pressed my palm to the door. The wood was cool beneath my fingers, grounding in a way that only unsettled me further. I pushed it open, carefully in case they were asleep.

Empty.

A sigh escaped me, making it apparent how much weight I had carried and how tightly I had held myself together. My fingers curled around the leather-bound journal at my side, but it did little to soothe the knot in my chest.

I should have known he wouldn't be in their room.

Oberon had always been restless, always wound too tight beneath his skin, a blade always waiting to be drawn. After last night, of course, he vanished into the early light. And Garrick likely sat recovering from another half-drunk misadventure or nursing the bruises that came with trying to pry answers from Oberon the way he always did, mischief trailing after him in that charming, exasperating, and predictable smoke.

I could go looking for them... or—

My gaze flicked to the window, where the faintest brush of sunrise kissed the crooked rooftops in hues of gray and pale gold. The village lay cloaked in the hush of early morning, its silence feeling sacred and untouched. Mist coiled between buildings and slithered along the cobblestone. The slow, steady breath of a slumbering beast curled along the shoreline, breathing with the rhythm of the vast and unknowable sea.

If I couldn't find them, I had to go alone.

The thought should have stirred hesitation, caution, or that familiar echo of Oberon's voice telling me to wait. To *think*. But there was no time to second-guess. The stillness had a sharp edge, the breath before something terrible happened.

Parchment whispered against the leather of my journal as I pulled it free. The soft texture beneath my fingertips was worn smooth from use and smudged with ink. I dipped the quill from their desk and scrawled a quick note, my writing fast but clean, just in case.

Because I wasn't reckless the way he thought.

The ink hadn't yet dried when I placed the note on the desk. Its weight was featherlight, yet final, a quiet farewell that said, *I tried. You didn't stop me.*

I stepped out into the corridor, out of the inn, and into the bite of morning air. The tavern stood silent behind me. It, too, had chosen to rest a little longer. The village held its breath. The usual clang and shuffle of merchants setting up stalls was absent; the marketplace was cloaked in canvas and dew, with creatures curled beneath blankets, waiting for warmth to return. The scents of salt and damp wood drifted through the air, clinging to the surroundings.

I followed the path in silence, the crunch of gravel beneath my boots the only sound for several long minutes. Even the birds hadn't yet stirred. Only the distant silhouette of a fisher moved along the dock, hunched and slow, casting off lines with quiet efficiency. His figure seemed to blur in the fog, more shadow than man.

My hand ran down my face, and frustration prickled beneath my skin. *Where were they? If they weren't at the inn, the market, or the tavern, then where?*

A low, familiar voice echoed through the mist.

Oberon?

I stilled, tilting my head to listen. His voice was a low thrum carried on the damp morning air, half-swallowed by the fog, the words too muffled to catch. *Strange.* He didn't speak aloud unless there was a purpose behind it. Even in battle, he was more steel than sound. His orders were usually sharp, concise, and measured.

But something about his tone, rhythm, and the quiet reverence laced into each syllable felt different. It wasn't a command, not a conversation. It was deeper.

I turned toward the docks, boots brushing against the wet stone path as I followed the sound. Mist curled around my ankles, swallowing shapes and softening edges. The village was still asleep. Every shadow stretched long and strange in the gray light of dawn.

Maybe they had seen me searching. I swallowed the sudden tightness in my throat. I had been wandering long enough, checking the usual places. Perhaps they came out to find me, to make sense of the morning like I had.

But each step was heavier than the last.

The wooden planks stretched into the sea like the ribs of something ancient and forgotten. My boots creaked when I stepped onto the docks. The air was colder, crisper here.

It echoed again. Clear this time.

"Dilthen Doe."

I froze, and a slow, crawling unease unfurled in my gut. It didn't announce itself with panic or fear. That instinctive hum beneath the skin that warned something was watching.

I didn't *want* to go toward the sound. I couldn't explain why, but I *had* to.

Each step felt heavier. The fog pulled me back, whispering that I didn't belong here. That this place, this moment, wasn't meant for me. Still, I followed the voice, legs stiff with dread, until I reached the furthest dock that disappeared into the thickest part of the fog. The pier's edge was indiscernible, swallowed whole by the pale gray curtain that rolled in from the sea. Everything beyond it felt muted, like I had stepped into a world half-asleep, half-submerged.

They might have found something. Maybe that was why they were here. Perhaps they followed a trail I missed.

The mist became denser. It slithered around my legs like fingers in thin, damp tendrils that crept up my heavy and cold skin. My breath fogged the air, and the familiar smell of salt and wet wood filled my lungs, but beneath the comfort of the sea was rot.

It wasn't the sour tang of spoiled fish or stagnant tidewater. It was more profound, denser, and more elduven. It was like something had died beneath the waves and continued to rot there, hidden just below the surface. A sickness tainted the air, faint but persistent, threading through the fog like poison. It settled on my skin, soaked into the fabric of my clothes, and seeped down into the marrow of my bones.

Decay filled my mouth with each new breath I took. The silence was broken by the brittle creaks of my boots on the old planks as the water below lapped against the pylons. It should have been a comforting, familiar sound. Steady and reassuring. Predictable. Yet the hairs on my arms prickled, and my fingers tightened on the leather of my journal.

A figure, half-formed in the mist, stood farther out than it should have been possible.

My heart lurched.

"Oberon?"

I squinted and leaned forward, but he wasn't on the dock, perched on one of the fishing boats, or leaning against a piling. He stood on the water.

Or... did he?

My breath slowed, my heartbeat loud in my ears. Maybe there was a rock beneath the surface. A sandbar I was unaware of. Perhaps it was Fae magic that Oberon hadn't mentioned—anything to explain why he appeared so impossibly poised above the shifting tides.

The fog swirled and thickened around his form with a deliberate, slow rhythm. The weight of the air pressed down as it breathed. The way he stood was so still, too rigid. His posture was unnatural. He waited. *But for what?*

My stomach churned as the first tremor of genuine fear slipped into my chest.

"Sinclaire!"

His name tore from my throat with desperation. It shattered the silence in the way only true terror can. The waves continued to lap against the pylons. A single gull cried out in the distance, the sound thin and far away.

But the figure didn't move.

The air shifted again. Thicker now. Denser. Like it had heard me and was listening.

I swallowed, trying to overcome the dryness in my throat. My boots creaked on the damp dock as I took another cautious step forward.

"Oberon!"

His head jerked back, snapping too far, too fast. A puppet's head yanked by invisible strings and without the grace of muscle or control. A cold jolt slammed through me, and I stilled. My breath became trapped in my throat, locked behind my ribs. My body refused to move, function, or breathe.

Slowly, the figure tipped its head to the side. Not like Oberon, but like something that mimicked him, playing at being him and chilled my bones.

Blue eyes flickered with an ethereal glow in the dim light. Their light seared through the fog. A pulse slithered through my nerves like a knife dragged across my skin. It wasn't just the horror of the sight, but the wrongness that bypassed logic and language, going straight to instinct.

The wind shifted, carrying the sharp smell of salt and decay. The figure stood there, waiting, with the stillness of a predator's patience. Its gaze clung to me as if it could see inside of my soul.

The world had gone silent. The sea had stilled, and the birds had vanished. The dock beneath my feet felt suspended between life and death.

My stomach lurched.

Run.

RUN!

My breath was ragged and shuddered through my lips, body locked in place, frozen by fear. Every nerve screamed at me to move, but my limbs, rooted in place, refused to budge. Then the figure's mouth opened with an unnatural, wrenching stretch. A scream erupted in a cacophony of drowning, gurgling, and wailing voices.

The scream echoed across the pier, tore through me, burrowed into my ribs, and crawled up my spine with icy, rotten fingers. It was suffering. Despair. It was death dragged from the throats of a thousand lost souls and forced into the air.

It ripped the breath from my lungs and left me gasping. My chest constricted as if the air had been stolen from me.

The pier trembled beneath my feet as the world blurred, its edges smeared like paint running in the rain. The mist slithered as it rushed toward me, alive in a way that made my skin crawl.

A shadow stretched behind the figure. It expanded and unfurled, far darker than the fog. Tentacles whipped toward me. I staggered back, and my foot seized on a warped plank. The rotting wood betrayed me, snapping beneath my boots as I fell backward.

Black, gleaming limbs wrapped around my legs sent a searing cold jolt through my body, sinking into my bones and veins like ice. The pressure locked around my ankle and thigh, pulling me closer to the end of the pier.

Panic clawed its way up my throat, strangling me as I screamed. My body fought against the pull, but I was no match for its strength. The dock blurred past me when the tentacles dragged me, scraping my skin against the rough wood. Splinters tore into my hands as I clawed for something to hold on to. But it didn't matter. I wasn't strong enough.

A sickening crack echoed, followed by blinding pain that exploded through my skull, a firework of agony exploding behind my eyes. The world fractured, my thoughts splintering into shards as I fell into darkness.

A familiar voice echoed through the fog, but was too distant to make out over the pulsing in my skull.

Oberon?

The void swallowed me whole, and I became weightless, drifting through nothingness. The roar of distant waves faded, leaving my body untethered from reality, pain, and fear.

I gasped, desperate for breath, desperate to move, as the darkness slipped away too fast. The sharp bite of air in my throat was the only thing that anchored me to what little of the world remained.

My eyes snapped open just as I plummeted.

The freezing water swallowed me with no time to breathe. Saltwater surged into my mouth, slammed up my nose, and burned through my senses. I choked, my body jerked, my muscles locked, and my lungs screamed for air that wasn't there. Panic erupted inside me as I fought against the dark water and tentacles still tight around my legs. But the ocean's mass constricted me.

My chest burned with a searing pain that cut through my ribs. The instinct to breathe overtook me, and I became desperate. When my mouth opened, water surged inside, and I gagged, my body spasming as I fought to survive against the icy salt. My lungs seized, the last of my breath stolen while my vision slipped away.

The darkness curled tighter at the edges of my sight. Freezing numbness spread through my limbs as I sank. Distant ripples of blue light flickered through the dark water, distorted and shifting with the ripples. Oberon's face broke through the surface above me. His eyes, glowing, haloed in silver. I reached for him, but he was too far.

The last strands of my consciousness slipped away as the darkness claimed me.

TO BE CONTINUED

*Continue reading for an excerpt of
the next book in the Oathsworn Saga!*

COMING SOON
BY BLOOD AND SOVEREIGN FLAME

By Blood and Sovereign Flame *is the second book in the Oathsworn Saga of cursed bloodlines, monstrous rituals, and the violent, aching bond between two souls who were never meant to survive, let alone love.*

All books in this series are read in sequence. They are not intended to be stand-alone books.

OBERON

THE STATUES' WHISPERS had faded, and in their place lay a glowing path. Veins of dim light coursed beneath the stone, guiding me deeper. *How long have I been walking? Minutes? Hours? Days?*

The lanterns that floated in midair hadn't shifted. There was no sun, no sky, just endless stone, arched bridges above, and buildings that blurred at the edges as if they were half-faded dreams. My boots made no sound on the path anymore; only my pulse remained.

I passed the same spiral towers, the same glimmering canals, and the same hollow market stalls. They looked different each time, familiar, yet foreign. *Shouldn't I have reached an end by now?* I frowned. My boots echoed oddly against the stone. It was muffled, yet echoed.

How large is this city?

Why am I here?

What am I looking for?

My fists clenched at my sides. My whole body buzzed as if something had awakened beneath my skin, a deep, vibrating pressure coursing through my blood and my bones. My senses thrashed, desperate for direction, but each time I reached inward to grasp them, they slipped away. They were sealed, restrained in an unfamiliar manner. I had spent my entire life sealing them. Now it made me restless.

The deeper I ventured, the more the city seemed to shift alongside me, with subtle bends in the path and lanterns flickering just out of sync. My vision blurred. Stone crumbled in the distance, and a dull pulse reverberated through the ground beneath my feet.

You're searching for her.

I paused, searching for the source of the whisper before continuing forward, drawn by the voice. The glowing path curved into a circular plaza, wide and open, framed by elegant columns entwined with flowering vines. A shallow pool glimmered at the center, reflecting the soft sky above.

Everything fell still, and reality flickered with my next step. The flowers turned to ash, the stonework cracked, and the water darkened. Then it vanished. The plaza returned: pristine, quiet, and vibrant.

What was that?

My reflection stared back from the pool, rippling when I touched the surface. The world flickered again, longer this time. The sky blinked out, replaced by a heavy void pressing down on crumbled rooftops. Lanterns flickered to life with unnatural green flames. The walls were half collapsed. Ivy had turned brittle and black, and beneath my feet.

Silt. Mud. Bone. Ruins. Rot.

The truth.

My heart thundered as I stepped back, causing the illusion to snap back into place. Flowers bloomed again, water ran clear, and the false sky shimmered. *It's not real.*

Whatever life the city pretended to have was a mask stretched over a corpse, and the deeper I walked, the less the mask held. The stone path shimmered beneath my boots. Shadows skittered in my peripheral vision. Lanterns were snuffed out mid-step, only to reappear a moment later, as if nothing had changed.

The illusion unraveled like a silk curtain, severed thread by thread. Scraping echoed around me, claws dragging across the stone. The sound followed me and then surged ahead.

I turned a corner and stopped in front of an ancient, towering palace. Black spires, ornate and spiraling with veins of obsidian and bone, climbed into the shifting sky. Ivy wound around its columns. Great stone doors, engraved with unknown symbols, waited at the top of an endless staircase.

When did that arrive? I didn't notice it before, even from a distance. I had taken no path that led to this.

My Fae senses slammed into me with such a violent pulse that I saw white. My knees buckled, and I crashed to the stone, catching myself with one hand as I scowled and pressed my fist into the cold cobbles. The magic inside me rioted.

The scraping stopped, and the city froze.

The muffled sound of crumbling stone echoed through the plaza. Cracks split the façade of the palace when I blinked. Chunks of masonry flaked from the high archways, ivy withered, and the gold shimmer of false sunlight flickered like a dying flame.

The hair on the back of my neck stood up as a ghostly, pale figure stepped forward from the dim haze of an alleyway.

My Fae senses surged again, as if recognizing a presence, slamming against the barriers of whatever held them and threatening to break free. I bit down harder, fighting to control them and prevent myself from unraveling. The figure's voice was muffled, as if it spoke through the weight of water. "We have waited for you, Fae." Another pulse rippled through the streets as the city breathed with its words.

"What is this?" I hissed.

The figure stepped forward, its form shifting and flickering between substance and shadow. Molten iron burned through my veins, causing me to groan from the pain. *"This is Vaelthorin,"* the voice intoned. *"The city that perished by the magic of your bloodline."*

I lifted my head, glaring at the ghostly form through the pain clawing at my insides. "I'm not them."

"You are their last lineage."

A deep snarl tore from my throat as my instincts fought against the force trying to claim me.

The figure tilted its head. *"You flee what you are. That is why the Queen stirs. Why the Veil cracks."*

A pulse surged through the air, rattling the lanterns and making the ground beneath me feel unsteady. I ground my teeth, my fists pressing harder into the damp cobblestone. I growled, fighting against the pull and the fire burning through my veins. "Why am I here?"

The figure stepped closer, its form rippling like a mirage. *"You are the key."*

My vision blurred, and I winced as another surge of pain ripped through my body.

"The fuck does that mean?" I gritted out.

It took another step forward.

A deep rumble erupted from my chest as something visceral shook loose from my core. Another shockwave slammed through the city, rippling outward and shaking the foundations. A ruined building in the distance collapsed, its remnants swallowed by the dark depths of the lake. I forced myself to my feet, swaying as my entire being thrummed with rage.

I was losing the battle with myself.

"You must let go, Fae."

The figure stopped, silent for a moment. Then, its head tilted, as if considering me. It stepped forward again, nearly close enough to lunge. Its presence pressed against me, and its voice was cloaked in finality.

"Unshackle the oath, or she will bleed."

The specter shattered in a breath of mist, torn apart by the flow of something greater.

I staggered forward as the pressure in my chest surged, molten and ragged. My pulse roared in my ears, louder than thought and the cracking stone. The chains that bound my magic trembled before splintering.

It wasn't enough anymore. Magic coiled in my gut, snarling for release. I dropped to one knee again, my hands splayed against the damp cobblestones. The stones steamed beneath my palms.

Don't lose control. I gritted my teeth so hard that my jaw ached. *You don't know what you are.* The Fae were said to be wretched manipulators and monsters. Beasts that spoke in beauty and bled corruption.

Something I fought not to become.

The shadows stirred, and my head snapped up. The lake rippled in the distance as dark water rose in a slow, elegant spiral. The air thickened, growing sweet and sour at once. From the deepest part of the ruins, through the cracked arches of what might have once been a temple, she emerged, draped in damp, drowned lace. The figure glided through the air rather than walking. A veil clung to her face, yet her gaze burned through it.

I didn't know her, but my instincts recognized her the way my bones knew the city.

"Stormborn," she murmured. "Even now, the name fits your skin." Her voice was honey poured over stone, beautiful and uneven with too many echoes.

My eyes narrowed. "What are you?"

"A keeper," she said. "A witness. One who remembers your kind when the world has forgotten." She drifted closer, the mist clinging to her.

"You don't know me," I ground out.

"But your body does," she answered gently. "Your power does." There was a pull beneath my skin, a thread behind my ribs. My Fae instincts surged with warning, rage, and response. "I could make you whole again," she whispered, tilting her head. "What you were meant to be."

"I don't need to be made whole," I gritted.

Her veil shifted slightly, and the edge of her mouth curved beneath it. "Don't you?" she purred. "You, the broken heir hidden in human courts, cloaked in lies, chained beneath mortal titles so your blood wouldn't stir the storm."

My fists clenched, and my magic shuddered. Light flickered faintly beneath my skin along the veins, like lightning trapped behind flesh. "What are you talking about?"

She came closer. "Her blood is the lock," The Widow whispered. "Her body is the threshold." A deeper pressure rolled through the elduvaris. "From her blood, you may rise with the gods, Stormborn."

The magic sealing me snapped. Light flared across my chest and down my arms as my veins ignited like fire given shape. "What the fuck does that mean?!" I staggered back, heat searing through me.

The meaning lingered in my mind, but it was just out of reach. It was too real to forget, yet too distant to grasp. *A girl. Herbs. Blood in the water.*

My chest clenched. My magic surged as I lost control.

The Widow's head jerked back, her veil rippling like a curtain caught in an unseen current as she gazed upward.

A muffled sound rolled through the water. *A voice?* The ground beneath my feet pulsed again before memories crashed through me.

The woman beneath the garden archway, wrapped in patchwork and moonlight. The defiant tilt of her chin. The blush when I glared at her. Her blood on my hands, slipping through my fingers. Her body, soaked, lifeless, on the docks, and my mouth to hers in unprecedented panic.

"I am not afraid of you, Oberon Sinclaire."

A profound voice, thunderous and fluid, pierced my thoughts. *Eden.* The light crackling beneath my skin flared brighter, searing through my arms, up my neck, and burning behind my eyes.

The Widow turned back toward me and stepped forward again. "The herbalist must bleed to wake the god."

"No," I snarled, my voice a low rumble. The specter's words echoed through me: *Unshackle the oath, or she will bleed.* My hands trembled, and my pulse roared in my ears as the magic scorched through me.

"You are the key," The Widow said. "But the door must be opened with her."

The veil over the city fell, and the golden shimmer faded when I stepped back. What was once luminous stone and floating lanterns had become rot and ruin. Cracked towers, split bridges, and buildings that had sunk sideways under centuries of weight, covered in glowing silken webs, were all that remained. The sky turned black, and the cobblestones were coated in silt and bone.

The Widow stood in the center, a grotesque creature larger than Neryth, with many brittle legs, a bulbous body, and a human-like torso.

"Take me back to Eden," I growled, lightning buzzing along my fingertips.

Her veiled head tilted, disappointed. Pitying. "Your heritage is wasted on you," she whispered. "You could have held the world, yet you let your sacrifice live."

A violent, scorching pulse exploded in my chest. *Sacrifice?* Light tore through my veins, casting bolts of lightning down my arms and splitting into the cobblestone and silt.

"She is not a sacrifice, and I'm done listening to ghosts."

The Widow lifted her arms in warning. The storm within me awakened. A current howled through the city. Lightning danced from my fingers, crackled across the sky, and struck the ground. The stones shattered, and buildings groaned.

The cobblestone shattered as I drove the power downward. A fracture surged through the sunken city, splitting along the street and into the foundations. The lakebed fissured. The pressure shifted.

A scream echoed through the city.

The Widow vanished in an instant, like mist scattered by a gale. Water surged in from the shattered floor with a force that slammed into my chest and threw me backward. Stone cracked behind me as I hit a crumbling wall.

Look for *By Blood and Sovereign Flame,*
coming soon to Kindle and paperback!

ACKNOWLEDGEMENTS

To my husband, Adrian, thank you for surviving bedtime battles, snack negotiations, and diaper-related disasters, all so I could write. You took the night shift without complaint, listened to me rant about fictional people like they owed us rent, and somehow pretended to follow the plot even when I lost it myself. This book exists because you kept the chaos at bay, and because coffee exists. But mostly you.

To my friends from Discord and the Tokyo Debunker Maple guild—Mr. and Mrs. Meowsti, Future, Ashu, and Ace. Thank you for cheering me on, dragging me back to writing when I was procrastinating in side quests (both literal and emotional), and reminding me that even when I doubted myself, I had a squad ready with hype, memes, and occasional threats of accountability. You didn't just help me finish my books, you made the grind fun. And slightly unhinged.

To my mom (aka Ma'am) and my brother, thank you for hosting Tiki Nights, which doubled as my weekly jailbreak from domestic chaos and tripled as free therapy via Milo sweet tea, junk food and background music. You let me escape just long enough to make progress without filing a missing persons report, and you listened patiently as I monologued about plot points and morally gray characters you absolutely did *not* sign up for. Your support means everything, even if my genre isn't your cup of tea.

To my readers, thank you for taking a chance on a chaotic little book by a chaotic little author. Whether you cringed, laughed, cried, or questioned my sanity (all valid responses), I'm grateful you stuck around for the ride. If your emotional damage even slightly mirrors mine while writing it, then I've done my job. Thanks for letting these unhinged characters live rent-free in your head with me.

Remember that everything isn't always as it seems.

I hope to see you all in Aurelith again soon.

H.L. Rillon

ABOUT THE AUTHOR

H. L. Rillon writes slow-burn, adult dark romance woven with threads of fantasy, horror, and emotional grit. A hopeless romantic at heart, she crafts stories where love is hard won, danger lurks in every shadow, and healing comes with both tenderness and teeth. When she's not writing, she reads with a cold cup of coffee nearby or wrangles three children, two cats, and a retired service dog with the grace of a seasoned chaos coordinator. Living with CPTSD and multiple chronic illnesses, she infuses her work with themes of survival, resilience, and the quiet strength it takes to keep going, even when the world feels unkind. She believes in love that bleeds, heroines who bite back, and magic that comes with a price.

Made in the USA
Middletown, DE
01 June 2025

76252601R00260